PRAISE FOR JENNIFER PROBST

PRAISE FOR *LOVE ON BEACH AVENUE*

"*Love on Beach Avenue* was such an adorable, funny, emotional, and wedding-y enemies-to-lovers New Jersey beach town love story! Just beautiful!"

—*BJ's Book Blog*

"The perfect enemies-to-lovers, best-friend's-brother romance! I laughed, smiled, cheered, cried a few tears, and loved Carter and Avery!"

—*Two Book Pushers*

"There's a reason Probst is the gold standard in contemporary romance."

—Lauren Layne, *New York Times* bestselling author

"*Love on Beach Avenue* is a three-layer wedding cake of best friend's brother, enemies to lovers, and just plain fun. Another yummy confection by Jennifer Probst!"

—Laurelin Paige, *New York Times* bestselling author

"I could feel the ocean breeze on my face as I turned the pages. *Love on Beach Avenue* is chock full of magic ingredients: a dreamy seaside, a starchy hero with a tiny dog, sparkling wit, and fabulous female friendship—a must-read romance!"

—Evie Dunmore, author of *Bringing Down the Duke*

"*Love on Beach Avenue* is the perfect enemies-to-lovers romance with well-developed characters, sexy banter, and so many swoon-worthy moments! Jennifer Probst knocked it out of the park with this book! Looking forward to the rest of the series!"

—Monica Murphy, *New York Times* bestselling author

"Fantastic start to a brand-new series from Jennifer Probst! *Love on Beach Avenue* is beautifully heartfelt and epically romantic!"

—Emma Chase, *New York Times* bestselling author

PRAISE FOR *ALL ROADS LEAD TO YOU*

"Funny, sexy, emotional, and full of scenes that make your heart swell and the tears drop, *All Roads Lead to You* is a beautiful story set in hometown America and one you will want to read again and again."

—*A Midlife Wife*

"Harper's story was everything I wanted it to be and so much more."

—*Becca the Bibliophile*

"Ms. Probst has a way of writing that I can't help but be 100 percent invested in from the first page!"

—*Franci's Fabulous Reads*

"Jennifer Probst expertly blends humor, sexiness, and emotion, keeping the reader delightfully addicted. She entwines these elements, evoking a hope that fate will align and bring love and happiness between two characters that seem to be at once perfect yet ill fitted for one another. I enjoyed this story; its plot, backdrop, characters, and romance gave me the warm fuzzies."

—*TJ Loves to Read*

"Jennifer Probst shines when she talks about her animal rescues in real life, and the saying is true: write what you know, and it will always be the best story. The same goes for this one; it's one of her best stories to date."

—*AJ's Book re-Marks*

"JP writes beautiful words, and I just loved this story. There was enough action, adventure, passion, and swoon factor, not to mention romance."

—*The Guide to Romance Novels*

"A read that will not only fill your emotional romance need but will fill your heart with the fulfilling need to care for a goat that needs to be hugged and to be besties with a horse to feel safe."

—*The Book Fairy*

PRAISE FOR *A BRAND NEW ENDING*

"*A Brand New Ending* was a mega-adorable and moving second-chance romance! I just adored everything about it! Run to your nearest Amazon for your own Kyle—this one is mine!"

—*BJ's Book Blog*

"Don't miss another winner from Jennifer Probst."

—Mary from *USA TODAY's Happy Ever After*

PRAISE FOR *THE START OF SOMETHING GOOD*

"The must-have summer romance read of 2018!"

—*Gina's Bookshelf*

"Achingly romantic, touching, realistic, and just plain beautiful, *The Start of Something Good* lingers with you long after you turn the last page."

—Katy Evans, *New York Times* bestselling author

Temptation

on

Ocean

Drive

OTHER BOOKS BY JENNIFER PROBST

The Sunshine Sisters Series

Love on Beach Avenue

The Stay Series

The Start of Something Good
A Brand New Ending
All Roads Lead to You
Something Just Like This
Begin Again

Nonfiction

Write Naked: A Bestseller's Secrets to Writing Romance &
Navigating the Path to Success

The Billionaire Builders Series

Everywhere and Every Way
Any Time, Any Place
Somehow, Some Way
All or Nothing at All

The Searching for . . . Series

Searching for Someday
Searching for Perfect
Searching for Beautiful
Searching for Always
Searching for You
Searching for Mine
Searching for Disaster

The Marriage to a Billionaire Series

The Marriage Bargain
The Marriage Trap
The Marriage Mistake
The Marriage Merger
The Book of Spells
The Marriage Arrangement

The Steele Brothers Series

Catch Me
Play Me
Dare Me
Beg Me
Reveal Me

Sex on the Beach Series

Beyond Me
Chasing Me

The Hot in the Hamptons Series

Summer Sins

Stand-Alone Novels

Dante's Fire
Executive Seduction
All the Way
The Holiday Hoax
The Grinch of Starlight Bend
The Charm of You

Temptation

on

Ocean Drive

JENNIFER PROBST

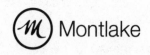

Text copyright © 2020 by Triple J Publishing Inc.
All rights reserved.

Published by Montlake, Seattle

www.apub.com

Amazon, the Amazon logo, and Montlake are trademarks of Amazon.com, Inc., or its affiliates.

ISBN-13: 9781542018647
ISBN-10: 1542018641

Cover design by Caroline Teagle Johnson

Printed in the United States of America

For Layne—a.k.a. Lauren Layne . . .
Thanks for the advice, the laughs, and the support along
the way in this crazy journey.
And the cocktails, of course.

It's time to start living the life you imagined.

—Henry James

To be yourself in a world that is constantly trying to make you something else is the greatest accomplishment.

—Ralph Waldo Emerson

Chapter One

"Mommy, do you like my outfit?"

Bella Sunshine-Caldwell finished stacking her daughter's lunch box, water bottle, and folder into her Fancy Nancy backpack and gave one final time check. Thank God. She despised lateness and usually did well with her organization skills, but the winter months were difficult to get both of them out of bed. Something about the lazy darkness and biting cold made her want to snuggle back under the blankets and beg for five more minutes. She'd even missed her normal morning run, sacrificing exercise for sleep, and still found herself behind. What if they missed the bus? She'd have to drive Zoe to school, and she didn't want to be late for her appointment.

"You look beautiful," she said, barely glancing over. Where were her brown boots? How could she keep losing things in such a small space? She rummaged through the cramped closet, dragging one out of the pile of discarded shoes and pulling it on. "Let's go, pumpkin. Coat on."

It was the sound of Zoe skipping across the floor that alerted her to trouble. Bella did a few hops to work the tight leather over her calves—was she gaining more weight?—and finally studied her five-year-old daughter, who tugged on her bright-pink jacket.

"Hold it, young lady." She snapped her tone into disciplinarian mode, shaking her head. "What do you think you're wearing?"

"My pink dress. You said you liked it." The defensiveness in her daughter's squeaky voice pegged her guilt. She knew better, but chose to ignore the rules.

"Zoe, that's a summer dress. It has no sleeves, and I packed it away. We agreed if it's in your closet, you can wear it. And you are not allowed to wear white dress shoes in the winter."

Stubbornness tilted her chin. "I found it on the bottom of my closet in a garbage bag with the shoes, so that counts. I want to look pretty today. We have show-and-tell, and Emma said she's wearing a pink dress and we could be twins. This is the only pink dress I have."

Bella reached up into the cloud and grasped for patience. Sometimes the cloud was full, like it had rained overnight and spilled out gifts like humor, positive attitudes, and flexibility. Other times, it was empty and dried up, and the only things it contained were frustration and PMS.

Bella prayed for the gifts.

"Our deal was for clothes hanging up in the closet," she corrected. "It's twenty degrees out, and you'll get sick if you go out like that. Why don't you wear your pink stretchy pants with the white sweater?"

Zoe's lower lip trembled. "It has to be a dress! We pinkie promised— please, Mommy!"

Zoe rarely had tantrums. They were more like intense discussions, which allowed Bella to be reasonable when something seemed important. She mentally clicked through various options to solve the problem as quickly and painlessly as possible. "Okay, go put your long-sleeved white shirt on under the dress. I'll get you some tights, and then you can wear those pink boots I just bought you."

Zoe's eyes widened. "You said they were for special 'casions."

"Well, I declare show-and-tell a special occasion. But from now on, no more sneaking out summer dresses. They stay packed up. Deal?"

"Deal!"

"Good. You have to move fast or we'll miss the bus."

Zoe rushed back into her room, and Bella hurriedly ripped open a new package of pink tights. When they went on sale, she bought them by the bucketload. With deft motions, she helped re-dress her daughter, grabbed her stuff, and rushed out the door.

Stomping on the accelerator, she got to the end of the road as the bus was beginning to pull away. She honked, practically fell out the car door, and ran out, scissoring her arms wildly in the air. The bus screeched to a stop, and she caught the dirty look the bus driver shot her. "Thank you!" she yelled, giving Zoe a quick kiss and watching her cross the street to board. She waved as the bus pulled away and disappeared.

A sigh spilled from her lips. Just another day in the life of a single mom.

Oh, Matt, I wish you were here.

She listened for a sign like she always did—a whisper in the trees, a honk of a horn, a shiver of cold awareness—anything to feel that he'd heard her and was here, but there was nothing.

Rolling her eyes at her drama, she trudged back to the car and pumped up the heat. Her husband had been taken way too early, but it had been five long years since he passed away, and she'd learned to do things on her own. God knew she'd made plenty of mistakes, but with the help of Bella's sisters, Zoe was a happy, stable child. Bella had learned after losing Matt to be grateful for all the good, and her daughter was a gift that allowed her to love a piece of Matt for the rest of her life.

Shaking off her somber thoughts, she headed toward Sunshine Bridal to meet with her coworker Gabe. Her two sisters were away for a few days, so she and Gabe were in charge of the Royal wedding, and she needed to be sharp, not mooning for a life with her late husband she'd never have. Eloise Royal demanded a postholiday celebration to rival the gaudiest Christmas imaginable, and Bella needed to impress. Her oldest sister, Avery, had been the driving force behind their family's successful wedding-planning business, but now that she was getting married and taking some well-deserved vacation time, Bella intended to step up and take over more of that role.

If only she didn't need to work with Gabe.

Why was she the only one suspicious of his intentions? He'd been a full-time assistant for years, mostly working with Avery, but lately, he'd been pushing for a bigger stake in the company. Just last month, everyone had agreed to give him a promotion so he could take on his own clients. Bella knew he deserved it—he was well respected by vendors and clients, and he worked hard—but part of her was a bit resentful because he wasn't family. Bottom line: she didn't trust him not to bail one day. Maybe try and open up his own business elsewhere and become their competition—which would break her sisters' hearts and Zoe's. Her daughter was crazy about him. Hell, there wasn't a woman on the planet who wasn't crazy about the man, which made Bella even more leery.

She made her way through the streets of Cape May, the usually vibrant New Jersey beach town mostly shut down for the winter. Holiday lights were still strung happily around trees and lampposts, illuminating the colorful bed-and-breakfast cottages throughout town. The water was a simmering gray monster, moody under the low-slung clouds, but a few residents still braved the boardwalk for their regular breakfast and morning run.

She pulled up to the familiar yellow-and-pink scrolled sign announcing SUNSHINE BRIDAL and gathered her stuff. Of course Gabe was already there. The man was as much a workaholic as Avery. She hurried up the stairs and headed straight to the conference room, following the scent of strong coffee.

"Morning." The deep, velvety voice drifted in the air like smoke, caressing her ears. "I picked you up coffee and a yogurt parfait."

She studiously ignored the sexy pitch of his tone and wondered why some men got all the sex appeal. Was it a gift from God at birth?

Did he zap his fingers at certain males and bestow all the traits to make women drop to their knees? Even worse? Gabe was nice. He was always thoughtful and willing to do what was necessary to make everyone happy. At first, she'd believed it was part of him being a good assistant, but over the years she'd learned it was just his personality. He was a bit of a caretaker.

Bella tucked away the thought and deliberately chose the seat across the table so there was plenty of distance. "Thanks. I was running a bit behind today." She focused on getting her laptop out and set up, giving her a few moments to put up the usual barriers before risking a full stare.

"I hope you didn't rush," he said, sounding concerned. She imagined a frown between those strong brows, his carved, defined lips pursed a bit in thought. "No reason we couldn't have started a half hour later. How's Miss Zoe?"

She shook her head with a sigh. "Insistent on wearing a sleeveless pink dress to school today."

His laugh was rich and filled the air with life. "Ah, was it show-and-tell?"

She jerked her head up too soon. Her gaze crashed into his, and those dark eyes pulled her in tight, the sooty depths flaring with a focused intent that threw her off. "How'd you know?"

"She's got a thing about dressing up for big occasions. How'd you win the argument?"

"The art of compromise—the foundation of my existence. I let her wear her brand-new pink boots, and she allowed me to winterize her dress. I can't believe I forgot to get her a pink winter dress for Christmas. Purple and red won't cut it."

"She got everything she wanted on her list and more. You gave her an amazing holiday."

She nodded, accepting the praise that meant more than he could imagine. She was always trying to make up for Zoe not having a father, especially around important holidays. Though she tried to remind herself her daughter had an extended family that gave her all the security she needed. "Thanks." Her next words were uttered grudgingly. "She's still crazy about that American Doll you gave her. The others have been neglected, but she plays with yours all the time."

"I'm glad."

"I still think it was too expensive." Watching Zoe's face light up with delight after she tore open Gabe's present had caused a slither of unease. Bella was afraid he was becoming too familiar—dropping by out of the blue, showering Zoe with unexpected gifts, weaving his way into the folds of her family with his carefree charm. He was even tight with her future brother-in-law, Carter, and they went out on a regular basis. Bella worried that Gabe would hurt too many people when he eventually decided to leave their small beach town.

He winked. "Nonsense, it was my pleasure. Gotta know what girls want, right?"

Her insides cooled. Oh yes, Gabe Garcia knew exactly what females wanted. He'd been dubbed the Bachelor of the Cape for two years in a row—a designation started by the magazine *Exit Zero* that spread into the New Jersey blogs and papers. He'd gotten even more publicity when they found out he worked for Sunshine Bridal, and for a while, clients had poured in just to work with Gabe. His escapades with women were famous, and excited gossip swarmed around him on a regular basis. He was their own local Jake Gyllenhaal, with a long line of females begging to end his single status.

Not that she blamed anyone. The man was like walking kryptonite. One look and women wanted to drop their panties.

Gabe nailed the tall, dark, and handsome vibe like no one else. His hair was thick and coal black, with a natural wave that set off his high forehead and bold brows. Inky eyes were framed by thick lashes and highly slashed cheekbones, slanting down to an honest-to-goodness square jaw—with a cleft. That manly jaw seemed to be consistently shadowed with a hint of stubble, giving him an edgy pirate look. With his impeccable clothes, charming smile, and graceful, lean body, the combination was lethal.

Her sister Taylor had pronounced him bangable on sight, but acknowledged she didn't want him to fall in love with her and ruin their work relationship. Avery was more attracted to his brain and easy ability to dazzle brides and grooms by the dozens and grow their business.

As for Bella, the moment she looked at him, she'd scented danger. He was too much to settle down in a small beach town for long. Eventually he'd be courted to a bigger wedding company and leave them all behind with a casual wave and a sexy wink.

He'd take their business with him, and they'd be forced to deal with the fallout. God knew she was an expert in that territory. She had no desire to visit that place again, so she'd learned to keep her distance and watch for any signs of restlessness. She needed to protect her family.

Over the years, as Avery and Taylor grew closer to Gabe, Bella had made sure to always be polite, nice, but professional. No late-night cocktails after work together or long, serious chats about their hopes and dreams in life.

Just business.

Oh, he'd tried to close the distance many times, but she'd refused. Even when she caught the flare of hurt in his eyes and the flicker of confusion on his face. After a while, they'd eased into a cordial yet tepid relationship that worked for both of them. It would have been perfect except for one small problem.

Zoe.

Her daughter worshipped Gabe, and he worshipped her right back. They'd fallen into a relationship that frustrated Bella, but there was nothing she could do. Now that he was a full-time wedding planner, there'd be even more contact. She had to make sure the business-only rules between them remained steadfast.

Mostly, it worked out. Bella usually handled the majority of her clients alone, pulling in Taylor when she needed extra help. Gabe had offered his assistance in the past, but she'd always declined, claiming she was able to handle everything. Eventually, he got the hint and stopped asking, and though Avery got frustrated with Bella's stubbornness, her sister finally conceded, accusing her of too much pride.

Unfortunately, Bella was stuck this whole weekend working the Royal wedding with him, but once Avery and Taylor returned, they'd go back to their normal schedule.

Bella sipped her coffee and began bringing up her files on her laptop. "I'm sure knowing what females want has made you good at your job."

His look was full of self-mockery. "It's definitely an asset. Unfortunately, my poor father almost disowned me when he discovered I was putting that type of talent toward helping brides."

Her curiosity was piqued. Gabe rarely spoke about his parents or past. "He had a problem with it?"

"Thought I was gay. Let's just say that talk didn't go well, because even though I wasn't, it pissed me off he had a problem with it."

She winced inwardly. She'd been guilty of thinking the same thing when he was first hired, but it hadn't bothered her. It had been a good six months before his female exploits became legendary. "What about your mom?"

"She had no opinion of her own. Whatever my father said was law. Don't get me wrong—he wasn't abusive. He just wasn't . . . warm."

She picked her words carefully. "I think it's sad that even in this day and age, people want to pigeonhole others. I think there should be more men in this business, and it's ridiculous certain careers are discouraged because of someone's gender."

"Agreed. But you all took a chance on me, and here I am, freshly promoted." He shot her a dazzling smile. "I think painful things in the past can be valuable lessons for the future. Do you feel that way?"

The thoughtful question and genuine interest in his gaze warned her they'd gone too far. Opening up his past was an invitation to deepen their relationship—an expert trick in forging intimacy she wasn't interested in.

She gave a bland smile and focused on the screen in front of her. "Sure. Listen, we have tons of work to get through. Shall we start?"

The air thickened. As her fingers clicked over the keys, she silently held her breath, then heard him take the seat across from her.

"Of course," he clipped out. "I'm sure you want to get through this weekend as quickly and painlessly as possible."

She tried not to wince at the double entendre of his words but refused to feel guilt. They had a job to do, and allowing herself to be vulnerable to his good looks and charm wasn't good for Sunshine Bridal. The less time they spent together, the better. Having her sisters under his spell was plenty. Someone in the family had to look out for their business interests and be practical.

So she didn't react to his words. She just got to work.

Chapter Two

She was doing it again.

Gabe tried to ignore the spurt of frustration ready to explode like a shaken-up can of soda once freed. He'd hoped working with Bella on this wedding would give them time to build some camaraderie. He'd been working for Sunshine Bridal now for three years, and he wasn't any closer to breaking down her walls than he'd been when they were first introduced and shook hands.

Why the hell didn't she like him?

Switching to autopilot, he began going down the multiple check-lists for the upcoming weekend, his brain going over and over their exchange. She'd actually asked him a personal question. Usually, she stuck to general greetings, work, or talk about the weather. But he'd been too eager, believing she was actually interested after inquiring about his mom.

Avery usually ran the morning meetings and always started them with enthusiasm, positivity, and genuine questions on everyone's mental state. Maybe this was Bella's way of trying to stay focused while her sisters were out of town. Except he was now full-time with his own clients, and she was still treating him like an afterthought.

Politely, of course. Bella was never rude or wanted to hurt feelings. Too bad every time she dismissed him, another piece of his heart crumbled off and blew away like dust.

"Gabe? Did you take care of the flowers?"

He shook his head and reminded himself there was a huge postholiday wedding to pull off. His plan to impress Bella so she was dazzled by his expertise was already failing. "Yes, we'll have the garland, mistletoe, and pine trees decorated and ready for both the ceremony and reception."

"Good. I confirmed with the sleigh driver, and he'll be out front to take Eloise from the hotel to the reception."

His lips twitched. "We actually have horse-drawn carriages in Cape May, yet she insisted on a sleigh. Do you know how long it took to find one of those?"

He enjoyed watching her face relax into laughter. "I know. There's been no snow, so they had to pay extra to mount wheels, or they would've been scraping the roadways with that awful sound the entire way."

He shuddered. "Never been a nails-on-the-chalkboard type."

"Me, either. What about the Santa Claus? Is Frank confirmed and set up with the toys we delivered?"

He winced. "Frank broke his leg last week and had to cancel. I had a hell of a time trying to find a replacement. Seems most Santas retire after the holiday until next year or the Salvation Army calls."

A crease furrowed her brow. "Who'd we get?"

"Paul Traipse finally agreed to step in."

Her face didn't register disapproval—she was too much of a professional to allow emotion to show—but he caught the flare in her china-blue eyes. He'd spent too much time imagining what those eyes would look like drugged with passion, chin tilted up, pupils dilated, staring at him. Only him.

Right now, though, there was only a faint judgment that drove him batshit crazy.

"Is he able to do the rap song they requested? He needs to perform the dance, remember?"

Yeah, he remembered. The bride had requested that Santa surprise the kids with a dance coordinated to DMX's "Rudolph the Red-Nosed Reindeer." It had taken him a while to convince Paul it'd be short and painless. It'd helped when they told him they'd pay double. "I checked and he's been practicing. Said he's ready to go."

She still looked doubtful. "Paul is known to enjoy too many cocktails during a celebration," she pointed out. "Are you sure he can be professional enough at a wedding? Should we hire a backup just in case? The Santa Claus dance is key to the reception, so there can't be any errors. There are too many children to disappoint."

Once again, she didn't trust him to do his job, and it stung. "I understand," he said tightly. "I believe he can pull this off. I'll be watching him carefully until his appearance, and I've already hired a car to take him directly home after his role. He won't be hanging out and partying with the guests at the bar."

She nodded. "Then let's move on to the next item."

He wondered if she ever lost her temper. The woman rarely gave in to tantrums, whining, or a bunch of other human emotions that were displayed by her sisters. She flowed like cool water over rocks, luring him to delve deeper to see what lay beneath.

He'd spent the past few years trying to unearth the heart she kept stubbornly locked up from him, yet freely offered to others. The moment his gaze had first met hers, something woke inside him, like a sleeping giant rising from a long slumber, suddenly ravenous to feed. When he'd gripped her hand in his, the electric spark sizzled under his skin, causing him to jerk back—he'd been shocked by his reaction. He expected the same surprise from her as their fingers slid apart and dropped away, but she'd barely given him a second glance. Obviously, he hadn't made the same first impression.

He'd figured it was just a physical connection that would fade. He'd never experienced a jolt of awareness with a woman before, as if a part of him recognized her. Hell, he didn't believe in love at first sight when

99 percent of the time it was simple lust. But as the months had passed, his feelings grew each day.

Avery brought a strong sense of leadership to the team, and Taylor the daring, creative wit. Bella was different. Her calm focus and gentle heart seemed to be the piece that held them all together. Her talent for supporting and nurturing a couple's needs impressed him, and she was no pushover. The woman was able to handle the worst of PITAs—Pain in the Asses—with a firm hand that caused the majority to back down immediately. It was the same expert way she handled Zoe, her arguing sisters, or the daily chaos that inevitably surrounded a thriving business built on customer service.

Initially, he'd believed she was dependent on others because of her quiet demeanor. The joke had been on him. Her ruthless independence bordered on obsession—the woman despised asking for help. She never dated, and never stepped out of her inner circle. She lived in a permanent comfort zone.

Was that another reason why she tried so desperately to avoid him? Did she disapprove of his lifestyle? Believe he was a player when he'd tried many times to show her it wasn't true? He'd hoped his relationship with her daughter would prove he was a man to be trusted, but she still had issues with him babysitting or trying to help with Zoe.

If it weren't so messed up, it'd be laughable. Yesterday, he'd picked up Chinese food and found a woman's phone number stuck to the outside of a fortune cookie. There were a thousand women out there he could date happily, maybe even settle down with or at least have a damn good time with for a while. Why did he have to be stuck on the only woman in the world who barely knew he existed?

Pathetic. Just like Dad used to say.

He shut the voice down from years of long, hard practice. He kept the rest of the meeting brisk and professional, though inside his gut churned. They had a packed event schedule beginning this evening, and the unspoken tension between them had to be dealt with.

She sipped at her coffee, staining the white plastic lid with an imprint of red lips. Her Goldilocks white-blonde hair was pinned up in a casual bun, and she wore black leggings with an oversize fuzzy gray sweater that seemed to swallow up her entire figure in warmth. Her appearance matched her temperament—she preferred an easy, casual style that fit into every situation, whether it be a luncheon, reception, or client appointment. He admired the way she juggled each piece of her life to fit into the whole, excelling at every role: mom, sister, friend, and businesswoman.

He wondered if she got tired of being everything to everybody.

The laptop clicked shut. "Good, we seem to have everything covered. I'll meet you at the Grand Hotel at three p.m. Text me if I need to pick up anything."

"Did you hire another nanny?" he asked. Bella had used a part-time caretaker to help with school pickups or late-evening weddings, but the woman ended up having twin granddaughters and had recently moved down south to be with her own daughter.

"Not yet."

"Then who's watching Zoe?"

Her gaze snapped to his, and her cornflower eyes seemed to whirl with a bunch of emotions before clearing. He would have given anything to know her real thoughts, or what made her suddenly hesitant, turning away as if she was afraid he'd see too much. "She's sleeping over at Daisy's house tonight. I appreciate your concern, but I have it covered."

Frustration simmered. In her stubbornness to always take care of things herself, she refused to even consider the ways he could help out. But every time he offered to babysit, she politely declined. It was past time he confronted her about it. "Yeah, I don't think you do."

"Do what?"

He gave her a level stare. "Appreciate my concern. I'm not questioning you as a mother, Bella. I'm just trying to help. As part of this team, I thought I got to care about Zoe, too."

She gave a slight jerk as the words hit. The tiny crack in her armor pleased him, but he didn't want to punish her. Maybe it was past time he gave up on this ridiculous hope she'd wake up one morning and finally have feelings for him. It was depressing as hell.

"Of course you can care about Zoe. She's always been crazy about you. I just don't think your job should include checking on who's baby-sitting her. It's not like you're family."

The direct hit and hiss of pain finally cleared his head. Bella would never let him in, either to her heart or her inner circle. He'd always be an outsider, and no matter of time or effort was going to change that.

He nodded, ducking his head quickly to clear up his space so she wouldn't spot the hurt. "I get it. I'll mind my own business from now on."

"Gabe, I'm sorry. I didn't mean—"

"I know what you mean." He forced a smile, finally acknowledging he was half in love with a woman who'd never feel the same. It was time for him to stop torturing them both. "We're good. I'll see you tonight, and we'll kill it. No worries."

From now on, he needed to focus on his career at Sunshine Bridal and follow her rules. He couldn't fight for something she didn't want in the first place.

He headed out quickly, and she didn't try to stop him.

The Grand Hotel held an impressive ballroom that boasted 360-degree windows in order to view the beach. The usual classic wedding theme of beach, sand, and sun had been replaced by a winter wonderland, combining the bride's slight obsession with Christmas with just enough elegance.

The ballroom was decorated with hundreds of twinkling white lights twisted around frosted twigs, zigzagging throughout the rooms and dripping from the ceiling. Mistletoe, mini pine trees, and poinsettias filled the tables and empty spaces. A giant evergreen decked out with decorations and tinsel was the main draw, and huge boxes of gaily wrapped presents were crowded underneath. Fake snow floated down and burst over the dance floor in timed intervals. Bella had to admit, it was one of her masterpieces, completely transporting guests back to the magic of the holidays.

As she checked in with the staff to make sure everything was running smoothly, she watched the groom lead the bride into a faulty yet enthusiastic spin on the dance floor. Their joyous laughter rivaled the soaring music of holiday carols and reminded her of why she loved her job.

She'd certainly never planned to work at Sunshine Bridal. None of her sisters had, but each of them had been forced to pick up the reins in different ways, especially once their parents retired. Her vision of life had always been simple—revolving around her childhood sweetheart and his dreams, rather than hers.

Matt had been working his way up the ladder at an investment firm, and she'd planned to happily settle down and be a stay-at-home mom. When she got pregnant with Zoe, they'd excitedly planned to have at least three more, both craving a big family. With his eye on yet another promotion, she'd never worried about them financially. Hell, she'd never worried about them emotionally, either. They'd been as madly in love after twelve years together as the first day. So when a drunk driver took his life, she'd had no road map for how to take care of herself, let alone a baby.

Thank God Avery and Taylor had stepped in to take over the business, and her sisters had slowly allowed her time to heal before bringing her on board. Since she needed a job, the business had been a lifesaver. But lately, Bella realized besides being good at her job, she also found that planning weddings satisfied something in her soul. Watching her work help give a newlywed couple a happy beginning reminded her of all the good things in life.

It also reminded her there was hope for some people. Being a part of a love story soothed a raw piece inside her she'd lost since the accident.

A child dressed in a bright-red dress tore past her, and Bella shook her head. It was always more challenging when children were invited to a reception. She and Gabe had come up with a fun list of activities throughout the evening to keep them entertained, but so far most of them were dancing and seemed to be having a good time.

She glanced at her watch. Almost time for the Santa surprise.

Her gaze scanned the room and snagged on Gabe. She studied his lean, pantherlike body clad in an elegant black suit, reluctantly admitting he was a perfect male specimen. He was chatting with a bunch of women at the bar, but even from this distance she spotted the invisible armor he wore while he worked. He handled guests with a deft expertise that balanced the sharp lines of friendly competence while deflecting overfriendly gestures. As he spoke, pointing across the room to answer some type of question, he'd already retreated a step back, keeping that essential one foot of space between him and the clients.

Guilt pricked. She'd hurt him today. Dammit, she hadn't meant the words the way they came out. But being in that conference room alone with him, those dark eyes probing her gaze, she'd been desperate to push him away and keep her sacred space. She wasn't comfortable blurring the lines of personal and work. She needed to keep them clear.

She'd apologize later. Preferably over a text message after this wedding weekend was behind them.

He pivoted on one heel and walked across the room toward her. The suit fabric seemed to bend to his will, emphasizing cut muscles and stretching across broad shoulders. One rebellious curl spilled over his forehead, practically begging for a woman's fingers to smooth it back. From the crowd who watched him hungrily from the bar, Bella figured he'd have enough volunteers.

He reached her and cocked his head. "You okay? You look like you could use a drink of water."

She heard her sister Taylor's voice gleefully sing in her head: *Yeah, a tall cool one. Like him.*

"I'm fine." Sometimes his sheer physicality affected her like any other woman, but she always mastered it quickly. She cleared her throat and refocused. "Is Paul ready? We need to get this done before the cake."

"Going to get him now. I situated him in the back room with a pitcher of water and snacks. We're good." He winked, his trademark gesture.

Irritation shot through her. Was he always performing for a crowd, or did he ever allow himself to be offstage? "I'll let Eloise know and signal the DJ."

Eloise had taken off her white fur stole and detached the collar from her dress so she could dance comfortably. She clapped her hands with glee, her scarlet nails flashing. "Let's get the children gathered up, Bella. I'm so excited about the dance—the kids are going to love it!"

Bella smiled with a confidence she still didn't feel. For some reason, she had that strange flutter in her gut that told her something was going to go wrong. So far, the instinct of disaster had led her to three previous wedding-nightmare scenarios, and she didn't want another one tonight. Probably another reason why she'd been on Gabe's case to double-check everything. "Our Santa will dazzle them."

The moment the vow left her lips, her ear speaker beeped. "Code red, code red. I need you in here, Bella."

She didn't miss a beat. "I'll be right back. We can situate the children over there."

It took her only a few seconds to find Gabe in the small back room where he was holding Paul. Literally.

And it took only a few seconds to realize Santa was drunk.

Paul lay flat on the floor, his padded belly sticking up in the air, snoring through his white beard. She glanced over and saw the pitcher of water, a glass, some half-empty plates of various snacks, and a silver flask that had rolled under the chair.

Ah, crap.

"How bad?" she asked, kneeling to study the man's slack face.

Gabe shook his head. "Bad. He must've had the flask hidden—I didn't think to look. It was filled with vodka. I can't believe I didn't see it. Last time I checked on him, he was fine."

"Can we sober him up and delay the Santa bit?"

Gabe muttered a curse. "Doubt it. Also, I'm afraid to risk him breathing on those kids."

"True." She mentally ran down her list of contacts, but no one came up as a Santa Savior. Then her gaze fell on Gabe. "Only one option left. Strip him and put on the suit."

Chapter Three

Her words seemed to ricochet across the room like a spray of bullets.

Shock flickered over his carved features. "What? Me?"

"You have a better idea? This is the highlight of the reception, and I'm not about to let them down. Are you?"

He groaned. "Shit."

She stood up. "Use those extra pillows from the couch for padding. Do you remember any of the dance moves? If not, you'll just have to freestyle."

He stared back at her with growing horror, his olive-toned skin blanched of color. "I'm not dancing, Bella. I'll sing the song. That should be enough."

"You have to do the dance. Look, don't worry about being professional. Just make it look entertaining. Let's go—we're running out of time. We'll let Paul sleep it off and get him home after the performance."

She headed to the door, but his frantic words stopped her short.

"I can't dance!"

She turned and studied him in confusion. "What are you talking about? You go out to clubs all the time. You're the damn beach bachelor— you have to know how to dance."

That perfect square jaw clenched. "I don't go out all the time, and I never dance at clubs. I hate dancing—all dancing. I can't do it."

"I'm sure you can dance; you're just not used to doing it for a crowd."

"I can't," he said again, his voice slightly strangled.

Her heart began to beat madly. "Gabe, Eloise has been talking about this forever. You have to try!"

He ducked his head and began tugging off Paul's beard. "Fine. I'll sing and sway back and forth and hope it will be enough. Let's do this before I change my mind."

She left him and spent the next ten minutes corralling stray children, then double-checked that the DJ was ready for the intro. "Gabe, are you ready?" she whispered into her earpiece.

He blew out a hard breath. "Yeah."

She signaled to the DJ, and the music began to blare. "Go on three."

Palms damp, heart beating, she waited as the DJ introduced Santa Claus. Gabe strode in with a red bag thrown over his shoulder, waving to the kids as he made his way to the dance floor. Clapping ensued, but Bella noticed most of the older children looked a bit bored, as if Santa at a wedding was lame, and they just wanted the whole episode to be over.

The rap song began, and Gabe dropped his bag. The strains of "Rudolph the Red-Nosed Reindeer" hit the speakers, and Gabe began to sing. He had a good voice, deep and strong, but as the lyrics continued, he just swayed back and forth, nodding his head now and then with no rhythm.

Bella glanced around. The crowd was obviously unimpressed. Eloise was frowning, waiting for the big dance number she'd counted on, and her husband muttered something in her ear.

And then it got worse.

Gabe began to clap, trying to get the audience more involved, but everyone just looked at him with a bit of awkwardness as the classic rap song blasted around them, contradicting the lameness of his performance. Eloise glanced around, her gaze finally latching on to Bella's, and she put up her hands in question, basically asking what the hell was happening.

Oh, this was bad.

Please, Gabe, she prayed silently. *Please do something to save this before it's too late.*

As if he'd heard her mental plea, suddenly, he exploded into a bunch of bizarre dance moves that made no sense. She watched in horror as the graceful, smooth man she knew morphed into a combination of old-school John Travolta with shades of Miley Cyrus twerking. His red velvet suit flashed, and his shiny black boots pounded the floor in a bad *Saturday Night Live* sketch parody. He moved his hands like a giant wave, snapping his fingers, and suddenly began to salsa, shaking his shoulders and hips like a sick bird trying to die in peace.

Dear God, he was right. He couldn't dance at all.

A drunk Paul would have been better than this.

She craved to close her eyes and make it stop, but she forced herself to keep watching. How was she going to salvage the rest of the reception? What excuses could she make? Would Eloise blacklist Sunshine Bridal, write bad reviews, and tell everyone she knew that her wedding had been ruined by a crazed, dancing Santa?

As the final quarter of the song mercifully began, she noticed a strange thing. The kids who'd looked bored were clapping and calling out encouraging words. A blur of phone lights blinked furiously as people took photos. Eloise looked delighted, laughing hysterically with her husband, as pockets of onlookers pointed and sang with Gabe.

They thought it was a joke. And they loved it.

Gabe spun on his heel for the climax and, with a hearty whoop, slid across the stage on his knees.

The crowd roared.

He took his bow, blowing kisses and throwing out some *Ho ho hos*, then smoothly transitioned into pulling out presents from his bag and calling out names. He distributed the gifts to the now-enthusiastic audience and finally made his exit.

Her knees almost buckled in relief.

Eloise raced over to her, beaming. "That was amazing!" she squealed. "How did you know changing the number up would be so successful?"

"I'm glad you trusted us to know when we feel something will work better," she lied smoothly. "With the age of your crowd, Gabe and I decided to go vintage and comedic. I'm so happy you enjoyed it."

Eloise shook her head. "You two are a dream team. Instead of hiring a Santa, he took it on himself to make sure it was done right. Thank you, Bella. Everything tonight has been just . . . perfect."

Bella's heart squeezed, and she said a quick prayer of gratitude that this disaster had flipped to a good outcome. "You and your husband deserve perfect."

She watched Eloise flit back onto the dance floor. Gabe's voice purred in her earpiece, like a high-performance sports car sparking to life. "Getting Paul home now. Back in fifteen."

"Got it."

The rest of the evening went smoothly, and after the cake cutting and custom dessert bar, the happy couple began their official last dance. By the time all the guests had left, her body ached and she wondered if she'd ever have enough energy to coordinate another wedding.

"Right now, I don't know if I'd give my right arm for a cold crab cake or a shot of tequila."

Her lip twitched and she turned toward Gabe. He'd stripped off his jacket and tossed it over a chair as he stopped behind her. Weariness carved out his features, and he arched his back until he got a satisfying crack.

She leaned against the wall and flexed her foot. "Crab cake, definitely," she said.

"Agreed. Let's go to the kitchen and grab something to eat before we head home."

She hesitated. Whenever she completed a wedding with her sisters, they retreated to the war room back at the office so Avery could go over all the high and low points. If Bella was working solo, she usually pulled something indulgent together in her own kitchen—either grilled cheese or an omelet. She'd never been alone with Gabe after an event before.

"Oh, I'm really not that hungry." Her stomach let out a loud growl, announcing her lie.

He arched a brow. "Really? You dislike me so much you can't even eat some leftover wedding food with me? Or are you still pissed about me screwing up with Paul?"

Shock barreled through her. "I don't dislike you, and I'm not pissed. That was a mistake anyone could have made. I just usually make myself something to eat when I get home."

He nodded and scratched his head. "I get it. But just this once, will you sit with me? I'm buzzing too high. Avery and I usually talk a bit to give me some time to come down."

She understood what it was like. People who worked late nights sometimes had screwed-up sleeping schedules due to the adrenaline. And even though being alone with him made her uneasy, she needed some food and downtime before she'd be able to sleep. "Of course."

They headed to the kitchen and spoke to the staff they knew well. Before long, they'd gotten plates with salad, seafood risotto, and grilled veggies. Gabe came back with two cold beers, and they sat in a small corner in the back on wooden stools.

"So are we going to get it over with?" he asked, tipping back his bottle.

She watched the strong column of his throat work, then tore her gaze away. "What?"

He snorted. "My dancing, of course. I told you I didn't know what I was doing."

The thought of his wild movements on stage hit her, and a giggle escaped. "I thought we were dead," she admitted. "But at least you finally did something, even if it was a strange mating dance for extinct birds."

He shook his head. "I froze up there. But then I looked at you and caught the panic on your face, so I knew I had to step it up."

"You saw me?"

"Yep. And you're always unflappable, so when you looked like you were about to vomit, I knew the wedding was at stake."

She forked up some risotto, and the delicious mix of seafood and carbs sang in her mouth. His words repeated in her mind. Yes, he was right. She rarely let her emotions take hold, especially with work. Usually, she was proud of her ability to take it all in stride and maintain her control, but lately, she was wondering if she'd taken it too far. Everything was so well planned in her life, there was no longer any time or space for impulse. What would it be like to lose control in a safe way? Was that even possible? Or maybe she was destined to keep things exactly as they were to avoid trouble. After all, she needed to provide stability for her daughter. A single mother didn't pair well with risk. She pushed the odd questions from her head and refocused. "Well, once again, you managed to charm everyone, even in a Santa suit. They thought the whole performance was rigged and on purpose."

He laughed, and the warm, rich tone caressed her ears. "Damn, did we get lucky. I'm going to start vetting new vendors for next holiday season so we don't run into this problem again."

She took a sip of her beer and enjoyed the sluggish warmth in her blood. "Good idea. But I must admit, it was nice seeing a part of you that wasn't perfect. I didn't believe you about not knowing how to dance."

"You think I'm perfect?" he asked with an edge instead of his usual flirtatiousness.

"Let's just say you seem to have it all together."

His gaze was a laser that dove deep and lit up her insides. Something gleamed within the dark depths, challenging her to look further. "I'm not perfect, Bella. There are things I don't have. Things I want so badly I can taste them."

Confusion swamped her, along with a sudden pulsing heat between her legs. She clenched her thighs to get rid of the sensation and reminded herself this was his MO with every woman. Somehow, all his words morphed into seduction. She was positive he didn't mean it specifically for her. Gabe just seemed to ooze sensuality naturally.

The question hovered on her lips, then fell out. "Why don't you go after them?"

"Because it can destroy what I do have, and I'm not brave enough yet."

She ached to ask more questions and analyze his words, but her instinct screamed danger, so she cleared her throat and refocused the conversation on safer, professional subjects. "Well, Eloise was quite pleased and said her cousin has been looking for a planner and is going to contact us. The Santa debacle ended up working out fine."

Frustration carved out the lines of his face, as if he wasn't ready to go back to talking about work. He took another swig of beer, and thankfully, followed her lead. "I'm sorry if I let you down. You warned me about Paul, and I thought I had it covered."

She sighed. "Giving Paul a body search to look for hidden alcohol isn't in the job description. I heard he was going through a rough time with his wife leaving him, so he probably succumbed to the postholiday blues." She shrugged. "Plus, I get these weird feelings when something bad is going to happen at a wedding. I should have realized ignoring it is never a good idea."

"You seem to have an instinct for this job. A sixth sense. Did you always want to work in the family business?"

Her mind flashed over the past. All the dreams she'd had for a future that was never meant to exist. "No. I was only focused on being a wife and mother. It wasn't until later that I realized how lucky I was to have a place to step into. This job may not have been my original calling, but I've made it mine. Does that make sense?"

He smiled. "Yeah, it does. It's one of your many talents." When she frowned, he continued, "I noticed a long time ago that you don't wait for opportunities or answers—you make them. Or find them. Maybe it's part of being a single mom, because you have to rely on yourself all the time to give your daughter what's needed."

The words shocked her, but even more so was the pride gleaming in his eyes while he gazed at her. Where had that come from?

A sense of shame washed over her. He was wrong. She'd always been reactive in her life—not proactive. It was just the image she presented, the surface of what she hid from the world. How badly she'd craved to have Avery's leadership skills, or Taylor's creative talent. Instead of a badass, she was the weak one. The one who needed protecting and being taken care of because she was always worried she'd never be enough for Zoe. It was as if when Matt died, he'd taken all her confidence and the core of who she was with him.

God, how she hated it. But she didn't know how to change, or where to start.

Suddenly, he frowned. "What's the matter?"

He was more in tune with her than she imagined, as if he sensed every flicker of her mood before she did. She forced a smile, refusing to let him in any further. "Nothing. I appreciate the compliment, though." She glanced at her watch. "It's late. Probably time to call it a night."

His gaze narrowed and he crossed his arms in front of his chest. "Back to being polite coworkers, huh? Did I hit a nerve with that comment?"

She refused to get flustered. "No, I'm just tired."

"What are you so afraid of, Bella? That if you opened up a little, you may actually realize I can be your friend?"

"We're friends," she said stiffly. "For goodness' sake, you're part of the team. You come over for dinner. You're close to my daughter. What else do you want?"

His jaw clenched. His hair was slightly mussed. He'd loosened his tie and unbuttoned the top button of his dress shirt, giving her a hint of dark chest hair. He was like a classic Pierce Brosnan James Bond—all sleek and sexy. Why was he being so pushy tonight and not respecting her need to keep things professional?

Tension pumped the air between them with something more— something that she didn't understand and didn't want to. Her skin prickled in awareness, and his spicy male scent rose to her nostrils. She raised her chin and glared back, annoyed at him for his strange words and intense stare and for challenging the damn status quo that worked so well between them.

"Do you really want to know?" he finally asked.

Her heart banged against her chest. Her mind screamed *Code Red*. The question held too many unknown factors she didn't want to analyze. She knew he got frustrated with her refusal to lower her guard, but she needed to protect her family. God knew she seemed to be the only one whose brain didn't fall to mush in his presence, or believe he walked on water.

It was her fault for agreeing to stay and share a beer with him. She should've known it'd send the wrong message and confuse their professional relationship.

Tomorrow, in the bright light of morning, he'd be glad of her dismissal. He had enough women to pick from who eagerly did his bidding. He certainly didn't need her.

"No," she said. "I don't."

He flinched, but recovered nicely. Slowly, he raised his beer in a mocking type of toast. "Then that's the only answer I need." He took a sip. "We better get back."

She jumped up. "Yes. Let's go."

They worked together to close the wedding, then went their separate ways. And Bella refused to think of the strange encounter between them or the question that reminded her of Pandora's box.

Better to keep it closed.

Chapter Four

She hadn't wanted to know.

The sting of Bella's rejection last night still throbbed like an open wound, but Gabe had no time to steep himself in regret.

He fell automatically into his role as host, working his side of the room in perfect complement to Bella. The postwedding champagne brunch was held at the Mad Batter, where the specialty omelets were perfection. Glittery icicles edged the enclosed porch with strings of white lights, fake snow, and pine-scented candles. Heaters kept the guests warm and merry. Eloise had arrived in a horse-driven carriage, sporting a luxurious red-velvet coat and matching boots, reminding Gabe of a sexy Mrs. Claus. She was an over-the-top bride but no PITA. Gabe had actually taken to her sense of lavish style and her refusal to care what anyone thought of her obsession with Christmas.

He admired a woman who owned her issues.

On cue, Eloise headed toward him with her arm tucked into that of a cute brunette whom he remembered as her close friend. He tugged on his memory vault for the name as they stopped right in front of him.

"I hope you're enjoying the brunch," he said with a warm smile.

The bride grabbed his cheeks and pressed a smacking kiss on his lips. "Gabe, you have been amazing," she said, pointing up at the mistletoe that hung above them. Usually, he had strict standards for space with clients, but the kiss held no heat, just friendly affection. "The wedding and brunch are perfect. I wanted to introduce you to my friend—"

"Jing," he finished, reaching out to shake her hand.

The woman's dark eyes widened, and a pleased smile curved her lips. She was a tiny thing, with towering four-inch heels, her body clad in a little black dress with a festive red scarf. Her long sleek hair fell like a waterfall over her shoulders. "I'm honored you remembered," she said teasingly. "I just wanted to tell you personally how much I enjoyed the wedding."

"I'm glad. Bella and I know how important it is to look back at a significant memory and have no regrets."

Her dark brow arched. "Handsome, and with a heart," she murmured.

Eloise gave a tinkling laugh and waved her hand in the air. "Why don't you two get to know each other for a bit and I'll be back?"

Gabe held back a sigh. Another matchmaking attempt by another bride. He was becoming an expert at deftly avoiding handpicked women for him he'd never see again. Still, he knew it was important to be polite. "Do you live in New York near Eloise?" he asked.

She shook her head. "I'm actually in Philly. I own a restaurant there."

He cocked his head, impressed. "What's the name?"

"Fins. It's mostly seafood, but we play with a lot of vegan recipes. It's a miracle I got to take a weekend off for the wedding."

"Hey, I've worked in restaurants before, and it's a hell of a gig. Hard work, and not many can handle the hours. How long have you had it?"

"Going on my fourth year and making a profit, so it's all good." Her stare deepened, and she took a casual step closer. "I'm in town for another two days before I head back home. I'd love to see you again. Grab a coffee. Chat?"

He hesitated. She was close by, had a great career, and seemed like his type.

His ears tuned to the sound of warm laughter. On cue, his gut twisted with longing. Someone had made her laugh. He mourned the fact he hadn't been the one to do it, and his next words came out instinctively. "I'd love to, but my schedule is jam-packed with events the rest of the week. I'm really sorry."

She eased back, smile still in place. "I understand. Do you happen to have a card?"

He pulled out his business card from his suit pocket. She plucked a pen from her clutch and scribbled on the back. "Call me if you change your mind. Or if your schedule opens up." She handed it to him, her fingers curling intimately around his.

He smiled. "Got it."

He watched her walk away and tucked the card back in place.

Great. Another possible love interest thrown away because of his obsession with Bella.

His heart still yearned to spill all his private secrets. To release all the pent-up emotion he'd been stuffing for the past few years and deal with the fallout. To stare into those gorgeous blue eyes and declare he wanted so much more from her than a casual business-colleague relationship.

Of course, odds were high she'd be shocked and walk away. God knew Bella had never showed him any interest before. The occasional glimpses of sexual attraction were brief and strictly physical. She wasn't interested in the man he was. Hadn't he been told his entire life that women fell for him based on his appearance? It wasn't ego—just fact.

After all, his father had repeated it like a mantra.

He turned to go check on the table, then stopped when he caught Bella's familiar scent. The light floral teased his nostrils, making him crazed to explore every inch of her skin. Her black pants and turtleneck sweater shouldn't be so sexy. Of course, the woman owned some killer curves, and those white-blonde tendrils of hair clung to her nape, begging for a man's lips to press against the sensitive skin. The tall cream boots emphasized the sleek length of her calves. She was the perfect package, yet she was completely unaware of her effect on men. Including him.

She gave him a dazzling smile for the benefit of the guests, contradicting her whispered words. "Uncle Arthur is beginning to get a bit overzealous with his political discussion. We need a distraction."

"I'm not doing another dance," he quipped. Humor danced in her blue eyes, and he couldn't help the rush of pride. He loved making her laugh.

"You'd never be able to duplicate such success. How about a toast? Should I grab the MOB?"

He glanced at the mother-in-law, used to deciphering the acronyms to describe each role, and shook his head. "No, definitely the FOB. He likes to talk."

"Good idea. I'll make sure the staff pours everyone a mimosa."

They split up, and soon the father of the bride was in his element, and all talk of politics had faded from the group.

Too bad they rarely worked together. Other than the benefit of enjoying her company, she was just as good as Avery during an event—sharp eyed, quick to make a decision, and able to smooth over any bumps with an easy smile and calm demeanor.

As the witching hour of one p.m. neared, when Eloise and her prince would be whisked off for their honeymoon, a large woman with bright-red hair in a flashy yellow dress marched toward him. He didn't recognize her from last night, so she wasn't within the bride's or groom's immediate family tree.

She jabbed a finger in the air at him. "You! You planned this wedding for Eloise, correct?"

Uh-oh. He flashed a grin that hid the sinking feeling in his stomach. He was really not in the mood to hear complaints or fix any big issues when he was twenty-seven minutes away from freedom. "Yes. My name is Gabe, and I work with Sunshine Bridal. I hope you enjoyed everything?"

Her face was quite fascinating—a rather large nose set off sharp, high cheekbones; intense golden-brown eyes; and red-painted lips. Her features weren't classically attractive, but she had a presence that made you want to keep looking. Energy buzzed around her figure like a nest of bees. She was taller than he was, colorful, and larger than life. This was a woman who would not be easily dismissed, so if she had a problem, Gabe was in trouble and he'd better fix it.

Instead of a blistering tirade, she threw her head back and gave a loud, joyous laugh. "Darling, I absolutely loved it! Your Santa routine was classic, and every single detail was perfection. Oh, how I despise cookie-cutter weddings, and though Eloise likes that princess trope far too much—I mean, really, a horse-drawn carriage?—the rest of it was unique and so enjoyable."

He relaxed. "I'm glad. Our goal is to always give couples the wedding of their dreams."

"I'm Eloise's second cousin, Adele," she said, offering her hand.

He respected her firm, short shake.

"I happen to be getting married myself and would love for you to do mine. Now, who is your lovely partner?"

Surprise shot through him. Usually brides requested a detailed planning session before jumping on board. Still, business was business. "Bella Sunshine-Caldwell. She's one of the owners. Let me call her over so we can chat."

He spoke briefly into his earpiece, and Bella quickly flanked him, introducing herself to Adele.

"I was just telling Gabe how much I adored the wedding and that I must have you both for my own."

"How wonderful! I'm honored you'd choose us. How long are you in Cape May? Would you like to come in for a meeting?"

Adele waved a hand in the air and straightened her fuchsia shawl. "Oh, I have no time for that, darling. I'm just so over the stuck-up planners I've met, and Eloise has told me how nice you've both been—not fake nice, there's a difference you know! Anyhoo, I can send over all my preference sheets. It's March second, so of course we'd need to celebrate the theme. We already have the reception place booked—I just need everything else done."

Gabe was used to overenthusiastic clients and tried to pull out more important details. "What is the reception venue?"

"The Housing Works Bookstore Café. I absolutely adore old things. Charm, vintage, character. Why do new when you can polish up old?" She winked. "Kind of like me, right?"

Gabe grinned. Damn, he liked her. She was so unpretentious, and fun. Planning her wedding would be a pleasure, but her venue was definitely not in Cape May. Not something he'd usually take on, but if he had the time, it might be nice to expand his client list.

"Where's the bookstore located?" Bella asked.

"It's in Manhattan."

Gabe nodded. "Well, we usually only do weddings in Jersey, but I'd be happy to discuss. It may sound like a year is far out, but it's never too early to sit down to go over some details. You said there was a theme?"

Another hearty laugh. "Darling, it's this March, not next! And our wedding date is on Dr. Seuss Day, my favorite author on the planet, so we'd need to do *all* the things to celebrate. Nothing is too outrageous; we must do something to liven up the crowd. Edward's friends can be a bit stuffy."

He shared a knowing glance with Bella, and his initial enthusiasm drained away. *Damn.* Why did the interesting brides and grooms have to be outlandish? There was no way they could plan something in two months, especially with a theme like that.

Bella spoke warmly, with the perfect touch of regret. "Oh, Adele, I must apologize, but we simply won't be able to take on another wedding only two months away. It sounds wonderful, and I know it will be a perfect day."

"Don't be silly, you must. I've already fired my last few planners, and I can't do it alone." She flashed a brilliant smile and did another wave of her hand. "I'll pay whatever is needed, of course. Now, I don't want to ruin Eloise's brunch by talking about my business, so I'll call you, and we'll get moving ASAP! Thank you, my darlings, this shall be epic!" She blew air-kisses and drifted back into the crowd, her red hair and bright clothes a beacon.

"Now that would've been my greatest achievement," he said, still a bit bummed he wouldn't get a crack at the unconventional wedding.

Bella grinned and shook her head. "That would be something, all right. Let's just be grateful we can decline this one smoothly. Can you imagine squeezing in another wedding this quarter?"

He shuddered. "No. Though I do have more openings than you." He hesitated, but forged ahead, ignoring his mental warnings. "I'm happy to help you out with anything. I know you're probably glad this weekend is over, but I liked working with you."

He expected her usual dismissive response, but for one moment, emotion flared in her powder-blue eyes, and the breath whooshed out of his lungs like a lovesick teen desperate to hear the answer to his prom proposal. Her lush lips parted, poised to say something; then she blinked, half turning away, as if she'd changed her mind. "Me, too. Eloise mentioned she made a love match. At least you got Jing's number. Not a bad reward, huh?"

Her words were delivered with a mocking lightness that tore through him. He wished Eloise hadn't mentioned it, especially since he had no plans to call Jing. Did Bella really think he was constantly searching for women to date? "I'm not calling her," he said, desperate to explain. "I was just being polite."

She laughed. "It's okay. The wedding's over, and she's not a client. I can't imagine how you keep track of everyone, though. Good thing your phone holds unlimited contacts."

Annoyance skated through him. "No, I don't—"

But she'd already disappeared into the crowd without a glance back. *Shit.*

Soon, the bride and groom waved goodbye from their covered carriage. Gabe watched them lean in for a kiss while the horses pulled them to their happy ending, wondering if there'd ever be one for him.

A few days later, he walked into the conference room at Sunshine Bridal for the regular morning meeting. Avery already had her favorite breakfast in front of her—a perfectly baked chocolate croissant and coffee. She was the leader of the crew, and he'd been lucky to learn the business under her guidance—her perfectionist ways equaled a perfect wedding, and he'd instituted a lot of her tricks of the trade. With her wildly curly hair, hazel eyes, and curvy build, she was like a firecracker always on a slow simmer, ready to launch.

"Good morning, Gabe!" she boomed out, a big smile on her face.

"Morning, Avery." He took his usual seat beside her and propped open his laptop. "How was Texas?"

"Amazing. Hot as hell and I adored every moment. Did I miss anything?"

Taylor sat at the end of the table, combat boots resting on the opposite chair, crossed at the ankles. Her diamond nose stud winked in the light streaming from the window, and pink hair shimmered with more enthusiasm than her words. "It's Cape May in the dead of winter. There's nothing to miss, dude."

He tamped down a laugh at Avery's sisterly sigh. "Well, it's rare that we're all gone an entire weekend."

Taylor smirked. "Your control-freak tendencies are showing. Admit it. You loved taking a vacation, didn't you?"

Avery was a proud admitted workaholic, but since meeting Carter last summer, she'd begun to ease away from her crippling schedule. She bit her lip in guilt. "I did," she whispered. "So much that we planned another one. What's happening to me?"

"It's called love," Bella sang out, entering the room. He automatically stiffened as the energy swirled around her—a feminine, light cloud that he wanted to savor. She grabbed her coffee and took her seat across from him. "Enjoy, you deserve it. Let the commoners take up your slack."

"Speak for yourself," Taylor said. "I have one year left on my prison term, and I don't intend to spend it working nonstop every weekend."

Gabe caught the worried glance Avery shot her sister. When Taylor had joined the family business, she'd always been clear it wasn't permanent. She'd never been interested in settling down in the small beach town where she grew up, and now that the time for Taylor to leave drew near, Gabe knew they had to make some hard decisions. Bringing in another employee was a big risk, especially since they were a tight-knit crew.

As usual, Bella smoothed things over. "We'll work it out. In the meantime, the Royal wedding went off beautifully, right, Gabe?"

He nodded. "Perfection. We almost recruited another client for March."

Avery perked up. "Oh, next March is a great time—we have openings."

"She wanted us for this March." He almost laughed at Avery's horrified expression. "With a Dr. Seuss theme."

Taylor groaned. "Nightmare. Bet you had fun saying no to that one."

"She was lovely," Bella said firmly. "Just not in her right state of mind. She said she'd fired all her other wedding planners."

"That's a code-red situation," Avery said. "Thank goodness we didn't have to deal with her. Taylor, how was the expo in Atlantic City?"

Taylor shrugged. "Pierce and I got a bunch of new-client leads, so I'd term it a success. Even better? I won two hundred and fifty bucks on the slots."

"Nice. Which machine?" he asked.

"*Sex and the City.*"

He rolled his eyes. "They haven't retired Ms. Bradshaw yet? I prefer the *Hangover* or *Walking Dead.*"

"Well, you didn't win the money on those, did you?" she quipped.

He laughed and wondered if he'd do better with a woman like Taylor—more snark than sweet. Then again, maybe not. He didn't know too many men who could handle the youngest Sunshine sister except Pierce Powers, a longtime friend of Taylor's and the best wedding photographer on the Cape, who insisted he and Taylor were no more than friends.

Avery clicked through her screens, then pointed her pen at Bella. "I forgot about the next agenda item we need to discuss. It's about getting caught up in a couple's sob story."

Taylor grunted. "I have no issues with that. What did Bella do now?"

Avery sighed. "Vera called. Seems our softy sister paid for a dress the bride couldn't afford."

Bella squared her shoulders, but her skin flushed with guilt. "I can't believe Vera tattled—she's the one who split the extra cost with me!"

"Dude, you need to stop giving away our profit," Taylor said. "What was the story this time?"

Her chin jutted out in pure stubbornness. "It wasn't a lot of money, okay? But she's on a strict budget, and she fell in love with a Jenny Packham that looked gorgeous on her. I watched her tear up."

Taylor rolled her eyes. "Cue the poor grandma sitting in the waiting room, telling her she can't afford it. Then she takes the dress off, cries some more, and Grandma begs for help to make it more affordable. Why was the dress shown when it wasn't in her budget?"

"There was no grandmother," Bella said. Her normally bright blue eyes grew shadowed. "She had her nine-year-old sister with her. Her sister found the dress on the rack and begged her to try it on. When she saw the price, she quietly took it off and settled for a cheaper dress. But when she picked it, there wasn't the same joy in her eyes."

"It does happen a lot," Avery said gently. "It's difficult, but we can't buy all our couples wedding dresses they can't afford."

Gabe sensed there was more. "What else happened for you to make the decision, Bella?"

Her gaze flew to his. Understanding passed between them. "She's in remission for breast cancer. They decided to get married right away, even though she has no hair. Her fiancé said he wanted their wedding photos to reflect the real woman he loved." Bella paused, emotion shining in her eyes. "I just wanted her to have something that made her feel beautiful and whole. Every bride deserves that on her wedding day. To be special. To feel special."

Yes. This was why he'd fallen so hard. She was a woman who needed to give and thrived on making others happy. If a man was ever lucky enough to gain Bella's love and trust, she'd shower him with everything she was. There would be no lies, no games, and no holding back. It was rare to find that type of deep caring in the world. She reminded him of all the beautiful things when he looked into her face.

In the stunned silence, Gabe spoke. "Sounds like a damn good reason to me. What do you guys think?"

Avery cleared her throat. "Sorry, Bella. I'll split it with you."

"I'm in," he added.

"Me, too," Taylor mumbled. "Can we move on now, please?"

Bella smiled, her body relaxing back into her chair.

They spent the next hour confirming schedules and various details for upcoming events. As they wrapped up, Avery waved her hands in the air. "Guys, I got a Google alert for Sunshine Bridal! Let me read it out loud."

Taylor rolled her eyes. "Probably just a news blog from the Expo."

"No, the heading says Sunshine Bridal to plan wedding of the year! Oh my God, it's from *Page Six*!"

He frowned. "Are we doing any celebrity weddings this year?"

"I didn't think so," Bella said.

"Wait, I'm clicking on it now. Hang on." They waited as she brought up the link. He became concerned when her excited expression slowly drained away. She grew dangerously pale and unusually quiet, staring at the screen like a Stephen King creature was about to jump out at her.

"What's the matter?" he asked, his hands clenching involuntarily into fists.

"Oh. My. God," Avery breathed, blinking furiously. She shook her head and stared at Bella. "We're in trouble. Big-ass trouble."

"Would you stop being cryptic and tell us?" Taylor demanded with her usual impatience. "Spill."

"Did you tell Adele Butterstein that we would handle her wedding?" Avery asked, glancing back and forth between Gabe and Bella.

"Who's that?" he asked. His mind spun to grasp the name the same time his gut lurched with impending disaster.

Avery narrowed her gaze. "The famous New York City heiress. The one who inherited the City Skyline publishing empire and only wanted to run the children's arm of the company, so she gifted her shares to close friends and family to run it instead? The one who's worth billions and has a bigger social media following than Taylor Swift?"

Bella gasped. "Wait—and she's marrying that big executive over at Tesla?"

"Whose name is . . . Edward," he said, meeting Bella's stare. The implication of that innocent conversation at the Royal brunch washed over him like doomsday. "Oh, shit."

"Bella. Gabe. Is this the woman who wanted you to plan her wedding this March? With the theme of Dr. Seuss?" Avery turned the screen around, and right there, in Technicolor, was Adele, the one they'd spoken to at the Royals' wedding.

Dead quiet blanketed the room.

Then Taylor burst out laughing, her fist helplessly hitting the sleek conference table with glee. "You guys are so fucked!"

Oh, they were.

They really, really were.

♥ ♥ ♥

After coffee refills and bumping some appointments so they could extend the morning meeting, Bella sat with Gabe and Avery, discussing the options. Taylor had left the room, still laughing.

Within minutes of the story breaking, Eloise Royal had sent a long text about her famous second cousin and how happy she was that the wedding was finally in good hands. Then Adele's assistant reached out, warning Bella of the massive amount of spreadsheets, pictures, and contact lists she'd gathered to send over so they could start working on the wedding ASAP. The reception venue left a message, asking for direction on setup, catering, and a thousand other details. Immediately, they were trapped in a nightmare situation and had no idea how to get out of it.

"If we take on this wedding and fail, our reputation will be ruined," Bella said. They'd worked so hard to build up a successful business; she hated the idea that one impulsive heiress could slander them while the world watched. "We need to decline and say it was a misunderstanding. I'll talk to Eloise about it and explain."

Avery shook her head. "It's too late. Even if we didn't sign a contract, Adele believes we verbally took on the gig, so if we try and back out, it will look worse. Our best bet is to clear all decks and make sure this wedding is perfect."

"Is this even a possibility with our current schedule?" she asked. "We'd need to be in New York and deal with new vendors. It's a huge undertaking, not to mention the pressure of the press. I think this is a mistake."

"It's definitely a gamble," Avery said, biting her lip. "But her assistant got the go-ahead to accept any late-planning fee we billed. She said price is no object, so we can double our normal charges for the inconvenience. The profit we'd make will give us a huge cushion for when Taylor leaves."

Dammit, she knew how important financial security was to all of them in this business. But when she thought of the risk, it still seemed better to say no.

Avery stared at Gabe. "What do you think?"

Bella studied him, waiting for him to agree with her since he'd met Adele personally, but then the glint of challenge sparked in his dark eyes.

A small smile rested on his lips, as if he'd just decided to take on Goliath and was looking forward to the battle. "We can do it. I'd have to move the Silverman wedding to you or Taylor, and Bella would need to rework her entire schedule. It'd mean overtime for all of us and a hard quarter, but I'm willing to tackle it. How can we pass up an opportunity like this? To finally show the world what Sunshine Bridal can offer?"

Avery grinned and high-fived Gabe. Bella watched them with a growing uncomfortable emotion she rarely experienced.

Panic.

"Wait, are you serious? You really think we can do this?" she asked, her voice a bit too high. She preferred working alone. Plus, she'd never taken on a last-minute high-maintenance client like Adele before. That was Avery's territory.

"Of course we can do this," Gabe said calmly. "Don't you think this is our moment?"

Bella's breath deflated from her lungs. Gabe's confidence practically shimmered from his aura, in complete contradiction to the unease flooding her body. "What about Zoe?" she asked.

"We'd all have to help out," Avery said. "Carter will love being able to spend more time with her."

Gabe nodded. "It's temporary, but we can pull it off if we all work together. Like a family."

Family.

She took a step back, suddenly overwhelmed. Gabe was slowly integrating himself into their day-to-day world, but slinging the word *family* around felt dangerous. He was a full-time employee—not a partner. Maybe he wanted to take on this wedding in order to boost his résumé? It'd be the perfect wedding to gain him more exposure, especially if it took place in New York City. Not to mention the fact that they'd be stuck together for endless hours, working side by side. There was a certain amount of intimacy that would be forced upon them, especially with the time constraint. Did she really want to take this on, knowing how much time they'd spend together?

Most troubling of all, she'd be dependent on others for her daughter's care. She'd always been careful not to take on too much at work so she could balance being a single mother with the responsibilities of a family business. But this was too much. Cramming in months of preparation in a few weeks. Holding a wedding beyond the safe confines of Cape May, with vendors and people she didn't know. It was a recipe for failure.

Hadn't she had enough of that in her life without reaching for more?

"I'm sorry, guys. I'm not comfortable with this. I'm going to have to say no."

Silence fell. She waited for recriminations and resentment, but when Gabe captured her gaze, she only saw a gentle urging and confidence. "I know it's a lot to take on," he said. "But you can do this, Bella. We can make this wedding special, and I think you're the perfect person for it."

"I agree," Avery said mildly. She glanced back and forth between them. "Gabe, do you mind if I speak to my sister alone?"

"Sure. Just call me when you're ready." He walked out of the conference room with his usual graceful, long-legged stride.

Bella crossed her arms in front of her chest. "I'm not changing my mind."

"Duly noted." Her sister studied her face with bold curiosity. "How did it really go with you two and the Royal wedding? Did something bad happen?"

The memory of Gabe's piercing dark eyes and demanding question slammed through her. *Do you really want to know what I want?*

A shiver shot down her spine. She cleared her throat. "No, it was fine. He's a hard worker."

"Yes, he is. I recently realized you rarely work together. In fact, I began realizing how capably you manage to avoid Gabe. And then I got to asking myself why."

She frowned. "I don't understand."

"Everyone loves him, except you. Many times, I've noticed you seem to deliberately ignore him. I was hoping working on the Royal wedding together would help you bond, but if you're uncomfortable, we can work out a different arrangement for Adele's wedding."

Bella half turned around to gather her thoughts. She'd never voiced her real opinion to her sisters. When Avery brought up a possible promotion for Gabe, she'd been a bit reluctant since she was afraid everyone would become dependent on him, especially if he decided to leave. But his work deserved recognition, so she'd immediately backed down.

"I'm fine working with Gabe," she finally said. "I have no problem with him personally, and I think he's an amazing wedding planner. But I'm concerned he's not cut out for small-town beach living. Not for long."

Avery tapped her lip, seemingly analyzing her words. "So you think he's going to leave? Steal our clients?"

"I honestly don't know. I worry that he's going to leave eventually for a bigger opportunity, and I don't want everyone shocked when the fallout happens. Plus, do you see how the entire female population follows him like the Pied Piper? He picked up a woman at the Royal wedding like it was nothing—and he didn't even seem excited about it! He's too used to getting his own way, all the time. That can be dangerous."

She waited for the hot denials from her sister. They'd formed a tight team working together, and Gabe had become a close friend along the way. But Avery let out a loud laugh and shook her head. "I love it. You think Gabe's dangerous."

Bella sighed with impatience. "You know what I mean! I'm trying to be truthful here."

"I wonder if you are," she murmured under her breath, pacing the room. "Listen, babe, I understand you're nervous about getting Zoe the care she needs while taking on a last-minute critical wedding. But now that I know you're comfortable working with Gabe, I think you need to do this for yourself, and the company."

"You'll be better at it," she said. "Why don't you take my place?"

"Because Adele specifically asked for you and Gabe. Your work on the Royal wedding is what closed the deal. Bella, don't you realize how talented you are? This business wouldn't be half as successful without you. I think it's time you grab this opportunity to be creative and think big and show how really fabulous you are. I know it will be hard, but I promise we'll be there for you and Zoe."

Bella took a deep breath, considering her sister's words. She was needed. And wanted. How could she say no to something that was this important to Avery? She'd be able to bring in a financial buffer for the business, and maybe prove to herself she could do this job just as well as her sisters. Wasn't it time to challenge herself and step out of her usual safe boundaries? Yes, the question that spilled from Gabe's sensual lips still haunted her, but she'd just be her usual focused self, and soon they'd both forget about the incident.

Avery narrowed her gaze, suddenly intent. "And as for Gabe, I think you're wrong. But I'm not about to try and argue with you or change your opinion. That will have to come from you."

The words had a strange foreboding, and a shiver raced down her spine. "This is important to you?" she asked softly.

Avery smiled, crossing the room and squeezing her hands. "I think it's important for all of us. Will you do it?"

Bella knew in that moment she had no choice. "Yes."

"Then let's get Gabe in here so you can get to work."

Chapter Five

"Mama, can I stay up a bit longer?"

Bella took in her daughter's big puppy-dog eyes and tried not to laugh. Zoe was snuggled under the blankets on the couch, watching TV.

"Nope. You have a spelling test tomorrow and need all your brain cells sharp. Why? What's on?"

Zoe sighed with deep mourning. "*Scooby-Doo on Zombie Island.*"

"Oh, that's my favorite! But it's spooky. Have you seen it before?"

"No, but my friend Zane said it's really scary and that I'd love it. He wants to be a zombie for Halloween. What should I be?"

"Well, we have a while before we need to decide. Tell you what—how about we record it and watch it together this weekend?"

"Yes!"

Bella set up the recording and Zoe scrambled out of her blanket fort.

"Go brush your teeth and I'll come tuck you in."

"Mama, can we get a dog? You said when it's something important to both of us, we can discuss it, and I don't think it's fair you just say no all the time."

A mix of humor and tiredness washed over her. Zoe loved to ask a million questions and delve into deep subjects right before bed.

She began straightening up, folding blankets and throwing away the leftover cups her daughter left behind in a constant trail. "No, we can't get a dog, because it's too much responsibility for me right now, but yes, we can discuss big things together."

"I'm big now. I can take care of it." She heard the water running in the background. "It can sleep with me."

"You're forgetting all the hard stuff I'll be stuck with. Like walking the dog at five thirty in the morning, or late at night, or cleaning up all the poop."

In between brushing, her daughter's mumbles floated down the hall. "Aunt TT can help since she lives with us."

That idea made Bella hoot with laughter. She shared a two-family home with her sister to save on the mortgage, but Taylor was fierce with her privacy, and had made it well known she wouldn't be sharing her space with anything covered in fur. "Aunt TT prefers fish over dogs."

"Ugh, fish are boring!"

As Zoe went on to back up her case for a dog they'd never get, Bella heard her phone buzz. She picked it up from the table and read the text from Gabe.

Can we talk? In person?

Her nerves tingled. She stared at the phone, torn, but Gabe never reached out to her with an emergency. She texted back. When?

Three dots appeared. I'm at your front door.

Belle gasped and looked down. Old yoga pants, bare feet, and a faded T-shirt. Hair in a scrunchie. No bra. No makeup.

Crap.

She forced herself to take a breath. It was about work, and there was no need to try and impress him. Better for him to realize she wasn't the sexy sort, lounging around in panties and a crop top. She was an unglamorous, messy, tired, single mom.

She responded before she changed her mind. Putting Zoe to bed. Come in.

She grabbed a fleece hoodie and slipped it over her T-shirt to take care of the no-bra situation but left the rest as is. Unlocking the door, she stepped back as he filled the space with clean, cold air, spice, and the heady scent of man.

"Thanks. Sorry about barging in, but it couldn't wait," he said in that deep, sexy voice. He dumped a plastic bag on the chair and shrugged out of his wool jacket. His off-the-clock outfit consisted of worn jeans that cupped his ass and a long-sleeve black Henley that brought out the depths of his eyes. His chiseled jaw sported a bit of stubble. His hair was windblown and mussed, like a woman had run her fingers multiple times through the thick strands.

Damn him. His sex appeal was beginning to mess with her head a bit. He made her feel juvenile, and she hated every second of her body's reaction.

"No problem," she said, shutting the door and walking as far away from him as possible. She tugged the hoodie down farther. "What's up?"

His gaze flicked over her. "Want me to wait till you get Zoe down?"

On cue, her daughter screeched Gabe's name and flew into his arms. Bella's throat tightened with emotion as she watched them interact with an easy affection that had only grown with time.

"What's up, buttercup?" he asked.

"Mama and I are gonna watch *Scooby-Doo on Zombie Island* this weekend. It's really scary, though."

He gave a shudder. "What's on the island? Vampires? Witches? Ghosts?"

She giggled. "Zombies, silly. Wanna watch it with us? We'll make popcorn."

"Hmm, sounds good, but let me check if I'm working, okay? Hey, I heard you didn't have any winter dresses to wear for show-and-tell. What'd you do?"

Her face pulled into a sad, adorable expression. "I have no pink ones. I tried to wear my summer dress, but Mama said no, but then she let me wear my cool pink boots. Wanna see?"

"Maybe later, I know you have bedtime. But I brought you something. Wanna see?"

"Yes!"

He set her down and handed her the bag.

Zoe carefully reached in and pulled out a bright-pink sweater dress with a high neck and flowers stitched down the side. "Oh my gosh, look, Mama! A pink dress I can wear in the winter!"

Raw emotion slammed through Bella. Even though she'd only made a short comment about that crazy morning, he had gone out and bought Zoe a dress because he cared for her. Dammit, why did he have to be so nice to her daughter? It only made it harder for her to keep a safe distance from him.

Her voice came out rough. "It's beautiful. What do you say to Gabe?"

Zoe hugged him. "Thank you so much, Gabe, I love it! Can I try it on?" She began jumping up and down.

Gabe easily cut in. "In the morning. I have to talk to your mom about work stuff, and you need your sleep."

She looked at the dress longingly but gave a sigh. "Okay. I'm going to wear it tomorrow. Can you tuck me in?"

Bella hesitated. It was rare he was around Zoe at bedtime, so she'd never had the opportunity to ask him before.

Gabe looked at her. His expression was patient, waiting for her decision, but it was the gleam of longing in his eyes that she couldn't deny.

"Of course. But no reading tonight. Straight to bed." She kissed her daughter and watched the pair head up together.

The moment they disappeared, she turned away. An emptiness yawned inside—vast and deep—and lately, she didn't know how to deal with it. Having Gabe in her house, with her daughter, only reminded her of all the things she'd once had with Matt and ached to experience again. It had been so long since she'd had male companionship, someone she could trust and love and laugh with. Would it always remain like this? Was she destined to be alone forever?

Low voices echoed down the stairs. She took the time to gather herself back together, along with her strength. Gabe was an important part of her daughter's life. It wasn't fair to punish Zoe for her slowly softening feelings for her coworker. Zoe had already been robbed of too many things. Somehow Bella needed to be more comfortable with them having a good relationship while she kept her distance. But the same questions haunted her.

Was it easier keeping them both safe from heartbreak?

By the time Gabe came back down, she was calm and the walls around her heart were safely barricaded.

"Sorry again about barging in so late." He gave her a smile and hooked his thumbs in his jean pockets. "Hope I'm not interrupting your plans."

A genuine laugh escaped. "Are you kidding? My agenda includes a *20/20* episode while I try to stay up past nine and fight the endless battle of chips versus cookies for a late-night snack I shouldn't eat."

"Chips should always win," he said seriously. "I didn't know you liked those shows. I'm obsessed—I watch them all. Did you see the one with the woman who supposedly murdered her husband, but they pinned it on her sister because they were having a secret affair?"

She snapped her fingers. "Yes! But the jury didn't convict, so that poor guy got murdered, and no one paid for it."

"I still think it was the wife, not the sister. The detective was a bit shoddy—he didn't seem to care as much as some of the others."

"Yeah, I agree. If I get murdered, I want one of those all-in type of cops who dedicate the rest of their career to catching the killer."

He nodded. "Me, too. Of course, you have Taylor and Avery in your corner. They're scary as shit. They'd find him and do their own justice."

"You're right. But Avery would do the same for you."

"Just Avery?"

The question had teasing undertones but probed just enough to make her turn away. She busied herself with dumping the rest of Zoe's cups in the sink. "All of us, of course," she said lightly. "Now, tell me what's going on."

He paused, then dove straight in. "We didn't have a chance to really talk around Avery. I wanted to check in with you about Adele's wedding. To see if you truly want to do this or if your sister pushed too hard."

Surprise flickered. The obvious concern in his voice didn't seem fake. She turned and stared at the gorgeous man before her, then pivoted on her bare foot. "I need wine. Want something?"

"I'll have the same."

He followed her into the small kitchen and slid onto the stool by the island. She uncorked a buttery chardonnay, filled two glasses, and leaned her elbows on the counter opposite him. He seemed to be studying her uncertainly, as if he wasn't sure what she was about to say.

"Are you worried I can't handle the work like Avery would?" she asked bluntly.

He gave a snort that was somehow endearing. "Hell no. Personally, I think you're the best match for Adele. I just want to be sure you feel comfortable taking this on. With me. If not, I'm sure Avery can step in."

Once again, he seemed in tune to her emotions. How did he see so much when she was careful to keep her distance? She figured he'd wanted to do this wedding for the résumé-building experience, but sitting in her kitchen a few feet away, she was suddenly confused about his real intentions. "Is it really just concern for me that brought you here, Gabe?"

"No." He shrugged, managing to make even that gesture elegant. "I also know Zoe will be affected by your absence and that you worry about her. Sometimes I think it's easy for all of us to forget how much you juggle being a single mom. You do it so well, we assume that nothing bothers you."

She reached for her wine with shaking fingers. God, how often she looked in the mirror and wondered if anyone truly saw her. She worked hard to try and keep centered, appreciating every small thing now that she knew about real loss, but sometimes she felt overwhelmed—as if there weren't enough hours in the day to accomplish what needed to be done. She was proud everyone thought she had it all together, especially her sisters, but alone in her room at night, she was plagued by self-doubt. Wondering if she was good enough at her job, or a supportive-enough sister, or the type of mother Zoe deserved.

Right now, she felt seen, without the surface gloss. By Gabe.

A tiny shiver crawled down her spine. She took another healthy sip and tried to regain control. "I appreciate you checking in with me. I already confirmed with Carter and Daisy they could help me out when we're in Manhattan. I also talked to Zoe to get her approval. It may seem silly to you—"

"It's not silly, Bella." His forceful tone resonated with a deep passion that made her tummy dip. Those dark brows lowered in a frown, and that one errant curl fell messily over his forehead. "She's the most important person in your life—as she should be. Why would I ever question that?"

A sigh escaped her. How could a man have the looks of an Adonis and such heart? No wonder he was able to charm anyone in his path. She had to be extra careful not to slip under his spell. "Because there's a lot of money at stake for Sunshine Bridal. Plus, this could be an amazing opportunity for your résumé and put you at the next level for your career. Unless we fail."

"We won't fail. But it's only worth it if we both want it." The word *want* fell from his lips and ricocheted like a gunshot.

She pushed away the wineglass. Maybe all her future interactions with him needed to be in complete sobriety.

She thought about his statement and the implications. This wedding would test all her skills and stretch her comfort zone. Yes, she wanted to do it for her sisters, and the finances, and even Gabe, but for the first time, she realized how badly she wanted to succeed for herself. Because deep inside, she was still unsure of herself. Wasn't it time she took a career risk and proved she was worthy of being an owner of Sunshine Bridal?

She spoke firmly. "I'm completely committed to this wedding. Zoe was excited about the Dr. Seuss theme and promised to help."

"Good. We'd all make a hell of a team."

Their gazes met and locked. In those inky eyes, something bigger loomed, something that made her insides a bit shaky.

She slid off the stool and turned away, placing her glass in the sink. "When do you want to meet to go over the initial plans?"

"How about Wednesday at ten? Your schedule was free. Does that work?"

"Yes."

He took one last sip and stood. "I better let you get some sleep. See you tomorrow."

She watched him put his glass in the sink next to hers, then shrug on his coat, the fabric pulling taut to stretch over his broad shoulders. He headed toward the door.

"Gabe?"

"Yeah?"

She crossed her arms in front of her chest. "Thanks for the dress. You didn't have to do that."

He gave her a long, lingering look. "I know. I'm just happy you let me."

He left.

She thought about his words for a long time before she headed to bed.

♥ ♥ ♥

"Three o'clock. You're being seriously checked out."

Gabe turned his head just enough to follow the direction of Carter's voice. Sure enough, there was an extremely attractive brunette stirring the straw in her drink, her gaze boldly meeting his. "She looks familiar."

"I think it's Vera's granddaughter. She's here for a visit, so you probably saw her around town." Vera was the owner of the famous bridal dress shop in the Cape.

He broke the gaze, checking to see if anything stirred beneath the belt. Nothing. "I don't need to be fooling around with anyone related to Vera. She'll kill me."

Pierce, the third of his guy crew, shook his head. "She was a prima ballerina in France and openly talks about her famous affairs. She's probably had more sex this past month than you have in the past year."

Gabe turned back to the bar and snorted. "Did you have to give me that visual? She's like in her seventies. Don't need that in my head."

"Sorry. I'm just saying she'd probably be open to her granddaughter living her life—she's not overprotective."

Carter leaned his elbows on the table and took a long swig of beer. "She's pretty. Go talk to her."

Gabe let out a half laugh. "Why are you two suddenly pimping me out?"

Pierce and Carter shared a look. Pierce was the one to speak. "'Cause you've been in a mood lately. Ever since you worked that wedding with Bella."

He jerked back in surprise. He should've figured his friends would notice. His emotions had been up and down like a jackhammer. She'd seemed so casual about Jing and his imagined "little black book" that was stuffed to capacity. She probably believed in his damn reputation as a player.

Ever since that stupid beach-bachelor tag, the town had cast him in the role of wicked seducer. He hated how so much seemed to revolve around his looks. Hated being flirted with and treated like he had no brains in his head. Hated the giggles and whispers when he walked into a bar, and the constant stream of women who approached him for some fun, rarely looking for more. It was a catch-22—women automatically thought he wasn't interested in a relationship, so he attracted the ones who only sought a one-night stand.

His reputation in Cape May was overrated and false, but it didn't stop the rumors from spreading. Last week, he'd heard he was part of a shocking threesome with a couple from out of town, when in reality, he'd spent his weeknights watching HGTV and working on weddings. For a long time, he'd laughed off the rumors, finding amusement in the gossip, but lately he was only feeling defeated.

Did any of it matter, though? Bella didn't seem to care. He was grounded in the work zone. Maybe he had a chance at a promotion to the friend zone, but he wasn't getting to the next level with her.

Except that one moment in her kitchen last night. When he'd talked about Zoe and how he admired her as a mom, she'd finally seemed completely connected to him. Her focus and attention made his head buzz like he'd guzzled a bottle of champagne, all fuzzy and bubbly with pleasure. If only she had a clue about the power she held. How he ached to feel her hands on his cheek, to smooth back her hair, to hold her in his arms and give her the comfort he knew she sometimes needed but pushed away. He wanted to be that man for her.

But she wouldn't let him.

"Sorry," he grumbled. "I'll just drink my beer, and we'll talk about sports and keep things simple."

Carter let out a curse. "Stop being so damn dramatic. Have you told her how you feel yet?"

"Are you crazy? I can't suddenly announce I've been crushing on her for years and ask her to try out a relationship."

"Sure you can," Carter said.

Pierce made a rude noise. "Nah, Gabe's right. Can't just announce how you feel all the time. It worked for you with Avery, but Bella may freak. She's been guarded since Matt died and has a kid to protect. She probably thinks Gabe is all wrong for her."

"Prove you're not, then," Carter said simply. "I've seen you with Zoe. You'd be an amazing father. Is she afraid you won't want a serious relationship?"

"Probably. Damn Beach Bachelor thing is killing me. I deliberately stayed away from dating to show her I'm not a player, but it doesn't matter. She thought I picked up someone at the Royal wedding, but I was just being polite. The gossip is ridiculous. I think everyone likes the idea of me wreaking havoc on the hearts of the innocent here."

The guys burst out laughing.

"Damn, that was good," Pierce said, patting him on the back. "Very descriptive."

A reluctant grin curved his lips. "Screw you. Both of you are useless."

"I still think you may need to be clear with your intentions," Carter said. "Tell her how you really feel. Get a '*Yes, I'm into you, too, and want to give it a try,*' or a '*No, go away or I'll scream harassment.*' You can't keep going on like this, dude."

"And if she says no, she's not interested?" he asked.

Pierce drummed his fingers on the bar. "It'll suck, but you're wasting too much time going back and forth with her. Maybe Carter's right. Get a yes-or-no answer, and work from there. If she says no, you start dating other people."

Carter nodded. "Good plan. Just swipe left, buddy. Or is it right?"

He groaned. "If I do this, I need to find the perfect time. I just can't declare my feelings across the conference-room table."

"You'll find it. After all, Valentine's Day is coming up. Cupid may help," Pierce said.

"I hate V Day," he grumbled.

"So does every other man in America," Carter agreed. "But if it makes Avery happy, I'm in."

"Spoken like a true poet," Pierce teased. "Actually, Taylor despises V Day. Says it's a holiday constructed for commercialism and to make females feel bad about themselves if they don't have someone in their life."

Gabe laughed. "Of course she'd say that. Gonna be a real bitch when she decides to move on."

Pierce cranked his head around and stared. "Why? Has she said something?"

"Not to me. But she made her intentions pretty damn clear she doesn't want to do wedding planning much longer."

Pierce muttered something under his breath, and a frown creased his brow. Taylor had always made her intentions to leave Cape May known, but maybe the upcoming reality was giving Gabe's friend pause. He suspected Pierce harbored hidden feelings for Taylor but didn't want to ruin their close-knit bond. They'd grown up together. Moving from friends to lovers was tricky, and many times it just didn't stick.

Another reason he was worried about pushing Bella. But maybe his friends were right. He'd hinted of his interest and hoped she'd want to hear more, but she'd quickly slammed the door shut. And he'd given her the out. He'd never asked her straight out on a date.

All his pep talks about moving on were bullshit. Until he knew where Bella's head and heart were, he couldn't date another woman.

"If you're feeling more for Taylor than friendship, maybe you need to take Carter's advice, too," Gabe said.

"Just call me Oprah. Or Dr. Phil. Or—aw, hell, who's the big advice guru this decade?" Carter asked.

"Ellen," he said. "She's the only successful talk-show host left."

Pierce lifted his beer and took a slug. "There's nothing between us," he finally said, staring into his glass like it held the future. "We're just friends. And she's been unhappy here a long time."

Gabe looked at Carter, who shrugged. "Okay. So now that we're all talking about our emotions like a bunch of girls, how about we discuss real stuff?"

"Like what?" Gabe asked.

"My wedding. Avery said she wants Lucy at the ceremony, but all I keep picturing was that other dog pissing on the runner at that wedding last summer." Lucy was Carter's Yorkshire terrier, who had given Avery a hard time in the beginning but now adored her. They treated the canine like a pampered only child. "I think she should sit this one out, and we'll bring her home some wedding cake. What do you guys think?"

Pierce rubbed his face and groaned. "Is this what it's come to with us? Are we old? Do we all need to get laid?"

Carter snorted. "Speak for yourself."

"I'm off the clock and refuse to talk about weddings," Gabe said. "Spring training for the Phillies is coming up. What do you think our chances are?"

After a slight hesitation, they all fell into a safe, manly conversation about America's favorite pastime. He had another beer, and by the time he got home, he'd made the decision to finally tell Bella his true feelings.

It was possible she'd never imagined him in a romantic way, and maybe the thought of hooking up with a man dubbed "the local stud" horrified her. But if he never asked her, he'd always wonder, and his life would be filled with regret and what-ifs.

It was time to take a risk.

Chapter Six

Gabe glanced around at the explosion of papers, folders, photos, and iPads on the table and groaned. "Why Dr. Seuss? No one in history seems to have had a wedding with this theme, which makes it impossible to borrow any good ideas."

They'd finished the conference call with Adele's assistant and were still struggling a few hours later. Bella tapped her fingernail against her pursed lips in a steady rhythm, which he tried not to focus on. He needed no distractions today. The first hit of creative juice and adrenaline had worn off. Now he struggled with the cold reality that this was going to be really hard to pull off well. He felt as if they were grasping at random items in the Dr. Seuss world to please Adele, but they had no true idea who she was or what she'd love.

In Taylor's words, they might be seriously fucked.

"The guest list is stellar," he said a bit grumpily. "Wall Street tycoons, writers, and philanthropists I've only seen in the news. They'll tear us apart if we screw this up."

"The real problem is how to avoid a childish birthday-party scenario and make it into a sophisticated wedding," Bella murmured, her gaze seemingly fixed into the distant future. "I think our scope is too wide. We're trying to grab ideas from too many books and characters. We need to narrow our focus."

"You're right. I'm overwhelmed—I had no idea he had this many books. I love color, but there's no way we can pull off a rainbow wedding here."

"Agreed. We need to stick to one theme and pull it all together."

"Well, the Grinch is out. How about Horton? He seems like a nice sort."

Bella raised a brow. "Think broader."

"You said to narrow the field."

"Not by sticking with elephants. It needs to be something everyone can support," she whispered, tapping her lip faster. "A lesson wrapped up in fun, but for an adult. Then we layer it through."

"Alcoholic beverages in bright colors?" he suggested. "Neon blue? Bright yellow? We can have signature cocktails that look fun to drink."

"Definitely. But what's the lesson?"

He blinked. "Don't drink unfun things?"

Her glower was adorable, and he'd realized in the past few hours he enjoyed baiting her a bit. She was zen most of the time, but when he scratched the surface, she had a bit of a bite. Probably the mother within her, which forced her to be a disciplinarian. She had steel underneath.

And he found it sexy as hell.

Suddenly, she froze, cranking her head around to gaze at him with a fierce intent. "*The Lorax*."

He flipped through the images on the iPad screen and quickly zoomed in on the book cover. "Yeah, I remember this. Save the trees, right?"

A radiant glow beamed from her face. "Recycling. Saving the environment. Truffula trees!"

"Truffles, like chocolate?"

"No." She excitedly tapped on the keyboard and began pulling pics from a folder. She slid over a mock-up print of fluffy vibrant-colored flowers with long stalks. They looked like cotton candy stuck at the end of a stick. "These are Truffula trees. We can find flowers that resemble them and use a nature theme throughout the entire reception. Adele wants to celebrate the world of Dr. Seuss, so let's step into the one he created in *The Lorax*. It can be both whimsical and elegant. I think this will work, Gabe."

He went to the stack of hardcover books she'd brought over from Zoe's bookshelf and took out *The Lorax*. As he thumbed through the pages, he got her vision, and it was like a zap of lightning finally reignited his tired brain cells. The possibilities suddenly seemed reasonable and plentiful. "It's brilliant," he finally said, slamming his fist on the table with victory. "I see exactly where you're going with this. Do you think we can get Maria to do the cake?"

Maria was the master baker of the Cape and their first choice for all weddings, which meant she was double-booked most of the time. Fortunately, the woman adored a good challenge, and a Dr. Seuss cake would be the one to make her consider. Especially with a sky-high budget. "We'll go and beg today if we can grab an appointment. Did you talk to Pierce about doing the photography?"

"Yeah, unfortunately he has another job booked. We'll have to find someone else."

"We're starting with a blank slate here, so let's go through the vendors we want to work with. We can transport the cake and flowers, but we'll need a caterer close to the venue. What's her bridesmaid-dress colors?"

He practically beamed with excitement. "There are none! It's just her and the groom."

Her excited grin hit him in his solar plexus. He loved sharing the thrill of planning a wedding with her. For the past few years, she'd refused to work with him, always insisting she didn't need the extra help or preferring Taylor or Avery to step in. Being able to get to know her on this level was a gift. "Oh, thank God. I was terrified we'd need to deal with neon colors and patterns."

He clicked on an image and expanded to full screen. "Here's the layout of the bookstore. We're dealing with a lot of mahogany wood, shelving, and columns, but if we brought in the tree element, we could accent the natural decor rather than trying to mask it."

"Yes, we can focus on the books as a main element instead of an afterthought."

He nodded. "Birch would work. It's light enough for contrast, has interesting texture and form, plus, it pairs beautifully with white lights."

Her face scrunched a little in thought. Some strands of white-blonde hair escaped her topknot and lay against her cheeks. "We use all recycled materials—from the place settings to the favors. Set it all against the natural beauty of the environment with—"

"Color for pop," he finished. "I think we finally have our theme."

"Let's get on the phone with our vendors and start mocking up designs," she said.

"I'll order in. Grilled chicken Caesar salad with unsweetened iced tea?"

For a moment, her blue eyes locked on him, an odd intensity radiating from her figure. "Yes, thanks."

He cocked his head. "You didn't think I knew what you wanted?"

She shifted in her chair but didn't break the gaze. "I guess not. We've never been as close as you and my sisters." An awkward shrug moved her shoulders. "Sorry. I only meant—"

"I know what you meant," he said softly. He studied her face. The graceful curve of her cheek, the lush pink of her lips, the startling blue of her eyes framed by thick lashes, the heart-shaped mole on her jutted chin. "I've always been listening. And I've always been here, waiting until you needed me."

She jerked back, but the tiny flare of awareness in her eyes told him there might be more. Maybe she was finally allowing him a peek inside a place that had been locked up tight.

Perhaps working together on this wedding was a way to get close and finally confess his real feelings. The thought caused cold sweat to prickle from his brow.

There was so much to lose.

But there was more to win. The conversation with Carter and Pierce reminded him if he didn't try, he'd never know if he had a real shot with her.

He was tired of playing it safe. Yes, things were easier as casual friends, but what if he could make Bella happy? What if they were meant to be together and he'd been wasting all this time? His heart already belonged to her, and the idea of spending another year afraid to admit his feelings, living like a monk, made his gut clench.

If he could use planning Adele's wedding to build a solid connection, he might be able to man up and ask her to take a chance on him. He'd noticed a softening this past week toward him. Spending time with her was key.

But it was still too soon, so he decided to lighten the mood. "And you finally do need me," he added with a teasing wink. "I'm crucial to dazzling New York society with the wonders of Seussland. Hey, how about we have Sneetch greeters at the doors? They can have big bellies and one will wear a star—the other won't. It can be a subtle dig at the have and have-nots, right?"

She groaned, and the heaviness in the air drifted away. "That's truly awful."

"I'll work on it."

He called in the lunch order and tried not to hope too hard.

"How's Adele's wedding going?" Avery asked.

They were gathered in Taylor's part of the house for dinner. They tried to schedule regular family dinners twice per week, but lately Taylor and Avery had been traveling, so they'd been missing each other. Bella was looking forward to a chill night with her sisters.

"We got a handle on it," she said, expertly stirring multiple pans of sizzling vegetables and seasoned chicken. "Can you get the toppings?"

"Sure." Avery set up a makeshift assembly line and began dumping shredded cheese, lettuce, and chopped tomatoes into bowls. "Did you decide on any details yet?"

"We're going with a *Lorax* theme."

Avery nodded, but Bella noticed the obvious frown. Her sister was a true type-A personality who thrived on details. And though her intentions were always good, she loved to offer suggestions. What made it even more frustrating was that her older sister was usually right. "*Lorax* is great to pull from. Is that Adele's favorite Dr. Seuss book?"

Taylor took out the wine, filled three glasses, then poured milk for Zoe. "Can we please not talk about work tonight? Did anyone see the new *Bachelor* pick? Talk about yumminess."

Bella added another dash of garlic to the peppers and onions, then removed the pan of chicken from the burner. Damn, why hadn't she thought to ask Adele what her favorite Dr. Seuss book was? Her sister would have gotten that detail.

She tried not to sound defensive. "I don't know. But we have enough feedback to know *The Lorax* will be perfect." She refused to second-guess herself now. Besides, Gabe had been just as enthusiastic, and she trusted his instincts.

"If you include *Oh, the Places You'll Go!*, you can focus on travel, and there's tons to pull from. Maybe even more than *The Lorax*."

Bella tried not to slam down the pan, reminding herself Avery was only trying to help. "We're mimicking the Truffula plants in our decor. We're going to use birch trees and place settings with recyclable materials. It's going to be fresh yet focused."

"Hmmm."

She cocked her head. "What does that mean?"

Avery waved her hand in the air. "Nothing. You'll do great—Gabe is amazing to work with and has so many ideas."

"Meaning I don't?"

"Of course not. Why are you getting so weird? Do you have your period?"

Bella gasped. "That's something a guy would ask! Shame on you. Maybe I'm just tired of being questioned on my own projects."

Avery's mouth fell open. "I'm not questioning you! I know you were worried about taking so much on, so I wanted to help. I don't want you to feel overwhelmed and alone in this, that's all."

Avery's concern only caused more irritation. It made no sense, but sometimes Bella was resentful of her older sister's unfailing confidence and belief that she could do anything she set her mind to. She hated that Avery would think of her as the sister who always needed extra help.

The awful words popped out of her mouth before she could tame them. "Don't worry, Avery. I can handle things on my own. I won't embarrass the family."

"What kind of crap is that? I—"

Taylor cleared her throat. "Did you see that Jason Momoa has a new movie out and he's naked in it?"

They both turned at once. "Totally naked?" Avery asked after a brief pause. "Full frontal? Or just the butt?"

"Momoa has a new movie out?" Bella asked.

Taylor grinned. "Nope, I just needed a distraction for you psychos. Enough about weddings and Dr. Seuss—I refuse to ruin Taco Tuesday. I'm hungry and ready to eat. Plus, I have some news and want to be the main focus of attention."

Bella shared a glance with Avery and settled down. God knew she didn't want to fight, and her insides were all tangled up with a bunch of messy emotions she needed to sort out. She'd do a long meditation tonight, and maybe a good night's sleep would settle her back. Lately, all her zen calm had been deserting her. She needed to figure out why.

"Fine with me," she said. "Can you get Zoe?"

Taylor nodded and went to get her while Bella transferred the food onto platters and put out the warmed fajitas. A tug on her hair made her turn.

"I'm sorry about the period comment," Avery muttered. "I'm getting stressed about planning my own wedding. Isn't that stupid?"

Bella sighed. "No, sweetie, it's not. It's perfectly acceptable, and I'm just being overly sensitive lately. How about we all get together and do a planning session? We do it for our clients—why shouldn't we do it for you?"

Avery sniffed. "Thanks. I think that's perfect. But can we leave Carter out of it? He did so good with helping plan his sister's wedding, he now thinks he's an expert. He's driving me nuts sending me all these new ideas, and my vendors keep calling me to go over his suggestions. I think I created a monster."

Bella bit back a laugh and squeezed her sister's shoulder. "We'll take him down a peg. Let's eat some tacos and hear Taylor's news."

Zoe raced in on Taylor's heels. "Tacos!" she squealed. "I don't want any peppers or mushrooms or onions or zucchs."

"That's zucchini, and you have to pick at least one veggie."

Her daughter made a face and slid into the chair. "Fine. Red peppers."

They dug into their tacos with gusto while Zoe chatted about her day in school. "There's going to be two dances at school for Valentine's Day. I can wear my new pink dress, Mama!"

She smiled. "Yes, you can. There's two this year?"

"Uh-huh. The first one is for mommies and boys, and the second one is for girls and their daddies. But Mrs. Wooley says it doesn't have to be a real mom or dad that goes. She said there can be friends or aunts or uncles or two mommies and two daddies. She says families are made up of all sorts of people, so I want to go with Uncle Carter."

Her heart squeezed in both pain and gratitude. She hated that Matt wasn't here to experience the magic of his beautiful daughter, but knowing Avery was marrying a wonderful man who could bring a strong male presence to the family was a gift.

"Oh, honey, Uncle Carter will love that! He's going to be really excited. Make sure you text me the date, Bella."

"I will."

Taylor finished her last taco and wiped her mouth. "Well, I don't know how I'm going to top a V-Day dance, but it's time to announce my news. I have been officially invited to participate in an art show."

Bella gasped. Taylor had always wanted to travel and study art abroad, but she'd been pulled into the family business after Matt died, and then their parents had retired. She'd committed to working another two years in order to make the business strong before moving on. Bella knew what a sacrifice her sister had made to stay. Taylor had never wanted to settle in the small beach town and craved a bigger, more glamorous lifestyle. Her painting had always been a passion that she termed more of a hobby, but in the past year, Bella had seen her spend more time in her studio. Carter had bought her first painting last summer and introduced her to a few contacts.

"Are you kidding me?" Avery asked, clapping her hands. "T, that's amazing! Tell us all the details."

"Well, Carter hooked me up with a big art dealer who takes on brand-new artists. He saw some of my work, and wants me to join in for an introductory exhibit in Paris." Her eyes sparkled with excitement. "He's interested in fresh perspectives and thinks my work has the edge he's been looking for."

"Paris?" Avery gasped. "This is amazing news."

"Wow, Aunt TT, you're gonna be famous!" Zoe announced.

"Doubtful, babe. But it doesn't matter as long as I try my best, right?"

Zoe nodded. "Right."

Bella swallowed back the lump in her throat. Pride resonated through her. It was finally going to be Taylor's turn to shine. "This is the best news. When's the show? How many pieces does he need?"

"The show is in September, and he wants five more canvases. No matter what happens, I have the opportunity to expand my audience. He's well known internationally, and mentioned if there's demand for my work, I can stay in Paris and work from there. I never thought it was a possibility since I'm not classically trained."

"You always had a raw talent," she said. "And you've been painting for years, learning on your own, self-taught. I'm so damn proud of you."

"Thanks." Her happiness seemed to fade a notch. "This means my time is officially up."

Avery sighed. "You're leaving Sunshine Bridal."

Taylor nodded. "I'd stay till the end of the year, but it depends on the show. I may need to leave earlier, so we may need to plan a September exit."

Bella's heart shredded at the idea of losing her baby sister, but she also knew Taylor needed to go. "We understand, babe. It's not a surprise—and God knows it's overdue."

"Wait. Aunt TT, where are you going?" Zoe asked with an edge of panic.

Taylor leaned over the table, stretching her arms out to grasp her niece's small hands. "I'm going to travel for a while, sweetheart. I want to see some of the world out there, and when you grow up, you may want to, also. But I won't be gone forever. You're my family—I will always come back to you."

Zoe blinked. "Is Uncle Pierce going with you, too?"

Taylor jerked back. "Um, no. He's going to stay here with you, just like Uncle Carter and Gabe."

"What if I don't know the right way to mix my colors? I forget a lot, and you're the only one who knows."

Taylor smiled, her brown eyes filled with emotion. "You text or FaceTime me. I will always make sure you get the perfect color. Deal?"

"Deal." She turned hopefully to Bella. "Mama, can we get a dog once Aunt TT leaves? I think we'll be too lonely, so we need something to make us happy."

Bella shared a glance with her sisters and burst into laughter.

Taylor grumbled. "Dude, I'm not even gone yet and you're replacing me with a canine."

Bella winked. "Hmm, not a bad idea. I was thinking of turning your place into a yoga studio."

"Oh, can I keep some of my storage here?" Avery cut in. "There's never enough space."

"Okay, Abbott and Costello. Real funny."

Amid the bittersweet sentiment, Bella was once again reminded of the beauty within the power of family. For her, it was enough. As long as she and Zoe had this, they didn't need anything else.

Her mind flashed to a picture of Gabe's face, his dark eyes gleaming with a banked emotion she didn't understand, his words echoing in her mind like a mantra.

"I've always been listening. And I've always been here, waiting until you needed me."

He meant as a friend, of course. There was nothing else between them except for a growing respect for his professional skill.

Funny, his words caused a deep longing to uncurl from within, but it had been so long since she'd been with a man, she chalked it up to loneliness.

It couldn't be anything else.

Chapter Seven

"I can't believe we scored a face-to-face meeting with Adele," Bella said. "I've never met such a hands-off bride. Are we sure her assistant isn't getting married instead?"

Gabe cupped her elbow and guided her over the high, uneven curb just as a bright-yellow taxicab roared past them, inches away. "I know. We need to use our time wisely."

He'd found a thirty-minute hole in Adele's nonstop schedule, and her assistant suggested a pub she liked that was a few minutes away from a previous appointment. He was used to dealing directly with brides and grooms who demanded a hands-on approach, refusing to delegate such details to an assistant. But Adele had been happy to relinquish her power, too busy to even pop on a quick conference call. It was a bit disarming to plan a wedding without direct client approval.

On the other hand, he was enjoying the limitless freedom to create and brainstorm an entire wedding. With Bella.

"When's our appointment at Housing Works?" she asked.

"Not till two p.m., so we should have plenty of time. Watch the puddle."

Her leather boot landed safely a few inches to the left. It was a cold day in Manhattan, with brisk winds and dirty snow edging the sidewalks.

"Here's the pub," she said. "I'm getting an Irish coffee. Don't judge me."

He laughed and they stepped inside. The old-fashioned Irish pub had a giant bar, lots of dark wood and brass, and spacious booths. He'd expected to meet their client at a fancy five-star restaurant, but it was a reminder that Adele Butterstein was different from the usual heiress and someone they didn't know well.

Which made today's lunch meeting especially important.

Weddings were extremely personal, and so far, they only knew surface information about the bride. He hoped with a face-to-face dialogue, they'd be able to tap into something deeper to give her ceremony and reception something special, beyond the Dr. Seuss drinks and Truffula trees.

They settled in, starting with water, and within five minutes, Adele's deep, booming voice rang out. "Darlings! It's so wonderful to see you!"

He grinned at her greeting. It was as if she were surprised to find them here instead of having an arranged meeting. She was dressed in a wraparound dress that emphasized her generous curves, the color a shocking pink. Her red hair was a glaring contrast.

She threw her canary-yellow raincoat on the coatrack and beamed at them from across the table. "I'm starving. Do you know they only give you tiny cucumber sandwiches at fundraisers? And fruit. I asked for a cracker, and they looked at me like I'd shot someone. When were carbs and cheese made the enemies? They did nothing but give women pleasure, and look what we did. Ostracized them."

Bella laughed. "Agreed. There hasn't been a bread basket I met I haven't loved."

The waitress came over, and they spent a few minutes ordering food, with both Adele and Bella going for an Irish coffee, extra whipped cream.

"Now, I cannot wait to hear all the details. Tell me what we still need to do."

Gabe kept his smile pinned, but his gut lurched. "I'm assuming your assistant has kept you abreast on everything? She's been approving things for us."

"Oh, my, of course! Stacia is a treasure. She sends me all the details, but I mostly skim them. After all, that's why I have you two working for me—to bring your amazing skill and vision to my wedding, right?"

Bella jumped in. "Exactly. And we've loved taking the lead on this. But taking some time to talk in person helps us focus on the details that will make your wedding truly personal. We don't want to miss anything that's important to you."

Adele put her hand to her heart, gaze full of emotion. "And that is why I picked you. That's just so lovely." The bread came, and Adele dove in, slathering on the butter and eating with the same type of gusto she seemed to have when attacking other areas of her life. "Darlings, talk to me about the things I'll love most. Stacia said our theme is *The Lorax*, and I think it's divine."

Gabe shared a look with Bella and dug in. Deftly parrying back and forth, they went over some highlights. "For the food, we've arranged an elegant sit-down, but Stacia seemed unsure about the menu. She mentioned your guests prefer a lighter touch, but we have an amazing chef at our disposal and would like to give you an array of food for your taste."

Her face lit up. "I'm so glad you mentioned it! No boring salmon or chicken or endless salads with beets, no matter how many of my guests pretend to be on a diet. I want to indulge at my wedding. The theme word should be *decadent*. Cheese, truffle oil, pasta, butter, anything that gives pleasure. Are we doing green eggs and ham?"

Gabe stiffened. "Well, no, but—"

"Thank God!" She laughed. "All of my other planners insisted we put green eggs and ham on the menu. Ridiculous, right? I'm looking to integrate the magic of Dr. Seuss into my wedding, not bash people over the head with overdone ideas. That's why I've loved everything you came up with so far."

"We're so glad," Bella said, obviously relieved. "Now, about favors—"

"Oh yes, let's give away trees."

Bella blinked. "Trees?"

"Of course, it goes with the theme. For the cake, I want it to be multilayered and toppled over in true Dr. Seuss form. And we definitely need a dessert bar with Dr. Seuss treats."

Uneasiness trickled through him. He figured she'd be a challenge, but trees were a tall order for any planner to fill. Literally.

"Can we do a specialty cocktail that smokes? I've seen some before, and it reminds me of the mist in a forest. Wouldn't that be wonderful?"

Gabe nodded. Yep. Wonderful.

Bella took advantage of the brief pause and leaned in. "Adele, is there a reason why you picked this theme for your wedding?" she asked curiously. "Is there something specific about the books or author that you love?"

Adele let out a long, dreamy sigh, as if caught in the past. "My nanny and housekeeper mostly raised me. My father insisted—said it wasn't proper for my mother to be taking care of children when she could be helping the world, or him. But at night, she'd sneak into my room, and we'd read Dr. Seuss books together. Oh, how we laughed!

"She promised we'd read every single one together, and we'd come up with fun rhymes and try to talk in a secret language only we understood." She took a sip of her drink, staring down at her cup. "I used to pretend my father was the Grinch and that one day his heart would grow big. It never happened.

"When my mother died, the only thing that made me happy was when I read Dr. Seuss and thought about her. She was with me when I read those books. Especially in *Oh, the Places You'll Go!* My mother would quote it all the time, reminding me I'm in charge of my destiny, and I have everything I need to follow my path—my feet and my brains. And then she'd tell me to never be trapped in a life I didn't want when I grew up. I could be anything, do anything, and act any way I wanted, as long as it was from my heart."

Empathy crashed through him for that lonely rich girl in her big, opulent house, looking for her mother in books that made her happy. He thought about his father and how many years he'd dedicated to trying to make his dad love him. He might not have grown up in a mansion, but in that tiny house, in his back bedroom with the drafty windows and threadbare quilt, he'd prayed too many times to be worthy of his father's approval.

Adele had learned from her mother that she was enough just as she was.

Gabe had taught that lesson to himself.

The missing piece they'd needed to plan this wedding suddenly fell into place. He'd been excited to plan a whimsical reception for a vibrant, interesting woman, but knowing the true feelings behind her love for Dr. Seuss would help them bring the event to a whole other level—one filled with emotion and memories that were important to her past.

Bella reached over and squeezed her hand. "Thank you for sharing that, Adele. We'll find the perfect way to make your mom part of your day." Bella paused. "I know how hard it is to lose someone you love. I promise, we'll make this wedding everything you dreamed of."

"Thank you, child," she said quietly. "I know you will."

Gabe cleared his throat, struggling past the emotional moment and getting back to logistics. "We've gone over the guest list and see you also want to skip the rehearsal dinner. Are you sure?"

She giggled, joy returning. "Lord, yes. I can't stand to see most of these people the day of the wedding, let alone the day before. They'll need places to stay, though. Penthouses, private suites, spa dates, et cetera. The usual to keep them happy."

Bella typed out the notes on her phone. "And what about Edward? Is there anything specific he'd like to see at the wedding . . . or not see?"

"Ed wants to show up so we can finally make this legal. We've been living in sin far too long for his poor aristocratic heart. He's asked for Courvoisier cognac, a safe place to smoke a cigar, and for me to be happy with the rest." She sighed. "Isn't he sweet?"

"He definitely is," Bella said.

The waitress dropped off their food. Gabe almost groaned at the perfect bacon cheeseburger. "How would you like us to handle the press?"

"Most of them want to write about my wedding and tear me apart," she said good-naturedly. "I want to be sure they don't get through the door."

"I'll coordinate with Stacia and get some security," Gabe said.

They chatted about a few more specifics; then Adele took a call and made her apologies. "I must run, darlings. Thank you. From now on, you have my approval to do the rest as you see fit. I barely have time to show up that day, let alone deal with cake and food tastings, appointments, or questions on my opinions. All I ask is you give me a day of great joy but with personal touches that will make it special."

"We will," Gabe said.

She blew kisses, grabbed her yellow jacket, and flew out the door.

Bella collapsed back into the booth. "She just gave us carte blanche to do her entire wedding, Gabe. She doesn't even want to hear from us! Has this ever happened to you?"

He scoffed. "Are you kidding? Most brides insist on a full explanation if I change the brand of chardonnay. This is beyond my usual pay grade."

Her eyes sparkled with excitement. "But now we know how to make this wedding perfect. The Dr. Seuss theme is about her mother."

Gabe nodded. "It's more important than trying to throw a wedding no one else has done or satisfying a fun theme. It's about what Dr. Seuss meant to her. Which means we can—"

"Bring her mother's memory into the wedding and—"

"Make it whole."

They stared at one another in complete satisfaction. His insides burned to reach over and touch her, make her understand how well they worked together and that they could be so much more. But he swallowed it all back for now. "I'm just not sure about the best way to do it," he finally said.

"Neither am I. But we'll figure it out."

He liked the term *we*. She was getting more comfortable in his presence. Sometimes he'd catch her staring at him, then quickly turning away and morphing into business mode. But the look in her eyes told him she felt more than she showed. His only problem was balancing what he really wanted from her.

Everything, the voice inside him whispered. *Anything she's willing to give.*

"We better go," she said, interrupting his thoughts.

He picked up the bill with a sigh. "Guess we pick up the check even if our client is richer than God."

Her giggle surprised him. "At least it's a tax write-off. We'll put it on the business card." She tucked it in the leather folder, then gasped as she studied the bill. "Eighteen dollars for an Irish coffee? Are they serious?"

Amusement cut through him. "Welcome to city prices. It's pretty standard."

"It had more coffee than alcohol! It's not even a fancy place. How much do you need to make here in order to survive?"

"Too much."

They paid and he escorted her out. The wind whipped with mad fury, and Bella rushed to cross the street, probably desperate to get back into the warmth of the car. He grabbed her arm and hauled her back just in time, barely missing a screeching taxi hauling ass down the other side of the road. His heart stopped in his chest as he looked down at her beautiful face, her cheeks flushed pink.

Bella gasped. "Oh my God, that car almost hit me when I was in the crosswalk! Pedestrians have right of way!"

"Not here. That's just a technicality." He kept a firm grip on her until she was safely in the car and wondered if his hair had turned gray. He needed to remember she wasn't used to being someplace other than Cape May.

He pulled out into the crazy traffic and slowly navigated them toward SoHo.

"I don't know how you drive here," she muttered after a few minutes of weaving in and out from double-parked cars, buses, and endless construction. "I complain about the summer tourists, but driving here is like playing Russian roulette."

He laughed. "I worked in Midtown for a while when I just started out. You learn quick."

They hit a pothole, and the car bumped. "You'd think with the high city taxes, they'd fix the roads."

"Agreed. But more money doesn't necessarily mean better resources. Or better anything."

"Isn't it interesting how money doesn't necessarily make you happy?" she asked, directing the heater to blow on her full blast. "Hearing about Adele's father was really sad. I can't imagine stealing time with my mom, like it was against the rules."

His mind flashed back to his own childhood. His father's consistent rip-downs and verbal abuse had almost torn him apart. He'd ached for the protectiveness of his mother, which rarely came. "Actually, I can. My father believed I was weakened by my mother, so he tried to keep us apart. But sometimes, when he wasn't around, she'd hug me and tell me to be strong."

Her soft gasp made him glance over. "Gabe, that's terrible. I know you mentioned problems with your dad, but I had no idea it was that bad."

He rarely talked about his past. It had nothing to do with the man he was today. He'd pushed forward and committed to a job and lifestyle he loved. He tried not to think about his father, but seeing her obvious pain for him soothed some of the rawness. "My dad liked to tell me what a loser I was. That I'd never be a real man. I know my mom felt bad, but she never did anything to try and stop him. After a while, I couldn't accept her excuses. I mean, shouldn't a mother protect her child?"

"Yes." Her voice broke, then strengthened. "God, yes."

He felt her gaze probing, but he kept his attention on the road. He didn't want her pity, but sharing such a core part of his past with her felt right. Wasn't this what he'd been longing for? To be able to get beneath the surface with Bella and show her who he truly was—even the rough parts?

"Children don't realize what's good or bad because they don't know any differently. It was when I visited my friends' houses and saw how their parents treated each other and their kids that I realized my home life was screwed up. As soon as I was able, I got out of that house. Left them both behind and chose to follow the type of life I wanted."

"Like the Dr. Seuss quote," she murmured.

He laughed. "Yes, exactly."

She shook her head. "I didn't realize how lucky I was. I grew up with sisters I was close to, and my parents taught us early about how to love. You had no siblings or other family?"

"No, I was an only. My father had two brothers, but one was in jail, and the other wandered off somewhere and never got in touch. Mom has a sister in California I saw once."

"You must have been lonely."

The words held a thread of understanding and an invitation to know more. She rarely asked him personal questions, so he gave her it all freely. "I was, but I found solace in beautiful things. While everyone was obsessed with Snapchat and Insta, I became a Pinterest junkie. First it was nature and animals. Then I became fascinated by high culture—beautiful people in glamorous clothes, traveling the world. I wanted that type of life, but I didn't know how to get it. One day, I was in the park. The weather was warm—it was early spring—and I watched a bride and groom and their wedding party get out of a limo and begin taking pictures all over the grounds. It was like watching a fairy tale of happily ever after. The white dress, the way the groom looked at the bride. Their friends and family happy and smiling. They were drinking champagne and doing all these poses in front of the camera, and I remembered thinking how badly I wanted to be a part of it. To share in that one perfect day—to be part of a memory that was good and pure and beautiful."

He gave a half laugh, embarrassed at his emotion. "Anyway, that's how I became obsessed with weddings. I studied endless pictures online. I loved the perfection of it all, from the cake to the flowers—anything seemed possible. And it was wrapped up in this thing called love. What could be better? So I began researching careers in the wedding industry and decided I'd try to be an event planner."

"And your father didn't approve?"

He laughed with no humor. "Hell no. I shamed him. That was a woman's job—not a man's. Dad did manual labor. He respected work that paid by using your hands. But I was lucky—I scored a job in the food industry, made a ton of money, and moved out. I worked nonstop, went to community college for my degree, and finally scored a job as an event planner. Eventually, I found my way to Cape May."

"I have an idea it wasn't as easy as you describe." Her voice was soft and melodic, the car snug and warm, giving them a protective armor from the bitter cold outside.

"I'm satisfied with where I am now. It was all worth it."

"Satisfied, but not happy?"

He had never been truly happy—the type of happy that comes from love and sharing a life with somebody. The endless women from before he'd met Bella were flickering images that had not been able to touch his heart, no matter how hard he tried. But when he met Bella's gaze for the very first time, his soul had seemed to recognize hers. It was as if he'd found his missing half.

But she wouldn't want to hear that type of truth from him.

Not yet.

"Let's just say it's good to have goals." He deftly parallel parked into the tight space just down the block from the bookshop and cut the engine. "We're here."

She nodded, seemingly lost in her thoughts for a while. Then she got out of the car.

♥ ♥ ♥

She'd been wrong about him.

All through their lunch meeting, she'd been distracted by the revelations he wasn't the man she thought. It was easy to assign a past to someone who was continually charming and easy-going, with classic good looks to match. She'd figured he'd been the golden child—prom king and endlessly popular. Many attractive white males with his type of personality had an easier path than others. But the one he painted came with heartache, and the career he'd pursued put him in a role that was easy to make fun of.

I found solace in beautiful things . . .

His words haunted her. She'd wanted to stay in the car, in their cocoon, and learn more about the boy who'd turned into a man who treated her daughter with such love and care. A man who took each wedding he planned seriously, digging deep to find what the couple needed from the ceremony. What else would she find beneath that playboy surface?

"Bella? What do you think if we crisscross the lights through here?" he asked, pointing to the expanse of ceiling in the main aisle at Housing

Works. "We can wrap around that column. Maybe do birch decor above the shelves?"

She refocused. "Yes, that would look good. I'd like to use smaller, more intimate tables laid out in here," she said, walking into the adjacent room. The space was a bit cramped for the number of guests, but she loved the energy of the place, and the air was scented with paper and dreams. It seemed to fit Adele's vision. They just needed to make sure every detail was unique and personal, as she had requested.

Van, the coordinator for weddings at the bookstore, took them to the spiral staircase. "Many brides come down here for the official ceremony, which we can set up there. I'd advise no large floral arrangements or gadgets since that will take up too much of the room."

"Yes, that's perfect," she said, tapping her lip as she studied the setup, imagining the final product on D-Day. "We'll bring in our own bar and set up high tables for the cocktail hour. We'll be using your caterer and finalizing the menu next week."

He nodded. "That makes things easier—Shelley does excellent work and knows the space well. You know we don't have Dr. Seuss books here, right?"

Gabe grinned. "No worries, we'll be bringing them in for the setup."

She turned to Gabe. "Each table can feature a theme from a different book. We can do quote cards—"

"Incorporate the actual book into each centerpiece—"

"And do seeds for the favors because—"

"They grow into trees!" he finished.

Van looked back and forth at them. "You work well together. I can't tell you how many screaming matches I've had to deal with from wedding planners. They're worse than the brides."

Satisfaction unfurled. She was used to working by herself, with occasional help from her sisters, but she'd been enjoying both Gabe's company and the way he approached his wedding planning. They had similar styles, and there was a respect when he listened to her that wasn't fake. Lord knew she'd met enough males in the industry who liked to mansplain or talk over her ideas.

Gabe was different.

They coordinated the rest of the critical details, and when they left the venue, she was confident in how they'd decorate the space. Glancing at her watch, she looked at the clogged traffic and groaned. "Getting home's going to be a nightmare. Do you want me to drive back?"

"No, I'm good. Who's with Zoe?"

"Taylor. They'll order a pizza, so I won't have to worry about dinner. You?"

He shot her an amused look. "Me, myself, and I? No plans. I have a bachelorette party Friday night I need to tighten up. They're a bit of a wild crowd, so I want to be prepared."

"The Bailey wedding?" She shuddered. "How'd you get stuck with that mess? She's such a PITA. I thought Avery was in charge of that one."

"I wanted to give her a night off. I don't have a fiancée I want to spend time with." He tugged off his jacket and laid it on the back seat. With slow, graceful motions, he rolled up his crisp white shirtsleeves, exposing muscled, sinewy arms.

Her gaze roved hungrily over the olive-toned skin, wondering what it would feel like under the sweep of her fingers. Wondering what his body would look like unclothed.

Perfect.

He loosened the knot of his sleek silver tie, working it back and forth until he was satisfied he had enough room. Then he climbed in the car, started the ignition, and curled tapered fingers around the steering wheel. His hips shimmied back and forth as he adjusted for comfort before leaning back in the seat.

A shudder ripped through her.

The spicy scent of cloves clung to him. She imagined pressing her lips to his rough cheek, her fingers caressing the chiseled line of his jaw, lingering over the softness of his mouth, turning his head around so he'd be able to kiss her deep and hard and thorough.

Whoa.

Her breath squeezed her lungs, and she hurriedly flipped off the vent to stop the rush of heat. She was already wet between her thighs. Where had that come from? Sure, she'd always recognized he was an attractive, virile male, but she'd never fantasized about him like that before. She needed to get her act together. See what happened from too many years of celibacy? She was definitely using her vibrator tonight to take the edge off.

"Bella?"

She frantically grabbed at her purse so she wouldn't have to look at him. Her skin pricked with heat. "Want some gum?" she asked, her voice breaking on a high note.

"No, thanks. You too hot? I'll lower the temp."

She stuffed a piece of bubble gum in her mouth and chewed. This was the reason working with him was problematic. Besides slowly relaxing more around him, they were beginning to form a tentative bond. Now her body chose this time to rebel?

Not. Good.

"Carter told me about the school dance. He's excited to take Zoe."

She smacked her gum and reminded herself to focus on his words and not his perfect male body. "So is Zoe. I like that her teacher stressed the dance didn't necessarily mean dads and moms. She explained families are made up of all roles and sizes."

"It's true, most families don't have a mother and father living in the same household. And who's to say what love is or should be? Carter is crazy about her."

"We're lucky Avery's marrying him. We're a bit possessive in our family and don't like to let too many new people in."

"Is that why you were wary of me for so long?"

The question stole her breath, and she almost choked on her gum. "I'm careful with new people. We're a tight-knit family. I needed to be sure you were going to work out."

"I'm still here. I love Sunshine Bridal, love what I can bring to the business, and think you all are kick-ass businesspeople."

She warned herself to get off the subject, but she was too tempted. "Yeah, but you're young. You may not want to settle down forever in a small beach town."

His brow shot up. "How old do you think I am?"

Her spine stiffened. "Twenty-five?"

"I'm twenty-seven."

Okay, so she'd been two years off, but having been married and borne a child, she felt centuries older. She still had ugly stretch marks that had never gone away. The thought of all those tanned, supple, gorgeous bodies he probably had in his bed seemed to mock her. "Still young. I'm just pointing out you have endless options."

His silence struck her as a warning rather than a pause. "You seem to be stuck on the word *young*. My calculations put you at thirty-one, just four years older. An entire future ahead to do what you want. Like me."

"No, it's different for me. I'm stuck here. You're not."

His lips thinned. "No one is ever stuck, Bella. You have plenty of options if you want to change your life or career."

"So do you," she shot back. "Why do you love Cape May so much? You seem comfortable in the city. Don't you think you'd have more opportunities here than a beach town?"

Seconds ticked by. He seemed to be pondering his answer as if it were important, and when he finally spoke, his voice was like a smooth, velvet ribbon pulled over naked skin. "Trying to get rid of me?"

She tried not to stutter. "No! I'm just curious."

"I had two jobs in Manhattan before Cape May. And yes, I liked the excitement and fast pace, but I also felt more like a number than a person. I worked with a lot of other planners, and we'd be assigned our next client by a ticket. Like at the deli counter." He gave a humorless laugh. "I couldn't bring my own personal style to anything because I was like a factory worker, assisting the top-level planners who rarely accepted my input. That was never what I wanted. With Sunshine, I'm a valued part of the team. Many of our clients are residents who I've gotten to know over the years. People know my name. Cape May is special because for the first time in my life, I feel seen."

His words tumbled through her, breaking apart pieces of the wall she'd guarded around her heart. She had no idea he'd found his past employment lacking. She'd always believed he strode into her beach town on a whim and decided to stay awhile. Hell, she'd been shocked he hadn't left within the first year, figuring he'd get bored of the limited opportunities. But the way he described her childhood home touched something inside her. He saw the beauty in it.

"I didn't know."

"Because I never told you. Sure, if you're the top dog, New York can be an amazing place to work. But going up the ladder and being recognized is damn hard. All I'm saying is everyone has a choice, Bella."

She blew out a breath. "But I have a daughter to be responsible for. My parents created this business so their daughters would run it. Taylor will be leaving in September, which puts more pressure on Avery and me. I grew up here. I know how hard it is to get out. Taylor's been trying for years."

"I get it. Definitely a lot of responsibility. But answer this question for me: Do you want to leave Cape May? Or Sunshine Bridal?"

She stared at him, her brain clicking madly for the answer. Not the correct answer. Not the easy answer. The one she'd been avoiding—the truth she'd been afraid to unearth in fear of what she'd find. "I don't know," she finally said.

Instead of pushing her further, or questioning her lame answer, he nodded. "That's fair. But maybe instead of feeling trapped in a life, you should choose to make it what you want. Maybe it's right here with your sisters. Maybe not. But I think you owe it to Zoe to try, don't you?"

She shook her head. "Children need routine. Stability. Family."

"Yes, but they need a happy, well-adjusted mother more. Eventually, they'll end up figuring out you weren't authentic and not a whole person, and they'll feel cheated. Believe me, I know, and it's a hell of a thing to live with."

Shock jolted through her at his raw honesty and the way he refused to flinch when talking about his past or his ideas. How had she never known how passionate he was under all that smooth surface charm?

Her heart beat madly, and she struggled to gain control over the conversation that was becoming more intimate with each mile. "Do you think we can hit a restroom? I think I need a break."

"Sure."

He pulled over to a gas station. She took her time in the bathroom, trying to calm herself down. Talking about her dreams and her daughter threw her off-balance. She needed to get this car ride over with and retreat to her home and figure out why she was suddenly reacting like this.

When she walked out, he was in the convenience store with a bunch of stuff in his hands. "What are you doing?"

He shot her a boyish grin. "Car snacks. We still have a ways ahead, and I think we need some old-fashioned junk food. Pick your poison."

"Oh, Lord no. This stuff is so bad for you."

"Exactly the point."

She stared at him with pure horror.

"Oh, come on, live a little. What's your secret food crush? I bet I can guess."

She put her hands on her hips and tossed her head. "Oh yeah? I guarantee you'll lose."

"Challenge taken. I get three picks." Right away, he lifted a bag from the hook. "Combos. Just the right amount of cheese with the salt of a pretzel. I'm right, aren't I?"

"Nope. As if I'd choose such a common car snack. Try again."

He paced the aisle, frowning, then pointed at the bottom row. "Pringles Sour Cream and Onion. I know you like to eat them at night after Zoe goes to bed."

Her mouth fell open. "How do you know that?"

He rocked back on his heels with victory. "Taylor came in with them once, and she blamed you for eating the entire can. You denied it, but I saw you were lying."

"I can't believe you remembered that."

"I win."

"No, you don't. I do love them, but not on car rides. They are strictly for watching investigative news shows and getting a rise out of my sister."

"Damn. Okay, I'm going with the Slim Jim. You strike me as a secret Jim lover."

The giggle burst from her mouth at his ridiculousness. "Wrong again, Sherlock. Ready to be dazzled?"

"Dazzle away."

She leaped to the end of the aisle and snatched up the familiar green-and-yellow package with the worst snack in all history. "Funyuns."

He blinked. "No. Way."

She beamed. "Told you you'd lose. And to celebrate my win, I'm getting them."

"Fine, but I want the Combos and Reese's peanut butter cups."

"Oh, wait, we need M&M's—they're like the appetizer."

"Good call." He dumped the pile of junk on the counter. "What about to drink?"

"I'll get water."

"I want lime flavored!" he called out.

Bella grabbed the bottles and bounded back to the register.

The guy behind the counter grinned. "Road trip?"

"Yep." She watched him ring it all up with a touch of pride.

"Some good selections. Surprised you missed the number-one pick, though."

"What's that?" Gabe asked.

He jerked his head toward the display by the door. "Hostess Cakes. Sno Balls, to be exact. I got the pink ones in—they never last."

Bella gasped. Met Gabe's stare. And nodded.

"Add one package of those to the bill, sir," Gabe said.

They climbed back in the car like kids, ripping open their stash and settling back into the drive. Oh, she was going to pay for this indulgence, but the moment the sweet, sugary cake coated in marshmallow and coconut hit her tongue, she moaned. "So good."

"It's been years since I've had one of these," he muttered. "I should've gotten the damn Mountain Dew."

"Water is healthier," she pointed out.

"Oh, wait, are you one of those people who order a Big Mac, fries, and a Diet Coke?" he asked suspiciously.

"Well, yeah. There is such a thing as overdoing it. Speaking of which, we have our appointment with Maria tomorrow about the cake and desserts."

"How'd you match up Big Macs and soda with Maria?" he asked.

"Overindulging. Cake and Dr. Seuss desserts. You with me?"

"Yeah, I'm back. Sugar overload. Hand me the Combos, I need some balance on my palate."

She poured out a few into his palm. "I may need to leave a little early to get Zoe to dance, but we should know by then if she's going to take the job."

"Too bad Carter couldn't ask. Maria loves him."

Maria had done Carter's sister's wedding cake and had been charmed by his intent to pick a challenging, unique design that would dazzle Ally. She'd ended up creating a masterpiece using a 3D effect with silver-foil roses, impressing Carter. The two had become fast friends, and Carter frequently stopped at Madison's Bakery during the day to steal a chocolate croissant and talk shop.

"Maria adores you, too. We'll pull some ideas together that will tempt her to want to take on the challenge." She opened up the Funyuns and breathed in the sharp tang of onion and garlic. The moment her teeth crunched down, nostalgia swept over her. It had never been the cotton candy that tempted her—always the salt.

"You look so happy right now," he said, his voice warm. "You should let yourself indulge more."

"Trust me, indulging in Funyuns is not the answer to self-care." She shot him a grin. "But I wouldn't say no to an occasional spa date or evening off."

"How long have you been raising Zoe alone?" he asked quietly.

Usually, she'd pull back and distance herself from any personal questions. But the atmosphere was relaxed, and in this moment, she just felt like sharing. "Five and a half years. Matt died when she was three months old. Drunk driver hit him."

"Was it local?"

"No, he was coming home from a business trip in Pennsylvania. I know it sounds awful, but everyone became obsessed with the lawsuit. How much money we'd get. Kept saying I deserved every penny to raise Zoe."

"Money doesn't replace life, but I can see how they felt you deserved compensation."

"The driver died, too. One bad decision to drive after leaving a party, and two people lost their lives. I wasn't about to pursue his family for a lawsuit when we'd all lost so much. I tried hating him for a while, but I couldn't. I remember getting in a car with my friend when I was seventeen, knowing we were tipsy but feeling invincible. Later on, I realized how lucky we'd both gotten to not get into an accident or hurt anyone. The night Matt died, no one got lucky."

"Emotions aren't logical. You had every right to hate."

She shook her head, caught half in the past. "Oh, how I wished I could hate back then. Instead, I fell apart. Became so numb nothing could touch me, not even Zoe."

Suddenly, her cold hand was wrapped in warmth and a gentle strength that eased the tightness in her chest. "I'm so sorry, Bella, for what you and Zoe went through. But you're here now, and when I watch you with Zoe, and what you manage to give her every day, I'm humbled."

His words shattered through the chipped walls and tore down her defenses. She held his hand tight, closing her eyes against the rush of raw emotion that touched her deep down in her soul. The truth rang out in his voice and soothed the broken edges. The gesture meant more than he'd ever know, soothing the need of a mother to know she was enough for her child.

For the first time since Matt died, it was like a man *saw* her. And God, it felt good. Better than a compliment about her looks or talent or cleverness.

Slowly, she uncurled her fingers from his and pressed back against the window. The air in the car seemed to thicken with tension, both emotional and sensual. The feel of his skin against hers had burned an imprint into her palm.

Confusion swamped her. What was going on here? She'd never had these feelings toward Gabe. And why did his affection seem tinged with more than casual friendship?

She cleared her throat and tried to clear her head. "Thanks," she finally managed. "Hey, what's a car ride without music? Got anything good?"

A few beats passed. She held her breath, hoping he'd take her lead and lighten the subject. Their conversation had become too intimate. She wasn't ready to confront her burgeoning physical attraction to him, let alone the safety she suddenly felt confessing secrets.

"Sure. Depends on your mood. We can go modern with Lizzo, country with Jake Owen, or old-school Jimmy Buffett."

She popped another ring in her mouth and chewed, determined to put them back on track. "I say crank up 'Margaritaville.'"

He did. They spent the next few hours singing out loud, telling bad jokes, and eating the rest of the snacks.

By the time he pulled up to her house, her stomach was protesting loudly. "I shouldn't have finished the whole bag," she moaned, crawling out the door.

"Do you have any TUMS inside? I can drop some off."

She shook her head. "I have a five-year-old—my medicine cabinet is stocked. Thanks for driving and for the snacks and for—"

"You're welcome."

Their gazes met and locked. Something surged between them, hot and needy, and she took a step back on the pavement for safety.

"Bella?"

"Yeah?"

"Thank you for a perfect day. See you tomorrow."

She didn't respond. Just shut the door and went inside the house, where her real life was waiting.

Chapter Eight

Bella stared at the flowers on her kitchen table and wondered when things had changed.

It had been a week since their car ride from Manhattan, and each day they seemed to grow closer. Where there was once a fine-tuned tension and distance, now a lighthearted energy flowed between them. Gabe made her laugh. He brought a focused creativity and work ethic to every part of the planning process, and she began to realize she enjoyed working with him as a partner more than working solo. But it was the other changes that startled her.

She'd begun to stare at him when he wasn't looking, her gaze stuck on the fine tightness of his ass or graceful stride. She looked forward to lunchtime, when they'd take a break and eat together, chatting about various subjects that highlighted his sharp intelligence. Knowing the truth about his past made her see him in a different light. He was a man who'd transformed his pain into a life of his choosing. The type of man she admired.

Along with many women in Cape May.

Bella suspected he had no lack of female companionship, but she was still surprised by the consistent invitations whenever they were out together. He was hit on by a customer in the deli line, a new cashier at Acme Market, and the sister of a client who'd come in to see Taylor. She watched as he conversed politely with each woman yet kept a distance that clearly showed his disinterest. He was able to let them down with so much charm, it looked like they didn't even mind.

He'd turned rejection into an art form.

But why hadn't he taken their numbers? Because she was around and it made him uncomfortable? She'd begun to wonder about the women he did date. He never spoke about them at work. Did he like keeping his love life a secret so he could have more freedom?

Yet he'd mentioned how he wanted a relationship. Someone to love. It was completely contradictory to everything she'd heard or believed about him.

Bella reached out, her fingers brushing a delicate petal. He'd sent pink teacup roses for Zoe with a funny card. Her chest tightened when she read it, knowing how excited her daughter would be when she returned home from school.

The bouquet he'd sent Bella was something she would have picked out personally. How had he known what flowers she loved? The Stargazer lilies were creamy white, with a burst of hot pink in the center, their pointed petals both interesting and elegant. They were surrounded by crimson roses, which only emphasized the shocking beauty of the lilies.

She couldn't stop staring at them.

The knock at the door broke the odd spell. Avery walked in with a large bag and a big smile. "Happy Valentine's Day," she greeted. "I'm on my way to Peter Shields for the Gonzalez wedding but wanted to drop this by. Chocolate for Zoe, chocolate for you, and the new bridal catalog from Vera. You'll need a few hours—she's outdone herself."

She shook her head and hugged Avery. "You didn't have to do that! I think I'll hide Zoe's chocolate for a while, though. She's been waking up at three a.m. the past few nights and can't go back to sleep. I've been existing on four-hour sleep the last two days."

"Oh no! Bad dreams?"

"She says no and that she's just excited to start her day." Bella laughed. "The last thing I need to give her is additional sugar, though.

But I'm glad I don't have to wait to see the new wedding dresses. Next spring is already upon us."

"Don't even mention it. Oh, what gorgeous flowers—did Gabe send them to you?"

Startled, she stared at her sister. "Yeah. How'd you know?"

She waved a hand in the air. "Oh, he sent some to me, too, and probably Taylor. He's a sweetie. Aww, even Zoe got a bouquet! I swear, that man's a prince. Everything still going good with Adele's wedding?"

The trickle of disappointment caught her off guard. Seemed her whole family had received flowers and not just her. Which was great. She was happy Gabe treated everyone with such care. She gave her sister a bright smile. "We've been making wonderful progress. I'm enjoying working with him."

Avery clapped her hands together. "I knew you guys would make a good team! You seem to think alike, too. I think you have more in common than you originally believed."

"Yeah." She hesitated, thinking over their heart-to-heart chat in the car. "Um, Avery, do you know much about Gabe's past, with his dad and stuff? After we met with Adele, we started talking about our childhoods, and I was really surprised by some of his stories."

Her sister arched a brow and shot her a searching look. "He rarely talks about his parents. I just know his dad was an asshole and made him feel unworthy. His mom didn't seem to help much, either, so he had it tough."

"I know how close you both are, so I wondered how much you knew."

"He only told me the basics, so I'm glad he opened up to you." Avery tilted her head, regarding her thoughtfully. "There's a lot more under the surface if you take the time to really know him."

Bella nodded and hurriedly changed the subject. Her sister wouldn't stop probing if she got suspicious, and Bella wasn't ready to tell anyone about these burgeoning feelings for Gabe. It was too . . . new. "Well, thanks again for the gifts—you better get going."

She kissed Avery goodbye and shut the door, then stared back at the gorgeous flowers in full view across the room.

The flowers were a kind gesture from a coworker. Nothing more. Nothing less. She needed to stop analyzing things.

Dragging in a breath, she got back to work.

♥ ♥ ♥

Gabe glanced at his watch and slowed to a crawl on Main Street. Ugh, Valentine's Day brought everyone out, even a flock of tourists who wanted to spend a romantic weekend getaway at one of the popular bed-and-breakfasts. Red-and-white lights twinkled merrily on the streets, and cars were packed into the row of various restaurants offering specials. He'd stopped for a slice at Louie's, where he'd been propositioned by the new girl working there, then had to politely reply to a dozen texts from women offering to give him a special V-Day present tonight.

No, thanks.

All he craved were his sweats, a beer, and a bingeworthy series on Prime. But he'd promised Pierce he'd stop by Taylor's and get some equipment she had borrowed that he needed for his next gig. He was stuck in Atlantic City for a big wedding and couldn't get there in time.

He hadn't seen Bella today, but she'd texted him a polite thank-you for the flowers. His mind flashed to the conversation with Pierce and Carter. Gabe still hadn't told Bella how he felt, but when they'd been alone together recently, it hadn't felt like the right time to say anything. Their car trip had been a good opportunity to open up and let her see more of himself. Maybe moving forward, he'd just be open and sense the right time. Maybe he'd just *know*. After all, he'd never planned to share his difficulties with his father, but the conversation had flowed naturally and built another level of connection.

He eased to the curb and walked to Taylor's door. She answered with her usual scowl, dressed in pajama shorts and a faded Imagine Dragons T-shirt. "You didn't have to send me flowers," she said grumpily. "I hate V Day."

He laughed. "I know. But there's no way I'm ignoring all the women I work with and appreciate. Did you like the color, at least?"

She motioned him in with a sigh. "Yeah, that was pretty cool. How'd you get Devon to do black roses?"

"Seems there's a lot of morbidity around this holiday I didn't know about. She almost sold out. You have that stuff for me?"

"Right here. Want a beer before you go?"

"Oh, I just picked up—"

The adjoining door burst open, and Zoe came tearing through. "Aunt TT! Wanna watch *Charlie Brown Valentine's* with us?" she screamed.

Dressed in pink Fancy Nancy pajamas, with her blonde curls floating around her shoulders, she reminded him so much of a younger Bella, his heart surged.

She skidded to a stop on bare feet, blue eyes wide with recognition as she realized he was here. "Gabe! Yay—I love my flowers, Gabe, they're my favorite color pink, and I put the vase in my room and told Meg that I got real live flowers for Valentine's! What are you doing here?"

Taylor crossed her arms in front of her chest and gave her a look. "Zoe. I told you over and over you need to knock on my door and not burst in."

"Oops, sorry. Please don't tell Mama. She'll be mad."

"Well, I am mad, and I did hear, and you need to obey the rules, young lady," Bella said behind her, lifting a brow. "Aunt TT may have visitors, and we don't want to interrupt."

"Damn straight," Taylor muttered. "Naked ones."

Gabe pressed his lips together to keep from laughing.

"But, Mama, look! It was only Gabe. And I'm sorry, I keep forgetting."

"Well, try harder or I'll have to make you eat extra vegetables."

Zoe gasped in horror and moved close to him as if he were her savior. "That sounds awful."

"It is. So knock."

Zoe tugged on his sleeve. "Did you come to visit us?"

He smiled down at her precious face and tugged playfully on a wayward curl. "No, sweetheart. I'm picking up something your aunt had for me, that's all. But I'm glad you liked the flowers."

"That was so nice of you," Bella said, her voice husky. "It made Zoe's day."

He shrugged. "Good, because as the only princess in the family, she had to get flowers."

Zoe's giggle charmed and mesmerized him just like the boa constrictor from *The Jungle Book*. "Is Mama the queen?"

"Yes, I think she is." His gaze lifted and crashed with Bella's. She seemed startled by the impact, taking a step back.

"What's Aunt TT, then?"

"Maleficent," Bella quipped.

Taylor preened. "My fave. At least she's not boring."

"Gabe, can you please come upstairs and watch Snoopy with me? Please? Mama made popcorn, and you can have some with us! Is that okay, Mama?"

Bella cleared her throat and fiddled with her hands, a slight flush on her cheeks. "Well, um, yes, but I'm sure Gabe has things to do tonight."

Yeah, he had pizza and sweats waiting for him at home, but the lure of spending some quiet time with Bella and Zoe was too tempting to pass up. "Actually, that sounds great. I love popcorn, and Snoopy, so it's a win-win."

Zoe gave a whoop and danced around. "It's like a Friday night! I get to stay up late! Are you coming, Aunt TT?"

Taylor grinned and shook her head. "Sorry, I have to do some work in my studio. But have fun."

"I will!" Zoe grabbed his hand tight and began dragging him toward the door that led to their half of the house. "Come on, Gabe. Mama has it all set up."

He noticed that Bella had remained quiet, but now the flush of pink colored her whole face. Did his presence disturb her? And if so, was it for a good reason . . . or bad?

They settled onto the comfortable sectional with Zoe in the middle, holding the big bowl of popcorn. She'd made it like the movies—with plenty of salt and butter—and he munched out while chuckling at Snoopy's antics as the Red Baron. Once again, Charlie Brown screwed up, Lucy teased him mercilessly, and Linus backed his best buddy up.

It was perfect.

A commercial came on, and he savored the scent of strawberry shampoo, the soft flannel of Bella's pj's, and the warmth of Zoe's arm linked with his. Bella had her legs curled up underneath her, her laughing gaze on her daughter. Zoe chattered on about a snow-cone machine she really wanted for next Christmas, and the spark of fierce love in Bella's soft blue eyes hit him smack in the solar plexus.

Emotion choked through him, raw and real. Right now, right here, he had everything he ever wanted.

Soon, Zoe yawned and climbed onto his lap to finish the cartoon. The Valentine special morphed into a few extra shorts he hadn't seen since he was young. As the credits rolled, he gave a contented sigh. "That was great, wasn't it, Zoe?"

He looked down when she didn't answer. She was asleep.

Gabe smiled, smoothing a few wayward curls from her cheek. "Well, we lost one of the crew. Do you want to take her up and—"

He trailed off when he looked at Bella, who was curled up on the end of the sofa, cheek resting against a throw pillow, face relaxed in slumber. The sweetness of them being able to fall asleep near him caused satisfaction to hum through his blood, along with a trace of possessiveness.

"Guess Snoopy couldn't compete with sleep." He moved to shake Bella gently awake, then paused. He'd tucked Zoe in before. He'd get her settled in, then head out without disturbing them.

He scooped up the sleeping child and carried her upstairs. Her room was a pink paradise that perfectly matched Zoe's personality—from the stuffed animals, dolls, and glittery lamp to the bright artwork decorating the walls. He placed her on the bed, covered her with the frilly pink quilt, and turned out the light, making sure to click on the unicorn night-light before closing the door.

He came downstairs and turned off the television. Bella was still asleep, her limbs crunched up as if still trying to make room for her daughter. A wave of tenderness washed over him. She tried so hard to please everyone all the time and be the best mom to Zoe. He wished she'd let him help.

He grabbed the blanket from the chair and tried to stretch out her legs so she'd be more comfortable. A tiny frown creased her brow, and she muttered something under her breath. He wondered if she was a sleep talker. Smiling, he tucked the blanket around her and leaned in to adjust the pillow, which was at an awkward angle and crushing half of her face.

Suddenly, she turned and rose up, wrapping her arms around his shoulders.

Gabe froze.

His body went on high alert, but he knew she was half-asleep. Slowly, trying not to wake her, he gently pulled back.

She pressed her mouth to his neck and breathed in, like she was savoring his scent.

Ah, shit.

His voice ripped from his throat. "You fell asleep, and I didn't want to disturb you. Do you want to stay here or go to bed?"

"So tired," she murmured, snuggling against his chest like she belonged there. "You smell good."

A strangled laugh rose from his chest. His arms automatically hugged her back, savoring her closeness and the womanly curves pressed to his body. "And you're exhausted. Do you need anything before I go?"

"Don't go."

He groaned, giving in to impulse, and kissed her temple. "I can stay till you fall back asleep."

"Yes."

He stroked her back.

"Feels so nice. Just until—" Suddenly she stiffened, her head tilting back. "Zoe?"

"I put her to bed. I figured you could use the sleep."

She relaxed with a sigh. "Thank you. You're good to her. To us." She focused that heartbreaking gaze on him, her china-blue eyes filled with a longing that punched him in the gut. "You got everyone flowers for Valentine's Day."

Caught up in the fragility of the moment, he barely breathed, feeling as if something had suddenly changed. "Yes."

"Why?"

He hesitated. But right now, he wanted her to know the truth. "Because you're all important to me. Especially you."

The air tightened with sensual tension. She blinked, as if trying to register his statement, and then slowly brought her hand to his cheek. His muscles stiffened at the delicacy of her touch, the wonder on her face as she searched his gaze, and in that moment, he realized this was the moment he'd been waiting for. And he couldn't run or deny or pretend any longer.

He cupped her chin, his mouth descending until it was inches from hers. Those pink, plump lips parted with invitation. Her light floral scent danced around him. "I want to kiss you, Bella. I've wanted to since the first day I walked into Sunshine Bridal and saw you. The sun was streaming through your hair, and you had red paint smudged on the tip of your nose from playing with Zoe. You looked up at me with those beautiful blue eyes, and I knew nothing would be the same."

"Gabe?" His name was both a question and an answer, a prayer and a melody. He waited for her to pull away, but she was motionless, staring at him with a raw mixture of emotions.

His thumb pressed lightly against her soft mouth. "I think you're an extraordinary woman who rarely gives herself enough credit. And I've been trying like hell to get you to see me as a man, not a business partner or casual friend."

She shuddered.

Fierce need shook through him, and he repeated his intention, giving her one last time to walk away. "I want to kiss you, Bella. I've imagined it too many damn times in my head, in my dreams, and I can't wait any longer."

Slowly, savoring every moment, his lips pressed to hers, lightly, teasingly. He slid his mouth over hers in a gentle caress of discovery, tamping down a groan at the sweet taste of her, the sudden rush of her breath, the fingers that suddenly dug into his shoulders.

He let her settle in, sipping at her like she was a fine wine, a juicy nectar hidden by a flower's bloom. Already drunk on her scent and taste, his body ached for so much more. And then she parted her lips, and his tongue slipped inside.

He swallowed her throaty gasp and kissed her like he'd always dreamed. Long, and deep, his tongue tangling with hers, gathering every last drop of her intoxicating flavor of spice and sugar and sin all wrapped up in one. Her body melted beneath his, and he became half-mad at the feel of her hard nipples against the cotton T-shirt; her arched hips; her damp, soft mouth beautifully responding to his.

He pulled back slowly. Dropped tiny kisses over her lips as he broke contact, already mourning the distance. Then he stared into her dazed blue eyes.

He'd taken the risk of his life. Kissing Bella could cause a chain reaction that could either spell disaster or finally allow him to show her how good things could be between them. Either way, he had no regrets, not when her taste still burned his lips and his body still shook from her touch.

Now there was only one thing left to do.

He waited for her reaction.

♥ ♥ ♥

Gabe had kissed her.

She sagged against him, the taste of his mouth still imprinted on her tongue. Her body roared forth in pure feminine power, begging for more; her tight nipples greedy for his lips; the empty, wet ache between her thighs demanding satisfaction.

When he'd showed up at her door, she'd been surprised at how her heart leaped and how badly she wanted him to stay. They'd snuggled on the couch and watched TV like a family, and it had seemed so natural, she'd allowed her exhaustion to overtake her, feeling safe in his presence.

Caught halfway between sleep and wakefulness, she only remembered the strength and power of his arms wrapped around her, the hardness of his muscles, the intoxicating scent of his cologne. Safety turned into want, and a desperation to touch him. She'd wanted that kiss just as much as he had.

Oh God, the kiss.

He had tasted like sweetness and spice, emanating a fierce male hunger that made her want every bad, delicious thing he could do to her. But it was his words that ripped her safe world to shreds and rocked her foundation.

This wasn't about one kiss.

This was so much more.

He was looking at her as if waiting for an answer, an answer she didn't know how to give. She studied his gorgeous mouth, trying to unscramble her thoughts. Yes, his leading question at the Royal wedding hinted at something she hadn't been ready to hear. She'd suspected an admission of attraction. A cracked door where he dangled the allure of a brief physical relationship, nothing more. That would better match his reputation. And she would have been tempted—the man was a god—but that was something she could be strong enough to walk away from in order to protect their business relationship and burgeoning friendship.

She hadn't a clue he'd been having these types of feelings for her. Big feelings. Feelings he'd been hiding for a while. Feelings that threatened her safe, protected world because he wasn't offering just his body.

He was offering his heart.

In a flash, all those glimpses from the past suddenly made sense. The way their gazes would occasionally connect and linger. The time their hands had brushed when they both reached for the laptop, and he jerked back as if burned. The day she'd gotten toppled by a wave at the beach and suddenly found herself swept up in his arms, protectively cradled against his chest, his heartbeat thundering madly in her ear.

Dear God, had the signs always been there and she'd been too stubborn to notice? Or was it more about fear? Because if she *had* noticed, she would have had to make a choice, and that would have been so much harder.

Now he waited, his gaze fixed on hers, the words he'd spoken no longer able to keep him hidden. He'd taken a risk by saying these things, by expressing his want, a longing to see what could be between them if she was interested.

Maybe, if he'd kissed her weeks ago, it would have been different. She hadn't known the hidden depths of the man before.

Now, she did.

Now, she knew she'd craved his kiss just as much. Because underneath, in a place where she rarely visited, a low simmer burned—the fire of possibility. Barriers had crumbled she had no motivation to rebuild. It had happened slowly, but now as she stared back at him, her lips swollen from his kiss, she realized she owed him a deeper truth.

"I'm confused," she said, her voice husky in the quiet. "I didn't know."

He nodded. "You didn't want to."

He was right. "I don't want to hurt you, Gabe."

His jaw clenched but his tone was gentle. "And I don't want you to feel pressured because I decided I couldn't hold back any longer. I'd just like to ask if you'd think about things. About us. If there's any part of you that feels the same way about me . . ." He trailed off, his gorgeous dark eyes suddenly sad.

She trembled, the confession stumbling past her lips. "I did. I do. I felt something." Her face heated. "The kiss."

He lifted his hand again, his finger tracing the line of her jaw in a tender caress. "Good. I know it's complicated. But God, I want to give you so much, if you'd only give me a chance."

A shudder shook through her. Why hadn't she noticed such vulnerability when he looked at her? She had mistaken the fierce protectiveness that shimmered from his aura as arrogance. What other mistakes had she made judging him? It was as if the world she'd known had just been torn down to the foundation, and it was up to her to rebuild it.

And in that moment, she had a sudden need to kiss him again, to be held in his arms and experience the same pop of desire tangled within a beautiful safety—the perfect combination. The urge was startling in its intensity. This was brand new to her, and she didn't know what she was ready for.

"I think we both need to be open and honest. I wanted you to kiss me," she said, tilting her chin up. "I'm just not sure what comes next."

He nodded. "We can talk about it. What you feel comfortable with. I can give you time to think." A small smile touched his lips. "I'm not expecting you to suddenly admit you have the same feelings I do. I just don't want to hide mine anymore."

She touched his hand. "I don't want you to. But I need some space and time for a bit. Okay?"

"Okay." He turned to go, then paused. "We can talk more later, but I want you to know whatever happens, I won't let it affect Sunshine Bridal. I swear it to you, Bella." With a last, lingering look, he grabbed the bag he'd gotten from Taylor and walked out the door.

His words and his scent and his taste surrounded her. She groaned. Her body throbbed with an ache she hadn't felt in forever, and her head felt like it was ready to explode with her swirling thoughts.

Switching off the lights, she went to bed, hoping for a few hours of darkness and silence.

But she dreamed of Gabe, and the way he'd kissed her, and the sweet promises she suddenly wanted to believe in.

Chapter Nine

"We have a problem," Bella said.

Gabe tried not to panic, but it had already been a long-ass day. This morning, he'd driven two hours to the greenhouse to pick up the right tree seeds for the favors, not trusting they'd be delivered on time. He had hit traffic so he skipped lunch, then met Bella at Sally's Stationery Store, where they'd crammed together at a tiny table to pore through huge manuals of paper samples until they found the perfect bamboo parchment to create the Dr. Seuss quotes. They were heading to Aloha for an acai bowl when she stopped short on the sidewalk, gaze trained on her phone.

They hadn't mentioned the other night. Sucked immediately into work, he was grateful there wasn't any awkwardness between them. Of course, they'd been stuck in a small space, heads together, thighs touching, while he desperately tried to focus on paper instead of kissing her again. But he'd gone over and over every detail of their encounter, and he didn't regret a second.

Kissing Bella for the first time had been worth the wait. And now, there was nowhere for him to hide. The truth was out, and it was now up to her.

He shook his head and refocused. "Is it a problem that will delay lunch?"

"Maybe. I got a text from Adele. It says: Darlings, I forgot to mention the birds. I'd like Dr. Seuss birds. Kisses and thanks."

He waited for more, but she stopped. "Wait, that's it? She wants Dr. Seuss birds? What does that even mean?"

"I don't know, but let me call Stacia." She dialed, hitting "Speaker," as they walked.

Thank God the assistant picked up. "Bella, I figured I'd be hearing from you."

"Hi, Stacia. Can you give me more details than what was in Adele's text? What type of birds? Is she talking doves to release after their vows?"

"No, she's decided birds could be a fun touch for the reception, especially if they look similar to something from a Dr. Seuss book. She doesn't care how they are incorporated, or how many; she's leaving all the details up to you."

Bella halted in her tracks, staring at him in bemusement. "I doubt the bookstore will allow birds inside," she said. "That could cause a problem."

"Do your best, we believe in you. Sorry, have to go. Text me with any other questions!"

The phone clicked.

Gabe cursed. "You gotta be kidding me. She's pulling a prank."

"I don't think so."

"Why would she want birds swooping on guests and pooping on their head? I'm not doing it. I'm telling her no."

Her voice soothed. "Let's grab something to eat and see what we can do. You can't focus when you're hangry."

She marched in front of him like a woman on a mission, and his gut did that flip-flop thing. He liked that Bella knew his tendency to get irritable when he hadn't eaten for a while. It gave him hope that he was slowly growing more important to her.

They ordered two acai bowls and sat at a picnic table inside. The crunch of granola, tart berries, and floral raw honey began to calm his nerves.

"First, let me call Housing Works and see if it's even possible," she said. "You start researching bird types."

He ate, grumbled, and hit the internet. There were plenty of weird, colorful birds, but most of them were from overseas and couldn't be shipped over in time. Parrots were a possibility. They were vividly bright and some spoke, but nothing screamed Dr. Seuss.

He hit a few other key words and began getting dragged deeper into the bird world.

Bella sighed and dropped her phone. "Okay, we can have birds, but they have to be caged and can't be flying free around the store."

"I don't know if that's good news or bad."

"Me, either. Find anything?"

"What about yellow canaries, like Tweety Bird?"

She shook her head. "That's Bugs Bunny, not Dr. Seuss. I think she's looking for something unique. Adele would never choose something so ordinary."

"Flamingos are cool."

"They're also gigantic and can't be caged."

"Right. Well, I'm not getting into a damn bird costume. Santa was bad enough."

The giggles that exploded from her made him grin, the sound full of such abandoned joy he wished he could keep it on repeat. "I love your laugh," he murmured, caught up in the sparkle of her blue eyes. "It reminds me of all the beautiful things in the world that surprise me."

She sucked in her breath as the ease twisted into intimacy, the seething crackles of connection igniting between them. And this time, it wasn't one-sided. He caught the flare of heat in her eyes before she had time to hide it, recognized the tremble in her lips and the sudden flush in her cheeks. She was thinking about their kiss.

She was finally thinking about him.

He cleared his throat and backed off. For now. "Okay, I found a few, but they're not in the US. We can do parrots—maybe a toucan? Macaw?"

"Still too ordinary. But if we're forced to, maybe we can have a bunch of birds sing a wedding song? That's different."

He arched a brow, then caught the lift to her lower lip. "Thank God you're kidding." He chased a variety of bird images on his laptop, reworded some phrases, and clicked on a picture. "Hey, this one is the Victoria crowned pigeon. Damn, it looks like a Dr. Seuss bird. Check it out."

He turned the screen. The bird was a deep, vivid blue-gray, with a purple chest. Black ink framed its face like a mask. A magnificent sprawl of feathers fanned out on the top of its head, the lacy white-tipped scrolls forming an elaborate headdress.

"That's it," she said, tapping the image. "Where do we get them?"

"Originally from New Guinea—rare in the pet trade. Crap. Wait, there are some held at various zoos. Think Cape May has any of them?"

She snorted. "I doubt it. We certainly can't have birds shipped overseas. I know we have the budget, but that's just too much. Why didn't she ask for a tiger? It would have been easier."

"I'd still rather stick with birds—no liability issues. Hey, it says they have some in New York, at the Central Park Zoo!" He read the information with growing excitement. "That's doable. We can borrow them for the ceremony and return them the next day. If they allow us."

Bella tapped her lower lip. "The negotiations on this are going to be delicate. I'm sure they don't just rent out their birds. Do you know anyone over there?"

He shook his head. "Nope. But I bet someone in Adele's crew does. Let's call back Stacia."

Within the hour, they had a contact and had prepared the ground-work. By the time Bella was ready to pick up Zoe, they'd secured a plan to book half a dozen Victoria crowned pigeons for a total of eight hours.

They'd be delivered and secured, and Bella was already working on getting some large gilded cages to hold them. At the end of the reception, the zoo handler would take them back.

Victory crashed through him, spiking an adrenaline rush. Bella laughed in delight, and they high-fived, basking in the glow of rising to the challenge to deliver Adele the perfect wedding.

He opened the door. "Supposedly, the birds make this amazing sound, too. The guests will love this type of touch."

"Much better than a parrot yelling 'Polly wants a cracker,'" she said. "I better get Zoe. Great job."

She shifted her feet, as if wanting to say something else but suddenly shy. He took the plunge and spoke. "Do you think we can talk later? Or tomorrow? I'd like to spend a bit of time together."

He held his breath until she slowly nodded. "Yeah. I think that's a good idea."

"Why don't you see what works and text me? I can come over after Zoe goes to bed or meet you in the morning for coffee? Anything you want."

"I have an early-morning appointment, and Zoe has the dance tomorrow night, so I'm not sure."

"I can wait."

"I'll text." Her smile was sudden and sweet and full of something he'd never seen before—anticipation. "Bye."

She left and he watched her disappear around the corner, like the poor damn chump he knew he was. But God, he didn't care. For the first time, he had hope, and that was just about everything.

The next day was full of appointments and a bridal-shower luncheon that had taken all his energy. Bella had also been busy, so he figured maybe they'd be able to talk over the weekend. Right now, the only thing he could focus on was collapsing on the couch, opening a beer, and getting ahead of some work.

Yeah, the beach bachelor's life was real glamorous.

He'd just changed into sweats and an ancient T-shirt when his phone buzzed. He glanced at the screen and saw Carter's name. "What's up?"

"I'm sick."

A litany of coughing came over the line. He frowned at the phone. "Man, do you need a doctor or meds? You sound awful."

"Yeah, I feel awful. Came on late yesterday and been going downhill. You gotta do me a huge favor."

"What do you need?"

"Tonight's Zoe's dance. I'm supposed to pick her up at seven p.m. to take her to the school. You have to go in my place."

He stared at the phone in shock. "Wait, you want me to go? Did you call Bella and tell her about the change in plans?"

"No time. I waited to the last minute to see if I could get out of bed, but I can't. Avery has the Myers wedding tonight."

That's right, and Pierce was with her, so he wouldn't be able to fill in for Carter. He glanced at the time. "That's half an hour away! I'm in sweats."

"So change. I'll text Bella—just get your ass over there and save mine."

Gabe held back a groan since he didn't want to waste any more time. "Fine. Get better."

He clicked off and headed upstairs. He needed to focus. It was important to Zoe to have someone she cared about by her side at her first real dance.

He intended to bring it.

"Mama, where's Uncle Carter?"

She checked the time. "He should be here any minute, sweetie. You look beautiful."

Her daughter beamed with pride and twirled again, showing off the cute sweater dress Gabe had given her. She'd matched it with the fake UGG boots with pink fur and loaded up her arms with pink sparkly bangles. Bella had braided her hair and interspersed a pink ribbon with a tiny fringe at the end. She looked fashionable and adorable, and her mother's heart swelled and wept, realizing this was one of so many moments she wouldn't have a father to share with.

But Bella was here. And Carter was family. It would all be okay.

The bell rang.

Zoe squealed and opened the door.

"Gabe? What are you doing here?"

Bella stared in shock at the gorgeous man framed in her doorway. He was dressed in a sharp black suit, with a light-pink shirt and bold pink tie. His dark hair was slicked back, emphasizing his high brows, cut cheekbones, and chiseled jaw. Those dark eyes sparkled as he bowed in front of them and held something out in his hand. It was a wrist corsage with tiny roses the color of ballerina shoes. "My lady. Our chariot awaits for our big date."

"But I thought Uncle Carter was taking me."

His face pulled into mock sadness. "Uncle Carter got sick with a bad cold and had to stay in bed. But I jumped at the chance to be your escort for your first ball. Is that acceptable for you, my lady?"

A torrent of giggles escaped. "Yes! I'm sad Uncle Carter is sick, but I'm glad you're here! And look what I'm wearing!"

He put a hand to his heart. "You look so beautiful—just like a real princess. I can't wait to dance with you and step on your feet."

More giggles. "Mama said you're supposed to try not to step on feet when you dance, plus you'd hurt. You're too big."

"Oh, then you can step on my feet. Are we ready?"

"Yes, I just need my coat!" Zoe flew by Bella to grab it.

A mess of emotions twisted inside her. He leaned in, and she caught the smooth sweep of his jawline. She tried not to gulp in a big sniff from the delicious scent of his cologne. "I'm sorry, Bella. Carter called me and asked if I could fill in. I hope that's okay? He texted you, right?"

She shook her head. "No, I was just surprised. Didn't you have plans tonight?"

His smile was both masculine and sweet. "Nothing I couldn't break. I'm glad he asked me. Are you coming with us?"

"I'm on the refreshment committee, so I'll meet you there shortly— have to pick up the cupcakes."

Zoe hurried out the door. "Bye, Mama."

"Bye, honey. See you guys later. Have fun."

He reached out and grasped Zoe's hand. The two of them began chatting as he led her down the steps and into the back of his car, where he helped clip her into the booster seat he always kept available for her. Then, with an almost awkward wave, he got in the car and drove away.

Bella leaned against the wall and closed her eyes.

Damn. Why was this happening to her? She'd been thinking about him nonstop since that kiss. She was doing her best to sort through her feelings with a rational analysis and be able to talk frankly about what she wanted.

The problem?

She still didn't know. There were so many reasons to let him down gently and explain why a relationship would never work. It would be best to keep a solid work partnership paired with a newly burgeoning friendship and not cross the line where things could get . . . messy.

But now he was with Zoe at her first dance.

He'd shown up, with his usual enthusiasm, and he wasn't even family.

Yeah. Things were already getting complicated.

She grabbed her coat and headed out the door. For now, she needed to concentrate on the night ahead. It didn't take her long to grab the cupcakes from Pretty Tasty Cupcake Boutique—all nut-free and delicious—and head to the school. The brick building was decorated with endless red hearts and Cupids, and she made her way into the cafeteria, which had been transformed for the dance.

The decor was simple but effective: Lots of red and pink balloons, with brightly colored tablecloths and disco lights flashing on the makeshift dance floor. Tables crammed with festive desserts and a giant punch bowl. Bella greeted a few of the moms she knew and began setting out the pink frosted cupcakes with sparkles. "If I see another heart or Cupid, I'm gonna vomit," said a feminine voice behind her.

Bella laughed and turned, giving her friend a hug. "Agreed. Think they'd notice if we grab some punch and spike it?"

Daisy held up a bronze thermos and put her finger to her lips. "Brought my own. Rosé all day, baby."

"You are so bad. That's why I love you."

Daisy Draper was a single mom to Zoe's best friend, Meg. She'd lost her husband in Afghanistan to a roadside bomb when Meg was just two years old. With their shared experiences in grief, they'd gotten close and had become each other's backups when needed. Daisy's work as an online journalist allowed her the flexibility to raise her daughter since she worked mostly from home, but Bella had watched Meg many times during Daisy's research trips or late-night meetings.

Their friendship had continued to grow over years of playdates, school parties, holiday shows, and the famous PTO meetings. Bella had spent many an evening on her friend's couch, lamenting about their single-mother status. With her short, sleek copper-colored bob; lean figure; and big brown eyes, Daisy had been sought out for many dates, but they all came up lacking. It was hard to find a guy who wanted to date a single mom, someone who couldn't go out for spontaneous dinners or romantic weekends away. Relationships were hard enough without any extra issues, though Bella and Daisy would never consider their children anything but a gift. Still, it made the idea of dating Gabe even more worrisome. Would he really enjoy her routine lifestyle or consistently coming in second to the needs of her daughter?

"Did your dad drive up to take Meg to the dance?" she asked, finishing up with the cupcakes and wiping off the leftover frosting with a napkin.

Daisy nodded. "Yeah, he's so sweet. He's going to stay overnight so he doesn't have to make the trip back in the dark. His night vision sucks."

Bella smiled. "I love that she's going with her Pop Pop; it's so special. Carter got sick, so he couldn't make it."

"Oh no! Who's with Zoe? I haven't seen her come in yet."

"Gabe."

Her friend gasped. "Gabe took her? Oh my Lord, wait till a text leaks out he's here. I guarantee the attendance will double by all the moms who refused to volunteer."

As busy as they were, they both tried to do their part to keep active in the school community. But they'd both taken a stand against baking—they bought the cookies and cupcakes for parties and dances. It was their sort of compromise to not become one of those over-the-top PTO moms and get all judgy toward working moms who just didn't have the time.

Bella knew being supportive of all mothering styles was important. She didn't know why society still emphasized tearing other women down, but as much as she liked to joke with Daisy, they'd learned not to assume anything by the surface. Too many times, there was rot beneath a sunny, seemingly perfect family. After losing their husbands, they both had said forgiveness and nonjudgment came easier, and they tried not to engage in gossip.

Most of the time it worked, but small beach towns were riddled with juicy tidbits. Sometimes it was hard to resist.

Suddenly, her gaze caught on the subject of their discussion. Standing next to Meg's granddad was Gabe, who was dancing to some pop song the girls were singing aloud to. He did one of those canned disco moves, swaying his hips back and forth while he laughed with the girls. The lights spun on his coal-black hair, and he threw his head back, smiling, his teeth gleaming white, and the familiar shudder gripped her body like a fever, squeezing it with sheer longing.

"Holy. Crap." Daisy looked from her back to the dance floor with shock.

Bella shook her head and tried to clear it. "What's the matter?"

"You're into him."

She stared back at her friend with a touch of panic. "Who?"

Her friend jabbed a cherry-red nail in the air. "Gabe. I just caught the way you looked at him. Why didn't you ever tell me?"

She hesitated only a moment. She wasn't ready to confide in Daisy yet, especially since she didn't know if it was just a brief attraction or something more. She forced a laugh. "Gabe's one of my business partners, I would never get involved with him."

"That's a valid excuse, but you evaded my real question. Who cares if it's inappropriate? Are you hot for him?"

"Shhh!" She glared, then grabbed the travel mug and took a sip. The liquid slid down her throat with ease and gave her fake courage to lie. "You're being ridiculous. I mean, of course he's hot, I'm not dead. But there's nothing between us."

Daisy crossed her arms in front of her chest. "Still not an answer. Why are you so freaked out? It's normal to lust after a man. I'm just surprised because I've never seen that look on your face before, and you've been working with him for a while. Are you an item?"

She looked around to make sure no one was listening and leaned in. "Daisy, please let's not talk about this. We're not an item. He was nice enough to step in when Carter got sick because he's both a family friend and coworker. Okay? Can we move on?"

Her friend gave her a beaming grin. "Sure. Did you sleep with him yet?"

She let out a frustrated breath. "Forget it. I'm going to talk to Amy."

"Good luck. She's still selling tickets for her Brownies club, and I'm tired of getting pitched constantly."

Bella marched over to the other table, where Amy and a bunch of PTO moms had gathered to chat and comment on the dance. Most of the males congregated on the other side of the room, while the moms manned the various snack and raffle tables. The girls giggled and drifted from the dance floor to their dates before settling back into their own tight-knit circle of friends.

She smiled, recognizing the old-fashioned separation of males and females even today. Still, she thought the dance was good for the girls. Her father had always been an important influence in her life, and she wanted Zoe to both respect and love the men in hers. It was also good for the men to experience a school event and see the children in their element.

Bella bought another ticket from Amy for the Brownies, cursing Daisy under her breath, then focused on the new topic of conversation burning past her ears.

"I think he's with Zoe."

She turned at the sound of her daughter's name to see Lacey standing next to Amy—two moms who were a bit *too* enthusiastic over the PTO for Bella's taste. They also adored gossip and liked to dissect who was dating whom.

Lacey's dark eyes narrowed with greedy intent. "We're talking about Gabe. No one knew he'd be here tonight. He came with you?"

Bella stiffened but kept her voice calm. "He had to replace Carter since he got sick. Why?"

Lacey and Amy shared a smug look. "Nothing," Lacey said with a slight shrug. "It's just that I haven't seen him in a while. Vera's granddaughter, Marlaine, is in town for a few weeks and spotted him at Carney's. Seems she's found her boy toy for her vacation."

Amy giggled, her gaze voraciously roving over the man across the room. "Lucky girl. You know, he's known to pull all-nighters—and I'm not talking about work."

Nausea lurched in her belly. Her skin grew hot and clammy, but she forced herself to remain casual. "He hooked up with Marlaine? When?"

"This past week. They're going out again soon. How did the three of you manage to resist the temptation, Bella? Or did you?" Lacey asked with a lascivious gleam in her eye.

"What do you mean?"

"Well, we all assumed he was sleeping with Avery. Is that why you and Taylor kept your distance? Or is he fair game now that she's marrying Carter?"

Horror washed over her. Talking about Gabe like he was a piece of meat being passed around made her ill. "Avery never slept with Gabe," she said stiffly. "I think you're being unfair to him. In fact, I don't think he's had a date in a while." She added that last comment in the hopes of shutting down the whole conversation.

Amy and Lacey laughed. "I'm sorry, I didn't mean to upset you, but really, Bella, are you serious? He's banged every woman in the Cape, and he's working his way into Atlantic City now. Can you blame him? He's gorgeous, single, charming, and has money. Maybe he keeps his personal life to himself since you work together?"

Amy nodded. "That would make sense. I'm sure the three of you don't need to hear about his conquests at your regular conference meetings, right?"

Her thoughts whirled in her head, their comments painting a bold picture of Gabe she didn't want to think about it. She watched him lead Zoe into a few spins and pretend to fall over. A few of Zoe's friends surrounded him, giggling hysterically.

Lacey sighed. "My goodness, look at him. He can even charm them young. He's so sweet with Zoe. If he wasn't such a player, I'd be desperate to go after him myself, but Lord knows I need a responsible man in my life. I've had enough of cheaters." Her words took on a hard edge. Her last husband had left her for an affair with a woman years younger, and it still seemed to burn.

"Agreed. At least Marlaine will have fun," Amy said. "And it's nice to know if there's an itch to be scratched, he's a guarantee."

The floor seemed to tilt underneath her. Desperate to get away, she gave a fake smile. "Better get back to Daisy. I see a line by the cupcakes."

With every step back to the table, she cursed herself for the endless doubts. Was Gabe trying to play *her*, too? She'd always known about his reputation, but knowing he'd set up an actual date with Marlaine made her feel foolish. How many women did he regularly sleep with? He'd acted as if he wanted to know her better and be a bigger part of her life. Said he'd been waiting for her for three whole years. Why? So he could finally sleep with a woman he hadn't conquered yet?

But the things he'd said to her seemed so real.

Shame burned through her. Yes, she was attracted to him. Yes, she loved how he was with her daughter. But this was too much to deal with. She had Zoe to look after, and she wasn't about to let Gabe become part of their intimate life only to leave when he got a better offer. But if he was still sleeping around while he professed to be crazy for her, what did that really say?

She couldn't handle these types of games. Better to lock the door on any possibilities between them before it was too late.

She had too much to lose.

Chapter Ten

By the end of the dance, Gabe was tired but happy. Zoe and her friends had had a good time. He'd hooked up with Tony, Daisy's dad, and a few other fathers to keep the girls happy and conversation at an easy level. He noticed the moms stayed on the other side of the room, running the various activities and snack tables, except for a few brave stragglers who crossed the invisible line.

Of course, the three women who did made a beeline straight to him.

He was polite but distant, just like at work. He tried to avoid locals in Cape May—it only made things awkward. Honestly, he was more embarrassed by all the female attention, hating how it put a spotlight on him when he wanted to show Bella he wasn't like the man society had dubbed him. He'd tried catching her eye many times throughout the evening, but she had avoided his gaze and mostly stayed by Daisy's side.

"Fun night," Tony said, smiling at Meg as she leaned against him.

"Agreed. It was nice to see the girls have fun."

"Zoe's lucky to have you in her life," the older man said a bit gruffly. "Daisy and Bella had some hard cards dealt to them. They deserve to have some good male influences. I heard you got a promotion over at Sunshine Bridal."

He stiffened. He was used to older men like his father thinking his career was odd or flamboyant. How many times had his old man sneered and called him useless when he'd decided to go into wedding planning? He kept his response brief. "Yes."

Tony nodded. "Good for you. About time there was some male influence in that industry. Must have taken some courage to carve a name for yourself. Congrats."

Warmth spread through him. He wondered what it would be like to have his father say something like that to him. He smiled at Tony and inclined his head. "Appreciate it. I'm lucky the Sunshine women gave me a chance."

"Gabe, my feet hurt from dancing. Are we ready to go?" Zoe asked, tugging at his sleeve.

He laughed. "Sure, but I should be the one complaining. Look at these fancy dress shoes," he pointed out. "They pinch my toes."

She made a face. "Mine are worser. These pink boots are not good for dancing. I think next time, I'll get a pair of ruby-red slippers like Dorothy—she walked all the way to the Wizard in those!"

He couldn't help it. Affection overcame him, and he picked her up to give her a hug. The scent of her strawberry shampoo and the open way she hugged him back were everything. "I'll keep my eye out for them," he said. "Let's go get your mom. Maybe you can sneak in one last cupcake."

Her eyes lit up, and they crossed the room, where the tables were already being cleared and the surplus was being packed away in organized Tupperware bins. "Need any help?"

Bella jerked as if surprised by his presence, then shot him a weird look. "Uh, no, we're good. Did you have a good time, sweetheart?" she asked her daughter.

"Oh yes! Even though our feet hurted, we danced a lot and had fun. Can I have one last cupcake?"

"How many did you have tonight?"

"Just one."

"Okay, but you have to promise to go to bed when we get home and not run around the house all sugared up."

"I promise." Zoe took the treat and immediately dove into the top, not waiting to unwrap the paper.

Gabe grabbed her some napkins, grinning. "Did the PTO make enough to show up the other schools in the district?" he teased.

Instead of a smile, she narrowed her gaze, studying him for a few moments as if ready to give him a diagnosis. "Hopefully. Thank you for taking her. I'll bring her home so you can go."

He frowned, not understanding the cold vibe between them. What had he missed during the two-hour dance? Was she mad he hadn't come to talk to her? "Sure. Hey, I didn't come over because none of the men did, and I thought it was some type of unspoken agreement. We stay on our side, you stay on yours. Was I wrong?"

"Hmm? No, we do that so the girls really experience the night with their escorts. Kids tend to run back to their moms, so we try to discourage it."

Okay, so that wasn't it. "Did you have a good time?"

She ducked her head and began packing up tins of cakes and brownies. "Sure, these things are all the same. You can take off, you know. I'll text you over the weekend if anything comes up about the wedding."

WTF?

He hesitated, feeling awkward, while she ignored him and deliberately turned to talk to some of the other women.

He tried to think of something to say, but his mind went blank. He slowly turned away, dismissed, and said another goodbye to Zoe. He trudged out of the school cafeteria with his shiny, tight shoes and tie and wondered what he'd done wrong.

"How was the dance?" Avery asked, opening her laptop.

Bella avoided Gabe's gaze and focused on the stack of notes in front of her. He'd texted her multiple times over the weekend, but she'd only responded to the ones regarding work. She hadn't been ready to answer anything on the personal front, still simmering. If he'd actually had a date with Marlaine the same week he kissed her, she'd been completely wrong about him.

She kept her voice cool and calm, refusing to show she was upset. "Great. Zoe had a wonderful time."

"Carter really appreciates you stepping in last minute," Avery said to him. "He was sick most of the weekend."

Gabe gave a curt nod. "Glad he's feeling better."

Bella noticed Avery biting her lip and glancing back and forth between them. The tension in the room ran tight and thick. "*Okay.* Did I miss something? You're both acting weird. Is the wedding finally giving you a breakdown?"

Taylor came in, pink hair swinging, a bounce in her step. Everyone watched as she slid into her seat, propped her knees up on the opposite chair, and sipped her coffee. Her nose ring flashed in the light. "Hey."

"Where's your stuff?" Avery asked.

"Why do you look happy?" Bella asked.

Taylor shrugged. "I had a good weekend. I can take notes on my phone—I have a light week before the madness of spring comes. Any other questions?"

Gabe grunted.

"I guess we're ready to start. Let's make this a great morning, people!" Avery announced with her usual enthusiasm. "Why don't you give us an update on Dr. Seuss?"

Bella waited for Gabe to take the lead, but he remained silent. "Go ahead," she said, motioning for him to start.

His voice was ice-cold. "Maybe you should be the one to say. Because it seems to me I've been completely in the dark. I don't know what's going on."

She flinched but refused to back down. She'd been completely professional this whole weekend with their communications. It was his fault if he expected her to be all warm and fuzzy after finding out he was steadily seducing all the women in Cape May while pretending she was the only one who interested him. "Fine. We have two weeks left and remain on point. Good communications with all vendors. Cake, desserts, and favors done. Gabe is handling all the family's reservations at hotels and various activities. I'm finalizing the menu and place settings. DJ, bartender, photographer, and justice of the peace all confirmed. Are you still watching Zoe for me that weekend? I'll be gone Friday night and not home till late Saturday."

"Yes, no problem," Avery said. "Have you been able to agree on the right way to present this wedding to the press?"

"We're in agreement," Gabe said curtly.

Taylor whistled. "Man, you guys are pissed at each other. What's up?"

Bella sucked in a breath, and her gaze swung to his. Male temper and frustration simmered in his dark eyes. He slouched in his chair, moodily tapping his index finger against the edge of the table, regarding her in silence.

"Nothing," she finally said, pursing her lips in disapproval over his reaction. He was acting like a brat just because she wasn't all sweet and chatty with him. "Just a miscommunication. We'll address it later in private."

"Good. I've been asking you to tell me all weekend."

"We don't need to have lengthy conversations every half hour like we're dating," she hissed, her temper fraying.

His laugh held no humor. "Dating, huh? How about you treat me like a human being first, and then we'll move on to dating?"

"You're being overdramatic."

"And you're being cold for no damn reason."

"Oh, trust me, there's plenty of reasons."

"Which you won't tell me. Talk about a miscommunication."

"Hold up." Avery threw out her hands. "I'm kind of freaking out right now. You two are my calm ones—no temper, no fighting, no egos, remember? You need to get on the same page, or we'll never get through high season."

"I don't have an ego," Taylor pointed out.

Avery snorted. "Sure, remember when you sulked because we didn't use your idea to bring in a tattoo artist for the Lowry bachelorette party?"

"Oh yeah! Well, I just hate when brilliant ideas get wasted. They were all on board."

"Right. Getting a group of drunk women to get permanent ink is a smart idea. Can you imagine the fallout?"

"Whatever," Taylor muttered. "You never take risks."

Suddenly, Bella couldn't stand it. "Can we talk about this another time, please? I have a ton of appointments to get to and need to wrap up this meeting."

A shocked silence settled around the room. She realized how rarely she not only spoke up but had an edge of temper to her words. She was falling apart over the silly realization that Gabe was exactly who she'd thought he was. But they couldn't keep going on like this.

"Gabe, can I talk to you in private, please?"

"Sure." He turned to Avery. "Can we adjourn the meeting?"

Avery stared at both of them, finally nodding her head. "Yep. Not much to go over today, anyway. I'm here if either of you need to talk."

"I'm here if you just want to tell me what the hell is going on," Taylor called out. "Call me!"

Gabe shook his head, and they left the room. "How about we go sit at Harry's and get some pancakes?"

"Let's go."

They walked together without speaking. The wind was high on the boardwalk, whipping in late-February fury, but the air felt cold and clean on her face, giving her an energy boost. A few locals walked their dogs or hurried up and down the street on the way to work with their coffee, steam escaping from open lids. Soon, the crooked sidewalks would be clogged with tourists and the beach open, but in these quiet months of winter, the Cape belonged to them. The ones who made a daily life here, where ocean salt ran in their veins, and the view of an open skyline called to the soul.

Harry's was quiet, so they grabbed a back booth for privacy. Their server introduced herself as Valerie and immediately lasered in on Gabe. She had curly black hair, almond-shaped dark eyes, and a smile that clearly revealed her interest. They ordered banana pancakes and more coffee, which Valerie raced to pour within seconds. At least they'd be guaranteed good service.

"I'm sorry I was sharp with you," Bella began, cupping her cold fingers around the hot mug. "What you did for Zoe was special, and I hope I didn't make you feel like it wasn't."

His shoulders relaxed, and some of the tension drained away from his frame. His dark hair was windblown and messy. He sported a bit of stubble that roughened his jaw and hugged those full, kissable lips. He wore jeans and a cable-knit sweater since he only had vendor appointments. He seemed more approachable without his custom suit, and even more devastatingly handsome. Now, it was easier to recognize the automatic melt of her body, the hum of her blood, and the tingle in her skin when she was near him. But it was time she separated attraction from what he was capable of giving.

"Bella, what happened at the dance? We were getting closer. I thought we were going to talk about us, but now you're back to treating me like a distant stranger."

The conversation between Amy and Lacey echoed in her mind. But how could she express her discomfort over all the women in town proclaiming him the local stud? She struggled to put her thoughts into words. "I began to get uncomfortable with what was happening between us."

The food came, and they both took a breath to pour their syrup, slather on butter, and dig into the carb-filled delight. "Why?" he demanded, his gaze intent and filled with banked heat. "Because of me? You? Or the attraction between us?"

She stiffened, her heart smashing against her rib cage in an uneven rhythm. She had to shut this door between them now, even though a part of her mourned that fact. Maybe she'd have regrets. But keeping her family safe was critical. They had years ahead of working closely together.

"All of it," she said simply. "I've thought about what you told me, and I will always treasure those feelings. You're an incredible man, Gabe. Any woman would be lucky to hold your heart. But we have a business partnership I take seriously. I liked getting to know you better working on this wedding together. And I think you were right when you said I was being too distant beforehand. I tend to do that with people who aren't family, and it's time I admit you're an important part of our lives. Since Matt died, it's hard for me to open up. I seem to believe everyone is going to leave," she said with a humorless laugh. "Zoe cares about you. So does Avery and Carter and Taylor. But friends are all we can ever be."

"Why?" he asked softly. "We're good together. I'm crazy about Zoe and your family. I'm crazy about you—have been for a very long time. And I know you felt something for me when we kissed. I'm asking, why can't you give us a chance to see if there's more?"

Her tummy plunged. Primal need twisted inside her, desperate to get out. Oh, how she ached to say yes and follow the possibilities between them. To be able to freely touch him, set her lips over his, be wrapped in his embrace. That kiss would haunt her forever, but she just couldn't take the risk that he'd hurt her.

Her sigh was full of longing and endless regret. "Because I don't want to," she said. He jerked back at the brutality of her words. "We're on different paths. I'm a single mom, four years older, settled into a family business and small town. You have no responsibilities and no ties. You have so much still ahead of you."

Anger carved out his features. "You're assuming you know what I want without asking me. I'm not a child, I'm a man, and capable of making my own decisions on what type of life I want to lead. I crave a settled relationship. Marriage. A family. A home. You're wrong—we're on very similar paths."

The damning words buzzed in her head. *If there's an itch to be scratched, he's a guarantee.*

"Did you go out with Marlaine this week?" she asked.

He stared at her with confusion. "Marlaine? You mean Vera's granddaughter?"

"Yeah."

"We had coffee last week. She's visiting for a few weeks and wanted to chat. I think she's been bored."

She took a deep breath. "And are you going out with her again?"

He rubbed his head. "Yes, but not like that. She said her friend is engaged, and she wanted to talk to me about Sunshine Bridal. We're meeting at the Ugly Mug to discuss a few details—that's it. I'm not interested in Marlaine. I'm not interested in any other woman but you."

His words contradicted what Amy and Lacey had said. Yes, it could be gossip, but there was so much smoke, there had to be a flame of truth. His reputation as a womanizer was widely known. And even if he was interested in her for now, when would his attention be snagged by someone prettier, shinier, and younger? She'd be left with a broken heart and something even worse.

A heartbroken daughter.

Never again. She refused to go down that road.

"Gabe, I'm asking you to respect my decision. I don't want anything between us except work and friendship. I hope that's okay, because it's important to all of us that there's no hard feelings."

He studied her for a while, then jerked back as if he experienced a realization. "You don't believe me," he breathed out. "You think I'm sleeping around. Did you hear gossip at the dance? Is that why you suddenly treated me like crap? Because you heard rumors I was going after Marlaine?"

She didn't answer—couldn't.

He muttered a curse under his breath. "Holy crap, this is messed up. Nothing I say is going to convince you, is it? Then again, it's probably easier believing the worst. It gives you a free pass from trying and maybe getting hurt."

"That's not fair," she whispered.

"You're right, it's not. But neither is judging me for something I've never done. I'm not going to sit here and defend myself. I need a woman who believes in me, who takes the time to know my heart and stands by my side."

Her throat closed up. Emotion burned her eyes at his raw words that seemed to be ripped from his chest. Oh, how she wanted to get up from the table, wrap her arms around him, and tell him she was wrong. That she wanted to try.

But she didn't.

Instead, she sat in silence while the buzz of the restaurant played around them.

"I'm sorry," she finally said. "I don't want to hurt you."

He gave a quick nod and looked away. "Yeah, I know."

"What do we do now?"

He laid down his fork and pushed his plate away. "Finish Adele's wedding. Keep working together. I hope you'll let me keep interacting with Zoe. I love that little girl."

"Of course. We'll just go back to the way things were. We'll be friends." The word stuck like peanut butter on her tongue, but she forced it out.

"I'll always care about you, Bella. Just want you to know that."

Her smile wobbled. "Thanks. I better go. I'll text you later on some outstanding items—we need to go over the specialized cocktail list and make some final decisions." She stood and pulled on her coat.

Gabe nodded, but he kept his gaze down.

She walked toward the exit, eyes stinging. She paused with her hand on the bar and, for one moment, looked back.

Valerie stood by the table, leaning over in an obvious flirty gesture. Her curls bounced as she nodded at something Gabe said, then laughed. She was in her midtwenties. Fresh faced. Probably single and free with no one to worry about but herself.

She was everything Bella wasn't.

A quiet acceptance came over her, even though her chest hurt. It was better this way.

For both of them.

She walked out and didn't look back.

Chapter Eleven

Gabe wondered how losing someone you never had still hurt like a son of a bitch.

He headed to his next appointment to confirm the final floral arrangements and let his mind drift.

Since her brutal confession, he'd spent the last week focused on work and trying to dig Bella out of his heart for good. They had managed to work together on Adele's wedding, both being careful not to cross over the invisible barrier between them. Every time he weakened, he reminded himself of the things she believed about him. He could have spent time defending himself, proving the rumors false one by one, but he refused. If Bella wanted to believe the gossip that he was sleeping around, there was nothing he could do.

He couldn't seem to catch a break this week. Even Marlaine wanted to cast him in the gigolo role. He'd kept their appointment for lunch, and when he discovered she had no friend who needed a wedding planner, he made an early exit. Her bold offering to spend her vacation with him to play caused no desire—just disgust. With her, for not believing he had more to give than sex. With him, for not being able to break out of the mold Cape May had made for him.

Avery was consistently pissed at the way the town portrayed his bachelor status, spinning embellished tales of sexual conquests he'd never had. Even worse—most laughed when he tried to debunk the rumors, thinking men should relish such a reputation in all forms.

Not him. Not when it became a barrier to meeting a woman who could be his forever. He'd picked his career because he loved organizing one of the biggest party events of the year, but there was another reason.

He still believed in true love.

His father's face reared up in his mind, sneering with scorching disgust. *You'll never be a real man. You're just a pretty boy who relies on his face and body to make your mark. You're useless.*

He tried to silence the voice in his head, reminding himself he was successful. Strong. He'd created a life he loved, and he refused to let rumors and the loss of Bella bring him back to the brink.

He'd worked too hard to get here.

At least he had no regrets. He'd given her all he had, and it wasn't enough. It was time to accept her final decision and move on. He believed there was a woman out there who was his soul mate.

He just had to find her.

The moment he walked into the floral shop, he relaxed. Devon met him with her usual zen energy, her hip-length dark hair and slow, graceful motions bringing him down a few levels. They both had a thing for flowers, and when he'd first moved into town, they'd fallen into an affair, but it had lasted only a few weeks. She'd made it well known she didn't do marriage or believe in monogamy. He respected her decision but soon realized their future goals were completely contradictory. They'd easily parted with no drama and remained friends.

"You owe me big-time," she said, as they made their way toward the back. "I pulled a miracle for this wedding."

"That's why we insisted on using you rather than some froufrou city celebrity shop," he said. "I did a consult with two of them."

"Not impressed?" she asked, opening her display coolers to pull out some arrangements.

"You know how you go to some of those five-star restaurants, excited to eat? Until you get a grape and piece of leaf on the plate, drizzled with some famous sauce. You leave broke and starving, but you're afraid to admit to anyone it sucked, so you lie. That's how these shops were."

Devon grinned and shook her head. "Well, I'm glad you allowed me to take up the challenge. These are some of the samples I constructed. I've been existing in a made-up Lorax land since our consult, and it's reminding me of when I was continuously high in college. Lovely, whimsical, but a little bit too spacey to live."

He studied the delicate, gorgeous stalks topped with delicate, puffy blossoms. The colors were magical: a rich lavender, a blush pink, a buttery yellow. They were accented by various blooms that complemented the uniqueness but still held the interesting Dr. Seuss–like shapes the wedding was based on. "What are those?" he asked.

"Hollyhocks with types of allium. I know she loves color, so I think we can do more vibrant shades in her bouquet to pop the dress. The more subtle ones will go well in the centerpieces to offset the table favors. It will look like this." She laid out a combination of petals of aqua blue, lemon yellow, and hot pink. "I had to dye them to get to the perfect colors. It's daring and can become garish, but I want to accent with this cream and keep it tight, so it's more of a pleasant shock. I can tie with this birch twig, then do some bedazzling with a touch of diamonds around the center."

"Fake ones?" he asked with an arched brow. "Sounds tacky."

"I can do real ones if you have the budget, but mine are so good you'll never know."

"They have the budget, but get me a sample of the fake and see if I can tell. Wait—I have a great idea. Let's do diamonds in the shape of stars from the Sneetches. Adele will love that extra touch. Is there time?"

"Sure, like I said, it will just cost extra."

"That's fine, my budget is generous. It just needs to be—"

"Perfect," she said with a smile, finishing his thought. "I know. It's one of my favorite qualities I admire in you. I'm also doing balloon flowers so light and puffy they look like they'll float away. You can string them up the spiral staircase you showed me so it looks like they're floating in the room. What do you think?"

"Honestly? I love it. It's everything we wanted." He snapped a few pictures to show Bella the final product. "Anything else?"

"We're all set. How's things going with you?"

He gave the canned response without even thinking. "Fine."

She surprised him when she reached out and touched his shoulder. "I don't believe you." Her brown eyes gleamed with empathy and something else. "Want to go to dinner and talk about it?"

He blinked, then studied her face. Was she asking him for a date? They'd once joked that one of the saddest things about their breakup was the loss of the garden they'd been working on together. "Did I miss something, Devon?"

Her smile was warm and easy. "No. It's just that I always enjoy your company, and I miss you. And I've been thinking how much fun we had together."

"Three years ago?"

"Ouch." But she laughed. Her hand moved lower down his arm. She'd always been a touchy person, enjoying constant physical contact. "Maybe I've changed a bit. It has been a while. Or maybe I just want to go out and have a great conversation and connect with you again. Is that wrong?"

No, it wasn't. In fact, he'd been craving the same thing, desperate to have that with Bella for so long, he didn't know how to transfer it to another woman. But suddenly, the idea of having dinner with Devon felt like a sign.

Bella was off-limits. He needed to start somewhere and build a life without her in it.

"No, it's not wrong at all. Maybe it's exactly what I need, too." He made his decision. "I'd love to have dinner. How's Friday night?"

"Good."

"I finish up on the late side. That okay?"

"I'm flexible."

They wrapped up and walked back into the main lobby. Maybe a date with Devon would give him a whole new perspective.

He decided to grab a slice of pizza from Louie's for a late lunch, stopping to chat with a few friends, and headed down Beach Avenue. Lost in his thoughts, the crunch of metal hitting metal seemed to mingle with the fury of the waves hitting the sand and the gray misty afternoon, but when he turned his head, he saw the rear-end accident right in front of him. Thank God it didn't look too bad.

He took out his phone to call 911 for the police, and that's when he saw the familiar golden hair whipping in the wind. She stumbled away from the car, holding her head, and a low, keening wail seemed to catch in the air and echo in his ears, making his blood curdle in his veins.

Bella.

He ran the rest of the way over. Yelling her name, he reached her just before she collapsed.

♥ ♥ ♥

The moment she woke up, Bella knew it was going to be a bad day.

She completed a long run in the misty rain, which made her hair frizz to new heights and popped out one of her contact lenses because she was blinking too much. She managed to complete her exercise routine with blurry eyesight, then got home to wake Zoe and begin her morning ritual. She burned the bacon and had to make a new batch, lost the sneakers Zoe had to wear for gym, then missed the bus by a few seconds. By the time she'd switched to her calming station on XM filled with quiet waterfalls and chirping birds, her nerves were stretched thin.

It's just another day, she reminded herself. Thinking about it and dwelling on what-ifs would drive her crazy. She was determined to be calm, serene, and at peace with each hour that unfolded.

She was stronger now, far from that woman who'd splintered apart.

It was time to prove it.

She picked up a coffee at Madison's Bakery and headed to Vera's Bridal to meet for an initial consultation with her September bride. Dress shopping was her favorite part of wedding planning. They had the first slot of the day, so she'd have plenty of time to help Stephanie, who was only twenty-two, marrying her first love, and happily pregnant. When Bella arrived, her future bride was with her mother and MOH—maid of honor—chatting with Vera.

They hugged in welcome, and Bella spent some time going over specific possibilities based on her love of old-fashioned lace. They served Stephanie sparkling cider and the others mimosas, then began the try-ons. After three dresses, everyone was still torn and had not found the magic one.

Vera took Bella briefly aside. "She's focused on lace, but it's difficult to tailor with a growing belly. I think we need an intervention."

Bella's brain clicked through other pictures the bride had seemed to favor. "What about lace as a main accent rather than the whole dress?"

Vera nodded regally. "Yes, I have a new Mori Lee that could work, but it may be over budget."

Bella grabbed her tablet and brought up a dress she'd found on Pinterest that reminded her of Stephanie's style. "Do you have this one?"

"Yes, I'll pull both."

Vera went back to the racks, and Bella walked over to her bride. "We have two other dresses we think you'll love," she said smoothly. "You'll be six months at the time of the wedding, so we want a fabric that will easily accommodate your new curves."

"You mean my big belly," Stephanie said with a laugh, her hand resting on her still-flat abdomen. "That makes sense. I'm open to ideas as long as I get my long-ass train and style I love."

The MOH shook her head in amusement. "At least it's not a shotgun wedding. You were technically engaged before you got preggers."

"Hey, that should be our motto," Stephanie said. "'*Not* a shotgun wedding—we really are in love!' What do you think, Mom?"

Her mom groaned. "Awful. Your father told me he was terrified for you both the first time Adam picked you up for prom. Remember how you swore in fourth grade you'd go with him to the prom in a limo one day? For years, your father said it was a sweet little crush that would disappear. He's still in shock he's gonna be a grandfather."

Bella smiled. "You were smitten with each other that young?" she asked. "It really is a true love story."

The MOH leaned forward eagerly. "Steph and Adam fell in love in elementary school, started dating in high school, and continued through college. It was as if they were always meant to be together. Meanwhile, I'm still dating jerks and kissing toads. Some girls get all the luck."

Stephanie giggled and waved her hand in the air. "Don't be silly, your match is out there."

"Hope so. Still, I believe we only get one shot at that type of love you guys have," the MOH said.

The mother nodded. "Agreed. Your father is sometimes a pain in the ass, but thirty years later, he's the only one I want to wake up to."

A tirade of memories assaulted Bella's vision, crushing her lungs and making her stumble back a step.

Meeting his gaze for the first time in algebra class and going weak kneed at his smile.

The first time they made love in the twin-bed dorm room, clinging to his broad shoulders as she whispered in his ear that she loved him, and he whispered it right back without hesitation.

Holding hands at graduation.

Looking downward, him on bent knee, his brown hair gleaming in the sunlight as the diamond ring he held sparkled into a thousand prisms of radiance.

Walking down the aisle in a white dress, gaze trained on his with every step forward.

Tangled in his arms late at night, talking about their dreams, the baby, and the beautiful, big life they planned together.

The day she learned it was all gone, and her one true love was never coming back.

Vera appeared with two dresses. "Let's get you back in the changing room. I think we may have a winner." Her gaze narrowed on Bella, who fought to remain calm as needles of pain jabbed her insides. "Are you okay?"

She forced a smile. "Yes, just going to grab some water. Be right back."

She raced for the back room, where Vera kept a small fridge stocked with water, juices, and champagne for the guests. Opening up the bottle, she chugged the icy water and prayed for sanity. It was happening again. The slow breakdown of her body and mind that would send her to bed, weak and heartsick, the depression rolling over her in waves she was barely able to fight.

It'd been a long time since she'd fallen apart, but she remembered every broken moment like it was yesterday.

Sweat beaded her brow. She fought off the panic and tried to slow down her heartbeat. Bending over, she placed her hands on her knees and focused on one breath at a time until she slowly calmed. She kept her daughter's face firmly in her mind, and eventually, she stood tall again.

Grabbing a tissue, she blotted quickly at her face, finished the water, and went back to her clients.

The sight of Stephanie standing on the pedestal made her gasp. She was clad in a gorgeous satin dress with lace lining the deep-V back, then spilling into a long, intricate train. The bride's face said it all. Tears shimmered in her eyes, and her mom was openly weeping.

"It's beautiful," Stephanie whispered in reverence. "This wasn't even on my hit list."

Bella's throat closed up. Knowing all the amazing moments ahead for her young bride stirred the hornet's nest but also reminded her how fierce love could be, how she had once been the one clad in white, wildly in love and believing in happily ever after. Being part of Stephanie's love story soothed the rawness. It was as if she got to experience dozens of redos and keep a piece of her heart filled with hope.

"If we were on that TV show, I'd make you say the words," Bella finally said.

Everyone laughed. "You can thank Bella for having me pull this one," Vera said without any ego. "She seems to sense what a bride needs in a dress. I wish she'd quit and come work solely for me."

Bella tried to deny the praise, but Stephanie suddenly walked over and hugged her tight. "Thank you for helping me plan the perfect wedding," she said.

"Oh my goodness, you're going to make me cry," Bella said after stepping out of the embrace. "Remember, it's my job. I'm just happy you make it so easy and joyful."

Vera clapped her hands brusquely. "We've found the dress, ladies. Now, let's talk veils and accessories."

Bella left Vera's Bridal later, finished up her second appointment with the New York photographer for Adele's wedding, then headed back to the office for some conference calls and paperwork. She tapped her fingers against the steering wheel, thinking about the past week. Gabe had made it easy to slide back into their old routine. He'd erected his own walls, so when they were together, he was pleasant yet guarded. She was grateful, but a strange grief settled over her when they were together now. Everything had changed. He didn't look at her with the warmth and longing she was used to. His tone held no teasing or intimacy. He treated her exactly how she'd treated him, and she hated it. The growing bond of friendship and the promise of more was finally gone.

At her request.

She reminded herself she had a daughter to protect, and she wasn't in a place in her life to welcome dating games. Besides, there was no way he'd want to settle long term in Cape May as a wedding planner for someone else's family business. Eventually, he'd leave, and it was better to cut off any growing emotions now rather than later. Much better to protect her heart and daughter before she became more involved.

She'd done the right thing. The only thing.

The afternoon was still misty and cold. The ocean roared as she drove up Beach Avenue and slowed at the red light, pumping the brakes gently in case of ice. She listened to Taylor Swift on XM to rev up some energy, thinking about the locked drawer she'd finally open tonight, after Zoe fell asleep, alone in her bed. For a little time, she'd allow herself to steep in the memories and his image, and when midnight struck, it'd be over for another year.

The deafening crash seemed to hit her ears before the momentum threw her body forward. Her forehead jerked against the steering wheel, while her spine folded like a rag doll. Her car skidded a few inches, past the white line that guided the crosswalk, and then there was a strange silence.

Her ears roared. She sat there for a moment, blinking, trying to focus on her surroundings, then began to climb out of the car on shaky legs.

She stared at the crumpled bumper as the cold wind hit her face. She rubbed her forehead, which had banged the steering wheel, then touched her neck to see if it was sore. A woman jumped out of the car behind her, fingers mashed to her mouth, saying something over and over that sounded like "Are you hurt?" and "I'm sorry," but it was like she was underwater; the words had a low droning noise to them.

It struck her that she'd had an accident six years after Matt had died, on the same exact day. If it had been serious, she could have been rushed to the hospital and died, just like her husband. She could have left Zoe all alone, reneging on the promise to never leave that she'd made while Bella cried herself to sleep so many nights after the accident.

Bella blinked, noting she was detaching herself and knowing she wasn't as strong as she'd hoped for. Her name blew in the wind, and she turned slowly to see Gabe rushing toward her, panic in his eyes, getting closer and closer. Something inside her unfurled, relaxed, and for a few precious moments, she didn't feel bad anymore—she only felt safe with him by her side and able to finally let go.

So she did.

Chapter Twelve

"No hospital," she said for the third time. "I'm fine. There's hardly any damage, I barely hit my head, and it was just the shock that took me out. I'm embarrassed enough."

Gabe cursed. "What if you have a concussion? Whiplash? You passed out, Bella! Now is not the time to be stubborn."

She waved a hand in the air for dismissal. "For a few seconds. My neck doesn't even feel sore. Honestly, it was a bump, and if you hadn't been there, we probably wouldn't have even called the police."

They'd already gone through the dog-and-pony show, with the cops taking a report and Bella refusing medical attention. There was minor damage to both cars, so they exchanged insurance cards and drove away. He'd finally lost his shit and insisted they drive to her house so she could at least rest and decide from there. Under the threat he was calling Avery and Taylor ASAP, she'd grudgingly agreed to go home for a cup of tea and to prove she was fine.

She sat on the floral couch, her feet up on the ottoman, her fingers clutching the teacup. He'd insisted she cover herself with an afghan—he'd read warmth was good for shock—and already checked WebMD for all the horrible things that could happen to her after a minor rear-end accident.

He was freaking out.

"You need to report every accident in case something happens—it's Insurance 101. What if I call Dr. Petrosky to come take a quick look at you? Make sure you don't need a CAT scan."

He would've enjoyed her laugh if he'd been in a better space. "My pediatrician? Are you serious right now?"

"Why? He's fine for Zoe! He'll at least be able to confirm you're okay!"

She gave a long sigh and settled back onto the couch. "Gabe, I appreciate your concern, I really do, but you're starting to make me nervous. Can you just grab some tea and sit down with me? You can ask me a bunch of questions where I can prove I remember my name and family history. If you want to see my eyes dilate, there's a flashlight in the top drawer."

He rubbed his head, gave her a grudging stare, then stomped into the kitchen. He hated tea, but he made a quick cup of coffee with the Keurig and settled down next to her with enough space to make them both comfortable. "People don't pass out after minor car accidents," he muttered. "Trust me, I'm not the nervous type, but I think if your sisters hear what happened, they'll want you to get checked out."

Her sigh was soft and a tiny bit sad. She stared into her cup with a broody look. "Honestly, it was more my reaction to the noise. The crash startled me, and I'd been thinking about some stuff, and it just hit me all at once. You have to trust me. I'd never put Zoe at risk by being too prideful to go to a doctor. Okay?"

He relaxed a bit. She never messed around where Zoe was concerned. Slowly, he nodded. "Fine, but you have to promise to tell them."

"I will. How was the floral appointment?"

He made a face. "You really want to talk about work when you're recovering?"

"Yes, I really want to talk about work. Did you finalize the bouquet?"

"Devon did an amazing job. I was going to text you pics, but I'll show you now." He flicked through them, and she made low, murmuring sounds of approval that made his muscles clench. He switched to thinking about serial killers to give his poor body a break.

"Brilliant. Adele will love it." She sighed and glanced at her watch. "I have to leave at three forty-five to get Zoe from the bus, and I wanted to squeeze in some paperwork at the office first."

"Yeah, I was heading there, too, but I think you should just rest for a while. You can work on your laptop right here."

"I keep telling you, I'm fine. Stop trying to treat me like a delicate china doll that's ready to break."

He snorted. "You? Trust me—you're more like the WWE wrestler chick–doll that's ready to kick some ass. I just feel like you don't need to push your luck with a bad day."

Her sudden paleness made him worried again. Those blue eyes widened, haunted by something that leached away the normal warmth and sparkle.

"Bella? I was just joking. Did I say something?"

She stared out at something he couldn't see in the distance. She placed her tea carefully down. "I'll be right back. Just want to hit the bathroom," she said woodenly.

He nodded, watching her go, checking to see if she looked steady. Damn, it was as if she'd seen a ghost. He'd been half joking, but he did wonder if certain days were better cut short when one had a gut instinct of wrongness. Not that a minor car accident should scare her. But it was the way she'd looked at him right before she passed out in his arms. Like she was trapped in a horror movie of her own making. It'd sent a cold trickle down his spine. Well, it wasn't like it was Friday the thirteenth. It was just February—

His thoughts stalled out. A tickle of memory reared up and became a flash flood.

Six years ago.

February twenty-second. The day her husband had died.

He sucked in a breath and placed his own mug down. Son of a bitch. He remembered when Avery first told him. They'd all been acting weird and jumpy, and Bella had called in sick, so he needed to take over a last-minute consulting appointment. He'd made some joking comment about her going to play hooky, and Avery quietly told him this was the date Matt had died in the crash. She also said they never discussed it. The sisters remained silent witnesses of the anniversary that had taken the man Bella loved, allowed her the isolation she seemed to crave, and moved on the next day like nothing had happened. Each year was the same, so he'd followed the pattern and never questioned anyone.

He'd felt it wasn't a great way to deal with grief, but he was no therapist. God knew everyone needed something different to soothe the ravaged pain of losing who they loved.

He froze as the realization slowly leaked through him.

Her car accident.

She'd experienced a crash just like her late husband had years ago. What type of horrible nightmares had that dredged up? No wonder she'd passed out. Had she imagined her husband at that awful moment? And had she honestly expected not to be affected by any of it? To work and pick up Zoe and finish her day like it was a normal one? To be so deep in denial, she didn't have to fall behind or deal with those emotions that might be silently tearing her apart?

He heard the door open, and she walked back into the room. "I better get going. Thanks for being there, Gabe. I promise to tell my sisters about it."

He hesitated, wondering if he was going to push her down an unknown path that could either help her heal or destroy her more. His nerves prickled, and he cleared his throat, waiting for courage.

It was the blankness in her expression that made him act.

"I didn't realize today is the anniversary of when you lost Matt," he said casually, walking to the bureau. He picked up the one picture always displayed: the two of them staring down at Zoe wrapped up in a blanket. Their faces were full of the love and wonder of first-time parents at the beginning of their journey. He imagined getting that chance with Bella and losing her too soon. That type of anguish could morph and change every year but never disappear. "Makes a bit more sense now why you passed out. I can't imagine the type of memories that crash brought up."

The silence screamed. He kept his back turned to give her the space, not knowing what to expect.

"How did you know?" she ripped out in a half whisper.

"I should have remembered sooner. Avery told me when I first started working here when I began to ask questions. I never meant to invade your privacy, but she thought I should know." He slowly moved away from the bureau and jammed his hands in his pockets. "Thing is, she said no one talks about it. She said it's easier for all of you to try and forget."

"Forgetting is good in some ways," she said. "At least it helps you function in the world."

"Agreed. But other times, it's like there's this splinter throbbing under your skin, and if you keep ignoring it for long enough, it gets infected. That's how grief works sometimes. Letting it bleed clean hurts, but that's how it can heal better."

He dared a look. Her eyes were curious as she stared back at him. It was as if she were caught between two different reactions, and he wasn't sure which one would tip her over.

"I went to a grief counselor, and she told me the same thing. I began to journal things—memories I had about Matt when we were together. Suddenly, I was writing more and remembering all these tiny things that I'd forgotten. I began getting stronger. I got out of bed. Eventually, I even got back to work and was able to be alone with Zoe." A faint smile curved her lips, but it only made Gabe ache from the sheer pain it obviously masked. "Finally, I didn't need the journals anymore, and it was easier for all of us not to talk about it. Not on the day he died."

"It's been six years now?"

She gave a jerky nod.

"Do you ever miss talking about him?"

She spun on her heel and walked toward the window. Pressing her forehead against the pane of glass, she began to speak. "Yes, but I'm afraid if I think about it or talk about it too much, I'll go back to the way I was. When I couldn't cope. I can't be weak like that anymore. Everyone is counting on me."

"That's not weakness, Bella," he said strongly, trying to make her listen. "That's just loving someone so much, you need to go away for a while inside to cope. You fought your way back to Zoe. To your sisters. And you can do it as many times as you have to—no one believes you're weak."

She shrugged, a sob in her throat. "I never wanted to run a million-dollar business like Avery or travel the world and be an artist like Taylor. I just wanted my own home, children, and Matt. I was the simple one. But Matt was worried about money, so he took this job in AC and had to do a lot of commuting. I kept telling him it wasn't important, but Zoe was a baby, and he wanted so much for us."

"I bet he was stubborn."

"Oh yes, Zoe's so like him. But very kind. Do you know he wasn't that big of a guy? He got called Shorty a lot in high school before he sprouted senior year. Anyway, he saw this Hispanic boy getting beat up on the school grounds, and he grabbed this big stick and started smacking those bullies on the back of their heads. They got so pissed. They turned on Matt, but he was fast, so he got away. The school heard about it and started calling Matt 'Gump' in the hallways, so he joined the track team. The next year, he scored a whole bunch of medals and got offered a scholarship for cross-country."

He cocked his hip, settling in. "You were seriously dating then?"

"Oh yeah, we were crazy about each other since junior high. We hooked up officially when we were in freshman year because my mom wouldn't let me have a boyfriend until then. I followed him to college, and we both graduated. Got married and moved back home to see if we could stay close to our families. We were so happy when we got pregnant. I was young, and technically it wasn't the best time since we were just starting out, but God, we were so excited."

He was afraid to ask his next question, but that same gut instinct urged him forward. Somehow, getting her to open up today was important. He didn't know why or how he knew, it was just a sense he needed to follow. "What happened the day he died, Bella?"

Her shoulders jerked. She raised her hand and pressed her palm against the window where no light streamed through. "It was a gloomy day, just like this. Matt was heading home from a job in AC, but he'd gotten off early. We were going to order Chinese takeout and watch a movie. So simple, but I couldn't wait. Zoe made me tired, and I craved some downtime with Matt. I remember it was past six, and I was annoyed. I kept texting him, wondering if he'd hit traffic or got out late. He didn't answer. I remember Zoe was cranky and crying, and I was in a bad mood, and I thought of all the ways I was going to show him I was mad when he got through the door. And then my doorbell rang and there were two policemen standing there."

She paused, and he waited her out, not wanting to break the fragile thread between them.

"You know, it was just like in the movies. They were in their uniforms, wearing somber expressions. Asked if I was Mrs. Caldwell. Said there'd been an accident. I got ready to grab Zoe and get to the hospital, but when I asked over and over if he was okay, they just looked at me like they'd probably looked at a million other people before and said Matt was dead. I couldn't believe it. Kept wishing it was a bad dream or a prank, but they stayed there, and I don't remember much after that."

Her hand dropped. She turned around and stared at him from across the room, a fragility shaking her body that told him she was at the edge of a breaking point.

"How did you survive the pain?" he finally asked.

"I withdrew. Went inside myself to a place where I didn't have to face it or worry. I tried to come back for Zoe, and my family. But it was too easy to stay. I went to the hospital for a while, Gabe. They termed it a breakdown."

"But you came back."

"Yes. One day, Avery came to visit me, and she had Zoe. I held my sweet little girl, and I heard her crying. It was as if she was asking me to come back. After they left the hospital, I tried harder, and things became less fuzzy. Then I heard Matt's voice."

A chill leaked through him. "What did he say?"

"He said it was time to go back to my life. To be with Zoe. To be strong." Her voice grew faint. "I always listened to Matt, you know. He was really smart and had my best interests in mind. So I fought harder and got out of the hospital. Began therapy. Got better." She swayed on her feet, and her eyes took on a glassy sheen. "Do you think I'll always have something broken in me?"

Shock waves of emotion hit him full force. He didn't think, just moved.

In seconds, he'd crossed the room and swept her up in his arms, carrying her gently back to the sofa. Pulling her tight, he held her against his chest and rocked her like a child, stroking her hair, murmuring her name. She was stiff at first, then, inch by inch, her body folded in, and she let go. The sobs came later—huge, racking, horrible sounds from the depths of her, trapped for so long they exploded out. He was humbled by the force of her love, horribly jealous of Matt to have claimed her in a way that would transcend a lifetime, and fiercely determined to show her how damn strong she really was.

Finally, the sobs eased. He kept her close, tucking her head against his chest, offering her a physical comfort he knew she desperately needed. "Life breaks everyone at one point. But the survivors get up and keep going, even if they're a bit broken. That's the type of strength you have," he said quietly. "You'll love and miss him till the day you die. But you didn't give up. You fought back to give Zoe a mom, and flourished in a career that fosters happiness and love. Terming it as weakness insults both you and Matt. Don't do that, Bella."

She raised her head. Tears streaked her cheeks. Her lipstick was rubbed off. Her hair was a wild thing of curls and waves that exploded around her. But it was her eyes that stole his soul, those powder-blue eyes that stared right back at him with a surge of heat and life that made him desperate to lower his head and kiss her deep and long and hard until they burned like fire and melted into each other as one.

His muscles locked in an effort to remain still. She needed something else from him right now—something bigger than the physical—and he intended to give it to her.

"I could never cry on this day," she said. "I didn't realize by refusing to feel anything, I'd made the pain stronger. And you're right. Matt would have hated me calling myself weak."

He caressed her cheek, treasuring the silky feel of her skin. "Good, then we're in agreement."

Slowly, she lay back in his arms. He leaned back and shifted her slightly to the side so her cheek rested against his chest. He stroked her back, and they sat in silence for a long time. He knew it wouldn't change anything between them, but he savored the moment of closeness, happy to be the man who was able to quiet her demons for a while.

❤ ❤ ❤

When Bella finally extricated herself from his embrace, she expected to feel ashamed. Instead, there was a new lightness inside her that hadn't been there before. As if she'd been carrying rocks and had finally let them drop.

He immediately eased away, got up, and came back with tissues. She wiped her face, blew her nose, and let out a breath. "Thank you."

"There's nothing to thank me for. You're hard on yourself."

She gave a half laugh. "Aren't we all?"

"I guess we are. Just remember you're an extraordinary woman." He paused. "I wish you could see yourself the way I do."

Emotion choked her throat. God, he was beautiful, inside and out. He'd given her a precious gift, helping her crack open the darkness inside and let in the light.

Her gaze met his, and her breath caught when she glimpsed the raw fire in his eyes, but then it was quickly gone, replaced by a resolve and distance that tore her apart. A battle raged inside her between head and heart. When she opened her mouth to speak his name, the doorbell rang.

He turned and walked down the short hallway. "It's Carter. He's with Lucy."

She heard low chatter, and Carter came in with his small Yorkshire terrier in tow. A pink bow tied her fur back in a tiny ponytail, and she wore a sparkly pink collar. "Hey, Bella, how are you? I was just taking Lucy for a walk and figured we'd stop by."

Gabe blinked. "Dude, you live across town. You couldn't have walked that far."

"Well, we walked a bit, then figured we'd go for a relaxing drive, then stopped here on total impulse."

She narrowed her gaze in suspicion. "Who told you?"

He let out a breath. "Thank God. I can't lie. Ron Livery from the police station called Avery and let her know you were in a car accident. She's wrapping up an event, so she told me to come right over. Are you okay?"

She groaned and dropped her face in her hands. Lucy jumped on the couch and began licking her, thinking it was a great game. She fought her off, holding back giggles at the doggy kisses. "Isn't there any damn privacy in this town? It was a minor accident, Carter. I'm fine. The car is fine. There's no need for you to be here."

He shrugged off his jacket. "Well, I'm staying because Avery is on her way. But I'll text her now. Can I say you didn't suspect I knew anything?"

Gabe shook his head. "Pathetic."

Carter gave him the finger and began texting.

Within minutes, the door flung open, and Taylor marched in, her pink hair tousled from the wind, a scary frown resting on her face. "Bella! Holy shit, are you okay? Christina from Bagel Time said she saw an accident outside the window, and it was you, but I left my damn phone in the car and didn't see it until now. What happened?"

This was unbelievable. Gabe caught her look across the room and shook his head. Ah, the pleasures of living in a small town where nothing remained secret. "T, I'm fine. I got rear-ended, but there's no damage."

"Did you get checked for whiplash? What about a concussion?"

Gabe took over. "She refused to go to the hospital—says she feels fine. There's no bumps, and her neck's not stiff. I think we just need to watch her carefully."

Her usually stoic sister looked freaked out and stood before her like she wanted to hug her but refused to be overdramatic. "Okay. Let me text Pierce and tell him he doesn't have to rush over. I thought he could get here faster."

"You texted Pierce?" Bella shrieked.

"Well, Carter is here!" she snapped back. "I didn't know what was going on. How did Carter know?"

"Ron called Avery," Carter said. "Do you have any snacks? I missed lunch."

Bella pointed to the cabinet. "Trail mix, chocolate-chip cookies, and plenty of fruit."

"Why didn't Ron call me?" Taylor asked. "Am I the least important sister or something?"

Carter shrugged. "I guess."

Avery and Pierce raced through the door at the same time. "Bella, what happened? I freaked when I got that call—why didn't you call me?" Avery demanded. She sat down on the couch next to her and pulled her in for a tight hug. "Are you hurt?"

Caught between humor and frustration, she chose humor. "I'm fine. For the fourth time, it was minor, there's nothing wrong with me, and you all didn't have to leave your jobs to come rushing over here."

Pierce headed into the kitchen. "I hated my client consultation anyway, so I was glad when T told me to leave. Are those chocolate chip?"

"Yeah, Toll House," Carter said, handing him the platter.

"Cool."

"Why didn't Ron call me first?" Taylor demanded, jabbing her finger at Avery. "I should be just as respected in this town as you."

Avery rolled her eyes. "You dated Ron in high school for one weekend, broke up with him, and asked his friend out. He's still resentful. He'll never call you first."

"You were cruel, Taylz," Pierce said between mouthfuls of cookie. "A real bitch."

"Hmm, I forgot that. Makes sense. I feel better."

Bella looked at the clock. "I have to get Zoe from the bus."

"I'll get her," Taylor said. "Come on, Pierce, come with me."

"I'm eating."

"Bring the cookies with you. We'll eat in the car, and Zoe gets her snack."

Carter snatched one of the last ones before Pierce took them. Bella watched them go, knowing there was no way she'd win the argument. Her family was worried about her. Usually, she'd internalize that type of care and believe it was because she couldn't handle stress, but now she looked at it from a fresh viewpoint. She'd lost her husband, but her sisters had lost their brother-in-law. They had experienced the pain of her loss, and she knew they approached this day with grief, also. Maybe the way they hovered and fussed wasn't a sign of her weakness.

Maybe it was just a way to show they loved her.

After all, she was the peacemaker of the family. They came to her to solve arguments, and when they were seeking advice or confessing their secrets. Why shouldn't they be able to nurture her during a tough time? An accident on the anniversary of Matt's death had caused her to collapse. Her family wanted to be there for her, and trying to pretend she was strong all the time was exhausting.

Bella sighed. If they were all here, she'd do what gave her peace and what she was good at. "Enough with the snacks," she announced. "Since everyone is here, why don't I whip up an early dinner?"

Carter raised a brow. "Sounds good to me. Avery?"

Her sister hugged her again. "Perfect. I like that we'll all be together tonight."

Bella rose from the couch and snapped into parental mode. "I have some steaks in the freezer, and we can do baked potatoes with some roasted veggies."

"Oh, with that special marinade you make?" Carter asked.

"Definitely. Gabe, you're staying, right?"

She turned to look at him. He'd been quiet, and there was an aura of stillness around him, like he was observing the scene from a distance. His smile was lopsided and heartbreaking. "Thanks, but I have to go."

Carter waved his hand in the air. "You don't want to miss steak, man. Can't you reschedule the appointment or work later tonight after dinner?"

Gabe shook his head. "Sorry, I can't."

Avery frowned. "I thought you had a free evening—just paperwork."

"Something else came up. But I appreciate the offer. Have fun." He gave a half-hearted wave and headed to the door.

Bella stopped him before he left. Tilting her chin up, she stared into those sooty eyes. "I'd really like you to stay," she said quietly.

He reached out to touch her hair, then jerked back as if he remembered he had no right to touch her. "Thank you, Bella. But I don't belong here with you. Everyone you really need is right here. Don't be afraid to let them in."

"But—"

"I'll see you tomorrow. Make sure you rest." He closed the door behind him.

She backed away, her heart twisting in her chest. The loss of his presence slammed through her, and she took a moment to collect herself before facing her sister.

"What's up with him?" Carter asked. "Not like Gabe to give up a free dinner."

"I'm not sure," Avery murmured. "I'm not around him as much since he got his own client base, but he's been acting a bit off. Bella, is there something going on with him? Is his schedule too much but he's afraid to say anything? What do you think?"

Her throat closed up. The image assaulted her vision. Tucked against his hard, muscled chest; matching breath to breath; his spicy male scent rising to her nostrils. She'd felt the burn of his skin through the thin material of his shirt, reveled in the way his fingers pulled through her hair, pushing it back from her forehead. Being in his arms was like finding something she'd been searching for and hadn't known existed. A reminder of all the good things she'd believed she'd never find again.

She ducked her head and hurried into the kitchen to prep. "He seems fine. I've seen no issues in his schedule, and we've got a handle on Adele's wedding. Maybe it's personal."

"What do you mean?" Carter asked.

She took out the steaks and a bag of potatoes. "Well, you know how busy his dating life is. He's seeing Marlaine—Vera's granddaughter—and

I heard a few women at the school talking about his active social calendar. Maybe he's just tired."

Avery shared a glance with Carter. "Is he seeing Marlaine?" she asked him.

"No. Marlaine had him in her sights, of course. The poor guy never gets left alone. She tried to come up with this phony excuse of a wedding to see him, but she just wanted a fun time while she was on vacation."

Bella looked up, surprised. "So they never dated?"

Carter shook his head. "Nah, Gabe is looking for a relationship, not a weekend fling. Unfortunately, every woman he tries to date seems to think he's the Cape's mascot for fun. The poor guy got so frustrated, he stopped dating. He hasn't hooked up with anyone in months." A frown creased his brow. "I figured you'd know that, Bella. Thought you were spending more time with him planning this wedding."

Bella jerked back at her future brother-in-law's judging stare. "Um, we never really talked about his personal life. I just heard he's with a different woman every weekend."

Carter snorted. "They must be imaginary. Gabe, unfortunately, is part monk. Pierce and I are pushing him to get on a dating app that's geared toward relationships." His gaze narrowed. "Why would you believe small-town gossip anyway? That's not like you. Have you ever asked him?"

Her cheeks burned. She grabbed the potato scrubber and began cleaning. "No. We focus on work."

The arch of his brow said he didn't believe her.

Avery leaned over with curiosity. "You never told me what you guys were fighting about that time you needed to leave the meeting. What happened?"

"Just a miscommunication regarding the wedding."

When no one responded, she risked a glance up. They were both staring at her as if they knew there was another story brewing beneath the surface.

Carter gave a chuckle. "Well, damn, there *is* someone else who can't lie for shit."

She gasped. "I'm not lying."

"You're not giving us the whole truth, either. Let me just tell you one thing about Gabe. He puts on a good front and pretends nothing bothers him. But he's got a big heart, and he's looking for the right woman he can trust with it."

Shock kept her still. Her future brother-in-law stared at her with an intensity that was rarely directed her way. It seemed as if Gabe had inspired a protective streak in Carter that only made her respect for him level up a notch. His not-so-subtle message was clear.

She'd been making some wrong assumptions. And he knew more about them than she thought.

"He's a good man," Avery said quietly. "And he deserves the best. I just wish we could hook him up with someone who wants to get serious."

"Someone who'll give him a fair chance," Carter added. "Pierce and I are working on it."

She had no time to answer. Taylor and Pierce returned, and Zoe came rushing up for a hug. They fell into a mishmash of chatter as everyone helped with dinner, but the entire time, there seemed to be a space in the room asking to be filled, something missing.

Or someone.

Normally, she would think of Matt, keeping the sorrow buried until she was able to go to her room alone and grieve. But tonight, it was different.

Talking to Gabe about what had happened had leached some of the poison. She reveled in her family's warmth and care as they fussed over her, and she saw in both her sisters' eyes how they were thinking about Matt. But for the first time, he wasn't dominating her thoughts and emotions like so many other years.

For once, the only man she was thinking about was Gabe.

Chapter Thirteen

Gabe looked across the table at the woman seated before him. He was having a good time. He'd always enjoyed Devon's company—they had an easy camaraderie and attraction that was never complicated. It had only grown difficult when he'd decided he wanted more from their relationship, and she had reminded him of their agreement not to get serious. Tonight, though, new beginnings seemed to be in the air, and he was going to be open to each one.

He'd taken her to Iron Pier Craft House, a casual favorite. The place was known for its specialty crafted cocktails during happy hour, sushi, and tapas. The high-topped dining tables looked out over a ceiling-to-floor window with ocean views. It was a perfect place for a first date with an ex. It was busy but not crowded, the line for takeout always long.

They ordered some martinis and started out with some burger bites and spicy shrimp. "Are you still happy running your floral shop?" he asked curiously. "You used to talk about expansion. Maybe working on an island, doing only weddings, remember?"

Her laugh was throaty. "God, yes, I remember. It was also three years ago. I don't think I gave myself the possibility I'd love what I do so much. I never expected to love running my own business."

"Well, you have more freedom and control this way. Still, I always envisioned you barefoot on a tropical beach somewhere, with a floral crown on your head."

She tilted her head, face amused. "A romantic view, I'd say. But I've got more business in my blood than you think. If I do run off to that island, it will only be because I sold my shop for a crapload of money and I'm on vacation."

He nodded, impressed. "That good, huh?"

"That good. I'm always booked, my rent's low, and I've made some contacts that allow me to compete with those snobby boutiques from the city. You know, the kind you snubbed your nose at?" she teased.

"I remember. Good for you, Dev."

Their gazes met, and she smiled at him. He realized she had changed in many ways since they'd first dated. Her energy seemed more focused. She'd always viewed time as a free-flowing thing but used to hold an edge that was now softened. Gabe remembered her hunger to experiment and push him out of his boundaries, as if competing in a race to do more, or be more. They simply hadn't matched.

Maybe things had changed.

"What about you? Are you satisfied with your choices?" she asked, her long hair swishing past her bare shoulders. She'd worn a short cotton floral dress and white fringe sandals—her style a bit bohemian but always chic.

He sipped his martini and seriously pondered the question. "I'm happy at Sunshine Bridal," he said. "I feel like I found my niche and enjoy my work. I'm satisfied."

She arched a brow. "*Satisfied* is quite a vanilla-type word."

He chuckled. "Better than gray, I guess."

"But a cop-out. Not like you." She studied him for a moment. "You haven't been in a relationship since us, have you?"

He focused on his plate. Bella's face swam before him, but he firmly pushed it away. "No."

"Interesting. You always said you wanted to settle down—that was one of the main points of us breaking it off. Yet all I seem to hear about is your amazing weekend conquests."

Irritation prickled. "Overrated. Gossip feeds gossip around here. It's getting old."

"Ever think about working in Manhattan? Or Atlantic City? A place where you can spread your wings, so to speak?"

Before, he would have shut down the idea immediately. Now, even though the idea of leaving a job he loved with people who'd become family gave him pause, he wondered if he needed to seriously consider it. "Not really. But like you, things have changed, and maybe I'll be more open to opportunities."

"I think that's a good toast, don't you?" Devon lifted her glass and entangled her wrist around his, leaning in. "To new opportunities."

Her brown eyes gleamed, and though nothing inside him buzzed in reaction, he knew it would take him some time. Which was perfect, because he wanted to take his next relationship slow and steady. He lifted his glass. *"Salud."*

The toast was both a mourning for what would never be and a celebration of a new chapter.

He smiled at Devon and drank.

♥ ♥ ♥

Taylor groaned, wandering around the house with a pathetic slump to her shoulders. "I'm blocked. I'm going to tank the whole art show. I'll be stuck at Sunshine Bridal until I'm as old as Vera, dealing with PITAs and overly cute flower girls who can't follow instructions. I want to die."

Bella clamped her lips shut to keep from laughing. "Damn, girl, you are in a mood," she said. "Don't you have a wedding tomorrow?"

"Yeah."

"Then how come you're not attached to your laptop like Avery and me, double-checking everything to be sure disaster doesn't befall you?"

Her sister shrugged and dropped onto the couch. She wore slipper socks, faux-leather leggings, and a yellow T-shirt that said I Hate Love

& WEDDINGS, which had been a joke for Christmas. Unfortunately, it had now become her fave item of clothing. "Because I'm not dorks like you both. I'm a confident woman who knows everything will be fine. Why are you home?"

"I'm going to pick up Zoe soon. She's playing with Meg, and Daisy said she'd feed them. I have to do a luncheon tomorrow, so I want to get to bed early."

"Will you go get me dinner, then?" she asked, batting her lashes in an exaggerated gesture. "I'm craving sushi. And tacos."

She winced. "Bad combo. But sure, I'll pick it up, just call it in."

Her sister brightened. "Thanks."

"What piece are you stuck on?"

A shadow darkened her features. "All of the new ones. I'm a bit concerned I could be one of those artists that create when there's no deadline or pressure. I keep trying to force the image I have in my head onto the canvas, but it keeps shifting, which pisses me off, so I yell at the bitch in my head who—"

"The bitch in your head?" Bella repeated.

"Yeah, my muse. But then she just shuts up to get even with me, and I get nowhere." She picked at her thumbnail. "Maybe this isn't going to work out."

Bella sat down. It was so rare that Taylor worried about things, it just showed how important this art show was to her. Finally, something mattered, and it was freaking her out. "It's going to work out," she said firmly. "But it may not be the path you imagined. I think we like to sketch out these ideas of how our life is going to go, but when it differs, the majority of us don't know how to handle it. This is the first time you're learning how to cultivate your art on a schedule. It may not go easy, but you'll get there, T. On deadline. I know you will."

"How?" she demanded.

"Because you don't let yourself fail," she said simply. "You're too hot-headed and stubborn, and even if you wait till the last week, you'll paint night and day and show up with your quota. Did you honestly think you'd just paint a bit each day and stay on a perfect schedule like some robot?"

Her sister frowned, considering. "I guess not."

"I *know* not. If your muse mirrors you, she's going to make things interesting. Hey, why don't we hang out, and you can take some time off? Let your inner artist stew a bit."

"I don't wanna watch rom-com movies or Disney," she warned.

"We can play a board game."

"Poker? With real money?"

Bella sighed. "Fine."

"Cool." Her sister's phone rang. A hip-hop song that had been customized for Pierce screamed out with a bunch of lyrics. She watched as Taylor glanced at the screen, declined the call, and threw it back on the couch.

Bella's jaw dropped. "Did you just not answer a call from Pierce?"

A funny look crossed her face. "We got into a thing. No big deal. Just think we need to cool off."

"You guys never fight."

"We don't when he's not an asshole."

"Do you want to talk about it?"

"Do you want to talk about whatever happened with you and Gabe at the meeting last week?"

Bella got up. "I'll get the food."

"Good idea."

She drove to Iron Pier and wondered if Pierce had finally found out Taylor was moving away soon. They'd been close for so many years, Bella always wondered if they'd ever thought of crossing the line to be more than friends. But her sister kept declaring nothing had ever happened between them, and nothing ever would. She would have taken Taylor's word if it hadn't been for the way Pierce looked at her when he thought no one was watching. Or how Taylor sought him out in a crisis, sometimes over Avery and Bella.

But it was complicated. Kind of like her and Gabe. If they'd decided to pursue a relationship, that is.

Which she'd rejected.

This past week had been different. Gabe was different. They worked side by side, tightened up all the last-minute details, and spoke easily to each other. He'd checked in once to make sure she was okay, then let it go. But all she could think about was the tender way he'd comforted her when she cried. For so long, she'd barricaded herself within her loneliness, thinking it was strength, but his words had allowed her to finally open up.

She'd hoped their connection from that night would remain, but his gaze stayed shadowed and his aura distant. His words repeated over and over in her head like a mantra, slowly driving her crazy.

I don't belong here with you.

Why did his statement cause so much pain? It was as if a hammer had struck and drove away her very breath. Was it awful to admit she missed the way he'd been around her? She kept thinking about their road trip, and the way they had laughed and eaten Sno Balls and how he'd talked about his father. She wished she'd asked more, listened harder. She'd wasted so much time keeping him at arm's length, afraid he was someone she couldn't trust. Why had she been so hard on him?

To protect your family, the inner voice whispered. *Remember? The same reason you told him you could never have a romantic relationship.*

She parallel parked at the curb and sighed. The assurance she had done the right thing didn't seem to fit as well any longer, and she didn't know why. But she'd made her decision, and there was nothing else left to do.

She grabbed her purse and headed up the stairs. It was a lively night, with a decent crowd, and she had to wait in line for her order. "Be right with you, Bella," Sean said. "We're a bit behind. Want to grab a drink at the bar? Laura's working."

"Sure, thanks." She walked to the bar and slid into the last seat on the end.

Laura flashed her a grin and headed over. She had a blonde crew cut, large hoop earrings, and gorgeous ink scrawled down her arms. She always wore a black tank top, no matter what the season. "Good to see you, Bella. How's things at Sunshine?"

"Busy, which is good. Can't wait till the end of this winter, though."

Laura made a face. "Me, too. I keep picturing me at the Lobster House, drink in my hand, sun on my face, crappy weather behind us."

"We're on countdown. Ya gotta believe."

She winked. "Sure do. What'll you have?"

"Just a seltzer with lemon, please. Waiting on some takeout." They chatted for a while, until Laura slipped to the far end of the bar. Bella checked her phone, then sat quietly, taking in the low chatter around her. Her gaze swung to the beach, perfectly silhouetted against the glass windows, and then she frowned, seeing someone familiar.

Gabe.

Her heart sped up, and she leaned closer, squinting. He was with a brunette, and he was smiling. She stood up from the stool to get a better peek, then almost gasped.

Devon. He was with Devon, and they were definitely on a date. She watched in slow motion as they encircled their wrists together, holding martini glasses up, heads bent close together. They sipped from their drinks, laughing as he spilled some over the edge. Devon grabbed a napkin and wiped it up, her hand reaching out to pat his arm, as if she were already familiar with his touch.

Nausea lurched in her gut. They'd dated before. When he first came to work, she remembered he had gotten involved with Devon rather quickly, and they were together for a short time before breaking up. He was never seen in a steady relationship again, and gossip peaked now and then that they were sometimes casual lovers when they weren't seeing anyone else. Bella hadn't heard Devon's name mentioned by anyone recently, though, so she'd chalked it up to rumors.

But maybe not.

The image of them in bed together slammed through her brain. Her hand jerked, and her soda sloshed onto the bar.

"Bella! Your food's ready!"

Her name echoed loudly in the air. She ducked down on instinct, not wanting him to see her and think she was spying, or following him, or doing uncool . . . stuff. She shoved cash at Sean. "Give this to Laura," she whispered, handing him a five-dollar bill and grabbing the bags. "I gotta go."

"Sure, sweetheart, have a great night."

She raced down the stairs, refusing to look back, and didn't feel safe until she was almost home. Shock raced through her, along with a terrible ache—the type of ache when you lose something you really, really wanted.

Or someone.

Gabe had moved on, just like she had wanted. Yes, it felt quick—a bit of a sting—but if he was waiting for almost three years to tell her his feelings, then it must've seemed as if he'd wasted enough time. Maybe Devon was really meant to be his match after all. Maybe he'd get the happy ending he'd always wanted.

She picked up Zoe. Ate the delicious food while she snuggled with her daughter and sister. Played a few games of rousing poker and watched Zoe beat her aunt for the very first time. Then went to bed.

She had everything she needed. She'd made her choice and had no right to regret or ponder if she'd made a terrible mistake. No right to wonder if she had left something behind that was more than an attraction, too afraid to allow it to grow, just in case.

Her life was steady. Her daughter was happy. Wasn't it better to protect what she had rather than take a risk on someone who could hurt them?

She tried to go to sleep with that reassurance, but she dreamed about the kiss and the lure of possibilities.

Chapter Fourteen

They'd done it.

It was a Dr. Seuss paradise.

Bella worked the room, triple-checking every last detail before the ceremony began. The reporters spilled over the sidewalk outside, bulbs flashing, a few interlopers desperately trying to sneak into the bookstore to be part of the treasured few able to see the quirkiest wedding of the year.

To keep reporters from seeing her dress beforehand, they'd wrapped a huge velvet cloak around Adele and escorted her inside the bookshop and upstairs until her big entrance. Gabe had dubbed the whole thing "very Lady Gaga," and spent a few moments charming the press by dropping juicy hints of what was to come without giving anything away.

The crowd seemed sedate and curious, their necks craning around to take in the surroundings as they took their seats. The bookstore had been transformed into Seussland, a fantasy ground where Truffula trees popped from corners, and floral balloons drifted from the ceiling and dripped from the staircase. Giant gilded golden cages held the amazing Victoria crowned pigeons, who were paired in twos, and hung in places where guests could see but not touch. They made a wonderful whooping sound that delighted the crowd and reminded Bella of a Dr. Seuss character. Hundreds of white lights twisted around funky birch-like accents, including signs pointing to different corners of the room where guests could enjoy various pictures of the couple paired with Dr. Seuss quotes.

Gabe's voice rumbled sexily in her ear. "Ready for the main show. Bride ready?"

"Going up to check now. Guests seated."

"Good. Press is contained, and I'm ready with the groom on your call."

She pasted on a professional smile and climbed the circular stairs. Adele was surrounded by her sister and two cousins, who fussed and tugged at her dress. She stepped smoothly in front of them to give the bride space. "If you ladies will take your seats, we're about to begin."

They shot her matching sulky looks as they left. After they disappeared, Adele turned to her. "They want me to die so they'll have my money," she said with a sigh. "My sister married a deadbeat who took most of her fortune, and she spent the balance in record time. My cousins are useless and haven't done one nice thing for me ever. Now they pretend to be my best friend."

"Many people display their best behavior and their worst at a wedding," Bella said. "You look breathtaking." Adele had picked out the dress before they began working together, and it reflected the woman's heart and personality. The buttery cream fabric was light as gossamer and flowed like water, draping over her body in a mass of crisscross patterns. The long sleeves billowed like bells, and a bright-yellow sash cinched her waist, matching the whimsical colored bouquet tied with birch and studded with diamond Sneetch stars for the occasion.

Adele smiled and her face lit up. "Thank you. I feel it. Did Edward chicken out yet, or is he still downstairs?"

"He's a brave one. He's not going anywhere." She gave Gabe the go-ahead, and the music drifted up the staircase. "Any questions? Anything I can ease your mind about? Everything downstairs is perfect."

"I know! I took a peek when I was being whisked up the stairs. I can't wait to see all the surprises."

"We want you to have fun and enjoy the evening. Let's begin the walk down."

Bella had done so many weddings, she always wondered if this one was going to be the time she didn't cry or feel moved when she saw a bride meet her groom at the altar. But she was never disappointed. It always brought a rush of warmth, and a gentle reminder that love was the only thing to cling to in the world—once you found it, you needed to embrace every beautiful second. Weddings were a reminder that happily-ever-after endings still existed.

She watched them recite their vows, and her gaze snagged on Gabe. Looking breathlessly handsome in his dark tux and slicked-back hair, he was straight from a magazine cover. She'd already noticed how most of the women kept sneaking glances at him. Sexual masculine energy simply radiated from his frame, leaving a trail behind him. Kind of like the Pied Piper. Except . . .

Except she'd been wrong to assume she knew about his love life. Since Carter had challenged her on believing the local gossip, she'd begun seeing things in a different way. Was it possible everyone was so used to thinking he was a certain man, no one would allow him to show a different side? After all, who didn't want a hot single male to claim as their local beach bachelor? Small towns thrived on that stuff. But had anyone ever asked if that was what he wanted?

She certainly didn't.

Bella remembered how it was after Matt died. How she was looked upon differently as a single mother. She'd been held to a new, higher standard. Any type of dating would focus curious eyes on her, ready to assess and judge and rip apart. She'd been afraid of that type of scrutiny, so it'd been easier to protect her daughter by refusing to engage in the dating world. She'd kept to her house and family, refusing to let the messiness of the outside world in, especially any type of men.

Now, she wondered if it was out of habit that nothing had changed in six years. She had whined to her sisters that she needed a date but did nothing to pursue it. It might be time to look hard at her choices and make some changes. She'd reached a safe level of contentment but nothing approaching true happiness.

Once, she'd accepted that would never be hers to experience again. But maybe she was wrong.

Edward and Adele took turns reading *Oh, the Places You'll Go!*, and she caught a few guests wiping their eyes at the surprise sweetness between the older couple. Guess even the hardened society crowd was vulnerable to a tender sentiment.

They were pronounced man and wife.

Gabe's gaze caught and held hers across the room.

Then the room erupted with applause, jerking her away from those piercing dark eyes. They fell into transition work—getting the ceremony chairs tucked away to open up the room and bring in the other accent decor for the reception. They worked in perfect symmetry, directing guests to the special cocktails in tropical colors, including a rosé champagne—the perfect color pink—with blueberries. Each had a funny-sounding name and was served by a different waiter with a specialized Dr. Seuss tie to coordinate with the drink and paired appetizers.

By the time the reception was in full swing, Bella guessed the alcohol and comfort food had loosened up the crowd. Everyone seemed to have lost most of their stiffness and settled into lively chatter at the tables and danced.

Gabe eased to her side. "All good on the home front. You?"

"No issues yet. The cocktails were a huge hit. Everyone's drunk."

"Perfect, isn't it? I heard a lot of chatter about the stations we set up. They love the travel section."

"Avery actually gave me that idea. Great feedback on the flowers, too. I loved when Adele cried when she spotted the tribute to her mother." They'd carved out a quote into a birchwood frame with a picture of Adele and her mother and displayed it at the station titled *Who We Love*. Friends and family caught in various photographs made up a few collages of Adele's and Ed's lives.

His face softened. "That was a brilliant idea, Bella. Weddings are about emotions, and become bigger than just the couple. It becomes their pasts and the people they loved, too."

She blinked at the heartfelt statement. "You really do have a poet's heart," she said with a smile.

His hand brushed hers, and a sizzling heat cracked through her. This time, he was the one to step back. The loss was bigger than she expected. She remembered how it felt to lean on his strength to get her through one of the most emotional moments. He wasn't afraid to stand strong in the midst of messiness. Why would she have thought it would be easy for this man to walk away from anything that challenged him, including women?

"We have the cake and dessert. I'll do a walk-through and make sure we don't have any sloppy drunks to tame."

"I'll make sure there's no catty women ready to rip the bride and wedding apart. Why are they always in the bathroom where the bride can overhear?"

They smiled at each other and parted. The next hour passed uneventfully. The cake was a huge hit; the impressive ten-level topsy-turvy layered creation was accented with encircling birch twigs making an elaborate crown around the base and mini–Lucy Ball flowers setting off each layer. The outside was a subtle work of art, a pale pink and rich cream, but when it was cut, there was a gasp from the crowd. Every other layer boasted a different bold color hidden inside—canary yellow, cotton-candy pink, Tiffany blue, seafoam green, red velvet. It was sheer creative cake artistry, and Maria had informed them both it had almost killed her.

As flashbulbs went off and the dessert table with cake pops, macaroons, truffles, and specialized Dr. Seuss treats was revealed, Bella knew they'd outdone themselves. The pigeons called out, and Adele's delighted laugh echoed through the air. Joy unfurled inside her, along with pride from being able to be part of a day filled with love. It was these moments that reminded her how much she truly did love her job.

Bella was just heading for a quick bathroom break when she was stopped.

"Are you the wedding planner?"

Bella turned. A petite woman stood before her, dressed in a stunning blush-pink dress with intricate beading. With her cap of dark hair, she looked like a pixie creature from a mythical land. "Yes. Can I help you with something?"

"I'm Latoya with *Bride Style* magazine. I'm doing a feature on Adele's wedding, and I wanted to ask you a few questions."

"Of course. Congratulations on getting on the list. Adele was selective of who she invited to the wedding."

Latoya laughed. "Adele and I go way back, so she knows I'm not out to make front-page news by trashing her. But I am fair, so to forewarn you, if I don't like something, I'm going to put it out to my readers."

Bella's smile hid her nerves. They'd been featured on the Knot and in a few other high-style articles over the years, but *Bride Style* was the fashion magazine for elite weddings and society brides. Styles, trends, and new hot contacts were made there.

"I understand completely. You should meet my partner, Gabe. We worked together on this for Sunshine Bridal."

"Already did. Cornered him right before you. I wanted to interview you both separately."

Uneasiness struck. Was this a way to try and split them up, causing a bit of controversy? The press liked an angle that was click-worthy. She wasn't going to play those games, but Latoya seemed genuinely friendly, and she was trusted by Adele. "I'm all yours. What would you like to know?"

"I'm going to record this because I have no pen and pad that will fit in my purse." She picked up her small clutch, removed her phone, and hit the button. "Sunshine Bridal is run by you and your sisters, correct? Can you tell me a bit about how the company was started, then go into your individual styles?"

Bella took her time, making sure to give details of her sisters' different personalities and how their whole vision took their parents' company to the next level. They chatted in-depth about how Adele had found them, and some of the most memorable weddings they'd planned in the past. Finally, they got to Gabe.

"Hiring a male wedding coordinator is still unusual. Have you ever had any issues regarding your female clients not being able to relate?"

"No, I think Gabe has brought a fresh perspective we all need. After all, most brides are desperate to involve a man in their wedding planning, but most run in the opposite direction. Gabe is able to act as a stand-in for the groom, when desired, and is an excellent guide through the overwhelming process."

"Who did most of the work bringing Adele's Dr. Seuss theme to life?"

"It was equal," she said. "Each of our full-time planners brings a distinct personality and touch to a wedding, but Gabe and I were able to meld our ideas to execute the perfect vision. It's another thing we're proud of at Sunshine. We all help each other out, so you get the power of a full team."

"You haven't had any runaway brides once they worked with Gabe, have you?" Latoya asked, a wicked twinkle in her eye. "I could see how it could happen. He's so charming."

Coldness trickled down her spine. Her voice reflected the chill when she spoke. "No, that has never happened and never will. Gabe is a complete professional, just like all of us employed at Sunshine. He treats clients with care and compassion, as we all should. I also think it's a discriminatory question. Would you ask a woman that?"

The reporter didn't flinch, just treated her to a level gaze. "Probably not, but no question is off the table."

She nodded and remained calm. She'd said her truth but didn't want to piss off Latoya, either. "Understood. My answer stands."

"Noted." Latoya asked a few other basic questions, then clicked off her phone. "Thanks so much. I'll email you if we decide to run a piece."

She offered her hand and they shook. "A pleasure. Our main concern is always the clients. We just wanted Adele to have the perfect wedding."

"Looks like she did." Latoya grinned and disappeared into the throng of people.

Bella subtly glanced at her watch. Thank goodness. The night was almost over, and she was ready to crash. Half an hour left to avoid a disaster and retire this wedding into the books.

Needing more water, she headed to the bar where standard cocktails would be and caught sight of Gabe. He stood with his back to her, broad shoulders thrown back in an almost defensive posture. As she got closer, she saw a pretty blonde in a tight snow-white dress pressing against him. Diamonds dripped from her neck and ears and wrists like icing. Her hands were stretched out in front of her, palms running up and down his chest.

Horror mounted at the intimate position, but then she realized Gabe was trapped between the bar and a chair, effectively cornered.

The blonde's head tilted up. It looked as if they were about to kiss. "I thought it was your job to give me the favor I wanted," she was saying, her speech a bit slurred.

He gave a small laugh, then grasped her hands to push her gently back. "Ah, and you did get a favor that's quite special. It's on your table. Didn't you like it?"

"Not as much as I like you."

Suddenly, another woman joined them, obviously the blonde's friend. She sidled up, her hip touching the blonde, completing the threesome. "Who'd you pick up, Kelly? How do you always manage to find the hottest men at these things?"

"Ladies, I'm going to need to check on Adele, if you'll excuse me."

Gabe tried again to get himself loose, but the women refused to move.

"This one's mine," the blonde declared, running a hand over his biceps and squeezing. "He's my favor for the night."

The friend joined in on the action and put her hand on Gabe. "I want one, too."

"Get your own."

"You can share."

Bella closed the distance, grabbed the blonde by the arm, and firmly jerked her away. "Excuse me, I need to talk with my associate."

The blonde gasped. "You shoved me! Who the hell are you, anyway? We were just getting to know each other."

Gabe stepped out of his corner and back into safe, open space. "Sorry, we have a crisis to take care of. Our apologies."

He began to move away, but Bella stood her ground, shooting the women a cold glare. "Next time, make sure your physical advances are wanted by the other party."

"Hey, you can't talk to us like that!" the friend declared. "We'll get your ass fired, bitch."

Bella gave them a tight smile. "Since the wedding is over, we're past that. But I think if I explained to Adele that the staff was being accosted while trying to remain polite, she'll be on our side. Now, if you'll excuse us."

Without waiting for a response, she stalked off with Gabe at her side. Then noticed Latoya watching the entire exchange with open interest.

Ah, shit.

Chapter Fifteen

She'd defended him.

The thought spun in Gabe's mind as they walked inside the hotel and headed to the elevators. There were two ways he usually reacted after a wedding: either he was exhausted and craved to crash in bed to catch up on sleep, or he was jacked up and ready to party. As he stared at the silver doors, he realized it would be a long time before he was calm enough to settle in. Ah, well, maybe there was something decent on television.

"Hey, do you want to get a drink in the bar?" Bella asked.

Surprised, he turned his head to gaze at her. She looked hesitant, shifting her weight back and forth, as if afraid he'd say no.

He smiled. "I was thinking the same thing. Sounds good."

The bar was modern, with sleek black-and-red touches, and half-empty at the late hour. They picked a low red couch with plump pillows and accent tables on the sides. The lighting was dim, and low lanterns illuminated the lounge, casting her in shadow. A guy dressed in a suit with a fancy glass jar sat at a piano, playing familiar tunes.

The waitress came over. "Drinks?"

"Yes, please. One Stella. And . . . ?" He looked over at Bella.

"Extra-dirty martini. Tito's vodka. Straight up, chilled. Shaken, not stirred. Extra olives, please, preferably stuffed with blue cheese."

"Got it."

The waitress drifted off, and Gabe stared at Bella.

"What?" she asked.

"I've never seen you drink anything stronger than wine, yet you ordered like we're in a James Bond movie."

She shrugged, then tucked one leg underneath her. "I love a good martini for the right occasion, but they have to be perfect."

"Are you a high-maintenance person masked as low maintenance?"

A laugh escaped her lips. He savored the sound like an expensive aged bourbon. "I don't think so. Or maybe I am. Maybe I pretend to be calm and zen to escape the fact I really am a control freak."

"I think we all have those tendencies."

"What about you? You seem pretty chill most of the time."

He winced. "I am, but I don't like anyone messing with my stuff."

She cocked her head. "What do you mean?"

"Probably an only-child thing, I don't know. That's why I never hired a cleaner. I like to have my things in a certain place, and if they're moved, I get upset."

Her lip quirked up, and her blue eyes filled with amusement. "Oh, you are going to need to explain more. This image is not fitting with the Gabe I know."

"Forget it. The drinks are here."

The waitress set them on the table. Bella sipped hers and declared it perfect, and he leaned back to enjoy his beer. "I'm not going to leave you alone until you tell me the rest," she finally said, pushing the stirrer in tiny circles. "Get it over with."

He groaned. "Fine, but don't tell Avery or Taylor. They like to pull the occasional prank, and I don't feel like being the recipient."

"I won't."

"Well, I like to alphabetize things. DVDs, books, et cetera."

"That's not too bad."

"And the pantry is coordinated into sections so it's easier to find things."

A frown furrowed her brow. "Interesting. Each shelf?"

"Yes, they're color coordinated. And I have canisters that are labeled."

"Okay. That's a bit intense."

"Maybe, but I never lose time looking for something."

"Interesting. What about your closet?"

He winced. "They're hung according to categories. Dress, casual, summer, winter, et cetera."

"Do you leave things out on the counter? Table?"

A shudder shook through him, so he took a sip of beer. "Hell no. There's a place for everything."

"This is more hard-core than I originally thought. Funny, I never noticed it at work. I mean, I know you like your charts like Avery, but it never seemed outrageous." She contemplated her drink. "What happens if you have a visitor over and she drops stuff on the floor?"

"I rarely have visitors."

"But if you do?"

He hesitated, imagining her in his room. Clothes lying in a tangle on the carpet, bra thrown carelessly over the chair, heels kicked off and left without a thought. He lived like a monk, used to his single status and his ability to never need to compromise. The yearning for more crashed over him and churned his gut. He'd happily change to have someone he cared about in his life, interwoven in his daily routine, bringing a chaos that was messy but joyous.

His answer came out rough. "I'd forgive her."

A thread of tension tightened between them. God, he shouldn't have said anything. He should be imagining Devon in the room. Their date had gone well, and they'd left each other with a hug and a lingering hope for maybe more. At least, that's what he'd wanted to feel.

A group of men dressed in trendy shirts and dark-washed jeans came into the lounge, visibly drunk and loud. They crowded close to Bella and Gabe, cracking offensive jokes, obviously still ready to keep the party going. Bella's face tightened as one of them began talking about banging the hottie in the club in the bathroom stall, and Gabe stood up. "Come on. Let's take our drinks and go somewhere quiet. I don't think we need any more noise tonight."

"Good idea." She took her martini, and they passed through the lobby, but there were no good places to sit and talk. "We can go to my room," she suddenly offered. "I have one of those nice living-room areas that's comfortable."

He opened his mouth to decline. It wasn't a good idea to be alone with her. Not late at night, after a big wedding, when his heart was still raw. But she nibbled on that lower lip, like she was worried he might think something bad, and he found himself nodding.

They rode the elevator up and entered her room. It opened up to a spacious sitting area with two chairs, a couch, a desk, and a big-screen television. She clicked on some lights and sat down on the chair. He picked the couch, giving them space between them. He was surprised to even be invited to her room, but he figured she was confident enough that nothing would happen. Depression threatened, but he pushed it away. At least she wanted to stay friends and allow him to be part of her life. He was glad she trusted him enough for that.

He remembered holding her in his arms. The soft sweetness of her body, the silky tangle of her hair, the light floral scent that cloaked her and flooded his senses. Being able to soothe her pain had been a gift. She'd cracked open and let him see the messy, gooey center behind the glossy surface of the woman she showed the world. That was the woman he was half in love with. But it only made things harder, because she was officially off-limits, and he was moving on.

Yet she'd defended him tonight in front of the reporter.

They still hadn't talked about the incident.

He found the question rising to his lips and spilling forth. "Why did you make a scene with those women at the reception? You know I could have handled it, right?"

Her shoulders stiffened, but she took her time, sipping her drink before lifting her gaze. He fell deep into those powder-blue eyes and had no desire to resurface. "I know. I'm sorry if I embarrassed you."

"You didn't. In fact, I was oddly touched you defended my virtue. I just hope you know I get that a lot with this job, and though it's uncomfortable, I've learned how to deal with it."

Her chin tilted up, and fire shot from her eyes. "You shouldn't have to deal with women pawing you or thinking you're some extra favor for them to play with. Just thinking about what those women said to you gets me so pissed off."

He jerked back in shock. "Really?"

She gave a feminine growl. "Hell yes. If it was a woman being touched without consent, there'd be a lawsuit. You were on a job. You said no and asked politely for them to back off. The way they were touching you and pretending you were a piece of candy?" She shook her head. "I'm sorry, Gabe. I guess I didn't realize it was so rampant. We need to do something. I wanted to punch that blonde in her face."

Laughter at her adorable fierceness on his behalf burst out from him. Avery had stood up for him many times, ready to upset the bride or groom on his behalf if he was being mistreated. He'd always appreciated it, but Bella's reaction seemed oddly personal. "Now that would have made the wedding go viral," he teased. "Honestly, Bella, it was annoying, but I'm always careful to try not to get into those situations. This time, I got cornered."

"Now I understand why you keep such a distance between your clients and the wedding guests. Even Latoya made a comment about it."

"Ah, yes, the reporter. She asked me a bunch of stuff, too. If I had an affair with any of you."

Her jaw dropped. "What? She actually asked that? This is supposed to be a wedding piece!"

He set his beer on the table and shrugged. "She's still looking for a good angle. Affairs in the wedding business probably sell magazines. I kept it professional, and she eventually backed off. If she's Adele's friend, I'm hoping we'll get a fair shake."

"Until she saw me explode on that guest," Bella said, and groaned. "Still, I don't care. Maybe next time she'll think before she feels like attacking some hot guy at a bar."

He laughed again. A ramped-up Bella was sexy as hell. She was like a protective feline, all hissing and clawing on his behalf. Warmth flooded his body. When was the last time anyone wanted to fight his battles?

"I appreciate it, though I'm surprised you thought I needed help."

"Why?" she demanded.

He paused, then let the truth out. "Because from our last conversation, I figured you assumed all female attention was wanted. If I'm sleeping around, that blonde would have been a perfect weekend fling."

She flinched. Set down her half-drunk martini. Then dragged in a breath. "I made a mistake, Gabe," she said softly. "I did what I accuse others of doing in town: assume all gossip is real. I had a talk with Carter."

He tried not to sound bitter. "Ah, so Carter had to defend me."

"No, I was just mentioning how you may have had a date when you said no to dinner, and he said it's been a long time for you. I told them about what was said with Marlaine, and he set me straight. I'm sorry I didn't believe you."

Relief and a sense of justice settled, but it changed nothing. "I'm glad you realize I wasn't trying to sneak a relationship with you in amidst my multiple affairs," he said dryly. "But I guess it doesn't matter anymore."

"I guess not." Her voice held a touch of regret, but he refused to go there. "You're dating now, though?"

He stiffened. Then regarded her with a frown. "Why do you ask?"

She shrugged. "I saw you at Iron Pier with Devon. I was going to pick up food."

Suddenly, the air sparked with a simmering energy. She was fishing, and it'd be best to close up the topic and head back to his room. Keep things safe. He was moving on and couldn't deal with this constant push/pull of his emotions any longer.

He kept to the truth. "It's been a long time since I wanted to date, Bella. Now that you made your choice, I decided to open myself back up. So, yeah, I had a date with Devon. Maybe we'll go out again."

She nodded. Her fingers twisted in her lap, making her look heartbreakingly fragile. "That's good. You guys dated before, right?"

"We did, when I first got into town. But I'm sure you don't want to discuss my personal life. We agreed it'd be best to keep things professional."

She flinched, and he regretted his sharp tone. God, the want for her was still there, tearing at his insides, and he couldn't pretend to be cool enough to talk about his possible future lovers with her. Not at this point. Probably not ever.

"You're right," she said softly. "It's just that I've been thinking a lot since then, and realized I may have . . . well, I may have . . ." She trailed off, staring down at her trembling fingers.

His muscles tightened, as if he were a predator who'd just scented danger. Or prey. "May have what?"

She kept her gaze on her lap. "May have made a mistake."

Her words hit like a sucker punch. His lungs lost air, and it took a moment to realize she was on the verge of telling him something big. Something that could change everything.

His head told him to get out of the room before it was too late. He'd made a promise not to chase her any longer, to move on and find a life for himself.

His heart screamed for him to stay.

Following his instinct, he got up and knelt at the side of her chair. The air between them thickened and pulsed with unspoken want. He studied her profile—the graceful curve of her neck, the natural pout to her lips, the patrician nose as proud as she was. Her hands were now clasped together, the long, tapered fingers with peach-tipped nails seemingly delicate, but he knew the strength hidden beneath. At first sight, Bella Sunshine-Caldwell was a willowy, blonde Goldilocks figure, a woman who reflected a quiet, peaceful aura—a serenely smiling single mother and professional businesswoman who never went off course.

But it was the woman who had sobbed in his arms and told of her broken heart that was the most real. The woman who had fiercely protected him from a stranger's advances and refused to back down. The woman who shyly stared down at her hands, afraid to look at him and admit the truth they'd both been fighting.

"Bella, you need to look at me."

Slowly, her chin tipped up. He captured her gaze, holding it while he delved deep and saw the raw hunger in her blue-ocean depths, the naked want carved out in her features. He sucked in a breath, stunned at the intensity of emotion he found there.

His voice deepened. "I need to know: Why do you think you made a mistake?"

This time, she didn't hesitate. "Because I convinced myself you couldn't be the man I wanted. It was easier to push you away, believe the gossip, keep things the same between us. I got scared."

He could accept that. But he wasn't about to blow things up and risk his heart until she took her own risk. "And now? How do you feel now?"

A shudder shook through her. "I miss you. The way things were between us. When I saw you with Devon, I—" She broke off, shaking her head. "I hated it. Hated her touching you and thinking of you both together."

Sweet victory buzzed in his veins. Her words sang in his head, making him want to roar in pleasure. He ached to yank her in his arms and claim her mouth with his. But he needed all of it.

He needed to know she was all in.

"Tell me what you want."

She jerked back. Her tongue slipped out to wet her bottom lip. Her voice was barely a whisper. "You. I want you."

She stared at him, pupils dilated, ragged breaths panting from her lips, and he knew this moment would be carved out in his mind—the first time he saw her face reflect her open want for him.

He muttered a curse, then leaned forward, both hands cupping her cheeks, his lips stopping an inch from hers. He waited, his gaze diving deep.

This time she reached for him, her words a sweet breath rushing over him. "Kiss me, Gabe."

His mouth covered hers.

♥ ♥ ♥

The searing heat of his lips reached every inch of her body and started a fire between her thighs. She surrendered to the kiss inch by inch, like a flower slowly opening to the heat of the sun, her insides trembling. His body remained on the other side of the chair; the only touch was his hands on her cheeks and his lips on hers, making the contact even more swoon-worthy, as if they'd just nudged open the door of a sizzling attraction that was ready to erupt.

He tasted of sweetness and sin. The spicy scent of his cologne teased her nostrils, and she leaned forward, wanting more. He broke away, his thumb stroking her cheek, his dark eyes searing into hers. Slowly, he pressed his lips to hers, softly, firmly, pulling back and doing it again and again, until she whispered his name and reached for him, sliding her arms around his shoulders and offering more.

He took it.

His tongue surged in and stroked hers, playing a wicked, teasing game that thrilled her. Her nails bit into his shoulders, and a moan ripped from her throat. He moved, standing up and lifting her to her feet. She arched up, and his hands cupped her buttocks, easing her close. Their mouths fused hungrily, and she became mad to drown in the taste and smell of him, the feel of his hard-muscled body against hers, nipping at her raw nerve endings. In between ragged breaths, she ripped off his jacket, pulling off his tie and tearing open his shirt with clumsy, frantic fingers. The slow dance of their mouths became primitive, as if the beast had been released, and all she could do was hang on to him and follow the path to slake the wet ache in her core.

"Wait. Are you sure?" he asked, his teeth sinking into the curve of her neck, causing her to cry out in pleasure. "We can talk."

"Don't want to talk." Her tongue licked at his olive skin, savoring the taste of salt and man, her hands smoothing over his toned abs. "Want you. Now."

He muttered a dirty curse. She thrilled at the madness of lust carved out on his face, the trembling of his hands as he tried to control himself. But she didn't want the careful, gentle lover tonight—she wanted Gabe in all his primal glory, desperate to have her.

She reached down and squeezed his erection, reveling in the sheer power of his desperate groan. God, she'd craved this—the dirty, raw coupling with a man she hungered for, the stripping away of barriers to reveal naked flesh in all its vulnerability and beauty, a lovemaking that was on the edge of fucking and had no place in the nice, neutral world she usually lived in.

She wanted to feel beautiful. Alive.

She wanted to feel everything.

He gripped her hair and tugged back. His teeth ground together while his gaze raked over her. Slowly, he unbuttoned her blouse, tugged down her bra, and stared greedily at her naked breasts, her nipples hard and begging for his mouth. "You want rough?"

She gave him the truth. "I want real."

His gaze softened. His grip gentled, and he gave her a kiss that brought tears to her eyes, humbling himself before her as if he were a servant to her queen, his own personal treasure. "It already is, sweetheart."

Then he lowered his knees and lifted her up, carrying her into the bedroom and dropping her on the bed. They undressed quickly, throwing their clothes off until they were both naked. Gabe grabbed a condom from his pants and put it on the table, then climbed on the mattress. He spread her thighs and covered her, taking one tight nipple into his mouth, sucking and licking, nibbling with his teeth until she was so sensitive, she almost begged him to stop. He treated the other breast to the same attention, while her hands roved hungrily every-where: the tight buttocks, his powerful thighs, his hair-roughened chest, the broad slope of his shoulders.

He worked his way down, teasing her, lifting her knees high and widening her thighs so she was open to him. Panting with need, her skin tight and hot, she cried out at the first slow swipe of his tongue on her center. He murmured sweet words, parting her folds, licking her until she squirmed helplessly under each hot lash, her orgasm shimmer-ing just out of reach.

His lips closed around her clit, and he sucked, increasing the pres-sure as his index finger slid inside her channel, setting up a lazy rhythm meant to drive her to the brink of insanity. "So pretty," he whispered. "So beautiful. Let go, sweetheart. Let me watch you."

He sucked harder and slammed into a magical spot that shot her body upward. She came hard, screaming his name, and the hot stream-ers of pleasure shredding her kept going, her hips helplessly writhing beneath him.

When she managed to open her eyes again, he'd donned the con-dom. He knelt before her, hands on her calves, his eyes fierce with a masculine possessiveness that thrilled her, as if he were about to claim what was his. And then the past reared up, tangling with a raw need inside for a man she'd never expected, and she made a low noise in the back of her throat, clutching his shoulders.

He stopped, poised at her entrance. His jaw tightened, but his gaze was calm. "What is it?"

"I just—" She shook her head, searching for the words. "There hasn't been anybody else. Since Matt."

His touch gentled. "Do you want to stop?"

"No." Even now, she ached for Gabe to fill the throbbing emptiness, but it was also another door shut behind her, knowing she'd be giving herself to another. Tears stung. "I feel too much," she finally whispered, shutting her eyes.

"Look at me, Bella." She forced herself to meet his gaze again, and in those dark eyes he gave her what she needed. "I do, too. I've been waiting for you. Only you." He kissed her, slow and deep, taking her back under until her body screamed for his. "I'll go slow."

He eased in inch by inch, filling up all the empty spaces, until he was buried deep. She gasped at the shock of it, the totality of a man inside her again, and he pressed his forehead to hers as if he sensed her sudden hesitation, letting her get used to him. Her muscles gradually relaxed, and he slid in even deeper, wringing a groan from his lips.

"You feel so damn good," he whispered, his tongue slipping between his lips to tangle with hers. "I don't know if I can last."

She smiled, nipping at his plump bottom lip. "Don't know if I can, either."

"Good. I'll make it up to you later."

He swallowed her laugh with his lips, slid out, and then plunged inside her with one full thrust.

"Oh God."

He gritted his teeth. Sweat beaded his brow. The need uncurled inside, hot and hungry, and she wriggled to get closer.

"Give me a minute, baby. Trying to slow down."

"Don't." She arched her hips, forcing him deeper, and he muttered a curse. "No more slow." She wanted him wild, wanted him to take her over the edge so she could lose herself in pleasure.

He gave a half laugh. "Sure?"

"Now, Gabe."

He grabbed her arms, stretching them over her head and guiding her hands to the headboard. "Then hang on."

The thrill zinged through her, and dampness leaked down her thigh. She arched up with each rough thrust inside, meeting him equally, squeezing the polished wood between her fists as she struggled to keep the orgasm at bay. His rough thighs scraped her smooth ones. His hard chest teased her sensitive nipples. His hips snapped, his dick sliding across her clit with the perfect friction, bringing her closer, closer, until—

The orgasm shattered her inside and out, flinging her to a place where nothing mattered but pleasure. She heard a dim shout, and his body stiffened, but she was lost in her own sensual haze, every inch throbbing with sweet release.

He grabbed her hips and rolled so he wasn't crushing her with his weight. His skin was damp. The sheets smelled like spice and sex. Her muscles felt sore and used, and she savored the delicious feeling.

He kissed her cheek and pushed her tangled hair back, staring into her face. "You okay?"

She practically beamed with satisfaction and a slow, unfurling joy. "Yeah. You?"

He laughed, tucking her in close. "Yes. But I need to sleep. I'm not even close to being done with you."

A shiver trickled down her spine. She snuggled tight, loving the feel of his arms enclosing her in shelter. "Me, either."

She closed her eyes, enjoying the rumble of his chuckle against her ear, then fell asleep.

Chapter Sixteen

When he woke up, he was afraid it'd been a dream.

Gabe turned and immediately relaxed. Bella lay beside him, hand tucked under her cheek, an adorable frown on her face as if she were dreaming about something that pissed her off. Her hair was a tangled, glorious mess tumbling around her shoulders. A tiny snort escaped her lips.

Hmm, the precursor of a big-time snorer.

He traced the line of her puffy mouth, trying to memorize the beautiful lines of her face, the paleness of her skin, the way her chest rose and fell with each relaxed breath. She was everything he'd ever wanted, and she was finally his.

He hoped.

Doubt crept in. They'd woken up three times last night to reach for each other, their hunger not even close to being quenched. Morning light streamed through the blinds. He wondered if she'd wake with regrets. Wondered if the impulse of last night would cause her to pull back again, and this time, he'd have to live with knowing how good it was when she'd been his. Even for a little while.

He had no regrets. Last night, his fantasies had become reality, and he'd never forget. He just needed to convince her to take a chance on a future with him.

Slowly, her eyes flickered open.

He smiled. "Good morning."

Her answering smile was sweet and a bit sleepy. "Morning. What time is it?"

Relief hit. She wasn't about to jump out of bed with a long litany of excuses and explanations of why they shouldn't have slept together. "Only seven. Want me to go down and get you coffee?"

"Yes, please." She stretched out her hands, locked them around his neck, and brought him in for a kiss. She was warm and soft and cuddly.

His heart turned to mush in his chest. In moments, the kiss turned deep and hungry, and he tugged off the sheet to caress her bare curves, murmuring in satisfaction as he found her wet. "Before or after?"

"Huh?" She blinked, arching into his hand, her gaze beautifully blurred.

"Do you want the coffee before or after I make you come again?"

Her cheeks flushed. He loved the way she had little modesty in bed but was shy when she had to walk to the bathroom naked. She'd made him promise not to look.

He'd lied.

She nipped at his lip like a playful kitten and clung close. "After."

"Good choice."

He sheathed himself and slid home. This time, he brought her to the brink slow and easy, enjoying her broken cries and the sexy scratches she left on his back. He steeped himself in her taste and scent, and watched her fall apart with fierce satisfaction.

His own orgasm hit hard, slamming his body into an earth-shattering pleasure he'd never experienced before. Everything was different with Bella. The satisfaction reached beyond the physical, touching the empty place in his chest that seemed to never get filled. When he finally kissed her and got up from the bed to wash up, he felt like beating his chest like an ape, he was so damn satisfied.

He dressed back in his pants and rumpled shirt, rolling up the sleeves. "Gonna change quick in my room, where I left my clothes. I'll bring coffee and breakfast."

"Thanks. I'll check on Zoe. We leaving in about an hour?"

He shot her a grin. "Or two."

He shut the door on her laugh, reveling in the sound.

♥ ♥ ♥

She hung up the phone after hearing Zoe's voice and wondered what she was going to do.

Last night had changed everything. She was not one to ever do things on impulse. Her past loss and being responsible for her daughter taught her to step away from things that didn't make long-term sense. It had worked well for her since Matt passed.

But now, Gabe had stolen a piece of her heart. And she needed a plan.

Sex for her was more than a physical outlet—it always had been. Taylor had tried to get her to loosen her narrowed limits, but sex meant emotional connection. Even a kiss felt wrong unless there was a certain chemistry. That's why there had only been Matt, her first true love.

But now there was Gabe, too.

The erotic images of their night together flickered past her mind. She hugged them tight, and decided to take a quick shower before he returned. God, she'd kissed him and hadn't even brushed her teeth! But ever since she'd seen him with Devon, she'd been haunted by the knowledge she'd made a terrible mistake. She'd wanted more time with him after the reception, hoping to talk and be honest about how she'd been feeling lately. Maybe even trying to open up the door one more time.

Until she'd looked into his eyes and realized her heart was already invested. She sensed if she didn't take a risk, she'd lose him, and the possibility of what they could be together was too much to leave behind.

She scrubbed her skin reluctantly, not even wanting to lose his scent, then dressed quickly in jeans and a long-sleeve pink sweater. Putting her long hair in a casual ponytail, she sat down on the sofa to wait.

They had to talk. Discuss what they wanted from each other and how to proceed. She crossed her legs, uncomfortable in the cold light of morning, but she also didn't want to lose that thrill of finally connecting with the man who made her happy. Yes, there were obstacles, but she couldn't imagine returning home and going back to the way things were between them.

He opened the door with two extralarge cups and two platters filled with a variety of food. "It was a buffet, so I got a bit of everything," he said, putting it down on the table. His gaze raked over her with regret. "You got out of bed."

"I figured I needed a shower."

"But you're wearing clothes."

She laughed, feeling slightly giddy. "It's easier for me to eat and talk when I'm not naked."

"Funny, it's the opposite for me."

She tossed him a humorous look and sipped the hot brew. She speared a piece of fresh pineapple, dipped it in some yogurt, and ate with pleasure. They made short work of the breakfast since both of them were starving. Finally full, she crossed her legs comfortably and sat, sipping her coffee.

"How's Zoe?" he asked.

"Good. She loves sleeping at Avery and Carter's—they spoil her rotten."

"As does Taylor. And Pierce. And me. And Daisy. And—"

"Yeah, I get it. Hard not to, since she's rarely a brat. I'm lucky to have such a sweet kid."

"Definitely, but I also think being raised with extended family is special. She's always surrounded by people she loves, so there's no lack of attention. I love that you and Taylor share a home."

She sighed. "Yeah, I'm going to miss her. It will be like another hole in the family when she leaves, but not all of us were meant to stay."

"She'll always come back, and you'll get a cool place to travel to on vacation." His grin was full of sexiness and sunshine. He reached over and snagged her hand, entwining his fingers with hers. The familiar touch of his hand made goose bumps prickle. "Even though I'd love to take you back to bed, I think we should talk."

Her heart sped up, but she nodded. "Okay."

They looked at each other for a few seconds in silence. He rubbed his head, half laughing. "I guess I'll go first. Last night meant a lot to me. I want to be clear how much *you* mean to me. I don't want this to be a one-night stand."

As she looked into his handsome face, she saw the wariness lurking, the fear gleaming in the depths of his dark eyes. It hit her full force that he believed she was going to wave off their night as a fluke, a pleasurable experience that they needed to move on from. Her chest tightened at the idea of hurting him like that, using him to slake an itch, like so many women had labeled him before.

She got up from her chair, this time kneeling in front of him, her gaze locked on his. "I don't want a one-night stand, either," she said softly. "I wouldn't have taken you into my bed for a fling. Last night was special. I just think we need to figure things out when we get home about how we want to approach this. I'm hoping you understand when I tell you I need to go slow."

He cupped her cheeks and pressed his forehead to hers. "I can do slow," he said.

She covered his hands with hers. "I want plenty of time for Zoe to get used to me seeing someone. And to work out how we handle our business and personal lives. And the best way to tell my family. And—"

"I get it, sweetheart. There's no rush. I've waited this long to finally ravish that sweet body of yours," he said with a wicked grin. "I'm not going anywhere. We'll see what feels best for you. I won't push."

She let out her breath in relief. "Then we're in perfect agreement."

He kissed her, his tongue thrusting lazily, and soon he was scooping her up into his arms. "Let me show you how good I can do slow."

And he did.

Chapter Seventeen

"I need a night out," Daisy whined over speakerphone. "I'm going stark raving mad playing with Meg's Barbie dream house and watching movies every night. Please, Bella. Let's go out and drink and pretend we're fabulous single women."

Bella laughed. "You always lose it mid-March," she said, chopping up carrots and celery and putting them in separate baggies. If she didn't give Zoe healthy snack options, she went straight to the bad stuff. "I feel bad, though. I've run the gamut of babysitters because of the wedding, and I promised myself I'd be home with Zoe on weekends."

"One teeny, tiny Friday night? For your best friend? I'll personally call Avery and Taylor and beg them on my behalf."

"You are desperate."

"After St. Patty's Day passes, I get depressed. It seems like spring will never come."

She understood. March seemed like the last punch before they got some sunny days that gave them hope. Tourists began trickling in for spring break, and the wedding season exploded. Soon, she'd be working nonstop. She usually neglected Daisy during that time, so it might be a good idea to indulge in a girls' night out. "Can you get a sitter for Meg?"

"I'll pay the first stranger I see on the street corner, at this rate."

Bella laughed. "Liar. I'll make a few calls and see if we can go tomorrow."

"Thank you! I'm going to dress up! And we'll get an Uber so we can get drunk!"

She shook her head and dumped some hummus in a small bowl. "Whatever you want."

She clicked off with Daisy whooping, and quickly checked her planner. It'd only been two short weeks since Adele's wedding, and she'd tried to spend as much time with Zoe as possible. She explained to Gabe she wanted to ease into telling people they were together, but so far, she hadn't found the right time to tell her sisters. Every time she had their ear, she chickened out.

She rationalized that once their relationship was outed, things might change. Right now, it was like this supersexy secret. He'd come over and occasionally watch a movie with her and Zoe. Other times, he'd show up after her daughter went to bed, and they'd spend hours making love and falling into one another. Each time got better. It was as if pieces of her were breaking open after each encounter. He'd leave before dawn, pressing a lingering kiss to her mouth, and she'd snuggle in the sheets that smelled like him, giddy with joy.

During the weekly meetings, he stared at her across the conference-room table, the fire in those dark eyes properly banked in front of her sisters, but she recognized the look of desire. He'd sip his espresso and calmly share his schedule, and she'd imagine his lips coasting over her naked breasts, the dirty words whispered in her ear, the way he slid deep inside her body and claimed her.

So far, no one seemed to notice how their relationship had changed since the wedding. Of course, Avery was steeped in planning her own wedding for October, and Taylor was furiously working on her art. But her sisters never commented on the new lightness in her step or the easier way she laughed. She took it as a sign that it wasn't time yet to come out to the world as a couple.

Grabbing a pen, she scribbled in her date with Daisy, then checked the business schedule. Taylor and Avery had weddings that night, so they were out. Gabe had an afternoon function—probably best not to bother him. Pierce was working. She texted a few backup babysitters she trusted, but they all seemed to have something better to do than babysit on a weekend. Finally, she called Carter.

"What's up?" he asked.

"Listen, if I ask you this, you have to be honest with me if you don't want to, okay?"

"As Avery tells me, I'm a bit brutal with my honesty, so I don't think that will be a problem."

She dragged in a breath. "My friend Daisy is desperate to go out for a night—she gets a bit squirrely at the end of winter."

"Don't we all. Even Lucy is getting bitchy over this weather."

"She wants to go tomorrow for a girls' night, but everyone's busy. I'd need someone to watch Zoe. And I know you just took her recently, so I understand if you want a night to yourself."

"Bella, it's fine. I enjoy Zoe's company, and Avery is working a wedding all night. We'll order pizza in. Not a problem."

"Thanks, Carter, I can't tell you how much I appreciate it. I'll drop her off at seven p.m.?"

"Sounds good."

Relieved, she tidied up the kitchen and went to check on Zoe, who was coloring a giant poster board of Elsa from *Frozen*. "Mama, look, I'm almost finished!"

She appraised the artwork, legitimately impressed. "Honey, that's really good. You may have Aunt Taylor's gift for art."

"That's what she says. I'm definitely going to be an artist when I grow up."

She smiled. "No wedding planner? You don't want to work in the family business?"

Zoe scrunched her nose and considered. "I do like weddings, so maybe that will be my backup."

"I'm impressed by your logic. Everyone needs a plan B. But I'll be happy with whatever you become, as long as you're happy."

"Thanks."

"Welcome. How about carrots with hummus for a snack?"

"Any brownies left?"

"No."

"Cookies?"

"No."

A long-suffering sigh emitted from her small mouth as Zoe furiously colored in Elsa's gown. "I guess I'll take the carrots."

"Wise choice."

Bella set her daughter up with snacks, then pulled her laptop out to work. A text came in from Daisy, informing her with tons of sad emojis that she couldn't find a sitter and had to cancel. *Damn.* She knew how badly her friend needed an escape. Maybe she'd go over there with Zoe, and they'd come up with something fun to do. Maybe a spa night. She'd bring her polish and foot bath, and they'd get Chinese food.

Bella texted Carter to let him know it was off, and immediately her phone rang.

"What happened?" he asked. "I thought it was important."

"Daisy couldn't get a sitter for Meg, so she had to cancel."

"I can take her."

Surprise hit. "Wait, you're offering to take two little girls on a Friday night? Are you high?"

He laughed. "Honestly, I don't mind, Bella. They're good kids, and they'll keep each other occupied. Tell Daisy I'm happy to watch Meg."

"Have I told you you're my favorite almost brother-in-law?"

He gave a short laugh. "And your only one, but I'll take the compliment. See you tomorrow."

She quickly let Daisy know and was assaulted with heart emojis with champagne bottles.

Bella smiled. *Good.* She wanted her friend to be happy, and a girls' night out would be fun for both of them.

♥ ♥ ♥

Gabe got home late from the bridal luncheon, craving a cold beer, a shower, and a couch. The old-fashioned tea party was supposed to have been low key and an easy one to manage. Instead, it'd been like Disney princesses gone wild, with drama, family chaos, and hysterical tears from the bride, who insisted the MOG had been picking on her. He'd had to go into Code Red mode, and by the time it ended and everyone was happy again, he was ready to collapse.

He glanced at his phone, but Bella still hadn't texted. She didn't have any weddings tonight, so he'd hoped they could go on a date, or he could take her and Zoe out to dinner, but she'd never responded. As he showered and changed into casual clothes, he couldn't help the uneasy twist in his gut at her behavior since Adele's wedding.

She seemed in no hurry to announce they were involved in a relationship. Not even to her sisters. He'd figured she'd be proud and happy to tell everyone, but instead he was still a secret. Sure, he'd been over to the house to hang with her and Zoe, and been invited to her bed at night with open arms. He'd spent every precious hour wringing out her pleasure, his name spilling from her lips a symphony to his ears. But he left before morning because she didn't want Zoe to see him.

He understood. It was a big change for Bella's life, and he had sworn to be patient. He would not be the man who whined and asked why she was holding back—not after all the time he'd spent dreaming they'd be together. He just needed to take it down a notch and trust her. Go with the flow and ignore the tiny voice telling him she had no intention of making their relationship public. It was just his old insecurities cropping up, messing with his head. They'd talked everything through and wanted the same things.

When he got out of the shower, he saw he'd missed Carter's call, so he dialed him back.

"Hey, come over and have a beer. I'm bored."

He laughed. "Where's your woman?"

"A wedding, of course. I have buffalo wings, chicken fingers, and pizza here I'm ready to share."

"You had me at wings. Be over in five."

Figuring he'd hear from Bella later, he headed over to Carter's house, looking forward to some good eats, TV, and male bonding.

When Carter opened the door, he wore a pink pointed hat with streamers down the back. "Come on in."

Gabe stood still, staring. "Umm, dude. Is this what you do when Avery goes away? I mean, it's cool, I just didn't know."

His friend shot him a disgusted look. "As if. We're babysitting. Get inside, it's cold."

He stepped over the threshold and barely held back a girlie scream.

Carter's place had exploded. There were crayons, papers, and coloring books thrown on the floor. A pile of fancy princess gowns, shoes, and purses lay by the sectional. Zoe and Meg were perched at the dining room table with endless teacups, saucers, plates, and a big teapot that looked like the Mad Hatter. They wore matching pink princess hats.

"Gabe's here!" Zoe shrieked, running over and hugging his legs. "Now our tea party can be complete!"

Meg merrily waved to him. "Hi, Gabe! Would you like strumpets or scones?"

Carter coughed. "I think it's called *crumpets*, honey."

"Oh, right!"

Gabe hugged Zoe, waved to Meg, and sidelined Carter. "You suck. You said we were hanging tonight, not babysitting."

"We'll do both. Bella's out with Daisy—they needed a wild women's night. Blow off some steam. Figured I'd do them both a favor."

Gabe jerked back. Bella was out with Daisy? Not that he cared she went out—he wasn't like that—but she hadn't even bothered to text him. The doubtful voice inside grew a bit louder. More and more, he was beginning to feel like an extra bonus in her life—not *part* of her life.

He pushed the disturbing thoughts away and nodded. "Ah, well, that was nice of you, but I didn't volunteer."

"Nobody likes a whiner, man."

"It's time for our tea party!" Zoe yelled, pulling him over to the table. "Meg, can you get Gabe a hat?"

"Of course."

He was offered a shiny yellow hat with a veil. "Can I just hold it?"

"You have to put it on, silly," Zoe said. "Now let's sit and have our snacks. Uncle Carter, can we have the pink cupcakes yet?"

"Did you finish all your chicken fingers?"

"Yes," they both called out in unison.

Carter shrugged. "Then go for it. Let's pause our tea party for a few minutes, girls. Gabe wants to have some wings and a beer, and then we'll commence after you eat your dessert. Deal?"

"Deal."

They attacked the small white box, and Gabe shuddered, following him into the kitchen. "Where'd they get all that stuff? Did they bring it over?"

"They brought over the clothes and hats. I'd found the tea set and some games at the toy store, so we keep it in storage for when Zoe comes over. Came in handy."

Gabe shook his head and took the beer. "You got a lot of layers. Like an onion."

"Yeah, well, don't go getting emotional on me. What's been up with you? Haven't seen much of you since the Dr. Seuss wedding. Things good?"

He delayed his response by taking a slug of beer. He wanted to tell Carter the truth. He could use some solid advice, or at least another male opinion. But he didn't want Bella to feel uncomfortable, either. "Things are a bit . . . complicated."

Carter arched a brow. "Sit. Have a wing. Tell me everything."

He sat and grabbed one. The burn lit up his mouth, and he coughed. "So good."

"I know, I got extrahot. It's got to do with a woman, right? It always is. Are you finally seeing someone you're into?"

"Yeah, I am. The problem is I'm supposed to keep us a secret for a while until we get adjusted to the idea of being in a relationship."

He blinked. "Why? She married?"

"No!"

"A politician? Breaking up with a current boyfriend?"

"No."

"Then why the hell are you keeping it a secret?"

"I told you—she wants time to get used to it. If I say who it is, you can't tell Avery."

Carter groaned. "You kidding? I can't keep secrets from her—you know this."

"Just for a few days. We're probably going to make an announcement soon."

"Then we must know her. Avery doesn't gossip, so if you don't want her to know, it's because . . ." He stared at him. "Holy shit. It's Bella."

"Shhh! Zoe's here," he hissed.

"Sorry, you just took me by surprise." Carter leaned in and punched his shoulder, a big-ass grin on his face. "Damn, you finally took our advice and told her how you feel? I'm so happy for you. I've always thought you two would be perfect together."

Gabe relaxed, warmth infusing him at his friend's enthusiasm. "Thanks. We've grown closer while planning the wedding, and that night, well, let's just say we had a heart-to-heart talk. I heard you had my back, letting her know all those rumors about me weren't real. Appreciate it."

"Was only telling the truth. Gossip like that would trouble Bella. She's protective of her daughter."

"Exactly. I think we finally found common ground. I'm ecstatic, don't get me wrong, but I'm still worried this whole thing will end up like a big illusion."

Carter frowned. "What do you mean?"

He ate another wing and contemplated how to explain. "I guess I figured we'd be checking in with each other more, about our plans, spending time together, et cetera. I thought she'd be happy to tell her sisters about us. You don't think she's having doubts, do you?"

"No reason to. Bella's not the type to jump in without thought. You've been patient and honest with her, and you deserve to be happy. Both of you. Try not to worry about how it unfolds, and just enjoy."

"You're right. Thanks. I needed a kick in the ass."

Two adorable faces peeked into the kitchen. "Are we ready for tea yet?" Zoe asked, smiling prettily.

Gabe shook his head and shot a look at Carter. "Sure. And afterward, Uncle Carter said he wants to play dress-up, and I'll be the judge to see who looks the prettiest."

"Yay!" they yelled.

Carter shot him the middle finger, and they went to play tea party.

♥ ♥ ♥

"How about that guy over there?" Daisy pointed out. "He looks nice."

Bella laughed, taking another sip of her wine. "What does *nice* look like? They said Ted Bundy looked nice."

"Why do you have to be difficult? I mean, he's nicely dressed, not too young or old, and looks single. Plus, we don't know him, so maybe he's new in town. Let's send him a drink."

Her jaw dropped. "No! Come on, Daisy, that's desperate. And I thought we were looking for you, not me. You're the one who wants to get wild, remember?"

Her friend sighed and sucked on her straw. "Sorry, I was just trying to shake things up. There's no one good out. They're all young enough to be my son, and that's just icky. Should we try somewhere else?"

"We tried the Boiler Room and Carney's. At least Harry's makes your favorite cocktail, and they have good appetizers."

Daisy looked glum. "Sorry to be a bummer. I'm just frustrated. The dating apps are awful, and there's not a lot to do in the winter. I'll be better once the tourists and the sun come back. More possibilities. It's just that I feel trapped lately."

Bella squeezed her friend's hand in sympathy. "I get it, babe. It's hard when you're a single parent and doing it all on your own. But I promise it will get better, and tonight, you can get drunk and forget your problems."

Daisy grinned. "You're right. Cheers." She clinked her glass and leaned back in her seat. "So tell me about you. How are things with Gabe?"

Bella's fingers jerked around the glass, and wine sloshed over the rim. She dabbed at it with a napkin, wondering why she felt so awkward telling her best friend the truth. Maybe she just wasn't used to being involved with a man, so it was still new. "Well, funny you should ask. We're kind of . . . well, we're—"

"Oh my God, you bitch! You're sleeping with him!" Daisy laughed with delight. "About time you got some. How was he? As good as everyone talks about? Tell me every last detail, and don't leave a thing out."

Unease settled. She shifted in her seat. "No, you don't get it. We're not just sleeping together. We're dating. Formally. I mean, we're in a relationship."

Daisy stared at her in confusion. "Oh. You mean you slept with him but then decided to see where it goes?"

She hated the way Daisy asked the question, like she was surprised Gabe would be more than a one-night stand. "He's not the man you think. I know everyone talks about how he's with all these different women, but it's not like that. He hasn't really dated anyone seriously in a long time."

"I know, Bella. That's why he's a player. He's well known not to get involved in any relationships."

She let out a breath. "I'm trying to explain he's a good man, and he cares about me, and he has no interest in dating or sleeping with anyone else. Okay? We're happy together."

Her friend regarded her thoughtfully for a few moments, then nodded. "I get it. I'm sorry, I didn't mean to offend you. I adore Gabe. It's just that you haven't been out in a long time, and I want you to know you don't have to feel guilty about just having some fun. Sex doesn't have to mean commitment or ever after. No one will judge you if you slept with him and decide not to pursue a relationship."

Oh, this was bad. Frustration nipped at her nerves. What was it about Gabe that had every woman so desperate to pigeonhole him? "I hear what you're saying, but I'm telling you it's more than sex. There are real feelings between us. He's good for me, and for Zoe, and we're moving forward. I'd appreciate it if you didn't gossip about him, especially to the other moms."

Daisy gasped. "Of course not! I'm thrilled you're happy! Hell, if anyone can change a man, you can. I trust you know what you're doing—you are the least-impulsive person I know. We good?"

"Yeah, we're good." Bella smiled, ignoring her doubt that Daisy was as happy as she pretended.

The bartender dropped two fresh drinks on the table. "Ladies, those gentlemen are sending you these drinks." He motioned behind them. "Enjoy."

They shared a surprised glance and twisted their heads to look behind. Two men in jeans and casual button-down shirts sat at the bar.

One was blond, one was dark haired, and they both looked reasonably attractive. Bella raised her hand in a thank-you, but Daisy immediately waved them over. The guys gathered their drinks and got up.

"What are you doing?" she hissed.

"Oh, come on, let's have some fun! I can finally get my flirt on. Just be my wing woman."

Bella sighed. Guess she had no choice. She pasted on a smile as the two men reached them, a little disappointed she wouldn't just get to hang out with her friend. But this was for Daisy.

It was going to be a long night.

♥ ♥ ♥

Hours later, Bella got out of the Uber and escorted Daisy to Carter's door. Her friend was a bit tipsy, but it was nothing that would limit her ability to care for Meg that night. She rang the bell, and he answered.

"Have fun?" he asked. She narrowed her gaze and wondered if she'd knocked on the right door. The man she thought she knew was sporting bright-blue eye shadow and two perfect dots of rouge on each cheek. "What's the matter? You guys drunk?"

She shared a glance with Daisy, and they burst into giggles. "No, but are you? Why are you wearing makeup?"

"Ah, crap, I forgot." He rubbed at his face. "They seemed to have smuggled in a cosmetic kit and decided to practice their skills. I'm comfortable enough with my masculinity to allow them to apply makeup on me. Tell that to Avery, okay?"

Her heart melted. She stepped inside and placed a big kiss on his cheek. "I love you, Carter. I'm so lucky you're part of my family."

He jerked back in obvious surprise, then relaxed. "Welcome. Come in. The two terrors are asleep."

When they entered, the scene struck her full force.

Gabe was on the couch, his arm tucked around Zoe. A blanket covered her, and her pink princess hat tilted drunkenly on her head as she slept with her mouth half-open. They were surrounded by dolls and sparkly jewelry. As he lifted his hand to give her a jaunty wave, she noticed his nails were painted hot pink.

Her ovaries melted right then. Watching him cuddle her daughter, secure in a night of babysitting, made her realize how special the man was. Suddenly, her entire body lit up, and images of her future flashed before her.

Gabe holding Zoe on his shoulders as they walked in the park.

Making pancakes on a lazy Sunday morning.

Backing her up against the refrigerator as he kissed her with passion.

Gabe holding a newborn baby, staring down with pure love.

She jumped like an electrical shock hit her. *What the hell was that?*

Daisy walked over to Meg, who was curled up on the other side of the couch, snuggled with a matching pillow and blanket. "Guys, you are amazing. I can't thank you enough. She wasn't any trouble?"

Gabe smiled. "They were angels. We got them a bit sugared up with cupcakes, though, so I think that's why they crashed."

Bella stared at the gorgeous, sexy man sprawled on the couch, his sock-clad feet propped on the table. Her heart expanded in her chest, and a shiver coursed through her. She wanted to say so many things to him, but her words and emotions lodged tight in her throat. "Your nails are pink."

He winced and lifted them up. "Yeah, they wanted to practice makeup, so Carter and I played rock, paper, scissors to see who got nails and who got the face."

"You cheated," Carter said.

Daisy laughed. "Well, let me get her home so you can salvage the rest of your evening."

Bella spoke up. "Carter, can I borrow your car to take Daisy home? I can pick it up tomorrow—we took an Uber here. I'm good to drive."

"I'll take you," Gabe said. "I'm leaving anyway, and the two boosters will fit in my car."

"Are you sure?"

"Of course." He extricated himself from Zoe's arms, put on his shoes and jacket, and lifted her up in his arms, still wrapped in the blanket. "Daisy, you got Meg?"

"Yep, all set."

They said goodbye to Carter, set up the car seats, and headed to Daisy's house. The girls roused briefly, then fell right back to sleep.

"How was your night?" Gabe asked.

"We had fun," she said. "Hit a few bars, but not much was going on."

"Except at Harry's!" Daisy announced. "We met two hot guys!"

Uh-oh. She watched Gabe stiffen, but his voice was calm. "Good for you. Locals or out-of-towners?"

Daisy jumped to answer. "They're on a business trip from New York and decided to stay a few nights here. I really liked them. I got the blond, and Bella took the dark-haired one. She always had a weakness for brunets."

"Hmm, interesting. I had no idea."

Bella rubbed her temples and tried to salvage the awkward exchange. "I was just Daisy's wing woman," she said firmly. "But the guy asked her out, and they exchanged numbers."

"You got a number, too, Bella," she said teasingly. "He liked you. And he's a high school teacher. Divorced. Midforties. Perfect for her."

"Daisy," she hissed, "I told you I wasn't interested."

"No, you didn't, you said—" She trailed off, slapping her hand over her mouth. "Oh my God! I'm sorry, Gabe, I forgot. Bella said you two were seeing each other. I'm so stupid. And kind of drunk. Don't pay me any attention; she wanted nothing to do with that guy."

Bella wanted to drop her head in her hands. Now it sounded like Daisy felt guilty and was trying to cover for her. He'd sat with Carter, babysitting her daughter, and found out she'd been clubbing with strange men. She owed him an explanation.

"Totally okay," he said casually. "I'm surprised she told you in the first place. I think Bella enjoys keeping a juicy secret."

Silence fell, but thankfully, they reached Daisy's house. "Thanks for the ride. I'm sorry for my big mouth."

"It's okay," Bella said. "Need help?"

"Nope, we're good. Call you tomorrow."

She got out, and Gabe waited until she was safely inside. Then pulled away.

She waited for the inquisition, but he kept silent.

Which was worse. Much worse.

"How did you end up getting stuck babysitting?" she finally asked, trying to feel him out.

"I got home late, and Carter called to ask me to come over. Bribed me with wings and beer. Didn't tell me we were also having a tea party."

She winced. "I'm so sorry. You didn't deserve that."

"I had fun." He turned and gave her an intense stare. "I teased Carter about roping me into a nightmare, but I happen to love Zoe, and spending time with her was a pleasure. Even if my nails are now pink."

"Gabe?"

"Yeah?"

"Can I explain about tonight?"

"Sweetheart, I know you didn't pick up a guy at a bar. I'm sure Daisy wanted to cut loose, and you were just there to support her. I've been a wingman many a time. We do what we must."

Relief coursed through her. Each time she was with him, he captured more and more of her heart. He was a man she could really lean on, who was confident in them both not to play silly games. "I'm glad you understand. I told Daisy we were together, but I think I caught her by surprise."

"I'm sure you did." He paused, tapping his finger against the steering wheel. "How did she react?"

The thought of Daisy's disbelief and laughter bothered her, but there was no way she was sharing that with Gabe. "Fine."

He shot her a look and shook his head. "Why do I get the impression you're not telling me the whole story?"

She scrambled to cover. "It's been a long time since I've been with a man. Daisy's not used to it, so she was just a little wary, that's all."

"Well, as your friend, she should be. I'm okay with that, Bella. It's just . . ." He trailed off.

"What?"

"I just want to be sure you're still excited about us. That you actually *want* to tell your friends and family." He paused, and the brief silence around them felt like the deep hush before a storm. "That you just don't want this to be about sex."

Shock ripped through her, but she had no time to answer.

Zoe stirred in the back seat and gave a tiny whine. "Mama?"

She twisted around to see her blinking sleepily, looking around in the car. "Yes, baby, we're home. Let's get you inside and to bed."

They went inside, and she got her daughter settled. When she came back down, Gabe was waiting in the living room. "She okay?"

"Went straight to sleep."

"Good."

He slowly walked over to her, stopping an inch away. He wore jeans and a green fleece shirt that made his shoulders seem even broader. Hips cocked, feet braced apart, his gaze raked over her body with a hunger that lashed out at her and made every nerve in her body stretch and tighten. The spicy masculine smell of him wrapped around her in pure seduction. Her nipples tightened, and she grew wet between her thighs. In that moment, she realized he held a sensual power over her that made her crave him—his touch, taste, scent. It was as if her body was starved for contact.

"How do you feel about me staying tonight?"

She trembled and took a step forward so they were pressed chest to chest, in full body contact. "I'd like that."

His gaze darkened. His thumb traced the line of her lips, stretching out the delicious anticipation, until she was crazed to feel his mouth over hers. "Do you know I want you all the time? I've never been addicted to a drug before, but now I know how it feels. I go to sleep with your taste lingering on my tongue." His lips drifted over her cheek.

She grasped his shoulders and hung on.

"I remember the sting of your nails in my back when you come. The way your eyes go wide and heavy when you're aroused, like right now." His erection notched between her thighs, and he slid his hands down to cup her buttocks, lifting up and grinding against her.

Her head spun.

"But most of all, it's your laugh—that husky, sexy sound you make when I amuse you. I could spend the rest of my life trying to make you smile and laugh, sweetheart. But I'll take whatever you give me—that's how badly I crave you. If it's only sex, I'll make damn sure I keep you begging for more, until I convince you we can be so much more." His lips nipped at her jaw, and then his mouth was on hers.

He kissed her hard and deep, his tongue thrusting inside and taking full control. She clung to him and gave it all back, desperate to be skin to skin. He lifted her high, and she wrapped her legs tightly around him. He took her straight to the bedroom, closed and locked the door, then undressed her slowly.

"You can't make a sound," he whispered in her ear, his hands all over her body, tugging at her nipples, stroking her belly, thrusting inside her channel until she writhed and moaned and begged.

Greedy for all of him, she hooked her ankle around his and flipped him, sprawling over his naked body with pure satisfaction. "That's right," she said in a low, teasing voice. "Be very quiet."

She slid down and took him in her mouth. She sucked him deep, then ran the edge of her teeth down his pulsing length until his hands fisted in her hair and he cursed, shaking beneath her with a helplessness and need that made her feel like a queen. Finally, she rolled on the condom and lowered herself over him, inch by slow inch, until he was buried deep, and her entire body throbbed and shuddered.

His hands cupped her breasts. His gaze devoured her, lit with lust and a deeper emotion that filled her heart. "Ride me," he murmured, tweaking her nipples. "Take all you want."

She did. And when the orgasm hit, he covered her mouth with his in a fierce kiss, swallowing every throaty cry. His hips jerked, and then he followed her over the edge, never breaking the contact. When they finally fell back in a tangle of sheets and naked limbs, she knew the connection between them was so much more than physical.

"You're wrong," she whispered to him in the dark, her hand on his damp chest, thigh tucked under his.

"About what?"

She pressed her face to his shoulder and told the truth. "It'll never be just about sex. And I'm telling Zoe and my sisters tomorrow. Because you're important."

He smoothed back her hair and dropped a kiss on her head. "Thank you, Bella. Maybe one day I'll be able to tell you how I really feel about you."

She stiffened, her heart thundering against her rib cage, waiting for him to finish. But he was asleep, and she knew she wasn't ready to hear it.

Not yet.

Chapter Eighteen

"Gabe and I are dating."

Taylor coughed on her bagel and began choking. Bella calmly got up from her chair, stood behind her, and gave her one hard thump on the back.

The bagel piece dislodged, and her sister sucked in a breath.

Avery jumped up and stabbed her finger in the air with triumph. "I knew it!" she screeched. "Oh my God, this is fantastic! I saw the way you guys were together, and something was just off. I'm so glad I insisted you both work on Adele's wedding—I was a true matchmaker!"

Taylor swiveled her head around and glared. She shoved the plate away from her in disgust. "Does that make me the stupid sister? You're telling me this has been going on behind my back for how long—and I didn't know?"

Bella smiled at her sisters, a bit relieved by Avery's enthusiasm and Taylor's normal temper. It meant they were happy about her big announcement. "Sorry, but it took me by surprise. Until we began working on Adele's wedding, I only thought I had a crush."

Avery laughed. "Knew it. Then again, it's hard not to have a crush on Gabe. He's kind of perfect."

Taylor blew out an annoyed breath. "Okay, just stop congratulating yourself over there. If Gabe was so perfect, why didn't you fall for him all that time you both worked together?"

"Because we had no chemistry. And looking back on things now, I realize he's been crushing on Bella for a while. How come you didn't go for him?" she asked Taylor curiously.

Taylor rolled her eyes. "I adore Gabe, but he's much too sweet. When he started working here, I got the brother vibe—not the hot-lover one."

"Well, now that you both declared the reasons you didn't sleep with Gabe, we can move on with other stuff," Bella said.

"Hell no," Taylor said, getting up to refill her flute glass. "We are so going to analyze every part of this hot lust journey. How often do we get to have breakfast together without terming it a business meeting? Let's take advantage."

Bella had called her sisters to a special morning get-together with a promise of carbs and mimosas and an announcement. They'd come immediately, eating up all the food and drinks, and allowing her to take her time with her declaration. She settled into the inquisition, knowing it was best for them both to get all their nosy questions answered.

"When did you first sleep together?" Taylor demanded.

God, why was she blushing? This was ridiculous; she was a grown-up. "After Adele's wedding."

Avery gave a whoop. "Nothing like a Dr. Seuss wedding to get you all steamed up."

Bella gave her a suffering glance. "Are you really having this much fun torturing me?"

"Yes," Taylor said firmly. "So you've been seeing each other for a few weeks now without telling us?"

"I needed some time to process. You know how I am. I went from not dating to sleeping with him and being in a relationship. It's not my comfort zone."

Avery's face softened. "I know, sweetie. I'm so damn proud of you, though. You could have easily walked away from Gabe because it was messy and you had enough excuses."

"I did at first," she said with a sigh. "And I still worry about Zoe and how we'll work together, and even if I'm ready to dive into all these feelings. Especially after Matt. So I told Gabe I wanted to move really slowly, and he's been good with it."

"Did you tell Zoe yet?" Taylor asked.

"No, but I will today."

"I'm sure she'll be happy," Avery said. "She's crazy about Gabe."

"I just want to make sure she feels good about us. I've never had to discuss the ins and outs of dating before."

"It'll be good for both of you," Avery said. "I'm glad you listened to Carter and realized Gabe wasn't the player you believed. I can see how that would have held you back."

She hesitated, tapping her finger against her lip. "Yeah, but there's still gossip. Even Daisy was surprised I'd want to get involved with him due to his reputation. I don't know, I have to admit it's a bit weird. Another reason I'm going slow."

Taylor gave her a sharp glance. "Do *you*, babe. I get judgments all the time. I happen to like sex, but it doesn't mean I'm some type of man-eater. And if I want to settle down one day in the far, far future, that shouldn't affect my relationship, right?"

"Yeah, you're right. It's this small-town thing, I guess. But I'll work it out."

"Of course you will. Just enjoy yourself. You're having sex again!" Avery said.

"Stop," Bella said with a hand out. "You're making me feel like I'm sixteen. It's embarrassing."

"Tough. That's what happens when you break a six-year dry spell," Taylor said.

She grinned. "Well, I wanted to see if you guys wanted to invite the guys to Taco Tuesday dinner. We have no weddings, so I'm hoping everyone's free. Can you check with Pierce, T? I'd like him to join us, too. You're talking to him again, right?"

Taylor glared. "For now. I'll tell him."

"We're in," Avery said.

"Good."

"Are you going to hold hands at the conference table now?" Avery asked.

This time, Bella battled her red cheeks and reached for the champagne bottle. "Seriously, you both suck."

They laughed with so much glee, she eventually laughed, too.

After Bella picked up Zoe from school, they gathered in the kitchen for Toll House cookies and juice. She listened to her daughter's nonstop chatter about her school day while she sorted through the endless bulletins stuffed in Zoe's backpack, and fussed over the new drawing.

"I made unicorn land, Mama," she said, pointing at the rolling green hills, rainbows, and colorful unicorns romping around. "It's a place where they eat all the candy they want, and no one is ever mean."

She tacked it on the refrigerator. "I love it, sweetie. I wish it really existed."

Zoe munched on a cookie, looking somber. "Oh, but it does. I dream about it a lot. I just need to go find it, like an 'splorer."

"*Ex*plorer. Can I go with you?"

"Of course. We do everything together."

She dragged in a breath and sat on the stool next to her. A perfect transition she needed to jump on. "And we always will, as long as you want me. Nothing will ever change the love I have for you, no matter who else comes into our lives."

"Uh-huh." She finished her cookie. "Can I watch TV?"

"I'd like to talk to you about something first." Her tummy clenched with nerves, but she kept her face and voice calm. "You like Gabe, right, honey?"

"No."

She froze. "What?"

Her daughter smiled with radiance. "I *love* Gabe! He let me paint his nails and watches movies with us and all sorts of good stuff."

She laughed. "Oh, good. Because I want to tell you about Mommy and Gabe. We decided we really like each other, too. Even more than just friends. So when a man and a woman really like each other, they may decide to date. Do you know what that is?"

Zoe's eyes widened. "Oh yes! That's when you hold hands and go to fun places together, like you and Daddy did before you got married, right?"

Matt's face drifted in her memory, bringing more joy than pain. "That's right. So Gabe and I are going to be dating now. That doesn't change anything with me and you, but it means Gabe may be here more often or join us when we go out, and you may see us hold hands, or he may even be here for breakfast some mornings. How do you feel about that, pumpkin?"

She watched her daughter's face carefully, but there was only a childish excitement as she clapped her hands. "Can Gabe come with us to Great Adventure on spring break? Mama, you promised I can go on the roller coaster if I'm tall enough and maybe he can even win me a stuffed puppy!"

"I bet Gabe will definitely try," she said with a smile. "Do you have any questions for me? Anything you want to know? If you ever feel funny about something, you come talk to me. I know Mommy hasn't dated anyone before, so this is new for all of us."

Zoe nodded, her blue eyes flickering with a jumble of thoughts. "We'll always love Daddy, but since he's in heaven, maybe he sent us Gabe to help take care of us?"

Bella stilled. In that moment, she realized her daughter had an old soul and was able to see things in a light that would be a gift to her in this lifetime. Somehow, even through tragedy, Zoe had flourished.

Warmth flowed in her veins, and it was as if Matt was smiling down at them, proud of the daughter they'd made together.

She blinked away the tears and tugged Zoe into her arms for a big hug. "I think you're absolutely right," she said.

"Mama?"

"Yeah?"

"Do you think we can get a puppy now? Gabe can help us take care of it!"

She burst into laughter and hugged Zoe tighter.

♥ ♥ ♥

Gabe walked into the Acme supermarket. He headed to produce, swearing this time it would be a quick trip in and out. He refused to go to the aisle where his weaknesses flared—namely, junk cereals that held the most magical sugary crunch. And forget frozen foods. Each time he failed to walk past a pint of cookies 'n cream ice cream without buying it, the move cost him a minimum of fifty crunches. He needed some stupid fruit.

Shaking his head at his mental scoldings, he grabbed a few bananas, red apples, and a bag of almonds, which would give him some healthy options. His schedule was sometimes so crammed, a quick snack was crucial, and he'd been lax lately.

Of course, he'd been getting some extra exercise. It'd been so long since he'd had sex, his appetite was up, along with his libido.

The thought of Bella floated in his mind, and he had to stifle a grin. Now that her sisters and Zoe knew, he'd been able to relax. He'd been off base about Bella wanting to hide their relationship. Avery and Taylor had teased them about their secret liaisons at the last meeting but then quickly settled into work mode. He'd sensed no strange tension, and knowing they fully approved only added to his relief.

He headed toward the cashier, then spotted the bright blooms of various bouquets at the front. Hesitating, he pulled one out. The center flower was a bright-blue happy daisy and reminded him of Bella. The hell with it. He was already so far gone, why not just bring her some flowers for Taco Tuesday?

He grabbed them and spun around.

"Well, hi there, stranger." Devon smiled up at him, her gaze curiously taking in the bouquet.

Guilt pricked. Dammit, he'd called her after Adele's wedding and left her a message that they should talk, but she'd never reached back out. He'd been secretly relieved, hoping maybe she'd changed her mind about them and wanted an out. But he still felt he owed her an explanation, even though the date had been open ended with no promises. "Hi, Devon. How are you?"

"Good. Just picking up some dinner. Haven't seen you in a while. How did the Dr. Seuss wedding go?"

"It was a big hit, and the flowers were one of the highlights. I'm really sorry I haven't called again. I got busy, and distracted, and—"

"Fell for someone?" she asked teasingly. "I'm assuming that's why we never got to the second date?"

He reached out and touched her arm. "Did you get my message?"

"Yeah, but it was full of serious meaning and a tad of guilt. I figured someone else had stepped in."

He nodded. "Bella and I began dating."

She blinked, obviously startled. "Bella? Wow, I didn't see that coming. But I'm happy for you. Though I may wonder for a long time what I gave up."

Her words stung a bit, and though he hoped she wasn't hurt, he sensed Devon really was pleased for him. She had an energy that was open and giving, and didn't hold grudges. It was one of the things he'd fallen for initially. "Thanks, Devon."

She surprised him by standing on her tiptoes and pressing a kiss fully on his mouth. "She'll love the flowers. See you around." Then she walked away.

He paid and headed for his car. Heading home, he showered, changed, then packed up the flowers and a bottle of wine for Bella. When his email pinged, he checked it quickly, then froze.

Latoya had emailed him the link to the article that was running in next month's *Bridal Style* magazine.

He opened it, quickly scanned, then went back to the beginning. As he read, the discomfort grew until it was a low buzzing settling low in his gut. The title alone made him want to wince in sheer humiliation.

A Man for All Seasons: The Hottest Wedding Planner Is Making a Splash in Cape May and Beyond. Here's Why.

It was accompanied by a full picture of him dressed in a black suit, his chin tucked in, gaze staring at the camera as if he were a male model posing rather than doing his damn job. It got worse as the reporter detailed some of his clients, then cited that awful Beach Bachelor thing that still wouldn't die. Sunshine Bridal was listed, of course, and there were some beautiful pics of Adele's wedding, showcasing the details that had made it unique. But it felt more like a showcase for him—the attractive single male who worked in a female-dominated business and had all the traits a future bride would find titillating. Something to brag about to her friends while they ogled him and whispered behind his back.

It didn't feel like praise for his work. More like praise for the way he looked.

Again.

You'll always rely on that pretty face and body to get you by, the voice sneered. *You've never been a real man. Never will.*

Gabe closed out of the article and shoved his phone in his pocket. He'd talk to everyone tonight and see what they thought. Sure, it was publicity, and it certainly wasn't bad for Sunshine Bridal. He was just getting damn tired of being tossed around as the fun subject in town when he just wanted to concentrate on two things: Bella and work.

By the time he got to her house, the whole gang was already there.

"Gabe is here!" Zoe shouted, racing over and leaping into his arms, trusting he'd catch her. When he did, he held her tight, his heart exploding in his chest at the sheer love he had for this little girl. Staring into her big blue eyes, her tumble of golden flyaway hair around her face, he had the gift of seeing Bella when she was young. Even better were her sharp mind and wit, even at such a young age. He'd never had so much fun conversing with a six-year-old.

He caught Bella's gaze over her daughter's head. The barriers had been crushed between them. They connected on a physical plane, but it was the quiet talks afterward, holding her in his arms, that he cherished. The sharing of her daughter, and her family. The way her lips curved into a sweet smile when she caught sight of him.

Maybe he'd always known. Maybe he'd been destined to only love her. Because he did. He loved Bella Sunshine-Caldwell with everything he was.

He just had no idea if she felt the same.

"Aww, he brought flowers," Pierce teased, clapping him on the shoulder. "Are those for me?"

Zoe giggled. "They're for Mommy, silly! Gabe and Mommy are dating. Don't you know that?"

Pierce pretended surprise. "I always thought your mama wanted to date Thor?"

More giggles. "No, she can't. He's only on television. And I like Gabe better."

Gabe tossed her once in the air, then settled her back on the ground. "I'm so glad you're in my corner, Zoe. These guys are brutal."

Bella laughed and walked over, pressing a kiss to his lips. "These are beautiful," she murmured, as he handed her the bouquet. "Thank you."

"Reminded me of you. Couldn't resist."

"Umm, Bella, I need you here STAT," Taylor called out. "There are four pans here. Some are done, some may burn, and it's chaos."

Pierce laughed. "Taylz, how were you the only Sunshine sister not to learn how to cook?"

"Screw you. I haven't seen you channel any Bobby Flay, either. Your best friend is the pizza-delivery guy."

"At least I help support the economy. You force Bella to feed you," he teased.

She flipped her pink hair, saw Zoe had her back turned, and gave him the finger.

Bella shook her head, taking one last sniff of her flowers, then headed to the kitchen. "Coming. Here, put these in water and get the wine poured."

"That I can do," Taylor said. "Gabe, you want a Stella?"

"Yes, please."

Avery and Carter were talking quietly in the corner. He noticed they were looking at her phone, but he didn't want to interrupt.

"Can I help with the toppings?" Zoe asked.

"Of course," Bella said. "Your aunt Avery is slacking off. Have Pierce and Gabe help you pour the cheese, tomatoes, and lettuce into bowls."

"Cool!"

Gabe smiled at her enthusiasm and got the impressive row of toppings sorted out. His mouth watered at the smell of sizzling meat, onions, and the spicy taco sauce. He sipped his beer, chatted with Pierce, and finally Avery came over.

"So I have an announcement," she said, giving him a pointed look. "That reporter you spoke with at Adele's wedding? She wrote up an article about us in *Bridal Style*."

Bella expertly removed two steaming pans and laid them on trivets. "That's great!" A frown suddenly creased her brow. "Wait a minute, your tone sounds funny. Is it bad?"

Gabe could tell she was worried about the incident at the bar, and he was happy that hadn't been included in the article. Still, the slant that he was single and available had been highlighted in the article.

"No, it's good. But they took an angle I'm not pleased about."

"I saw it," he said. "Just before I came over, I got a notification and read it."

Avery tilted her head and studied him. "What did you think?"

He shrugged. "I like the exposure for Sunshine, but I'm not sure you wanted me as the main star."

She waved a hand in the air. "I don't care about that, I care about you. I wished it had focused more on your amazing work at the Dr. Seuss wedding and not that beach-bachelor crap you hate."

"Bad word, Aunt Avery," Zoe said.

"Sorry, sweetheart."

Bella distributed the meal onto a few platters and spoke up. "I didn't read the article yet, so you guys are driving me crazy. Avery, can you read it out loud?"

"Yeah, let's sit down, get settled, and hear it," Taylor said.

They put everything on the table, got in their chairs, and loaded up their plates. Bella got Zoe situated with a hard and soft taco, a few beans, and red peppers. They ate and listened as Avery read the whole article, then passed her phone around so everyone could look at the photographs.

He watched Bella's reaction, noting her tight lips and stiffened shoulders. Dammit, did she think he'd answered Latoya's questions by trying to grab the spotlight? It was more of a piece on him than Sunshine Bridal, and if he were an owner, he'd be a bit pissed.

Finally, she spoke. "Once again, they're making you the angle as a male wedding planner. Pisses me off. If it was reversed, readers would call out the discrimination."

"Agreed," Taylor said. "I don't like that, either. I do like the pics of the wedding, and how they mentioned our clientele and how we bring something special to the business."

"They hardly mentioned Bella," he said. "We did that wedding together, but they made it sound like I did it alone."

Bella gave a snort. "I couldn't care less about that—we're all a team here, so if one gets press, we all do. I just want to know how you feel about it, because I can call her up and demand she pull it. Threaten her with a lawsuit."

Avery nodded. "Definitely. We'll all back you up on this, Gabe. How do you feel about the article?"

He stared at the women around the table. A deep sense of relief and gratitude washed over him. They knew he hadn't tried to slant the article his way. And they were willing to fight for him if he felt the article wasn't fair, even if it gave the business an amazing amount of PR.

They weren't treating him like a regular employee.

They were treating him like family.

He reached out and squeezed Bella's hand. "Thanks for the support. I agree, I'm not happy with the way they slanted this whole thing, but as long as you're okay, I think we should let it run. Brides are still going to see that we pulled off the wedding of Adele's dreams. I think it's going to open up an entire segment of business for more top-rated clients. And then we can decide who we want to take on."

"You sure?" Avery asked.

"Yeah."

Pierce rolled his eyes. "Still don't know what the big deal is. Hell, I'll pose in bikini briefs if it will triple my clientele."

Everyone laughed. "You would," Gabe told his friend. "Maybe I'll officially hand over my title of Beach Bachelor to you."

"Bring it."

"I know the *Bachelor*!" Zoe piped up. "Mama and Aunt TT watch it together! But they say I can't watch 'cause it's too adult."

Bella winced. Taylor suddenly looked focused on her meal.

"Hmm, not quite feminist, is it?" Pierce teased. "Giving out a rose based on sex appeal and evening gowns? I'm shocked."

Avery threw up her hands. "I've never watched it, but they're addicted. Once, I was calling them in an emergency, and they refused to pick up their phones!"

Bella cleared her throat. "It's brain candy," she explained. "I don't really care about the outcome. I read on my Kindle while it's on."

Gabe laughed, loving her pink cheeks and the crap way she lied. "Sure, sweetheart. We believe you."

"What does *bachelor* mean?" Zoe asked.

Bella handed her a glass of milk. "It means someone who's single," she said.

"I like married better," she said with an adorable frown. "And no one is single at the table anymore!"

Bella cocked her head. "Yes, we are, honey. No one is married here."

Zoe puffed up her chest and beamed. "They will be. Aunt Avery is marrying Uncle Carter, and I'm going to be the flower girl. I've been practicing. Mama will marry Gabe, and I'll have a new daddy, and Aunt TT will marry Pierce 'cause they're bestest friends and love each other!"

Silence fell.

It was Taylor who laughed first. "Everyone gets our own happily ever after, huh?" she asked teasingly, reaching over and tugging on a wayward golden curl. "I feel like I'm a series installment in a romance novel," she said. "But I'm tired of being last, so my story would have to be told first."

Avery nudged Carter. "She's always bitched about being last, but if she's the youngest, her story would be third. We'd be first," she said with a wink.

Gabe blocked out everyone but Bella, focused on her reaction to Zoe's announcement.

She shook her head and laughed. "Let's not get ahead of ourselves, sweetheart," she joked. "We don't have time in our schedule to plan three whole weddings!"

"Ain't that the truth," Avery said.

When Bella's gaze swung around to meet his, it was obvious she expected him to share in her humor.

His heart dropped.

The idea of marrying him made her laugh. He almost wished she'd reacted in shock rather than a complete disregard for any type of permanent future between them. His insides stilled and numbed him in a clumsy attempt to ward off the pain while he forced himself to smile back, pretending to agree with her.

She didn't seem to notice his world had just exploded, and nudged Zoe's arm. "Why don't you finish that last bite so you can have ice cream?"

"Yay! Is it cookies 'n cream? That's my favorite, just like Gabe."

"Yes, it is. You're like two peas in a pod," Bella said. The words were lighthearted, but the damage had been done.

He swore he wouldn't humiliate himself at this table, even as his father's mocking laugh echoed in his head like a ghost, reminding him he'd always been unworthy. He pushed the hurt and the memory down hard, locking it away. "We just have the best taste, don't we, Zoe?" he asked with a wink.

"Yes!" She gave a wink back, which came out exaggerated, and everyone laughed.

The topic was swept away, and they spent the rest of dinner and dessert with light chatter. One by one, everyone left, until Bella went to tuck Zoe in, and Gabe finished up the dishes.

He tried to chill, but her reaction kept rolling around in his head like a stuck slot machine. He knew she was wary about marriage after what had happened with Matt, but was it specifically him or her past that caused such strong emotion? He'd told her that he'd take anything from her he could get. And he would. Every night Bella wanted him in her bed was a gift and an opportunity to cement the bond between them. She claimed they were in a relationship. But in her mind, was this always going to be short term, destined to fade out on her behalf? Was she still concerned about his age or his past, not believing he could be a good father and husband?

He pushed away the panic and reminded himself she just needed time. Time to be with him and allow her trust to blossom.

When she came back in, he'd just closed the dishwasher. She slipped her arms around his waist and leaned against him with a sigh. "Do you know that for women, real porn is a man who cleans up?"

He chuckled, savoring her light floral scent and the lithe length of her body. "Hmm, so you're saying if I meet you naked with an apron around me, it'll turn you on?"

"I'd devour you," she whispered, pulling his head down for a long kiss. "Are you staying?"

He paused. His brain told him it'd be better to go home tonight. Sit with his feelings and rebuild his defenses. Maybe she'd miss him.

But his big head wasn't going anywhere.

"Yes, if you want me to."

"I do." She cupped his cheeks and met his gaze head-on. "And I want you stay tomorrow for breakfast. To be here when Zoe wakes up."

He pressed his forehead to hers, accepting the offer. It was another tiny step toward him, and he'd savor each one. "I'd like that. But right now, all I can think about is porn."

She laughed softly, her hands dropping to his ass, squeezing tight. "What do you have in mind?"

"Me. You. And some seriously dirty . . ."

"Dishes? Laundry?"

He nipped at her bottom lip. "Exercise. I'll need to bathe you afterward. I've been dreaming of getting you in the tub with nothing but a bunch of bubbles between us."

She shuddered and he took full advantage, backing her up step by step into the bedroom. "Dirty exercise is good. We'll work off the ice cream."

"And next time I'll bring over my iron and G-string. Get you real hot and bothered."

She smiled up at him with joy. "I'm crazy about you, Gabe. I haven't been this happy in a long time."

"Me, either. Now get into that bedroom and make my fantasies come true."

He shut the door behind them, satisfied she'd given him as much as she could for now.

Chapter Nineteen

Gabe scrolled through his exploding in-box. Since the *Bridal Style* article had hit, Sunshine had been inundated with new clients. Unfortunately, a bunch of them were just curious to meet him, and some of his initial consultations had turned into awkward come-ons and brides bringing their best friends to meet the hot wedding planner.

Frustration simmered at a low burn. Usually, he took this crap in stride, but lately the small-town vibe that had charmed him the past few years seemed like a noose around his neck. Hopefully, things would settle back down, and he could do what he did best without being judged on his damn looks.

He stopped at the urgent flagged message from Endless Vows Bridal Agency. It was one of the NYC-based agencies Adele had fired for being too big-time, but their reputation was stellar. Celebrities used them, and they were known in the industry as being the Holy Grail.

Curious, he skimmed the email, then started again at the beginning. They wanted him to interview.

Surprise spiked through him. The agency had a strict policy of not hiring anyone without a minimum of five years' experience in big-budget weddings. Would he even qualify?

He glanced at his watch. He had half an hour before he needed to head out. He'd never been interested in being another number in a big company full of egos—that had driven him to Cape May for the small-town feel—but he'd be crazy not to call and see what they really wanted. On impulse, he quickly dialed the number, asked for Melody, then introduced himself.

"Gabe, we're thrilled you called back," she said with genuine enthusiasm. "You did Adele Butterstein's wedding, and we were stunned by the turnout."

"Thank you," he said politely. "Weren't you originally booked as her planner?"

Her laugh held a touch of self-derision. "Indeed, we were, and we screwed up royally. But our mistake could end up being our best asset. We'd love to invite you in to interview with Palmer Matterson. He thinks you're a fresh vision in this industry and wants the opportunity to pitch you."

He stared at the phone. Palmer was the actual owner of Endless Vows, which meant he wasn't going through a random HR interview. He knew the agency put out constant feelers to recruit, but this seemed different. "What exactly is he interested in?" he asked. "I'll be honest, I'm happy at Sunshine Bridal and wasn't looking to relocate at this time."

"We understand. He'd just love a chance to talk and see if he can interest you in a rare opportunity. He was quite impressed by the article in *Bridal Style* and all you have to offer. Can you come in this Wednesday?"

This was nuts. He had no plans to leave Cape May or his job. But he'd worked his ass off for so long to get to this point. How could he say no? He owed it to himself to meet with Palmer and see what he wanted.

"That's fine."

"Excellent! One p.m., at our office. I'll email you the specifics. We look forward to meeting you."

He clicked off. Guilt pricked his conscience. Should he tell Avery? Bella? Or would that just put everyone in a needless tailspin, freaking out Bella when things were good between them?

After all his dreams and hard work, he was being recognized by one of the top agencies in the industry. They wanted *him*. Those doubts that still lingered from all the years of his father's taunting suddenly quieted. Maybe this was an opportunity he'd be foolish to give up.

No. Better to keep it quiet for now.

♥ ♥ ♥

Bella grabbed a water bottle and checked the clock. She needed to get to the school for the PTO planning session, and dinner had run late. "Sweetheart, I need to drop you downstairs at Aunt TT's, okay? I have to run to your school for an hour."

"Is it for my year-end graduation party?" Zoe asked excitedly.

She smiled. "Yep. I cannot believe in just over two months, you'll be out of kindergarten. How did you get so big so fast?"

"Don't know. Is it gonna be a great party?"

"Well, of course, I'm the best party planner ever, right?"

Her daughter giggled, and everything lit up inside her like Christmas. "That's right."

"Good. Let's go." Bella took her hand and guided her down the stairs.

"Mama, what's a player mean?"

Bella froze, turning toward her daughter. Zoe didn't even look at her; she was focused on gathering the bunch of Barbie dolls she was taking with her, like the question was just an afterthought. "Where did you hear that, honey?"

"Well, when Gabe picked me up from the bus yesterday, my friend Theresa said her mom said Gabe is a player. I told her you were dating, and she said the word again and that her mom would never date a player. What does it mean?"

Anger unfurled, but she kept her face calm. "A player is someone who doesn't date just one person but dates a whole bunch of people."

"So Gabe's not a player 'cause he just dates you?"

"That's right, but we don't want to use the word *player* to describe someone, because it's hurtful. Adults are allowed to date many people, if they want. But Gabe and I decided we really like each other and want to only be in a relationship with each other. Do you have any questions about Gabe and me?"

She shook her head. "Nope. I love Gabe. I'd like him to be my dad."

It was the second time Zoe had mentioned Gabe being her father. Before, the idea had been unthinkable. Now, she blinked back the sting of tears and brought her daughter close in a hug. "That makes me happy. But right now, Gabe and I are just dating. And if we did get married, he'd never replace your dad."

"I know that. It's good to have a few dads or moms or grandmas or grandpas, right? Then there's more people to love."

She pressed a kiss to Zoe's head and wondered how she'd gotten so lucky. "That's right. Now let's hurry up, I don't want to be late."

The exchange with Zoe burned in her mind the whole drive to the school. She couldn't believe the moms were still talking about Gabe. Either way, she was going to have to decide whether or not she took a stand. She refused to be whispered about when she attended the school's functions or allow Zoe to be manipulated by her classmates who knew nothing. They must've found out about her and Gabe, but they had no right to make judgments on her without even asking a question.

She did some deep breathing in the car and calmed down. There was no use going in upset and defensive. She'd be cool and professional, and maybe after the meeting, she'd say her piece to Kelly—Theresa's mom—about keeping her mouth shut.

She wished Daisy had been able to come, but she'd called and said she had to work late. Bella had promised to not stick her with a crappy job just because she didn't show. They had each other's backs like that.

She knew most of the mothers there and greeted Amy and Kelly with polite distance, making sure to sit with some of the nicer moms.

Eventually, she relaxed and had fun with the planning. They chose the theme (Disney) and assigned different tasks. Bella came with a spreadsheet handy, and everyone seemed happy for her to take charge along with the president. They finally settled on the date, time, and details.

Andrea, the president, came over afterward to thank her. "I think you're our biggest asset when it comes to parties," she said with a laugh. "Has spring wedding season hit yet?"

Bella wrinkled her nose. "Yes, unfortunately, all of us are slammed, and it'll continue through the summer. Don't want to complain, though. Business has been booming."

"Well, of course—everyone saw the article written about Sunshine. So exciting to have one of our local businesses go national. Are you starting to do New York weddings, also?"

"We took on a few." She didn't want to name-drop, but signing a local television star who sang on Broadway was big news. After *Bridal Style* dropped its article, the phone had been ringing off the hook with queries.

Many specifically for Gabe.

"Huge congratulations. Hopefully you won't be booked up when my son finally decides to marry his girlfriend. They've been dating for years, and he's still not ready."

"Don't push him. But when he does pop the question, you call me. I'll make sure we take good care of him."

They laughed and Andrea left. Bella packed up her stuff and watched as Amy and Kelly caught sight of her and headed over.

"Hi, Bella. Thanks for helping us out—we loved your ideas," Amy said with a friendly smile.

Bella smiled back but remained wary. "Welcome. I like doing this stuff."

"Where's Daisy?"

"She had to work late, but I signed her up for decorations with me. She's good at that."

Kelly nodded. "We heard you were really busy with weddings, especially after that article. It must be nice to finally be recognized for your hard work."

"It is, even though it's hard juggling everything."

"Sure, being a single mom is hard," Amy said with a sympathetic gleam in her eye. "Speaking of which, Daisy was telling me the news about Gabe. We're happy for you. You needed a guy in your life. I know it's been a long time."

She stiffened, ready to do battle. "I'm glad you brought it up, because I wanted to talk to you both about something that bothered me. Zoe came home today saying Theresa was calling Gabe a player."

Kelly groaned and covered her eyes. "I'm so sorry! She must have overheard me. I'm really embarrassed."

Bella shifted her feet, still uneasy. "Apology accepted. I'd just appreciate it if you didn't talk about us at this point. I'm really happy with how things are going."

"Of course you are. That man is a machine," Amy said with a laugh.

"I really didn't mean to judge you," Kelly said. "I just hope you don't get attached. He's the perfect transition guy for you. But sometimes those men have this magical thing over us that keeps us from realizing the truth."

"You mean the magical penis?" Amy asked.

Kelly jabbed her finger in the air. "Yes, that!"

Their laughter was like mean pokes, hitting her in all the sensitive areas of her body. "What are you talking about?" she whispered harshly, trying to keep her voice low. "Gabe and I are dating, not having some cheap fling. I thought Daisy told you."

Amy blinked, looking genuinely confused. "She said you hooked up, not that you're seriously dating."

Her stomach lurched. Had Daisy really kept that information from them? And if so, why? "Well, I don't know why she said that."

"Oh God," Kelly said, looking chastised. "Seriously, Bella, we just assumed you'd never try and settle down with a guy like Gabe. You have a daughter, and you lost your husband, and Gabe is just . . ."

"Just what?" she asked tightly.

Amy sighed. "Just not long term. I mean, he was kissing Devon in the supermarket last week! That's why Kelly was calling him a player."

Bella stood her ground, trying not to grit her teeth. She refused to be goaded into some type of gossipy drama that centered around lies. "Devon? I can tell you with one hundred percent certainty that never happened. And I find it offensive for you to be spreading rumors about him like that. It's not fair to either of us."

Kelly and Amy shared an uncomfortable look. "Amy's right," Kelly said. "You can go ahead and ask Christina from Bagel Time Cafe. She was at the Acme supermarket, and Gabe handed Devon a bouquet of flowers, then she gave him a full kiss on the lips. I swear to God, I'm not lying. She saw it with her own eyes."

The ground shifted, but she held strong. A bouquet of flowers? Could it be possible he was stringing both of them along and bought them both flowers? No, Gabe wasn't like that. But the doubts had drilled into her brain and wouldn't quiet.

"Well, I'm sorry, I just don't believe it. Listen, I have to go."

"Sure, we're sorry. But hon, I gotta be honest. You're way too good for a man like that. He'll only end up breaking your heart," Amy said.

She didn't answer. She walked slowly away with her shoulders squared and back straight, pretending she wasn't dissolving inside. She drove home carefully, ignoring the nip of panic at her nerves.

She had to find out what the hell was going on.

♥ ♥ ♥

Gabe fished out his turkey club for dinner and settled down with his laptop. He'd had back-to-back appointments all day for the Alperson wedding next weekend, and he was beginning to worry. The FOG was flying in from Colorado, and a snowstorm was ready to hit right around the day he was supposed to fly out. He'd gone back and forth with the bride, who was seriously starting to lose it, and managed to get him an earlier flight out.

Gabe had felt like a fucking superhero. But had he gotten the deserved gratitude and high fives? Nope.

The FOG told him he refused to leave early due to some big business meetings. So now he was dealing with a hysterical bride, a pissy FOG, a frustrated groom, and a ticket that wasn't going to be used.

Wasn't he supposed to just plan weddings? How'd he get roped into making sure entire families kept his clients calm? It sure as hell wasn't in his job description, but then again, it's what made Sunshine the best. It wasn't just about the details—it was the entire experience. He was a support system.

He thought about having a beer, then settled on seltzer. When the phone rang again, he almost didn't look, not able to deal with another call from the bride where he did nothing but soothe her rantings. Lord, wasn't that what her fiancé was for?

Good, it wasn't her. He picked up. "Hello?"

"Gabe? It's Michelle from *Exit Zero* magazine. How are you?"

Ah, the famous glossy that had made his life a living hell two years ago. "I'm good. Say, if this is about the advertising, Avery's in charge of that."

"No, actually, I have great news. You've just been picked as the Sexiest Beach Bachelor for the June issue!"

No. Fucking. Way.

He cleared his throat. "Ah, Michelle, thanks but no thanks. I'm not interested."

A heavy pause pulsed over the line. "Gabe, are you kidding? This is an honor—we polled hundreds of people all the way down to Wildwood and Long Beach, and you were number one! This is our biggest issue, and we've booked out our ads way in advance. Everyone's waiting for the announcement!"

His temples began to throb. He could not go through this again. First *Bridal Style*, now this. He just wanted to be left alone. "Again, thank you, but I'm going to decline. Besides, I'm involved in a relationship, so that negates the whole bachelor thing."

"You are?" Her shocked tone irritated him. "Well, you're still not married, so it counts. I'm really disappointed by your reaction here. I guess this means you don't want to do a photo shoot?"

"Umm, no. Definitely no. But good luck to the new winner. Can't wait to see who it is."

"Oh, we're not picking another winner. We'll just run the article without your pic. How about a quote?"

His heart sped up. He looked at the phone with a touch of wariness. "Wait—I just said I don't want to be involved."

Her laugh reminded him of a tinkly bell he wanted to mute. "Gabe, don't be silly, we have to run the article! You were chosen whether you like it or not, and it's the biggest spread to kick off summer. I can use your picture from last time or pull it off the website. No problem."

"Michelle, listen to me. You know Pierce? Put him down as the new beach bachelor—he's perfect for the job. I don't want anything to do with this."

"Well, Pierce was definitely in the running, but you beat him good."

He closed his eyes. He was trapped in a nightmare that kept recycling. This would have never happened in a big city like Manhattan or Chicago or LA. Why did he have to settle in a quirky beach city that kept forcing him to be their local celebrity? He wasn't even rich!

"Is there anything I can say to change your mind?"

"Nope. But if you decide to send me an updated photo with a quote, we don't go to print till Friday. Thanks, Gabe!" She hung up.

Son of a bitch.

When another buzz came in, every muscle clenched, but he relaxed once he saw it was a text from Bella.

Can I stop by?
Yes, here working. Come save me.

He glanced around, but his place was pristine, as usual. He thought about how messy his living space could get with Bella and Zoe, but it brought a sense of warm anticipation, not worry. He'd begun to realize he enjoyed keeping his stuff organized because there was no one here but him. With people came chaos, but it also brought love. He'd been ready for a long time to experience all those things with Bella.

The tap on the door came a few minutes later. "This is a nice surprise," he said. "I thought you had a PTO thing." He went to pull her in for a kiss, but her head ducked and she stepped past him.

"It just finished. I wanted to talk."

"Good, I've had a hell of a day and need the company. Want some wine? Seltzer?"

"No, thanks."

"Sit down, you look all tense. Did you have a crappy day, too?"

She turned from him and pulled off her jacket. "You could say that."

"I want to hear about it, but I have to tell you something. I just got a call from *Exit Zero* magazine. Seems they had one of those ridiculous polls again and named me Beach Bachelor of the year. Can you believe it? I begged Michelle to leave me out of the whole thing, but she refused. Think I can sue?"

She sat down and regarded him from the couch with a strange expression. "Probably not."

"I probably wouldn't anyway. But paired with this *Bridal Style* thing, I'm getting sick of these ridiculous stories like I'm some kind of unicorn here. I tried to throw them Pierce, but she said maybe next year. Then I told her I was involved in a relationship and that should clear me from the list, but basically if I don't have a ring on my finger, I'm fair game." He shook his head and flopped down next to her, then continued, "Sorry, sweetheart, I'm sure this isn't fun for you, either. Add in a crazed, crying bride calling me every ten minutes and a mean-tempered FOB, and I'm ready to go to bed. Preferably with you." He leaned in with intent. "Do we have time?" he teased. "Or are you due back home?"

She didn't answer. Just kept looking at him with a polite distance.

A bad feeling crawled through him. It was as if she'd rebuilt the same barriers he'd battled before. The last few weeks of intimacy made him assume they were past such remoteness.

Or had it just been lying in wait?

"Bella, what's wrong? Did something happen?"

A flicker of sadness gleamed in her blue eyes. "Does a part of you like being written up as the local bachelor?" she asked. "I mean, I know you're protesting, but it wouldn't be wrong to admit it feels good to have so many women interested in you."

The bad feeling ratcheted up to borderline panic. He fought the emotion back and knew he needed to remain calm to get to the heart of the matter. "It wouldn't be wrong, but it would be a lie," he said carefully. "I feel like I'm missing something important here."

"I just think you may want to be able to flirt and date who you want without being imprisoned with a single mom who doesn't go out much. I know it gets boring." She twisted her fingers together, the telltale nervous gesture he'd come to cherish. He loved knowing all the tiny details that made up her body and mind and emotions, relishing the unveiling of each secret. Now, though, she was shutting down, and he had to find out why.

"Not for me. But I told you this before, and I thought you understood my intentions. I don't want any other woman, Bella. I want you, and I want Zoe. Period."

Her hand shook as she reached up and pushed back her hair. He wanted to take her in his arms but knew she needed the space to work through these doubts. "Do you want Devon, too?"

He frowned. "What does Devon have to do with us?"

Anger snapped from her gaze. "A lot, it seems. Especially when you're giving her flowers and kissing her in public places. I'm not sure what constitutes a relationship with you, but for me, it's complete monogamy." A wild laugh escaped her lips. "Honestly, this is my fault—not yours. I knew we were on different paths, but I got caught up in the intensity of it. Of us. I think it's time we got real with each other."

Suddenly, he was just as angry as she was. "Let's back it up. First, I did not give Devon any flowers. I bought one bouquet, and that's what I brought to you Tuesday night. Second, I told you exactly what happened between Devon and me. We had that one date. When I returned from Adele's wedding, I left her a message, telling her we needed to talk. She never answered, and we haven't seen each other since."

"Except at the supermarket when you kissed her?"

He blew out a breath. "No. I mean, yes, I ran into her at Acme. She asked about the flowers. I told her they were for you and we were serious. She was surprised, said she was happy for me and understood, and gave me a kiss before I could stop it. Then she walked away. There is nothing between Devon and me, Bella. I swear to God."

She slumped back in the sofa and bowed her head. "I believe you."

"Good. Monogamy is important to me. You're important to me. Where did you get this lopsided story from?"

The sigh that left her lips was full of emotion he was suddenly afraid to probe. "Some of the moms at the PTO were telling me that someone they knew saw you and Devon kissing. It didn't take long to jump to conclusions, especially when they keep constantly telling me you're not to be trusted for the long term."

He tamped down the surge of temper. It wouldn't do any good to freak out over lies and gossip. It never had. He just needed to convince

Bella. "It's not true. I've been lonely for a long time," he said simply, allowing her to see his heart. "I tried many times to see if there were any women who could give me what I was looking for. None came close until you. From the moment we met, it's only been you."

She tipped her chin up. Her lower lip trembled. "I feel so many things for you," she whispered. "But I'm still confused. Worried that this physical chemistry between us may flicker out, and there won't be enough for you to want to stay."

He tunneled his fingers through his hair in frustration. "You're asking for guarantees I keep trying to give you, sweetheart, but you obviously don't want to believe them."

She shook her head. "No. I do believe you about Devon."

"It's more than Devon. It's your constant belief that I don't want this. It's your reluctance to tell anyone we're together. When the moms told you about Devon, did you let them know that we're in a serious relationship?"

"I told them we were dating."

He nodded. "A casual word. Anything else? Did you come to my defense?"

"Of course!" she said hotly. "But I wanted to talk to you first to see exactly how things played out."

A fist slammed through his gut. The slowly dawning knowledge that she might always doubt him crippled his heart. "Now you know the truth. So my question is, where do we go from here?"

She jerked back, her features stark. "What do you want?"

Her answer told him what he didn't want to face. He was 100 percent invested in being the man for her and Zoe, but Bella wasn't there yet. Maybe she'd never be. Or maybe she needed more time, which was fine, unless she'd always planned to keep him at a safe distance. His reputation concerned her. And though he was damn frustrated by *Bridal Style* magazine, and *Exit Zero*, and the women coming on to him, those were things he couldn't control.

Even worse? They might never stop. Would it eventually erode everything good between them because of her constant doubts? Would she ever truly trust him enough to move forward, or was he going to commit to defending every one of his actions on a regular basis, hoping one day she'd finally believe in him?

Dear God, would he be chasing her love his whole damn life, just like he'd done with his father?

The realization crashed over him like a tidal wave. He couldn't do that to himself again. It had almost destroyed him the first time.

Yet how could he walk away from the woman he loved, without a fight?

He swallowed back the agony and gave her a smile. "Sweetheart, I want to move forward and be here for you and Zoe. I want that more than anything, but this is no longer about what *I* want. It's about your feelings toward me. You say you believe me about Devon, and the other women I've supposedly been with, but are you just holding back, waiting to see when I'm going to disappoint you? Is this a game I can never win?"

"No." She reached out, then jerked her hand back. "I don't know."

He nodded, knowing he deserved more, or at least the truth. "If the man I am isn't enough now, it never will be."

Her head flew up, and her eyes shot blue sparks. "You're plenty of man for me! Don't say that about yourself."

He stared into her beautiful face and gently stroked her cheek. "Maybe you can never feel the same way I do about you. Maybe that's something I have to face and learn to live with. I'd still like to try, but I'd need to know you not only believe me but trust me with your heart."

An aching regret lingered in her gaze. "I want to."

"But you can't right now because you still have doubts?"

"Not about Devon or the other women. Just about if we could work. I wish we could explore our relationship privately, without being judged or hassled all the time."

His throat closed up, but he forced out the words. "Out of the spotlight."

"Yes!"

He shook his head slowly. "Not really possible. And not the type of relationship I want. Do you?"

She pulled back. "Why do you need to pressure me right now? Can't we take our time and figure things out?"

In that moment, he wondered if he should let her go. Wondered if he was strong enough to keep trying to convince her of the man he was, the man he'd hoped she could love. But his heart remained stubborn, and so very hopeful.

He let his hand drop. "Take whatever time you need, Bella. I already know."

They stared at each other for a while, lost in a tangle of questions, what-ifs, and endless possibilities.

Finally, she stood up. "I better go. I need to think about things."

He walked her to the door, then dropped a soft kiss on her lips. "Good night. I'm right here if you need me."

For a moment, he thought she'd break. She stepped forward and wrapped her arms around his shoulders, holding him close. He savored her breath and her sweet scent and the silky feel of her hair against his skin.

Then she pulled away and left without another word.

Chapter Twenty

"Thanks for coming in. Been looking forward to meeting you."

Gabe shook Palmer Matterson's hand and settled into the lush red-velvet chair. His office was the type of space that a man dreamed of: Ceiling-to-floor windows overlooking the skyline of Manhattan. Rich textures of leather, velvet paired with deep mahogany wood, and a big-ass desk that proved whose dick was the biggest right from the start. A full bar took up the corner, framed photographs of his many legendary celebrity weddings were displayed on the walls, and a huge television/audio unit filled one corner.

The man himself was just as impressive. He was only about forty but sported a thick mane of gray hair, with pale-green eyes that seemed startling in his face. His Armani suit was exquisitely cut in a smoky charcoal, paired with an emerald tie. The Rolex on his watch gleamed, and his shoes were Italian, definitely handmade.

Gabe had expected a rich asshole, but he was surprised when they launched into a casual conversation, and he found him not only knowledgeable without ego but with a sharp sense of humor. Slowly, he relaxed, even more curious as to what the man wanted from him.

"Let me tell you why I reached out," Palmer said directly. His gaze gleamed with intelligence and honest enthusiasm. "When we lost Adele's wedding, I was disappointed. I immediately began digging to find out why and found the planners who were assigned were treating her like a cookie-cutter celebrity without personal thought or care. This disturbed me, so I looked deeper and found something that was running rampant, like a disease."

"What?"

"Complacency. The more planners I spoke with, the more I realized no one was excited about their job. Oh, sure, I still had some gems who'd been promoted along the way, but I realized my employees had lost the fire and needed restructuring. I've spent the past few weeks weeding out the deadweight, installing some new classes to ramp up creativity, and am excited about the new direction this company is taking."

Gabe nodded. "Sounds wonderful. I think if more companies took the time and effort to make hard changes, the market would be much better."

"Agreed. But you have to be willing to fail in order to succeed. You did that with Adele's wedding. You reached into corners the average planner can't even see and made it uniquely personal. That's why I want you on my team, Gabe."

"That's very flattering, but I did have a full partner on Adele's wedding. Bella Sunshine-Caldwell is one of the owners."

Delight lit the man's gaze. "Honest, too, huh? I like that. Yes, we knew from the beginning you were on a team, but I'm not interested in the owner. I'm interested in a top hire who has no family strings or responsibilities that can get in the way. If I hired Ms. Sunshine, I'd always be competing with her family business. You have the best of both worlds—experience, loyalty with a family firm, and a vision with no limit. You're the one we want."

Pride cut through him. His father's voice withered silently in his head. The top agency in New York City wanted him. All his work had paid off, and finally, he had hard evidence of his success. He was at the top of the chain, and he'd done it all on his own. "I appreciate the vote of confidence. But I'm still unsure what you want me to do here.

I'm not interested in leaving a thriving business where I work on equal terms with the owners just to take a job to be a cog in the wheel."

Palmer laughed, resting his hands on his knees. "Agreed. And I don't need another full-time planner. I'm talking about a management position with your own team to run. I want to offer you full gratis—the ability to pick your people, pick your clients, and run your own schedule."

His brain flashed over the possibilities. "What type of clientele?"

"Celebrities, billionaires, reality stars, even the power couples who rule New York. It may be a welcome change for you. Small towns seem to keep planners under a microscope, but here, it's the clients they judge. I'm creating an entire position just for you, Gabe. Now, you're going to tell me this doesn't interest you?"

Gabe stared at the man across from him. His heartbeat sped up, and the full implication of this job offer struck hard.

This was an opportunity of a lifetime.

He'd have the ability to create his own world at the helm. A team underneath him, ready to do his bidding and help him carry out his vision. No more small-town gossip. In the city, attractive men were plentiful. He could re-create his life with one word.

Yes.

"I'll need more details," he finally said, keeping a strict poker face.

Palmer grinned. "I figured. Let's talk."

An hour later, he headed back to Cape May, his head spinning. If he took the job, he'd be forced to give up Bella and Zoe, and a life he still loved. But what if Bella would never be ready to commit? Already, she'd distanced herself over the ridiculous rumors of Devon. What if he gave up an important work opportunity to chase someone who'd never truly be his? Could he take the risk, or was it time to be real with himself?

The questions battered his head and his heart the entire drive home.

"Bella, I can't make a decision. Do you think I should go with the vanilla, the eggshell white, or the butter?"

Bella shook her head and refocused on her bride, Winifred, who had three invitations laid out on the table. It took willpower to study each of them honestly and make a choice. The bride was a bit of a PITA, and every decision was not only lingered upon but obsessed over, accompanied by a painful whining that edged her nerves. Her partner, Sophia, was much more free flowing and relaxed, but had promised Winifred full control of the wedding planning. They made a beautiful couple, but Bella couldn't help wishing her primary contact were Sophia.

Still, she swore to give the young couple everything they dreamed of, so she relied on her professionalism, smiled, and pointed to the card on the left. "Definitely butter, it's the perfect shade. Elegant with just a hint of play."

Winifred nodded slowly, her French-manicured nail tapping against the embossed edge. "I think you're right. But we need to change the font to this other one and put our names centered in bold so they stand out."

"Of course. I have it all under control." Bella stood, desperate to wrap up the meeting, and busied herself with organizing the bulging folders in her bag. "We got a lot done today, Winnie, and are on schedule. I'll see you at the bakery for cake tasting next week."

Winnie looked back at the invites. "Are you sure the eggshell isn't more classic? Do you think I should call Sophia?"

She lowered her voice as if they were conspiring. "The eggshell is classic, but a touch boring. You are unique, which screams butter. And personally, I think Sophia will love to be surprised."

Winnie puffed up. "Yes, I guess I am unique! And you're probably right about Sophia, she hates being accosted with too many details. Oh, I'm so glad this is behind me! I'm literally exhausted, and I'm out all the time doing bridal planning."

Bella tried not to wince since she was doing the majority of the planning but kept her smile. "Just remember I'm here to do anything you need. Let me walk you to your car."

Winnie chatted nonstop regarding the shoes and whether she should purchase specialized slippers as a backup, keeping her another ten minutes. By the time she pulled away from the curb, Bella wanted to weep with relief.

It had been a week since her talk with Gabe, and every cell in her being missed him. He'd given her the space she needed and hadn't been in her bed. At the morning meeting, he didn't treat her with any type of resentment or give her the silent treatment. Instead, he greeted her, smiled, listened to the agenda, offered a few comments, and left. There was no sidelong seething look or open pleasure in his dark eyes any longer. No kiss, or hug, or even a brush of his hand against hers. He was completely professional. Just like his old self, before they'd begun a relationship. He'd given her exactly what she needed in order to decide how to move forward.

She hated every second.

The sun shone brightly in the sky, reminding her of the new spring season and the final death knell of winter. Weekends were booked with various weddings and parties, and new clients had poured in after the *Bridal Style* article hit the newsstands. She'd been taking on more responsibility, and Avery had finally hired a new assistant to take Gabe's place, which would help all their workloads. School was nearing an end, and the crazy, chaotic summer neared with the onslaught of tourists, late nights, long hours, and . . . loneliness.

She walked back to the office, her heart heavy. Last summer, she'd watched Avery fall in love with Carter, and Taylor rush headlong into her painting. She'd always felt like the true middle child. Not crazy creative or so passionate about work that it became her main focus. Zoe always tethered her to what was needed and gave her a joy no other person truly could.

Until Gabe.

She liked the woman she was when she was with him—the woman he saw when he looked at her. Her confidence had grown, and sharing the secret part of her along with her sexuality caused her to blossom. Why was it so hard to embrace this relationship 100 percent? Was she truly fearful of all the outside elements threatening them, or did it go even deeper? Was Gabe right when he said she was just waiting for him to fail so she could back away?

She needed to figure stuff out soon. Though she'd begged for time and insisted on moving slowly, he didn't deserve to be kept in limbo while she struggled for answers.

Zoe had asked why he hadn't been over lately, and she'd given work as the easy excuse. But it was obvious her daughter missed his presence, which had become steadier the past month. Bella seemed to hang on the precipice of backing away or leaping in fully with her heart, but the thought of her daughter getting hurt along the way froze her in place. Every decision she made affected both of them. What if the gossip about Gabe didn't stop, and Zoe took the brunt?

Her phone buzzed. Daisy's number flashed on the screen, and she picked it up. "Hey, how are you?"

"Good. Guess what?"

"What?"

"I have a date!" Daisy screeched. "With the guy from the bar. We're going to dinner Friday night."

She grinned, her mood lightening for her friend. "That's great! Do you need me to watch Meg?"

"Nope, already taken care of. My dad wants to take her for a sleepover, so he's picking her up after school. I'm so excited, Bella. I need to go out and get new underwear and Spanx."

She laughed. "Planning on getting to third base already?" she teased.

"Not sure, but if all goes well, some heavy petting is definitely on the schedule. I'll see you at the Lobster House beforehand, right?"

"Oh no, is the kickoff tomorrow?" she asked. It had become tradition to gather for a massive cocktail hour when the weather began getting nice. Most of the town had made it an annual event; everyone would stop by for drinks and to officially close the end of winter. She'd totally forgotten about it.

"Yes, and don't even think of getting out of it. I need you for moral support before my date."

"Okay, I'll be there. Zoe has a pizza party, so I can swing by and pick her up afterward."

"Perfect. How's everything going? Still hot and heavy with Gabe?"

She hesitated. She hadn't confronted her friend since the PTO disaster, and after her discussion with Gabe, she'd decided to keep things quiet until she made a decision. "We're sorting some things out," she said carefully. "But I'm okay."

Her friend sighed. "Oh, Bella, I hope he didn't screw with you 'cause I'll kill him myself. Was it the Devon thing?"

She jerked as if slapped. "No, that was all false. Is everyone still talking about it?"

"Kind of. I wasn't sure what to believe, though. Listen, I gotta get back to work, but I'll call you tonight so we can talk. I'm here for you."

"Thanks." She hung up with heavy trepidation. Her love life was being talked about and dissected by everyone, and she hated it. Would it always be like this? And if so, was she strong enough not to care in order to have Gabe?

She pushed the questions out of her mind and focused on work. Jessica, the receptionist, seemed to be overwhelmed today, juggling nonstop ringing phones and enough walk-ins to throw her usual organization off-kilter. Bella popped her head out. "Jess, did you eat yet?"

The young redhead shook her head. "No time. Man, that article really pumped up business!"

She laughed. "It's a good and bad thing. You're doing great—why don't you put the voice mail on and head out? I'll be here if any emergencies pop up."

She gave a relieved sigh. "Thanks, Bella, I just need some fresh air."

"Shoo, I got this."

The girl grabbed her purse, jumped up, and took a few steps when the phone began shrieking.

"Go," Bella said with a wave.

The door slammed.

She grinned and scooped up the phone. "Sunshine Bridal."

A cultured feminine voice came on the line. "Can I speak with Gabe Garcia, please?"

"I'm sorry, he's not here. Can I take a message?"

"Yes, thank you. This is Melody at Endless Vows Bridal calling to check in. We had an interview with him last Wednesday and wanted to touch base. We're hoping he's decided to take the position."

Ice trickled down her spine. She tried desperately to sound calm and professional. "Of course. Let me take your number, and I'll have him get right back to you."

"Wonderful. And you can tell him not to worry about references at this point."

"I'll do that."

She jotted down Melody's name and number, her fingers trembling around the pencil. When she hung up, her entire body locked up, as if trying to defend against an intruder. All her secret fears and suspicions burst forth in a tsunami of emotion.

He was going to leave.

Just like she'd always believed.

She stumbled back into the conference room, the receptionist desk forgotten. Wringing her fingers, she wondered if Avery suspected or if anyone knew. Had he told Carter or Pierce? Had he been planning to look for another job the whole time, or had she pushed him away?

He'd promised to give her time. Promised he cared about her and Zoe and had no intention of leaving. God, what if she'd taken too long to make her decision, and he figured he'd cut his losses?

Her stomach lurched. Gabe had told her he didn't like being a number in a big-city firm. Maybe this position was too good to pass up. Could she really blame him for taking on a job that would give him more money and prestige?

Yes. Because he'd kept reassuring her he was happy in Cape May and at Sunshine Bridal.

Bella picked up her phone to call him, then slowly placed it back down. She wouldn't say a word. She'd wait and see when he felt it was time to tell her and hear what he had to say. She'd be calm and listen to all the good reasons he needed to leave them all behind.

She stared out the window and chided herself for being so shocked. In a way, this was all her fault. All her fears and doubts had come true, and now Zoe and her family would be devastated. After all this time, hadn't she learned her lesson?

Everyone always leaves.

Chapter Twenty-One

When Bella reached the Lobster House the next evening, the outside bar was jammed.

The restaurant was an icon in Cape May, and during high season, people packed the open decks that held dozens of wooden picnic tables overlooking the water, feasting on buckets of oysters, shrimp, and lobster. Two outside bars added to the party atmosphere, and when ordering food for takeout, groups would linger over a specialty cocktail while waiting.

The weather cooperated with happy sunshine and a playful breeze. She stopped to chat with a few people before ordering a tequila sunrise—the drink special of the day—and took a deep breath of the salty ocean air. She'd been tempted to cancel, sick about seeing Gabe, but she refused to cower and hide. He owed her the truth—face-to-face. For now, she'd try to celebrate spring and reconnect with the people she cared about.

She waved Taylor over, who was the easiest to spot with her pink hair and diamond nose ring catching the light.

"Hey, glad you made it. Do you know if Avery and Carter are coming?"

"Avery's got a rehearsal dinner, so she's doing a stopover with Carter. Where's Pierce?"

"He's coming with Gabe." Taylor regarded her with narrowed suspicion. "Speaking of which—why are you not here with him? I haven't noticed his car parked by the curb this week. Something up?"

She looked away, not wanting to say anything. "Sorting stuff out, I guess."

Usually, her youngest sister backed way off. Her respect for privacy was legendary, so Bella was surprised when a frown creased her brow. "That doesn't sound good. I heard gossip in town, but I know it's not true."

"About work?" she asked, wondering if she wasn't the only one who knew about his big offer in New York.

"No. About Devon."

Irritation hit. She was getting sick of the Devon thing still going on. "Yeah, I know. Let's not talk about it, okay?"

Taylor opened her mouth to say something, but Daisy interrupted just in time. "Hey, gorgeous babes! Happy almost summer!" She laughed and clinked her glass to theirs, her copper hair turning to fire under the light. "How's it going?"

Taylor smiled. "Good. Heard you have a hot date."

Daisy rolled her eyes. "Lord, I just told Bella, but I guess my dry spell around here is legendary. Even my dad congratulated me and took Meg for the night. Nothing like getting a thumbs-up from your own father to get frisky."

They laughed. "Where is he?" Bella asked.

"Should be here soon. How's wedding season? Any fun disasters to entertain me with yet?"

"Would you believe it's been pretty easy lately?" Taylor said. "I haven't had a PITA in a while. Which means I'll be due soon for a doozy."

"Speak for yourself," Bella said. "I had an appointment with Winifred today."

Taylor winced. "The whiner and codependent?"

"Yep. Her partner, Sophia, is such a sweetheart, but she took herself completely out of the planning. How am I going to deal with six more months of this?"

"Get help?" Daisy suggested. "I'm sure your sister or Gabe can take the brunt."

Taylor snorted. "As if. Bella's the best to handle the difficult couples, anyway. She's able to translate a calm focus everyone can relate to. It's a gift."

She stared at Taylor in surprise. "I thought that was Avery."

"Avery is a driving force of energy and the backbone of Sunshine. But you? I think you've always been the heart."

She shared a glance with Daisy, whose mouth dropped slightly open at the compliment. "That was really nice," Daisy said. "And I agree."

Taylor shrugged. "I can be nice sometimes. No one gives me enough credit."

They laughed. A few minutes later, Daisy was tapped on the shoulder.

"Hello," Andrew said. Her date from the bar looked fresh in the light, with a simple white T-shirt and khakis. His slightly curly blond hair gave him a touch of a pretty-boy look, which Daisy adored. Bella watched her friend light up and hoped he'd be good for her. It had been a long time since she'd allowed herself to go out on a date—she was just as overprotective of Meg as Bella was of Zoe.

"Hi, Andrew." They did an awkward half hug, but they both laughed, easing the tension. "You remember Bella, and this is her sister, Taylor."

He shook their hands. "Nice to see you again, Bella. Nice to meet you, Taylor. Can I get you ladies another drink?"

Everyone declined, and they fell into casual chatter. A bunch of PTO moms caught sight of Daisy and rushed over, probably to get a handle on the new hot guy she'd seemed to lasso. Before long, the circle had grown bigger, and soon Bella caught sight of Avery, Carter, Pierce, and Gabe as they headed over.

Her heart thundered, and the boat deck rocked under her feet, throwing her off-balance. God, he was beautiful. He must've had a consultation, since he was in his suit, but he'd taken off the jacket and had rolled up the crisp white shirtsleeves to his elbows. He walked toward her, coal-black hair tossed in the wind, his overwhelming grace and sexuality stealing the very breath in her lungs.

But it was the look in his soot-colored eyes that made her knees want to buckle. They pierced hers, holding her hostage, pretending his heart was all hers.

Lie.

Avery handed her another drink. "I have one whole hour to cut loose before going back to work." In an obvious good mood, she wound her arm around Carter's neck. "Wanna get crazy with me, babe?"

He laughed and pulled her into his side. "Not before you need to juggle the Baker family. You'll need all your brain cells to get through that war zone. Hidden bombs everywhere."

Pierce shuddered and grabbed his beer. "I'm dreading tomorrow's wedding. They want a video, and I'm thinking nothing about this crazy family should be immortalized. They've had blowups in my office regarding the photo packages."

Avery winced. "They are a bit temperamental. And we're meeting the whole crew tonight. The MOG has been married three times, the FOG twice, and the FOB has four stepchildren, all pissed that he paid for his daughter's entire wedding. I expect fireworks. It will be a good test for Nora."

Gabe nodded. "She seems to be doing great so far. Avery finally found someone who loves color-coded tabs and Excel sheets as much as she does."

"I'll still miss you the most," she said, blowing air kisses at Gabe.

Pierce groaned. "You two are weirdly affectionate. No wonder Carter thought you were banging each other."

Taylor snorted. "I didn't know that!"

Gabe cracked up and pointed at Carter. "Damn, he's actually blushing. It still gets him irritated to hear he was intimidated by me."

"Shut up," Carter growled, grabbing Avery. "Come on, baby, let's go mingle."

"We'll come with you," Pierce announced.

Bella turned to head toward the big circle of laughing, chattering locals, but Gabe reached out to encircle her wrist. "Can we talk?" he asked quietly.

She jerked in his grasp, her body already piqued and ready to play. He'd made sure the physical bond was strong between them, wringing out endless orgasms and holding her tight in his arms until she'd believed it was all real.

The anger hit, and she tilted her chin up, nailing him with her gaze. "Do you have something to tell me?" she said, ready for the confrontation.

"Yeah."

She squared her shoulders. "What?"

"I missed you." His face revealed the familiar fierce hunger he'd been so careful to mask lately. "I've been hoping you had enough time to think. About us."

The breath exploded out of her lungs. "I've been doing nothing but thinking lately," she said coldly.

He flinched. "What's wrong?"

"Let's just say I'm finally facing the truth about everything. Especially us."

He leaned in to speak, but her name echoed across the boat. "Bella! Get your ass over here!"

With one last pointed look, she turned her back on him and headed over to Daisy. Trying to calm her shaking limbs, she lost herself in the big group, where everyone was loudly interacting, sipping cocktails, and picking on pails of peel-and-eat shrimp set out around the various tables.

Gabe eventually made his way over and stood beside her, stiff and quiet.

Andrew approached with Daisy. "Sorry, I don't think we met?" he asked Gabe, leaning over to shake his hand. "I'm Andrew."

"Gabe."

"Oh, you work with Bella?"

Daisy cocked her head in anticipation, as if she were expecting Bella to jump in and correct him or explain they were dating, but she fell silent after glancing back and forth between them. An awkward silence descended as Andrew waited for the answer.

"Yes," Gabe finally said.

Bella remained silent, too overwhelmed by the shaky anger inside, bursting to get out. If they were really involved in a relationship, he would've told her about the job. He deserved to feel rejected.

Just like her.

Daisy cleared her throat. "Bella, Gabe, Avery, and Taylor all work at Sunshine Bridal. They're a pretty big deal and even got written up in some big magazines."

"Cool," Andrew said.

Bella jerked as she caught the look on Gabe's face. A twist of pain and betrayal. His lips tightened, and he held his shoulders stiff, as if trying hard not to show how badly her silence had affected him.

Well, what had he expected? Why wouldn't he tell her the truth? Did she owe him anything at this point?

"Excuse me," Gabe said politely. He stepped away from the circle, walking across the deck while some more PTO moms drifted over to socialize. Bella tried to concentrate on the lively conversation, but Gabe's face haunted her.

She needed to find him and talk.

She crossed the room, looking, but didn't see him. She tapped Avery on the shoulder. "Have you seen Gabe?"

"He just left. Said something came up—everything okay?"

"Yeah, thanks."

She raced off the boat and through the exit. She caught the sight of his lone figure heading to his car in the lot and called out his name. He waited for her, but when she reached him, his expression stopped her cold.

It was barren. Closed off. The usual light and pleasure in his gaze were now replaced by stone-cold resolution.

"Do you need something?"

She swallowed and hugged herself for warmth. "I'm sorry. I wanted to talk."

He stared at her for a long time and then shook his head. A humorless laugh escaped his lips. "I'm sorry, too. For not realizing how hard this is for you."

Her heart slammed against her chest. "It's not. I was just angry and trying to get back at you."

"Why?"

The hurt ripped through her. "You lied to me. Endless Vows called. They said you'd interviewed for a position and they hadn't heard back from you."

He muttered a curse, then rubbed his head in frustration. "Dammit, I should've known they'd call. Palmer's a smart SOB, and he wanted to make sure my current job knew I'd interviewed."

A bitter laugh escaped. "Oh, so that's the only thing you're worried about? That your dirty little secret got spilled before you could tell us?"

"No. I was going to tell you, but much later. There was no reason to confuse us any further."

Her jaw dropped. "Are you kidding me? Am I someone you now try to handle to have the least amount of messiness? How dare you do this to my family? My sisters trusted you—if you were so intent on going to some big-time company for money and glory, you could've warned us. Don't you feel you owe us anything?"

"Bella, you don't understand. I was never looking to leave. I got a call that the CEO wanted to interview me, and yeah, I felt like I owed it to myself to hear what he wanted. But I was never going to take the job. I love my work, and I love Cape May, and I love—" He stopped, his face a hard mask, emotions ruthlessly banked between that icy wall.

He loved her.

The unspoken statement ripped through her. What was happening? She'd been so sure of his intentions.

He cleared his throat and continued, "When did you get the call?"

"Yesterday."

"And you didn't think to ask me right away? You waited until we were in a public place to finally show me you'll never be ready for this relationship?"

She jerked back. "No! How do you think it felt to hear you were pursuing a job that would take you away after all of your declarations? I have a daughter to protect. This isn't about just me, Gabe. You have the power to hurt Zoe in ways that you'll never understand."

His features softened with regret. "I'm sorry. I'd never hurt Zoe, or you, or your family. You mean too much to me. I didn't want to tell you I'd turned down a job when you were trying to figure things out about us. I thought it would only muddy the issue. The job means nothing to me. The only thing I want, and have ever wanted, is you."

Her legs shook, and the truth of his words crashed into her. She took a step forward, but he kept speaking. "But you already know that, Bella. You must. I've been telling you my feelings from the beginning, waiting for you to catch up. But tonight, I realized I'm not the right man for you—I've just been too damn pigheaded to accept it."

Panic nipped. What was happening? How had everything been suddenly flipped around?

"You've been looking for an excuse to pull away since the beginning. First it was Marlaine, then Devon, now the job. It's the gossip at the PTO and the way this town makes you feel because you're dating me. It's how you'd rather be dating someone other than the crowned beach bachelor." His face broke, and she caught a glimpse of a deep pain that tore her apart. "You need someone you can be proud to be with, and I need a woman who accepts all of me, no matter what the world tells her."

She shook her head. "No, I don't want another man. And God, yes, I'm proud of you—I just got confused," she whispered. Tears stung her eyes. "I don't want to lose you."

His smile was heartbreakingly sad and final. "We were never each other's to lose. Not yet. I love you. I will always love you, but I can't keep doing this."

"Gabe—" She was breaking apart. She took a step forward, desperate to touch him, but he remained stiff and unyielding.

"Do you know what it feels like to want someone to love you so badly, you'd do anything? Change who you are, make compromises, live on hope even when the reality reminds you you'll never be enough?"

"I didn't want to do that to you," she whispered in horror, wringing her hands together.

"You didn't. I did that, Bella. By placing unfair expectations on you and not remembering my promise. See, after my father, I swore I wouldn't settle for anything less than someone who truly saw me—the whole me, good and bad, right and wrong, and all the mess in between. It's a lot to ask someone, though, and I want so much more than you can give." He leaned down and pressed a gentle kiss to her lips. "I gotta go. I hope you find what you need. We'll be okay—it'll be hard for a while, but I care about you, and we'll find a balance eventually. Right now, though, I need some time alone."

She watched him leave, frozen in place. Tears ran down her cheeks. Agony tore through her. Yet she didn't go after him.

She'd managed to hurt the only man who'd begun to heal her and teach her about real happiness.

She'd managed to lose the man she'd fallen in love with.

Chapter Twenty-Two

The knock on the door surprised him. At first, his entire body clenched with anticipation, hoping and dreading to see Bella at his door. If she apologized again and tried to get him back, was he strong enough to say no?

Relief and disappointment merged at seeing his guests. Pierce and Carter stood at the door with a bottle of tequila, a bag of limes, and a gallon of cookies 'n cream ice cream. "You gotta be kidding me," he said, shaking his head. "What are you doing here?"

"Chicks don't get to claim the entire market on heartbreak," Carter said.

"Yeah, dudes feel shit, too. We're here to help," Pierce said.

Torn between laughter and the awful threat of sentiment, he went with the former. "Get your asses in here. Who told you?"

They came in and dumped the stuff on the table. Pierce got busy grabbing glasses, and Carter began dishing out ice cream.

"No one," Pierce said. "But I saw you fly out of the Lobster House looking sick, and no one's heard from you for the past week."

Carter dumped some spoons out and dispersed. "Avery said Bella's working around the clock, taking a bunch of Taylor's appointments and shutting herself in the house with excuses. It screams of a bad break."

Pierce cut the limes and dumped them in with the tequila. "Look, you don't have to tell us anything. We just want you to know we got your back, and if it hurts, get drunk. It's always better in the morning."

He gave a strangled laugh but took the liquor. "Something sounds a bit screwy with that statement, but I don't really care. I think I needed this tonight. Thanks."

They lifted their glasses silently, inclined their heads, and drained them in one gulp. Then they sat down at the table and dug into their ice cream.

"Do you want to talk about it?" Pierce finally asked.

"Nah," Gabe said. "I want to talk about stupid stuff and eat my ice cream."

"Done," Carter said. "Did you see the last episode of *The Curse of Oak Island*? Son of a bitch—I think they may find the treasure."

Pierce cut a hand in the air. "Nah, it's fixed. It's been on too many seasons, and the narrator is always getting excited. I'm afraid it's a setup."

Gabe considered it, scooping up a particularly large chunk of cookie. "I think at first they thought they'd find the treasure, but after so many seasons, they're trying not to look stupid now. Or maybe they just want to live like the characters in *National Treasure*. I should've been an archaeologist rather than a wedding planner. I may have had a better life."

Carter refilled their glasses. "I don't think Indiana Jones had it easy. Sure, he got to seduce a bunch of women, but most of them betrayed him. Plus, he had huge issues with his dad."

"So did I," Gabe said. "My father was a prick."

Pierce raised his brow. "No shit? I didn't realize that. Sorry, man."

"It's okay. He was always calling me pretty boy and saying I'd never be successful without using my looks. No matter how hard I tried, he just didn't like me, let alone love me."

Carter winced. "That's harsh. His loss. Not to get mushy, but you've become one of my best friends, and I don't bring people in lightly. As for work? I mean, you're a good-looking dude, but it's obvious you have an amazing talent. Otherwise Avery wouldn't have kept you on so long and promoted you. She even mentioned she wants to offer you partner down the line."

"That's good to know." He took another shot. *Hmm.* He was starting to like the ice cream and tequila together—it was more complementary than he'd originally thought. "What sucks is that I thought Bella was the woman I was going to marry. I know it sounds pathetic, but the moment I met her, I got this gut instinct like I knew I'd met my future wife. Took us all this time to finally connect, and now it's gone forever. I'll have to watch her marry someone else one day who will be a dad to Zoe." He looked up from his empty bowl. "I'm depressed."

Pierce poured him another shot. "Sucks. You sure you both can't work it out? I've known Bella a long time, and I've never seen her so happy. Taylor said the same thing. It was like a light went on inside her that had been dim. We'd all begun to wonder if she could feel the same way about anyone but Matt."

The image of her beautiful face floated in his mind. He braced himself for the slap of pain that followed. "It was too much for her," he finally muttered. "All the crap publicity around me. The gossip. But the bottom line? She's not able to let go of everything and dig into a relationship with me." He quickly filled them in on his job interview and their talk in the parking lot.

Both of them winced. "Ouch," Carter said. "Didn't know about any of that."

"I know she was upset, thinking I was going to take that job and leave. But knowing she wouldn't have even tried to call me and talk? It's the same thing she did every time she heard a woman's name brought up. I can't keep going around like a lost puppy dog in love with her while she struggles to figure stuff out."

"You're gonna hate what I have to say, dude," Pierce finally said. "But this is a classic 'It's her, not you' scenario. Maybe you scared the crap out of her 'cause her last husband died and left. That screwed her up for a while. She may need to figure out if she really wants to take another risk on love."

"Agreed," Carter said. "Also, even though you love her, she may not have made you happy. Not if you were always going to deal with her constant doubts about you. You deserve more. I hope you know that."

The truth of his friends' words hit him and eased some of the rawness. They were right. As badly as he'd wanted Bella, he couldn't go back to the person he'd been around his father, chasing someone's approval and love. It was time to truly let the past go and seize on a future that could make him happy.

"Thanks, guys. Appreciate you trying to get my head right."

"Will you think about taking that job now?" Pierce asked curiously. "Now that it's over between you both?"

Gabe had obsessed over the question all week. Signs seemed to point toward building a new life away from Bella and the small town that could be restricting his opportunities. But one morning, as he'd sat by the ocean and pondered his future, picturing himself working and living in a fast-paced environment again, the answer came from deep within. A peace that told him as bad as things were right now, he was already home.

He loved working for Sunshine Bridal, where he was looked upon as family rather than a sales check. The beach had soothed his soul, until sand under his feet became a vital piece of home. He loved dealing with small-town vendors and going into a restaurant where people greeted him with affection. Yes, it was also maddening sometimes, but when he thought of leaving, his heart rebelled. Over the past three years, Cape May had become part of him.

His fingers tightened around the glass. "I should. It's more money. I'd get to lead my own team. I wouldn't have to worry about small-town gossip, or be stuck working with a woman I'll probably always love who doesn't love me."

His friends stared at him. "Will you?" Pierce asked again.

He gave a long sigh. "Nah. I'd rather stay here, where I belong."

Carter punched his arm in male comradery. "Good. 'Cause we'd miss you too much, dude. Who'd be our third? A group needs at least three people, and I don't like anybody else."

"Is it okay to say I love you guys?" Gabe asked.

"Only if we're drinking."

Carter poured a few more fingers of tequila, and Gabe drank, feeling grateful for good friends.

♥ ♥ ♥

Bella heard her name, but she was deep into her closet project. She currently had every pair of shoes pulled out, along with every coat, loose scarf, pair of gloves, hat, and dress jacket. They lay in a heap on her bed, sorted into piles of keep, trash, and donate.

"In here!" she called out. Next up were her drawers, then the pantry, and her bathroom vanity would be the finale. She hadn't spring-cleaned in way too long, and it was time to get the place completely immaculate.

Taylor peeked her head in. "What's going on?"

"Spring-cleaning," she said, lifting up a red ankle boot with a large gold buckle. "Do you want these?"

Her sister wrinkled her nose. "Hell no. They're old and look like they're from the nineties. I wear combat boots."

Bella threw it into the donate pile. "What do you need?"

"To talk. Where's Zoe?"

"Playing in her room. We're going out for dinner later. Wanna come?"

"Nope, got a date."

A sliver of jealousy pierced her heart. "Good for you."

"We'll probably have amazing, mind-blowing sex later," she continued. "It feels good to cuddle with a man sometimes, doesn't it?"

The memory of Gabe surging inside her, gaze locked on hers, fingers interwoven while he took her to orgasm, crashed into her mind. She jerked, rubbing a fist over her eyes in an attempt to ward off the agony. "Sure. Have fun."

"Miss Gabe, huh?"

She let out a shocked gasp. "You did that on purpose! Why are you needling me? Is that why you're here—to stick your nose in my business just so you can sleep better at night?"

Taylor sat down on the bed. "Yeah. Tell me everything."

She glared at her sister. "At least Avery respected my privacy. I told you both it didn't work out, and we were just taking some time apart to deal with it. No big deal."

Taylor snorted and crossed her legs, like she was settling in for a good campfire story. "Liar. I gotta admit, you threw me on this one. Usually, you're the calm one, and sure, you like your privacy, but you've never shut us both out like this before. Not since Matt died."

Bella winced. For months, her sisters had desperately tried to reach her, but she'd shut herself into a deep, dark, silent hole where nothing could touch her. "That was different," she said stiffly. "This is just a breakup. I'm sure everyone knew it wouldn't work out anyway. I mean, look at us."

"I did. Gabe was your perfect match, and I think you screwed it up. I've been watching you guys for a while and trying to respect your space, but I can't let my sister lose the best thing that's happened to her. God, now I sound all dramatic and crap, like Avery. See what you're making me do?"

She rolled her eyes at her sister's words. "Oh, so you're coming to my rescue? A few relevant insights, and I'll change my mind and our relationship will be repaired, huh?"

"Hopefully. First up, what initiated the breakup?"

She was tempted to tell her to go away and keep her mess locked up tight, but Taylor seemed to genuinely care, and suddenly the invitation to share her heartache shook through her. A shaky breath escaped her lips. "I screwed up, T."

"It's okay, babe. Tell me."

She did. She went over the stuff with Devon, the PTO, what Zoe had heard about Gabe, how she'd intercepted the call from Endless Vows, and what he'd told her outside the bar. When she was finished, she felt a bit lighter inside and had to remind herself it was important for her to lean on the people she loved.

"I see where Gabe is coming from," Taylor said slowly. "But I'm more interested in you. Do you love him?"

For so long, she'd avoided the question even from herself. But now she just spoke from her heart. "Yes. He fills me up, T. It's so much more than sex, though that's beyond perfection. It's the way he listens to me and makes me feel good about myself. How he treats Zoe and seems to want to be part of our family. It all snuck up on me, and when he confessed his real feelings, I finally experienced all these emotions I thought I'd shut down after Matt. But I kept having so many doubts. I was sure he was going to leave and take that job, and now I've made the biggest mistake of my life."

"Why was it so easy to believe everyone else except Gabe?"

Startled, she stared at her sister. "I don't know, it all seemed to fit."

Taylor nodded thoughtfully. "It's interesting, you seem to make choices based on everyone else's opinions. I remember you told me once you worried about being judged if you went out too much because you were a single mom."

"That could have happened!"

"Yep. But does it really matter, if that would make you happy? I think you stopped asking what *you* wanted, because you always worry about everybody else. Aren't you tired of trying to please everyone except yourself?"

The memory of her conversation with Gabe during their car trip slammed through her. He'd asked if she was happy in Cape May and at Sunshine Bridal. Instead of answering yes, she'd given him all the excuses of why she was stuck.

"But maybe instead of feeling trapped in a life, you should choose to make it what you want."

Is that what she'd been doing? Making choices based on other people's opinions? "I'm so confused," she murmured.

"What are you really afraid of, Bella?"

She buried her face in her hands. "Not being enough for him. What if I gave him everything I had, along with my daughter, and he gets bored or interested in someone else, and we're left behind?"

"Or what if he dies like Matt did?"

She flinched, staring at her sister with betrayal. "How can you say something like that?" she hissed, anger shaking through her. "Why do you have to be so cruel?"

"I'm not. I'm just stating the facts. Matt was the love of your life, and he was killed. No one will ever know what type of pain you went through—it's something you can only experience and get to the other side to really understand. You're full of excuses about Gabe's reputation and how you're desperate to protect your daughter in case he leaves for bigger and better things. But I think it's time you admit, at least to yourself, you're really afraid Gabe can be taken away at any time and you won't be able to handle it again."

Shock barreled through her. Hot denials rose to her lips, then died. She took her sister's words and flipped them over in her mind, pulling their meaning and how she felt about the accusation apart.

Then realized Taylor was right.

Losing Matt had almost broken her. Zoe was the fragile thread that kept her sane and pushing forward. The idea of going through that type of pain if Gabe either walked away or was taken in a tragedy haunted her. She'd never be able to do it twice. Wasn't it almost easier to take the pain now and avoid a love that deep? A love that could wreck her very world and tear her soul apart?

She'd become a woman afraid of trusting her heart and afraid of making her own choices, and God, she was so tired of questioning herself, worried that she might never be enough for Gabe. Her emotions crashed down and exploded from her. Tears leaked from her eyes, and her body shook as she bowed her head and wept. Taylor came over and pulled her into a tight, hard hug. Her sister let her cry for a while, not saying a word, and when she was done, she took both her hands and squeezed.

"Listen to me, Bella. This is important. You have to stop settling for half a life out of stupid fear and decide to grasp what you want, even if it scares the shit out of you. Love is awful. But will the unknown ever stop you from loving Zoe, or me, or Avery, or Mom and Dad?"

She shook her head. "No."

"Exactly. Gabe is the same way, but this time, you get to choose, which is more powerful. You will never be the same person you were before you lost your husband. No one expects you to. But don't you dare hide behind excuses about gossip and age and a bunch of other stuff that doesn't matter. I've seen the way that man looks at you—like you're his damn sun, moon, and stars. Are you going to give that up for what-ifs?"

It was like the fog lifted, and she suddenly saw things the way Taylor did. The way she'd stacked her barriers to keep him out, rationalizing her excuses so they made perfect sense. Dear God, what had she done?

Had she lost him for good?

"You're right," she whispered. "What am I going to do, T? Should I try to talk to him? At this point, I don't know if he'll believe me."

"Hmm, I don't know. I mean, Avery would tell you conversation and communication is key. I'd tell you use sex to apologize and make him forget. But something's telling me you need to make a statement in a big way for him to truly believe you're all in."

Suddenly, she heard Avery's voice floating up the stairs.

"In here!" they both screamed together.

Avery walked in, looking at the explosion of stuff strewn around. "What's going on? Spring-cleaning? Oh, cool boots—can I have them?"

Taylor snickered. "I knew you'd take them."

Avery stuck out her tongue and flopped on the bed with them. She studied Bella's face with a worried frown. "Have you been crying? Did Taylor say something to piss you off?"

"I'm always the one to blame around here," Taylor grumbled.

Bella swiped at her eyes. "We were just talking about stuff."

"Okay, I've been meaning to ask you about what's going on, but I didn't want to pry. But I think it's time you open up. Oh, BTW, that stupid article in *Exit Zero* is running soon. I tried to help Gabe kill the story, but Michelle is claiming it's news." She shook her head with annoyance. "It's ridiculous—I told her it was bad for business, but she insisted all news is good PR. Hey, wanna go out for dinner? Where's Zoe?"

"Playing in her room," Taylor said. "I'm getting laid. But Bella and Zoe are going out to eat later."

"Good. Now, what's wrong. Can I help with something?"

And just like that, the lightbulb went on.

A big statement.

Beach Bachelor of the Year.

A way to prove she was all in.

"Oh my God, I know!" Bella said, scrambling off the bed. "Can you watch Zoe? I have to go into town real quick and do something. T—can you let her know what's going on?"

Avery gasped. "Wait! Taylor knows and I don't? What's that about?"

Taylor tossed her a smug look. "Maybe Bella and I are tighter than you know. Maybe she comes to me for all the advice now. What do you think of that, Miss Smarty Pants?"

"Don't fight!" Bella called out. "I'll be back!"

She had a man to claim.

Chapter Twenty-Three

Bella twisted her fingers and looked at the calendar.

Tomorrow, she'd know.

Nerves gathered in her belly, but they were entangled with a sense of satisfaction. For the past few days, she'd been journaling and really looking at her life from a fresh viewpoint. More and more, she realized how many times she'd been passive in a way to feel in control. Funny how losing Gabe had finally led to her greatest lesson of all.

Control was simply an illusion. No one knew what would happen in the future. It was today that was important. And she realized it was up to her to make the changes she wanted.

Taking a deep breath, she picked up the phone and dialed Daisy's number. Her friend immediately picked up. "Hey, girl. How are things?"

"Good. How about you? How's Andrew?"

Her friend actually giggled. "Really good. We're going out again this weekend. He's such a nice guy, Bella! But I'm taking it real slow and just enjoying his company. No talk about what it is or trying to analyze things. That always gets me in trouble."

"Ditto. I'm so happy for you. Listen, I wanted to talk to you about something important. Do you have a minute?"

"Sure. Hit me with it."

"It's about Gabe."

"Oooh, are you guys back together? Friends with benefits? Or did he do something to piss you off, which means I'll have to break his kneecaps or hire someone?"

"No, none of that. But I've noticed when we were dating, I wasn't really truthful with you, or myself. And even worse? I let other people guide me on what to think. Especially you."

Daisy's voice sharpened with worry. "Are you mad at me for something?"

"No, babe. I'm mad at myself, but I'm trying to make some changes. You see, I'm in love with Gabe. It's not his body or his hotness—it's his heart. I tried to tell you we were in a relationship, but I know you never really believed it, and I never tried to really talk to you about it. I screwed up, Daisy. So bad I lost the one man who can love me the way I was meant to be loved."

"Back up. I think you need to tell me all of it."

She did. She shared how their relationship had developed over time, her fears and doubts, and finally gave her friend what she should have from the beginning.

The truth.

"I'm so sorry, I didn't know," Daisy finally said.

"I know, and that's on me."

"So what happens now? Are you going to try to get Gabe back? Can I help?"

She told her friend what she had done, and silence came over the line. "Is it stupid?"

"No, it's brilliant. And it's going to be okay, no matter what happens. I really wish I'd known how you were struggling. You've always been my best friend, and I want to be here for you, like you are for me."

"I know. I'm tired of locking up all my problems and keeping them to myself. I'll try to do better."

"I'll try to listen better. And if anyone says a word about Gabe, I'll shut them up good."

She laughed, her heart lighter. "Thanks, Daisy. Love you."

"Love you, too."

She hung up and tried to feel hopeful, even though she knew it might still be too late. Either way, she wasn't going back to the scared, passive woman who let others dictate her life.

This time, she was going to fight for what she wanted.

♥ ♥ ♥

Gabe headed down Ocean Drive and tried to get his happy on. He had a bride who was counting on him to bring it big, and he didn't want to disappoint her. It'd been a rough week, but he was determined to claw his way back to some sort of contentment, even if it took gallons of cookies 'n cream and pints of tequila.

He winced at the memory. Not the best morning after, that's for sure. They'd all fallen asleep at his house, nursing wicked hangovers and a sugar high. They'd agreed for the night to be just like Fight Club.

No one would hear about it.

He stopped at the Bagel Time Cafe to grab lunch and go over his packed schedule for the weekend. As he got in line, he nodded at a few locals amid the tourists, wondering why they were staring at him and smiling like they knew something he didn't. When he got to the counter to order his turkey club, Christina leaned forward, her ponytail bobbing with enthusiasm.

"Oh my gosh, Gabe, I saw the piece in *Exit Zero*. It's so good!"

Ah, crap. He'd forgotten the magazine had hit stands today. Great, no wonder everyone was staring. Gossip would relaunch, and he'd be ogled and approached for endless dates like the stud he wasn't. Could his week get any worse?

He forced a smile. "Thanks. I'll wait over here."

He stepped to the side, scrolling through his phone, and glanced over. Justin from Louie's Pizza and Ron from the police department were eating lunch. When he caught their eye, they gave him a thumbs-up, pointing to their copy of *Exit Zero*.

He was going to lose his shit.

He finally got his lunch and hit his other two meetings, where more people commented on the "great" article and congratulated him with sly winks and grins. He was just deciding to sue the magazine for mental anguish when he ran into Devon.

Yep. Things could get worse.

"Hey, stranger. I read the article. I'm really happy for you," she said. "Are you still coming tomorrow at three for the Bailey wedding?"

"Yeah. Unless I decide to move and retire to an island where there's no beach bachelor," he said a bit grumpily.

Surprise skittered across her face. "Oh, you didn't like that article? I'm sorry—I thought you were excited about it. It seemed kind of sweet. Not very feminist, I must admit, but even I could forgive the intention."

He scoffed. "Devon, you know I hate that crap. Why would being declared the local beach stud make me anything but embarrassed? I don't even want to talk about it. You should throw it away."

She dug out the magazine from her beach bag, frowning. "Okay, now I'm really confused. You and Bella aren't together anymore?"

"What does Bella have to do with it?"

She stared at him like he was stupid. "Because she's the whole focus of the article. Are we talking about the same one?"

She shoved it into his hands, and he glanced down at the glossy pages. The title hit him first, like a sucker punch to the jaw.

TAKEN! Hands Off My Man, Local Business Owner
Claims. The Beach Bachelor Belongs to Me!

There was a big red *X* over his picture from last year, and next to it was an image of Bella, her gorgeous face staring back at him, smiling like she had a big secret.

His hands shook as he skimmed the article.

It held all the details of their growing relationship. How they had been fighting their attraction at work because they were worried it would ruin their professional relationship. How they had become close friends and finally couldn't fight their feelings for one another. Her frustration about how women seemed to gossip and claimed to have slept with him. How he was the perfect man, work partner, and male mentor for Zoe. And how she loved him and didn't want any woman on the Cape or beyond to think he was up for grabs, because he was hers.

He looked up at Devon.

Her mouth went into a little O. "You didn't know?" she asked.

He shook his head, the ground beneath him suddenly shaky. "I have to go. Mind if I keep this?"

She grinned. "Nope. Go get her, Romeo."

He took off at a dead run.

♥ ♥ ♥

Bella walked into the office and wondered how bad the fallout was going to be.

He hadn't contacted her. The story had hit the stands that morning, and she hadn't received even a text or a question about whether she was stark raving mad. The wait was slowly killing her nerves, so she decided to do some paperwork in a quiet room rather than be out in town. Already, she'd been approached by endless people, congratulating her as if she'd done something amazing rather than declare her love for a man who deserved everything.

She willed her phone to ring. Then decided silence was golden, especially if he'd changed his mind about his feelings for her. Maybe she'd hurt and denied him too many times for him to forgive. She needed to be ready for that.

She'd just opened her laptop when she heard the door fling open and footsteps pound on the floor. When she looked up, Gabe stood in front of her.

Sweat rolled down his forehead. His face was bright red. His shirt clung to him, outlining his lean muscles. He was panting, as if trying to gulp in air, and she jumped from the chair, worried he was about to collapse in front of her. "Are you okay? Do you need water?"

"Holy crap, it's like ninety degrees out there," he gasped, leaning over briefly. "I'm out of shape."

"What are you doing?"

"Needed to see you. Ran all the way from Beach Avenue."

Her eyes widened. "Are you kidding me? That's like fifty blocks—oh my God, sit down." She raced over, grabbing a bottle of water from the refrigerator and pressing it into his hands. "Drink."

He did, gulping down the water, then dropping the bottle beside him. "This isn't the romantic way I wanted things to go down," he said, still fighting for breath. "I wasn't supposed to be a half-dead, sweaty mess when I make my big declaration."

Her heart thundered. She dropped into the seat next to him, scared to ask but more scared not to ask. "Did you read it?"

"Yes. Just now. I was trying to ignore the whole thing and refused to read it, assuming it was the original feature. Then I ran into Devon, and she told me about it."

"Devon?"

"Yeah. Needless to say, I was shocked."

She bit her lip. "Shocked good? Or shocked bad?"

Suddenly, he turned, and there was no barrier between them. His dark eyes gleamed with a steady warmth and a searching question. "Shocked good. Sweetheart, you sure know how to get a man's attention. But did you really mean what you said?"

Hope sprouted. With trembling hands, she reached out. "Yes, all of it. Gabe, I'm so sorry. Sorry about the way I treated you and let my own fears drive me to believe others instead of you. I realize so many things now—how afraid I was about everything. Afraid I'd lose you like Matt. Afraid of living a life I wanted in case it clashed with anyone's judgment or might open me up to another heartbreak. I thought I wanted a safe existence, but I was never really living. Not until you.

"Losing you was losing a part of my heart. You pushed me to be more, want more, and love more. You are a man who deserves a woman who sees your heart and kindness and strength and never doubts you. And though I don't deserve it, I'm asking you for forgiveness." She blinked back the sting of tears. "I'm not afraid anymore. I'm ready to stand by your side, fight for you, treasure you, and make you happy. I'm asking for another chance to love you the way you deserve. Because I do love you, Gabe. With everything I am."

His gaze drilled into hers. For a few heart-stopping moments, he remained still. Then, he pulled her into his lap, cupped her cheeks, and kissed her.

She fell into his arms, and his kiss was like coming home. Clinging hard, she opened her mouth to his thrusting tongue and devoured him whole. Her body wept and sang for joy, as if the last piece of a puzzle had been missing and was finally found.

When he lifted his head, he was smiling. "Bella, I love you. Thank you for trusting me with your heart."

"Thank you for taking such good care of it."

As she stared down into his beloved face, she realized that life might not have just one happily-ever-after ending. Maybe there were many more, hidden in plain sight, but you had to pay attention.

Bella closed her eyes, leaned into her strength, and relished the unseen future.

Epilogue

"Gabe, it's my graduation party!"

He scooped Zoe up and whirled her around while she held tight and laughed hysterically. Her Goldilocks-blonde hair was caught up in a glittery pink bow, and she wore a pink princess gown he'd found in Lynn Arden's Children Shoppe. "You're so grown up now, you'll need to drive yourself to school in first grade!"

"I can't drive yet!" she said, her face screwed up with childlike humor. "I'm too short!"

Bella grinned and pressed a kiss to his lips. "I will not even think about my daughter driving, thank you very much."

"Not even in a very cool pink Jeep you can borrow?" he teased, tucking a wayward curl behind her ear.

"Not even then."

"A real Barbie jeep?" Zoe asked with wide eyes. "Oh, I can't wait to drive!"

"You will someday, sweetheart," he said. "Now go round up your friends—it's almost time for cake."

Zoe tore off across the room.

Bella crossed her arms in front of her chest and gave a mock glare. "Really? A pink Jeep?"

"The Jeep may distract her from the dog. You can thank me later." When she cocked her head in question, he led her to the window and pointed out to the front porch. A giant pink Power Wheels Jeep with a pink bow sat out front, charged up and ready to go. "I couldn't resist. Don't get mad."

Her face softened, and she stroked his cheek, her gaze full of his dreams and his future. "I'm not. I just love you."

"Even if I tell you it has a radio that's pretty loud?"

She laughed, spinning out of his arms and shaking her head. "Even then. I'll get the cake out."

"Love you, too!"

He wondered if this much happiness was legal, then decided he didn't care. The house was filled with giggling, shrieking little girls, Daisy and Andrew, and the rest of the family. He couldn't come up with a better way to spend a Sunday afternoon, which had been carefully blocked on the calendar so none of them had any events to attend.

He grabbed a refill of seltzer and watched Pierce in action. He'd seamlessly integrated himself into the group of girls, and no one seemed to notice him as he caught candid shots of their interactions and scenes at the party. He moved with a subtle grace, chasing light and shadow, working his way across the room.

Suddenly, he straightened and stilled, his head lifted in the air as if scenting prey. Gabe swiveled his gaze around and saw Taylor.

She was sitting under the window, which streamed in rays of bright sunshine. Her nose stud winked, and her sleek pink hair shimmered, giving off a punch of energy she exuded just by walking into a room. She was laughing at something Avery said, head thrown back, her face open and joyous in a glimpse of emotion usually masked under her trademark sarcastic wit and cynicism.

Curious, he watched Pierce stare at her, then slowly pick up the camera and begin catching the moment. He ducked to his knees and moved his body in a graceful dance, as if chasing something only he could see. The bulb flashed. When he uncurled from the floor, a fierce look flickered over Pierce's features as he gazed at Taylor.

Gabe walked over and stood beside him. "Wanna take a break? This isn't a work gig, you know. Have a beer."

Pierce shot him a grin. "Just wanted to grab the opportunity while it's here. I'm making a going-away scrapbook for Taylor as a surprise."

"She'll love it. It's gonna be hard on all of us not having her around, huh?"

His friend avoided his gaze and fiddled with the camera. "Yep. But it's what she's always wanted. She never planned to stay in Cape May like I did. This was just a side road for her."

"Sometimes side roads take you to the most interesting places."

Pierce shot him a look. "What are you now, a philosopher? You fall in love, get the girl, and suddenly you wax poetic?"

Gabe laughed. "Maybe."

Bella's voice rang through the air. "Cake time! Come gather at the table!"

Gabe clapped him on the shoulder. "Let's eat cake."

He walked with his friend to the table, and as they celebrated Zoe's rise to first grade, Gabe treasured every moment around the people he loved. Bella put a few candles on the cake for Zoe to blow out. "Don't forget to make a graduation wish," she said.

Somehow, he'd gotten a happy beginning. The difficult past with his father and the long road to claim Bella's heart seemed critical to get him to appreciate this exact moment. To be with the woman he loved, part of a family, and finally at peace with his doubts. Everyone deserved love and was worthy of it—he knew that now.

As Zoe closed her eyes to make a wish and blow out the candles, he found himself hoping Pierce would get his, too.

ACKNOWLEDGMENTS

A big thank-you to all the usual suspects!

To the amazing team at Montlake for the endless support—Maria Gomez, you are the best, and fingers crossed I'll be able to visit again for one of our famous long lunches! To Kristi Yanta, who always takes my writing to the next level—I'm so glad you're on my team. To my agent, Kevan Lyon, who helps propel me forward with both shrewdness and kindness. To Nina Grinstead at Social Butterfly—I appreciate everything you do to get my books into readers' hands. To my assistant, Mandy Lawler, for keeping it all humming well in the background as I write—I'd be lost without you.

To my husband, who cooks dinner faithfully every night so I can whine and write and make my deadline. To my boys, Jake and Joshua, who actually offer advice when I whine and eventually tell me, "Mom—just go write!"

And as always, to my readers. I hope you're enjoying your time with the Sunshine sisters in Cape May—thank you so much for reading!

ANOTHER SUNSHINE SISTERS STORY BY JENNIFER PROBST

Look for the next installment in the Sunshine Sisters series, *Forever in Cape May*, coming in April 2021.

Editor's Note: This is an early excerpt and may not reflect the finished book.

Prologue

"Dude, that was weird."

Taylor Sunshine and Pierce Powers were lying in her twin bed in the dorm room. The fraternity party had been the usual—loud jocks, giggly girls, and too much alcohol. She'd lost at beer pong—God, that game sucked—and been pretty tipsy when she left. Of course Pierce had spotted her and insisted on walking her back. He'd gotten her to the bed and turned to leave, and her hug/lunge ended up bringing him down on the mattress next to her. After a good laugh, she'd looped her arms around his neck to pull herself up, and he'd leaned closer, and they'd . . .

Kissed.

She'd waited for fireworks and the shattering knowledge that he was the one. Her sister Bella had met the love of her life in junior high and said she'd always known they'd get married. But with Pierce? Other than the softness of his lips and his familiar scent that always comforted rather than aroused, Taylor felt a pleasant hum and then . . . nothing.

He groaned into the red plaid pillow. "This isn't happening. You are not telling me my kissing was weird."

"That's not what I was saying! I said the *kiss* was weird, not your specific kissing style. Did it feel a bit like incest to you, too?"

He let out a noise into the pillowcase and rolled over. "I'm outta here."

"No, I'm sorry." She caught his hand and pulled gently back. "Pierce, stay. The room's still spinny, and I'm afraid I'll get sick."

She refused to feel guilt at his concerned expression. She only reacted on her need to have him close tonight, the boy she'd grown up with and the man who knew her best.

He sat back down with a frown. "Do you need water?"

"Not yet. Look, I attacked you, and it wasn't fair. We swore we wouldn't do that again."

His face tightened with irritation. "We were fifteen, Taylz. It was a miracle we didn't end up playing doctor earlier."

His use of her nickname softened the rough edges of his statement. "That's the point. We both felt nothing back then and promised we wouldn't muck up our relationship with crap like feelings and sex. I'm really sorry. Maybe it's the new cologne you're wearing. I was channeling Beckham."

He laughed, and she relaxed. Thank God she hadn't hurt him. They'd met freshman year in high school when they'd been assigned to be lab partners. He was an A student; she was a C. He'd ended up tutoring her all semester, scared shitless she'd tank his grade, and a friendship immediately bloomed. Other than that one experimental kiss, they'd been best friends who'd had each other's backs, all the way past graduation. She'd gotten accepted into Monmouth, and he attended Montclair a short while away. They'd been able to hang out on a regular basis and keep the same closeness from high school.

"You should be studying poetry, not performance art," he said with a roll of his pale-green eyes. "I swear, you're nothing like the other girls I know. And I'm not sure that's a compliment."

She fluffed up the pillows, leaned back, and motioned him over. "Come sit next to me, and you can insult me all you want. I deserve it for sticking my tongue in your mouth."

"We didn't get that far," he muttered, still obviously annoyed at the whole scene. But he took his place next to her, his arms crossed in front of his chest to make his point.

A relieved sigh ballooned into her lungs and went softly out. Warmth flowed in her veins from the alcohol, and the darkness masked the shabbiness of her tiny, cluttered room. She leaned her head against his broad shoulder, beefed up from lifting weights and boxing, and breathed in the scent of cotton, male sweat, and tequila.

His jean-clad legs were crossed at the ankles. She'd seen a ton of girls checking him out at the party, and she knew he never lacked for a date or anything else he wanted. Pierce was a good-looking guy. She also knew he was good in bed since many of his partners talked—and talked loudly—confiding all the details she didn't want to hear.

Still, she always knew she got the very best of Pierce Powers that no one else could ever claim.

Loyalty. Friendship. Trust.

"You forgive me?" she asked softly, nudging his shoulder. "I'm a bit drunk, and Will just broke up with me. I think I was feeling sad and kissed you on impulse."

His snort nailed her. "You broke up with Will, and we went out specifically to celebrate your freedom, remember?"

She scrunched up her nose. "Oh yeah."

"You're hopeless." But his words were softened with humor again, and she knew she was in the clear. "But I forgive you. Unless you think we should try once more in a few years? Maybe the third time's a charm?"

"Doubt it. Besides, it would be awful if we ever hooked up. If we had a fight, who would I call? It couldn't be you."

"Your sisters?"

"Ugh, I never tell them anything. I love them, but they chose lifestyles I despise. Bella's having a baby, and she's so young! And Avery is going for her PhD, which is boring as hell. No, thanks."

"Okay, how about this? We make one of those marriage pacts. If we turn thirty and we still haven't married, we marry each other."

"I'm not getting married at thirty!"

"So we'll make it thirty-five."

She pulled lightly at the crisp hairs on his arm. "Nah, that's so tropey. Like that movie—*My Best Friend's Wedding*? Best friends always vow to marry when they get super old. We should do the opposite."

"What do you mean?"

The idea hit her and she nodded with satisfaction. "We make a blood vow to each other that no matter how old we are, and how tempting it is to have sex, we never hook up. We swear to be best friends till the end—nothing more, nothing less. What do you think?"

He shifted his weight and gave her a funny look. "What if we change our minds? Hell, what if we want to have sex one day or decide to become fuck buddies?"

She shot him a glare. "We won't—we're better than that crap! We tested it twice already and know we're safe from the spark thing. It will be a way to protect our relationship forever. What do you think?"

He cocked his head. His long dark hair had escaped from its tie and fell loose against his cheeks. "Yeah, I guess you're right. Never thought about it like that."

"Let's do it. Make it official." She jumped up and grabbed a safety pin from her desk. "Stick out your hand so we can do a blood pact."

"We're not the kids from *IT*. I don't want a scar on my hand."

She grabbed his hand impatiently. "I'm just going to prick your finger."

He lifted both heavy, dark brows that gave him an adorable, surprised look. "Why are we doing this again?"

"Because you're important to me, Pierce. You're my best friend. My ride or die. I never want us to get tempted to jump into bed on impulse and ruin the best relationship I ever had. Are you with me?"

His features softened. "You're such a dork," he said with pure affection. "Be gentle."

She made the strike short and quick, then repeated the move on herself. They lifted their index fingers in the air, pausing a few inches away.

Their gazes met and locked.

The air shimmered with a current of energy.

They recited the words, their voices melding in perfect harmony.

Then touched their fingers together.

A hot bolt of fire shot through her body, crackling into a shock that exploded like she'd just touched a wet electrical outlet. She gasped and jerked back, her finger throbbing.

He yanked his hand away, glaring at her. "Hey, I told you not to hurt me!"

"I didn't." She stared at him, cradling her wounded finger, but when she shook it out, there was just the tiniest prick of blood from the needle. The air in the room eased, and she breathed deep. Probably the alcohol. She was imagining things. "Sorry, I must have pressed harder than I thought. I'm still tipsy."

His face relaxed, and he grasped her wrist loosely. "Come on, let's sleep it off."

They cuddled together on the bed, fully clothed, her head tucked in her favorite spot in the crook of his shoulder. "Pierce?"

"Yeah?"

"Where are you going after graduation?"

His heart beat steadily against her ear. "Not sure. I want to do photography. Maybe I'll take on an assistant position. Learn some stuff before I branch out and do my own work. What about you?"

"Paint and live anywhere but Cape May," she murmured sleepily. "I want to travel. London, Paris, New York. I feel like the entire world is out there ready for me to explore and conquer. Do you feel that way?"

He was quiet for a while. "I like Cape May; it's my home. I wouldn't mind settling back there if I had a place and work that was all mine."

"Not me. I'm never going back."

She drifted off to sleep with big dreams swimming in her head, the future mapped out like an adventure with buried treasure at the end of every path.

Until her mother called a few months before graduation.

Bella's husband had been killed in an accident, leaving her sister alone with a newborn baby. Things had fallen apart, and Taylor was needed.

So she went home and learned that some dreams weren't meant to be.